D0974506

Woof at the DOOR

Laura Morrigan

BERKLEY PRIME CRIME, NEW YORK

THE BERKLEY PUBLISHING GROUP
Published by the Penguin Group
Penguin Group (USA) Inc.
375 Hudson Street, New York, New York 10014, USA

USA | Canada | UK | Ireland | Australia | New Zealand | India | South Africa | China

Penguin Books Ltd., Registered Offices: 80 Strand, London WC2R 0RL, England
For more information about the Penguin Group, visit penguin.com.

WOOF AT THE DOOR

A Berkley Prime Crime Book / published by arrangement with the author

Berkley Prime Crime Books are published by The Berkley Publishing Group.
BERKLEY® PRIME CRIME and the PRIME CRIME logo are trademarks of
Penguin Group (USA) Inc.

For information, address: The Berkley Publishing Group,
a division of Penguin Group (USA) Inc.,
375 Hudson Street, New York, New York 10014.

ISBN: 978-0-425-25719-7

PUBLISHING HISTORY
Berkley Prime Crime mass-market edition / July 2013

PRINTED IN THE UNITED STATES OF AMERICA

10 9 8 7 6 5 4 3 2 1

Cover illustration by Maryann Lasher.
Cover design by Diana Kolsky.
Interior text design by Kristin del Rosario.

ALWAYS LEARNING　　　　　　　　　　　　　　　　　　PEARSON

To Blake.
Who needs Superman when I have you?

ACKNOWLEDGMENTS

This is my first novel and through the years I've amassed an avalanche of gratitude to express. I'll try not to ramble.

I must begin by thanking my seventh-grade English teacher (yes, really) Mrs. Sonja F. Nichols, who was the first objective person to call my writing a talent. I still have your letter.

Next, are the people who, by some miracle, agreed with her, starting with my agent, Elaine English. Thank you for your guidance and enthusiasm for this story. And to my editor, Faith Black, along with all the folks at Berkley Prime Crime who turned this manuscript into a real, honest-to-goodness book. Your hard work is much appreciated.

To my fellow writers in GIAM, the motivation and inspiration you all provide is a blessing. And the ladies of my uber-talented local writers group: Amelia Grey, Dolores Monaco, Frances Hanson-Grow, Geri Buckley Borcz, Hortense Thurman, and Sandra Shanklin. Thank you for keeping me on track. I truly could never have done it without you.

I must also thank my friends and family for all their love and support. Especially my aunt Oma Laura, a lifelong Jacksonville resident, who tirelessly provided detailed descriptions of random locations for this book. (Any errors or embellishments of these are mine, of course.) My brother, Dan, for his insight into all things lawyery, and my sister, Elizabeth, for challenging my vocabulary and never letting me give up. My mom, Frances, who gifted me with the writer's gene, sparked it by reading me mysteries at bedtime, and fanned the flames with endless encouragement. Thanks for teaching me the value of patience. (Or trying to, anyway.) And my dad, Ed, who told me I could achieve anything I put my mind to, and taught me that being a little different and more than a little stubborn were actually good things.

Finally, to my husband, Blake, for being brave enough to live with a novelist. Your understanding, patience, and love have made this dream come true. Thank you.

AUTHOR'S NOTE

Though this story takes place in a real city and involves a real sheriff's office, in order to spin a cohesive tale, I bent the rules and fudged as needed. Locations have been tweaked. DNA processing happens at the blink of an eye. Civilians are asked to help secure crime scenes. I ask you, dear reader, to forgive these and other uses of creative license. Happy reading!

CHAPTER 1

I got the call on a Sunday.

For most people, getting a call from the cops on a Sunday afternoon would be alarming. For me, it meant one thing—I needed to get the lemur off my head. Fast.

Not that this wasn't already a priority. The little gremlin was pulling my hair like, well, a panicked, four-month-old lemur who had escaped from his enclosure at the zoo and had mistaken me for his mama. He clung to me with the fervor of a tick on speed. To make things worse, it was July in Jacksonville, which meant I had long since sweated through my cotton tank top. Sporting a lemur hat was going to induce heatstroke in a matter of minutes.

My name is Grace Wilde, and technically, I'm an animal behaviorist who works with everything from elephants to schnauzers. The reality is much more complicated.

"Hold still, Grace. I'll get him!"

"No!" I sidestepped Hugh, the zoo's veterinarian, who was reaching out to try and disentangle Kiki-the-lemur from my hair. This, of course, alarmed Kiki. Whistling in distress, he scurried for a better grip, shuffling his weight around 'til my eyes were covered by a combination of my own dark hair and a lemur tail.

I stumbled blindly backward. "Hugh, do not try and get him off. Just . . . just . . ." I held out my hand. "Lead me back to the enclosure. I'll get him off once we're inside."

Kiki had escaped that morning. The zookeepers had been chasing him around for hours. Like so many times before, I got called in to resolve the issue. Because I, the expert, usually got the job done. Most of the folks at the zoo think I'm an anomaly, the outsider who bosses them around on occasion and does crazy things like walking up to an injured ostrich, or dealing with demented orangutans. But the truth is, it's not so crazy, not when you understand what's going on in their animal minds.

Which, fortunately—or unfortunately, as the case may be—is my gift. Like Dr. Dolittle and Ace Ventura, I can, and do, talk to animals. And more important, they talk back.

At the moment, I was trying to focus on calming, happy thoughts, in order to help the lemur do the same. A calm, happy lemur might loosen its grip on my hair, and might not poop himself in terror. Which, in the current position, would be worse for me than for him.

Kiki. It's okay. My mind reached out to his. Soothing. Calm. Many animals who live among humans have a wide vocabulary. Zoo animals, with some exceptions, do not. So rather than being able to use words, I had to stick with basic emotional conveyance and imagery. Usually, I am very good at this. Not, however, when I'm panting like a blindfolded bulldog.

No! I felt a surge of panic from Kiki and heard someone shuffling closer. Probably Hugh moving in to take my hand. Kiki's hind foot found my earlobe and he gripped with a prehensile toe that felt more like a grappling hook.

"Stop!" I raised my hands to the sides, as much a gesture to keep everyone back as a means of balance. "No one move. I need a minute to calm him down."

There were murmurs and more shuffling, but Kiki seemed to get that no one was moving in to grab him so he relaxed a fraction. I still couldn't see. My line of sight was obscured by the black-and-white rings of his bushy tail.

I reached up slowly, to move his tail, all the while issuing gentle thoughts. I sent him images of his enclosure, where his family was waiting for him. I envisioned bananas and oranges and any other kind of fruit I could think of. Bit by bit, I managed to reposition his tail under my chin. Kiki liked that, promptly snaking it around my neck.

Great.

I didn't want to think about how ridiculous I looked. I could see it reflected in Hugh's face. His lips trembled in an attempt to bite back laughter, his eyes watering with the effort.

I scowled at him, but apparently, scowling at someone while wearing a lemur hat was less than menacing. Hugh lost his battle and chortled loudly, which startled Kiki.

The tail tightened. I tried to focus again on being calm but my annoyance with Hugh was making it difficult. Hugh was one of those guys—the kind that knew how to seduce with a smile and pointed glance. The kind that women fawn over. Delicious from the sun-kissed tips of his brown hair to the steel toes of his Red Wing boots. He looked like the Marlboro man and saved cuddly animals. One cocky half smile and most women were toast.

I was unaffected by his charisma. Yeah, sure I was.

"Sorry," he said quietly, sparkling hazel eyes belying the word. "I'm sorry, but you look like one of those Russian guys."

I didn't bother to say anything. Instead, I squared my shoulders and, with as much dignity as I was capable of, walked toward the lemur house.

The zoo was quiet. I didn't see or hear anyone. No children running around. No haggard parents scurrying after them. And it made me wonder if they had evacuated the zoo because of one little lemur. Probably. As much for the sake of safety as from fear of lawsuits. I could imagine Kiki deciding to affix himself to some poor soccer mom.

The thought made me want to giggle. Kiki picked up on

my altered mood and released my ear, sliding down to perch on my shoulder. The enclosure was just ahead. I could see one of the zookeepers and shooed him away from the door. I could slip in and talk Kiki into reuniting with his real mama.

All right, little guy, we'll get you back where you belong in just a second.

That's when my phone rang. Or rather, began playing the Eagles' "Witchy Woman."

Kiki whistled in abject terror and plastered himself to my face. I fumbled with my phone, unclipping it from my belt and flipping it open. With my mouth covered by lemur belly, I had no way and no desire to try and answer, I just wanted to shut it up. I could hear a man's voice faintly, something that sounded like "homicide" and "police" and "assistance."

I ignored the words, my surprise and curiosity tossed aside until I could finish my task. I flipped the phone closed, focusing on calming the lemur while edging in the direction of Kiki's home. At least I hoped I was heading that way. I wasn't sure. I was blind and suffocating. It would have been funny if it hadn't been for the smell. Lemurs, as a whole, don't smell awful. But getting this up close and personal was a little too much for me. My eyes watered, my throat clogged, and I tried not to gag.

Kiki up. I patted the top of my head and sent the mental message—an image of him riding on my head. The lemur was young, and I was pretty sure he didn't understand much of what I was saying. I had to stick with images. I focused and tried to breathe through my mouth. I sucked in large amounts of fur and bumped into the side of the cage.

Home. As always, I translated the raw impression that flashed from the animal's mind to mine. And I knew the lemur would head willingly back into its cage. If it would just get off my face . . .

Air—fresh, clean air wafted into my lungs. I didn't think it was possible for ninety degrees to seem refreshing, but in that moment I couldn't imagine anything better. Kiki climbed onto my head and was reaching out to grab the cage.

In a move worthy of a ninja, I opened the door and lunged inside.

Kiki leapt up to rejoin his family. The lot of them stared at me with wide, golden-brown eyes. If I had been anyone else, I might have thought they were critically eyeing my Kiki-inspired hairdo. But the chorus of thoughts that streamed at me like a pulsing wave told the truth.

Shock. Relief. Fear. Wariness. Joy.

Guess we humans are the only ones with self-image problems. Go figure.

"Witchy Woman" started up again and this time I answered.

"Wilde Kingdom, this is Grace."

"Grace, this is Detective Nocera. I'd like to ask a favor, if you've got a minute."

· · ·

It doesn't really matter who you are, what you look like, or how much money you have in your 401k. Death, whether creeping down a back alley or waltzing through wrought iron courtyard gates, inevitably visits us all.

Even if you are Mark Richardson, the star quarterback for the Jacksonville Jaguars and son of the governor of Florida.

I could hear his dog's frantic barks from the front yard. Deep, relentless . . . desperate. A big guy. A guard dog. I was thinking Rottie or Dobie. Maybe a shepherd. I'd find out soon enough.

A young patrolman motioned for me to follow him, and I walked over thick St. Augustine lawn toward the house. The McMansion was one of those faux Mediterranean deals that hit the mark much better than most. Lush landscaping, a warm paint scheme, and a bubbling fountain in the entry courtyard completed the look. We walked through the open door into the foyer. Though it was cooler inside, it wasn't by much. I paused just inside the door. The patrolman was called back outside, and I was left to process the situation. The truth is, as crazy as my life might seem with the wrangling wallabies and whatnot, I'd never been to a crime scene.

It was not what I'd expected.

The house was as nice inside as it was out. The exception being that the place was messy. Not trashed, like there had been a fight, but there had definitely been a party. Wineglasses and empty beer bottles mingled with hors d'oeuvre plates and other debris on countertops and end tables. A jovial sign proclaiming JAGUARS, ALL THE WAY! hung above a large fireplace. The travertine tile floor was sticky, soiled with mud, and sprinkled with glittering confetti. The lingering odor of cigars and alcohol fused unpleasantly with the unmistakable metallic smell of blood.

That was the big difference. On TV you see all the blood and stuff, but there's no smell. My stomach rolled, and I stepped to the side. Two large columns flanked the foyer. I moved behind one so it blocked my view of the body. I wasn't ready yet. I shut my eyes and swallowed hard. This wasn't going to be easy. Not only was I going to be dealing with my reaction to the murder, I would be dealing with the dog's, too. I pushed everything out of my mind until there was nothing but white noise. Then I slowly opened my eyes.

Another part of my gift—one I've had to work really hard to hone—is that I have superior control over my own feelings.

I disconnected as much as possible and eased out partly from behind the column. A plump woman was bending over the body of Mark Richardson. He sat slumped on the white leather couch; a crimson line of blood bisected his face and pooled on his bare chest. The shot had passed through his skull, obliterating the back of his head.

Jesus.

I didn't want to look but made myself. I had to get all the shock out of my system so I could handle the dog.

The wall behind the couch was a gruesome splash of blood and brain matter. Two men flanked the coffee table. One I recognized. Detective Jake Nocera, at one time an officer with the K9 unit, whom I had worked with a while back.

Jake was a gruff, barrel-chested guy from Buffalo. Judging from the sweat beading on his bald head, I'd say he'd yet to acclimate to Florida summers.

The other guy, the one I brilliantly deduced was from the crime scene unit because of the CSU plastered across his muscular back, focused on the detective and asked, "Who found him?"

Jake pulled out his notepad and said in a familiar accented grumble, "The maid. Julie Martinez. Says she usually doesn't come on Sundays, with church and all, but Mr. Richardson offered to pay her extra if she would clean up after the party. She and her sister arrived around eleven a.m. She had a key and the alarm code. Turns out she didn't need either."

"Door wasn't locked, alarm was off," CSU Hunk surmised.

"Yep, looks like he knew whoever did this." Jake glanced at the body.

"We have a list yet of the partygoers?"

"Workin' on it."

I watched as the men moved over to a large bookcase. Jake's back was to me; CSU Guy had a nice profile. A bit exotic—strong angles and high cheekbones. His eyes scanned over the framed photographs and trophies that lined the wooden shelves.

He pointed to a photo. "If I remember, he and his girlfriend recently had a very public breakup . . ."

"Already on that, too."

The woman, who I assumed was the medical examiner, stood and turned to the men. "Liver temp puts time of death at around four thirty a.m. or so." She pulled off her gloves and began placing her equipment back in her case. "Looks like the single shot to the head is the cause. I'll know more once I get him cleaned up. I'll run a tox screen and page you if anything turns up."

"Thanks, Maggie."

"You got it." She pointed toward the back of the room, where a bank of French doors lined the wall. "What about him? The poor baby's going crazy out there."

"Animal control was supposed to be here an hour ago," CSU Guy said. "They got tied up out in MacClenny, helping Baker County deal with twenty-five half-starved pit bulls."

From where I stood, I still couldn't see the dog. Furniture blocked my line of sight. But I could hear him, barking with every breath.

"He doesn't seem very sociable," Maggie, the ME, said.

She was right. Anyone trying to get a leash on him would probably have ended up in the hospital. That, or the dog would be shot. Maybe both.

Jake let out an affirmative growl at the comment, waved a thick hand toward the doors. "The chief's already been chewing my ass, and now we got Cujo here wanting a taste of it, too." He mopped his brow with a limp handkerchief. "I got a call in to an animal trainer. She should be here soon."

That was my cue. No more stalling.

I abandoned my column and started forward, stopping just behind CSU as he said, "She? You really think a woman will be able to handle him? What's she bringing, a stun gun?"

So much for thinking he was cute. "That won't be necessary." My tone was crisp, and as he turned, I gave him a look that could, and in fact had, stopped a polar bear in its tracks. I let my gaze roam over him in appraisal and cocked my head. "I've handled much worse."

I'll say this, the guy had the good grace to seem sheepish and shot me an apologetic smile. I ignored it and turned to Jake. "Detective."

Jake made a quick introduction. "Grace Wilde, this is Sergeant Kai Duncan. Kai is with the Crime Lab."

I nodded curtly at Sergeant Duncan and turned back to Jake. "What's the story?"

Jake pointed at the back door. "Big Dobie in the backyard, seems to be trained as a guard dog. Got a nasty cut on his nose, and he's pretty freaked out."

Understatement. "I've got my medical kit in my truck. I could calm him down, get the kit, and sew him up, but it would probably be best if I take him with me until you find out who will want to claim him." I glanced at the body. "He doesn't need to stay here."

"I don't see a problem with that. Kai, you need to go over the dog for anything?"

Kai shook his head. "It doesn't look as though the killer would have made contact with the dog. If he had, we'd probably be processing two bodies."

Jake snickered at that and smiled at me. "Don't I wish. He's all yours."

Showtime. I walked forward, past the couch, to where I could finally see the dog. A slice of red ran down a cut on the side of the Doberman's nose. As he barked, blood and saliva were hurled at the glass between us.

I stopped and knelt in front of the French door. I had already calmed myself. Now it was time to work on him. With one final deep breath, I opened my mind to the dog. I was immediately overwhelmed with emotions—desperation, alarm, betrayal. Images of violence and pain flooded my mind. I pulled my thoughts away from the awful torrent and tried to drag the dog with me. *Okay, it's okay. It's not your fault.*

The Doberman stopped snarling. I filled the space in our linked minds with white haze. Calm nothingness pressed out the horror.

I whispered aloud, "All right, boy, I'm going to help you." Slowly, I stood and turned. "The officer that brought me in told me not to touch anything. Would you open the door and let me out?"

After a moment's hesitation, Sergeant Duncan stepped forward. "You sure?"

I arched a brow and waited. He moved to the door and turned the knob with a gloved hand.

I slipped out as the door swung in. Dogs communicate in several ways. Smell, touch, sound. But most important is energy. My energy was different than any other human the dog had encountered. I was connected to his mind. I sent him waves of calm, alpha energy. *I will lead you. I will help you.*

His master was gone. His job to protect fractured into uncertainty. Confusion and fear dominated his mind. I had to fill the void.

Again, I knelt in front of the dog.

It's all right. Good boy. I felt him relax measure by measure.

The cut on his muzzle wasn't that deep; a few stitches would work. I just needed to get him out of here. Reaching out slowly for his tags, I flipped past the license and looked over the two round brass plates. One was engraved with the word JAGUARS and what looked like a phone number. The second had what I was looking for—his name.

"Hey, Jax. That's a good boy." As I spoke in a soothing monotone, I sent wave after wave of my energy and moved to stroke his sinewy neck.

The giant dog slowly collapsed and rolled over to expose his belly. *Jax, good boy.*

I smiled down at him as I scratched his rib cage. "Yes, you're a good boy, Jax." After several minutes, I knew I would be able to lead him out of the house and to my Suburban. "Okay, let's go get you fixed up." The dog rolled onto his feet. I grasped his thick leather collar and walked him through the door. I made sure to position myself between the dog and the body as we walked by the couch. He hesitated, and I paused for a moment.

The Doberman whimpered softly. *Gone?*

I placed my hand on the dog. *Yes, I'm sorry, boy. He's gone.* I felt the massive dog begin to tremble. Taking a deep breath, I forced myself to ignore the renewed torrent of emotions that swirled through me. "Come on, come with me." Gently, I led the quaking dog out of the room.

As we reached the front door, I heard Sergeant Duncan say, "Well, that was impressive. Is she a dog whisperer or something?"

Jake grunted. "She's something all right."

I smiled. One point to Team Grace.

• • •

I stood under the near-scalding water and spread more of my sister's twenty-dollar shampoo through my long hair.

No matter how many times I lathered, no matter how hot the water, I just couldn't shake the feeling that I wasn't clean. The images of blood and death kept creeping in to pollute my mind.

I've never been very good at dealing with suffering. In veterinary school, I told myself I would get used to it. That I would be able to block out the pain, the nauseating fear. But I couldn't. I'd gotten better at dealing with it through the years, but it still took its toll emotionally. In the clinic, every time an animal had been brought to me, I knew its thoughts, felt its terror and pain. It should have made me a better vet. It didn't.

"But it makes you a damn good animal trainer," I muttered to the showerhead. I had yet to meet a creature great or small I couldn't work with. It was laughable to think that I couldn't handle a Doberman, as Sergeant Duncan had assumed.

I knew what he saw when he looked at me. A petite, curvy little *thing* who needed help opening her peanut butter jar.

Okay, so jars had been known to give me problems in the past, so what? I have small hands. But that's not the point. Hot guys think they can use their looks to make up for bad behavior. Like Hugh, who assumed he was smart enough not to get caught in his womanizing ways. It's funny the things people will do when they think no one is watching. Even people who work with animals every day don't count them as witnesses. I know better.

My ability to communicate with animals isn't exactly public knowledge. I don't talk about what I can do. For one, everyone would think I was a loon. For another, it comes in handy from time to time for people, like hot guys who've finally talked you into going on a date with them, to assume what they say and do behind the Elephant Barn is private. Not that I spy. I don't. Much.

My friends are like anyone else's—four legs and fur aside—misbehave and they'll tell me.

My sister, Emma, who hounded me like a beagle after a jackrabbit to go on more dates, would argue that I was being unfair. I had blown Hugh off countless times. Just because I'd finally decided to say yes the next time he asked me on a date did not a commitment make.

Details.

One male I do trust? My dog, Moss. Though being half wolf, he's technically a hybrid, interspecies mutt or not, the big guy never lets me down. He had even companionably sniffed the Doberman when I'd brought him to the condo. No territorial posturing, just an offer of friendship.

I turned off the water and stepped out of the shower into the steamy bathroom. The Doberman was lying on the sleek black-and-white marble floor. He raised his head and looked up at me.

"Hey, Jax. You feeling better?"

He wagged his nub tail. The cut on his face looked much better. The sedative I had given him so I could clean and suture the wound had calmed him down considerably. Now his thoughts were hazy. No shocking memories of violence and panic. Later, maybe tomorrow morning, I would try and make sense of the jumbled images he had communicated to me, but for now it was best to let him feel calm and safe.

The truth was, I didn't really want to know what he remembered. I assumed from where Jax had been in the backyard that he'd had a clear view of Mark Richardson's murder. I also guessed from the impressions he'd given me so far that he had, in fact, witnessed what happened. What I didn't know was if the cops had a suspect, or evidence that pointed them in the right direction. I hoped so. Telling the cops that their only witness was a canine was not something I wanted to do. Especially if said canine relayed crucial information for them through me.

I groaned at the thought of how that conversation would go.

The sound of the front door opening had Jax scrambling

to his feet. A low growl vibrated in his throat. Protective tension radiated from him like heat off asphalt.

Easy, Jax. It's okay. I quieted him with soothing thoughts. "That's just my sister, Emma—"

"Grace! I do *not* believe this!" My sister's annoyed voice streamed from the living room.

Crap. I grabbed a thick, oversized towel, wrapped it around me, and zipped through the bedroom I had been calling home for the last two weeks. My sister loved me enough to house me while I looked for a new home. She and Moss . . . different story.

Jax was close on my heels as I skidded down the hall to the living room.

Emma stood, hands on her hips, scowling at Moss. "That couch is made of Venetian silk, you beast. Off!" She shooed the dog and bent to pick up a displaced pillow from the floor. Her stylishly cut dark hair fell across her face, hiding her frown for a moment. "Grace!"

I shot a weary glance at Moss. *Really? Would it kill you to stay off the couch?*

He slid slowly off his perch and walked over to plop down onto the antique Persian rug.

"Sorry, Em. As soon as I find a place, we'll be out of your hair."

My sister continued to glare at Moss, who had begun to scratch fervently behind an ear, sending tufts of downy white fur flying. Emma shook her head. "I swear, he just does it to spite me—" She broke off as she turned and noticed the huge Doberman standing next to me.

Here we go.

Emma raised her perfectly pruned eyebrows and pointed at the dog. "What the hell is that?"

I plastered on a bright smile. "This is Jax." I introduced him like I would a long-lost relative. When Emma remained silent, glowering down at me like a lithe Amazon in four-inch spiked heels, I felt my smile falter. No one intimidated me like my older sister. It was genetic. I could stand up to wild horses, but Emma's scathing glare always made me flinch. "I'm sorry. I know I promised that I wouldn't bring any wayward animals to your place, but I had to. I got a call today—"

"I don't want to know Grace, really." Shaking her head, Emma turned and stalked into the kitchen. "Mr. Cavanaugh called again to bitch that Moss was howling. The geriatric old goat swears his life is being ruined because he can't watch reruns of *The Golden Girls* without having to come over here with his sticky notes. Now you bring home another dog?"

I ignored the comment about our curmudgeon of a neighbor. The man was an ass. If he heard so much as one bark from my sister's condo, he complained and wrote wacky notes and taped them to the door.

I followed Emma into the kitchen. Leaning against the smooth granite counter, I glanced down at Jax, who had dutifully trailed me into the room. "You heard about Mark Richardson?"

"Of course." Emma pulled a bottle of Chardonnay out of the wine fridge and began uncorking it. "It was all over the news. Why?"

I watched my sister pop open the wine and set the cork aside. "Jax was his dog. I had to pick him up from the crime scene."

Emma almost dropped the crystal wine goblet she was lifting out of the cabinet. "What?" Astonished, she looked from me to the Doberman. "Good grief, Gracie. Did he see what happened?"

"I've only been able to pick up some raw emotions from him. But yeah, I think so."

Emma stared at me a moment longer, her beautiful face made only more compelling by the concern in her dark eyes. "And they just let you take him?"

"Why wouldn't they? I'm licensed. He's being officially quarantined."

She slowly shook her head, poured two glasses of wine, and handed one to me. "Are you going to tell the cops?"

"Tell them what?"

"Grace—"

"What do you want me to do, Em? Tell them that I can communicate with animals telepathically? That Jax may have seen who killed the governor's son, and if he tells me who did it, I'll be sure to call?"

She frowned into her glass. "It sounds a little crazy when you put it like that."

"It sounds a *lot* crazy." I took a long sip of the cool Chardonnay.

"What are you going to do?"

"The only thing I can do. If I get anything clear from Jax, I'll figure out a way to tell the police." I sighed, swirling the wine. "Then they can put me in one of those nice padded cells."

"I hear they can be pretty relaxing." Emma smiled. "You know, like a quiet getaway. No phone. No Internet."

"No wine."

"I'll bring you wine." Emma tapped her glass against mine. "You know, not everyone thinks it's crazy to be able to talk to animals."

"You're right, the Pet Psychic even had her own TV show," I said with mock admiration.

"I'm serious, Grace. I think you should tell people."

I groaned. "It's not like when we were kids and it was fun to get the dog to spy on the Fisher brothers."

"You never know. I bet there are plenty of people who would think your ability is a real gift, but you never really open up to anyone. I mean, you never even gave Hugh a chance. He was perfect, a vet, who works at the zoo. He has to know what you do isn't just luck. Bonus—he's got that whole rugged manly-man thing going on."

"He was hooking up with one of the keepers!"

"Says the elephant."

"Who's a reliable source."

"Why would you care? You had already made it clear you wanted nothing to do with him. You never went on a single date with the guy, and you blacklist him because he didn't get himself to a monastery when you blew him off?"

"I didn't trust him."

"You don't trust anyone."

"And that's a bad thing?"

"It is when you won't give anyone a chance."

"Here we go." I rolled my eyes. The topic of my social life, or lack of it, was something my sister never tired of rehashing. That and bugging me to join her in her daily martial arts class. I wasn't sure which was worse.

"I mean it," Emma went on. "You never go to parties with me."

"Your parties are about schmoozing. I don't schmooze." Emma was *the* premier party planner in Jacksonville. She wasn't a social butterfly; she was a social condor.

"And you haven't been on a date in over a year."

"I have, too."

"Going to the New Year's Eve party with Wes doesn't count." Emma grinned at me. "Only dates with *straight* men count."

"I've been busy."

"I know, your social schedule is *sooo* demanding." Emma blinked at me in faux-wonder. "How do you manage it?"

I had just opened my mouth to snap out a retort when the phone rang.

Emma picked up the receiver. "Hello?" A sly smile slid across her face. Her voice turned to velvet. "Why yes, she's right here." Emma covered the receiver and teased in her best adolescent whisper, "It's a boy!"

I snatched the phone from her. "Yes?"

"Grace Wilde? This is Sergeant Kai Duncan from the Crime Lab; we met earlier at Mark Richardson's residence."

His voice was warmer then I remembered—more open. "I remember you, Sergeant Duncan." Too well, apparently.

"Please, call me Kai."

"What can I help you with, Kai?"

"It's in regards to the Doberman. We need you to fill out a couple of forms, stating that the dog is temporarily in your custody."

I did a quick mental check of my schedule. "I can stop by in the morning."

"That would be very helpful."

He told me his office was in the Police Memorial Building and that he would leave the paperwork with the receptionist. For some stupid reason, I felt a twinge of apprehension.

I shook off the feeling, hung up, and spoke to Emma before she could ask. "He's just a guy with the police who needs me to sign some stuff about our new friend here." I gently patted Jax on the head.

"He's got a nice voice." Emma held up her wineglass and swirled the light golden liquid. "Is he cute?"

Yes. I frowned at my subconscious's automatic answer and shrugged as nonchalantly as I could. "He's a cocky jerk. He didn't think I could handle Jax."

"Most people couldn't." She tilted her head. "You didn't answer my question, is he cute?"

"Is that all you think about?"

Emma grinned over the rim of her wineglass. "*You* should think about it more often."

"I'm not going there." I shook my head and turned to leave the kitchen. I was already spending way too much time thinking about my nonexistent sex life. "Order some pizza. I'm going to get dressed."

"That means he's definitely cute."

I whirled to face her. "What is that supposed to mean?"

"You always get extra pissy with the cute guys."

"Cute guys think they are God's gift to everyone."

"I guess it's your job to put them in their place?" Emma shot me a pointed look. She knew my MO better than anyone.

I crossed my arms. "I am not going to be seduced into stupidity by a perfect smile and nice body." Been there done that. Not looking for a repeat.

Emma's eyes widened. "Oooh, so he has a nice body?"

"Forget it." I threw my hands up and started toward the guest room.

"You're the one who was checking him out!" Emma called gleefully after me. I waved dismissively over my shoulder and turned down the hall.

"My sister has a one-track mind," I said to the dogs, who

followed me into the bedroom. I tossed the towel on the bed and pulled on a pair of baggy cotton pajama bottoms and a tank top. Jax flopped down by the doorway and grunted.

"It's not like I don't *want* to date," I grumbled. Of course, that was a lie—I didn't want to date. Dating made things complicated. For some annoying reason, my mind conjured up the image of Sergeant Duncan. Complications. Like going on a date with a handsome investigator and ruining the night by confessing my secret.

I could just see it: Nice dinner, nice wine, nice conversation, until I said, "By the way, I can communicate psychically with animals. Can you pass the salt?"

He'd be wondering when I'd gone off my meds. Sighing, I sank down onto the bed. Moss leapt up to sit beside me, nudging his head under my arm. He had picked up on my subtle mood change and, like always, wanted to make me feel better.

"Thanks, big boy." I sank my fingers into his thick fur. Moss, as keeper of all my secrets, knew what Emma didn't. I would never make the mistake of spilling my guts. Not again.

Years ago, I had stupidly opened up to the first man to make me melt like a sundae with extra hot fudge—Dane Harrington. He was gorgeous, rich, and smart. I'd met him in my first year of college and had fallen fast and hard. We spent one wonderful summer together at the end of the first term. Scampering off to the Bahamas . . . *on his family jet*. It had been a magical trip. Right up until the moment I told him about my gift.

I woke up alone to a note and a plane ticket home.

Being a quick study, I adopted a "don't ask, don't tell" policy. It had worked like a charm. Until today.

I glanced over at Jax, who was dozing in the entry to the room.

Today, the rules had changed.

• • •

That night, I was pulled from sleep.

I sat up and blinked bleary eyes, willing them to focus

on the bedside alarm clock—3:44 a.m. Moss, who had been sleeping next to me, raised his head off the pillow and studied me. I heard a soft whimper.

Jax.

He was stretched out in front of the bedroom door. His face and feet twitched in a dream. I paused a moment and then made my decision.

I closed my eyes and tried to merge with the dog's slumbering mind.

I entered his dream, saw through his eyes.

An image flashed before me—a ball, a tennis ball. I could feel the joy, the desire to play. Then, there was no ball. It had rolled under the sofa.

I tried to get the ball but couldn't reach it. Then I looked up. He laughed. "Get your ball, Jax!"

But it was out of reach.

One distorted memory leapt to another.

Now I was outside, looking in through the doors. I felt panic rise. I smelled fear and blood. I dug at the door and rammed the glass but couldn't get in.

A shadow moved toward the front door and then I saw: He sat on the couch. Unmoving. I felt my legs tremble as the scent of new death filled my lungs.

I threw open my eyes and gulped for air. Blinking, I scanned the room and noticed Moss was sitting up watching me intently. He sniffed at my face and then nudged under my chin.

I swallowed hard and tried to will away the wave of nausea. "I'm all right." But I wasn't. I could still feel the chill of death, taste it in the back of my throat.

I looked down at Jax. He was sleeping soundly now. The nightmare had come and gone.

I lay back on the bed and stared at the ceiling. Moss inched close to me and laid his head on my stomach.

I began stroking his soft fur and wondered how long it would be before Jax remembered the most important detail of that horrible night—the identity of the killer. I was betting it wouldn't be long. Then what was I going to do?

CHAPTER 2

After a dawn walk on the beach with the dogs and a gallon of coffee, I was finally coherent enough to come to a decision. I needed to find out what the cops knew. If they had a solid lead in Mark Richardson's murder, they wouldn't need Jax or, more aptly, me to tell them who the killer was. I could concentrate on making sure Jax was stable enough to be adopted, instead of trying to decipher garbled memories of a murder I really didn't want to see.

Just after nine o'clock, I scored a parking spot on the corner of Bay Street and Liberty. Though the city had lined the street with palm trees, nothing could soften the facade of the Police Memorial Building. Grayish-tan, blocky with dozens of terraced steps leading to the doors, it reminded me of a squashed Aztec pyramid.

As I began my trek up the stairs, I weighed my options. I'd thought about having the receptionist call Kai Duncan's office but shook off the idea. It would be better to contact Jake. I had his cell number. I could sign the paperwork on Jax and then call him.

I was so lost in thought as I scribbled my name over the forms, I wasn't aware anyone was behind me. Until I heard a warm voice say, "You should really read documents before you sign them. That could have been a confession."

I turned to find Sergeant Duncan standing there. Was he taller than I remembered? He shot me a smile that could probably charm the pants off a nun. If nuns wore pants.

I returned it with an indifferent nod. "Sergeant Duncan, I didn't expect to see you today."

"It's Kai, remember? I was on my way to grab something to eat. And you . . . caught my eye."

He didn't skim his gaze over me the way I had done to him the day before, but I got the feeling he wanted to. Instead, his eyes stayed locked on mine. It made me jumpy.

"I won't keep you." Turning away, I walked back toward the main doors. What was it about this guy that raised my hackles? Wasn't I supposed to be finding out what the police knew?

He caught up to me. "How's the dog?"

"Traumatized."

He maneuvered around me to hold open the door. The heat, even though it was still early, was a slap in the face. "It's still violent?"

"*He* still needs some time." I shot Kai a glare. "Jax witnessed the murder of someone he loved and was unable to do anything to prevent it. How would that make you feel?"

"How do you know that he witnessed the murder?"

That stopped me. "What?"

"You said he saw what happened and couldn't stop it."

I tried not to look as flustered as I suddenly felt. This was why I didn't want to talk to him. He was looking at me a little too intently. "It's obvious." I shrugged. "You've never had a dog, have you?"

"Not since I was a kid."

I nodded, as if that explained everything, and turned to walk away.

"Wait, Miss Wilde. Grace." He followed me down the

front steps. "I keep offending you when I don't mean to. Let me make it up to you. I'll buy you a cup of coffee." He motioned to the deli down the street.

"It's ninety degrees out, and you want to buy me coffee?" I kept walking toward my vintage skyline-blue Suburban. Like it was home base and I would be safe once I reached it. I knew I should say yes. If only to pick his brain and find out what was happening with the case. But there was something about him that sounded the alarm bells. Was I really just being pissy, as Emma had alleged, because he was attractive?

"An iced tea, then. Come on. I'll prove to you I'm not a jerk."

After lengthy consideration, I sighed. "Okay."

As we walked across the busy street, pausing in the middle to wait for a garbage truck to rumble by, I tried to think of a good excuse to ask questions about the case. I'd never had the social skills of my sister, but I had watched her in action. Flattery. Emma had used it to glean information; would it work on an investigator?

He held the door for me again as we entered the deli. The enticing aroma of fresh-baked butter biscuits made my mouth water.

The young man at the counter smiled as we walked in. "Hey, Kai, you want the usual?"

"Yeah. And a large iced tea for the lady." He glanced at me. "You want anything else? My treat."

My stomach grumbled and I ordered cheese grits and a biscuit with honey.

"Have a seat and it'll be right out."

We sat at a corner booth. As we slid in, my knees brushed his. I automatically scooted back on the bench, ignoring my reaction to the contact. The flush I felt creeping up my neck was because of the summer heat, not the man sitting across from me. Yeah, sure it was.

When I looked up, Kai flashed that killer smile and then began scanning my face, like a scientist studying a new specimen. I refused to let the scrutiny ruffle me and looked directly into his clear, glass-green eyes.

We sat for a moment, locked in a stare-down I was sure I would win. Though my heart had started to beat a little faster as I took in just how handsome he was.

Finally, Kai settled against the back of the booth and spoke casually. "Jake says you're an animal trainer, but you must be a veterinarian, as well, or you wouldn't be able to quarantine the dog."

I forced myself to relax a little. As long as he didn't get too personal, I would be fine answering his questions. Then maybe I could maneuver in a few of my own. "I keep my license current. It comes in handy with what I do."

"Which is to rescue traumatized animals?"

"If need be."

"What kind of animals do you usually work with, when you're not saving the wayward?" Again with the killer smile.

I tried to ignore the effect it had on me. Though honestly, since I had a pulse, it was a losing battle. Yep, I'd be much better off talking to Jake Nocera.

"I deal with family pets mostly. I do a lot of consulting."

"Consulting?"

"I specialize in problem behavior."

"So if Fido is eating the sofa, you're the person to call."

"Yep." I tried to figure out a way to artfully turn the conversation around. Ask a question, something.

"So I guess that Doberman yesterday comes under the category of having problem behavior?"

"Yep." Wow, I was really doing a bang-up job of gleaning information. Look out, Nancy Drew.

"How were you able to do what you did? Just walk up to that dog and . . . tame him?"

Suddenly, my imaginary dinner-date scenario flashed through my head. This was a little too close for comfort. I looked away from him, out the window at the busy street. "I'm good at what I do."

"Where did you learn? Did you have a mentor?"

"I'm self-taught. I've worked with animals all my life." I continued to gaze out the window, my mind spinning like the wheels of the passing cars. "After a while, I developed the ability to read them. Now I can work with them in almost any situation." My answer was the same I gave anyone else who asked.

"So you've just studied animals?" Skepticism laced his words.

I turned to face him, leaned forward, and folded my hands on the table. Time to nip this in the bud. "You're a criminal investigator, right?"

He nodded.

"When you go to a crime scene, there are things you know to look for—clues, or whatever."

Again, he nodded.

"But if I sat and watched you do your job, I wouldn't really know what you were doing, because I don't know anything about investigating crimes."

"And I don't know anything about working with animals."

I lifted a shoulder. "Most people never bother to learn."

"Is that why you don't like people?"

I paused to consider the question. "It's not a question of like."

"Then what is it?"

"Animals act in ways I can understand. Even wild animals that hunt and kill are motivated by necessity. Acting on instinct. People are different. So many times they are selfish and cruel—just because they want to be."

Kai's grin dimmed slightly. "I wouldn't argue with that."

"With all you've seen, I'm sure you wouldn't." For an instant, I felt a sense of understanding pass between us. I allowed a hint of a smile to play on my lips; it would be nice to think that someone like him could understand me. I liked people but didn't trust them. If anyone could get that, it would be a man who saw just how purely evil people could be to one another. Crime scene after crime scene.

I had a shot of inspiration. If I opened up, maybe he would, too. "Yesterday was hard for me. I mean, seeing everything." It was true. I'd seen death before—terrible, gruesome death— but even so . . . "I'd never been to a murder scene."

"First one is never easy." His voice was gentle.

"I hope it will be my last." Now I tried layering on the flattery. "How do you do it? I mean it's your job to look past the body and see clues and evidence—how do you do that?"

"I'm good at what I do." He mimicked my earlier statement with a half grin.

"Don't you ever worry you'll miss something?"

"I always worry that I'll miss something."

"I heard you say that Mark Richardson just broke up with his girlfriend. Do you think she killed him?"

"We don't know yet. We've got to talk to more people."

"I guess that's pretty common, for the murderer to be the lover or wife or whatever, right?" Did I sound like I was fishing?

Kai nodded. "Statistically, yes, most murders are committed by someone who knows the victim. The evidence will tell us."

I remembered hearing them say that Mark Richardson had let his murderer in. I also remembered how messy the scene was. "You say the evidence will tell you. How do you know what to look for? I mean, I saw the crime scene. The place was a mess."

"Parties make gathering important evidence a challenge. But we start with the most obvious point and go from there."

"Which is?"

"The body."

"So you get the bullet and do some analyzing like they do on TV?"

He made a face. "Yes and no. It doesn't work out quite like it does on TV. We can't analyze every bullet. Some are too damaged to run through the system."

"Damaged from what?"

"Hitting a reinforced steel stud." The look on his face told me that was exactly what happened with the bullet that killed Mark Richardson.

"That doesn't sound good." I had him going now. I was gearing up for another question when his phone chirped.

He flipped it open. "Duncan. Yeah, what's up?" He

frowned as he listened. I tried to make out what the other person was saying, but I was too far away to eavesdrop. "Well, the casing has to be there. I'll head to the scene and take a second look around. We must have missed it."

When he flipped his phone closed, I asked, "Do you have to go back to Mark Richardson's house?"

"Yes. I need to double-check something."

The waitress came and set our orders on the table.

I was trying to think of a way to nonchalantly ask about what he was looking for when he changed the subject. "Do you have a farm or something?"

"A what?"

"You know, for all the animals you work with. Do you live out in the country?"

"Oh. No, but I'm in the market. Right now I'm staying at my sister's condo on the beach." I took a bite of biscuit that was so slick with butter my arteries screamed in protest. It was fantastic.

"Was that your old Suburban?" He switched subjects again as he bit into a twice as greasy biscuit stacked with eggs, sausage, and cheese.

"Yep."

"'Seventy-three?"

"'Seventy-five."

"Nice."

As much as I appreciated a man who saw the beauty of my clunker, Bluebell, I didn't want to talk about my beloved behemoth. Kai was quickly devouring his breakfast, and I feared he'd be on his way back to work before I had a chance to get any more out of him. I had to get him talking.

"You know . . ." I leaned back and reflected on a few oddities I'd noticed as we talked. "You don't really look like a science guy."

"What do I look like?"

"Well." My gaze roamed over him. "You have a great tan."

"We live in Florida."

I ignored the comment. I was getting into my perusal of

him. "And you have a slight tan line around your eyes, so that means outdoor activities. Lots of sun."

"Maybe I like to mow my lawn."

I took another bite of biscuit, chewed thoughtfully while I examined him, looking for, what? Oh yes . . . clues. Dark hair, with just a touch of auburn, a little longish for a cop. Broad shoulders and muscular chest. Strong arms. "Developed upper body."

He set down his biscuit and shot me a lazy grin.

I glanced at his watch, a Nixon. "Surfer. You look like a surfer."

His eyebrows arched. "Not bad."

"Am I right?"

He nodded. "What made you think that?"

I pointed to his watch. "Nixon makes surf gear. And when you paid at the counter, you had a Hurley wallet."

"Very Sherlock Holmes." He gave me a full-wattage smile, and I have to say I was impressed. But being sucked into his good looks wasn't going to get me info.

"So tell me more about your job," I said. "What else do you look for at a crime scene?"

"Trace evidence. Fibers, hair." He shrugged.

"Did you find anything? I mean anything that will tell you who did it?"

He didn't answer and his gaze lasered into me. The force of his look was so strong, I actually leaned back.

"What?"

"Why are you asking me so much about the case?"

Uh-oh. "I'm curious."

"Curious? Are you trying to get me to tell you a tidbit you can sell to the press?"

"What? No!" This was going south faster than a herd of caribou in a blizzard.

"You sure about that?"

"I wouldn't do that. I just feel connected to this thing, I guess." I glanced down at my hands as if they held the answer. I desperately tried to channel my sister. Emma, the social artist, would work her magic in a situation like this. Kai would be eating out of her hand and spilling his guts. Maybe I needed a rubber bracelet. WWED?

"I don't think you're being honest with me, Grace."

Panic flooded heat to my face, and I blurted out the first thing that came to mind. "It's Jax."

"The dog?"

"If he can be adopted, he'll probably be claimed by a friend or relative. If Mark Richardson was murdered by someone he knew . . . I don't want Jax to be adopted by a killer. That would be awful!"

Kai looked at me like I'd just begun speaking in tongues. I knew it was a ridiculous reason, but it was one I could work with. Mostly because it held a whisper of truth.

"Look," I said. "It may not make sense to you, but it's true. I want him to go to a *good* home. Murderers do not rank high on my list of good."

I wasn't sure if he completely bought it, but he said, "Ooo-kay."

We finished our breakfast in silence, and when we headed across the street, he must have made a decision about me because, as we reached my car, he turned to me and sighed.

"Grace, I can't share any details of the case, so don't ask me to. But I will say this—keep Jax as long as you can."

"I only have him for ten days."

He glanced back toward the sheriff's office as his cell began ringing. "It may take us longer than that."

CHAPTER 3

I hauled myself into Bluebell, cranked the AC, and watched Kai walk into the sheriff's office. I drummed my fingers on the steering wheel and thought about what he had just said. It might take them longer than ten days to find who killed Mark Richardson. Not good. Not good at all. By then, Jax might tell me who the killer was. Then I'd have to tell the cops. Not that they'd believe me. But what other choice would I have?

I noticed a woman walking toward the building. Something about her was familiar. I squinted through the windshield as she got closer and tried to place where I'd seen her before. There was a man with her, leading her quickly toward the doors. He wore a suit and had to be sweating rivers, but he looked unruffled. His hair perfectly gelled, his head high, his suit pressed. The only defect in his confidant facade was his eyes. They darted around, as if he expected someone to jump out at them.

Before I knew what I was doing, I had slid out of Bluebell and followed them into the sheriff's office. I tailed them to the receptionist's desk I had visited earlier and loitered behind them pretending to be looking for something in my purse.

"Miss Jennifer Weston, here to speak to Detective Nocera." The man spoke for her, and I realized two things: He was her lawyer, and she was the woman in one of the photos I had seen at Mark Richardson's house.

The ex-girlfriend. I studied her as they waited for the receptionist to call Jake. She was slim and wore a yellow dress the same shade as her golden hair. A white cardigan covered her shoulders and arms. Weird. It was hot enough out to fry eggs on the sidewalk and here she was in a sweater.

She mumbled something to the lawyer and, ignoring his frown, headed toward the sign that said, RESTROOMS.

I waited almost a full minute, then followed.

As I hoped, Jennifer was just walking out of the stall as I entered the restroom. She glanced at me with big, blue, tear-swollen eyes and a face that made me think of baseball games and apple pie. I couldn't picture her blowing a hole in someone's head.

"Are you okay?" I asked as she dabbed at her eyes.

She nodded. Then shook her head, sniffling. "I—I just lost my best friend. He was . . . someone . . . someone . . . killed him."

The tissue in her trembling fingers was wadded up into a useless ball. I hurried into the stall and unrolled a long section of toilet paper. Ripping it off, I folded it and offered it to her. "I'm so sorry."

She took the tissue and wiped her nose. "Thank you."

At that moment I wished that my psychic gift extended to people. She didn't look like a cold-blooded killer. She didn't act like one either, but who knew? She could have killed Mark Richardson in a jealous rage or something and now her tears were from regret. Or guilt.

"Did you . . . are you here because you're a witness?" I asked, trying to saturate my voice with shock and sympathy.

She shook her head. "No, thank God. But the police are talking to everyone. I don't know what I can tell them. Mark was so wonderful. I can't think of anyone who would want to kill him."

Jennifer started sobbing, and I did what any good Southern woman would do when in the ladies' room with a crying stranger—I gave her a hug and patted her on the back.

After a few moments, she settled down and turned to the sink. She tugged her sleeves up to splash water on her face, and I noticed several deep ugly bruises on her lower arm. I'd seen marks like that before, and knew why she was wearing the sweater.

"Are you sure you're okay?" I kept my eyes on the bruises so my question would be clear. Handprint-shaped bruises didn't just happen. They could be the reason Mark's brain was plastered all over his wall. She might have gotten tired of getting knocked around and pulled the trigger, or she had a new, violent boyfriend who didn't like her thinking of her ex as her "best friend."

Jennifer followed my gaze to her forearm. "I bruise easy." She shrugged, fumbled with the sleeves, and pulled them back down to cover the marks.

I gave her the dubious, woman-to-woman eyebrow raise. She sighed and fussed with the sleeves some more.

After several beats, she finally said, "I know how pathetic that sounded. Like I'm some battered woman or something."

"Are you?" I didn't have to fake my sympathy this time. I had a history with domestic violence. My sister had been a victim. If Jennifer Weston was being abused, I wanted her to get help.

She shook her head, but avoided my eyes. "It's not like that."

Yeah, sure it wasn't. "Well, if you need to talk . . ." I handed her my card just as the door to the ladies' room creaked open a fraction. A man's voice echoed into the room.

"Jennifer? Everything okay?"

"I'm on my way." The door thunked closed, and Jennifer gave me an almost smile, the kind that you just knew would be great if it could break free of the grief and really shine. She looked very sad and very young. "Thanks."

"Sure."

She pushed the door open and walked out of the ladies' room. I thought about her and the bruises and contemplated calling Jake or Kai and telling them about the marks. I wasn't sure I wanted to do that. I didn't think the girl I had just met was a killer. And throwing suspicion on her because of a bruise seemed wrong. Maybe I was projecting. If my sister's ex had been killed and the cops knew her history with him, she would have been suspect. Hell, *I* would be suspect.

I decided to give it time. After all, the cops would do their job. I knew Jake—he was good at what he did. I assumed Kai was, too. They probably already knew more about Jennifer Weston than I'd learned in a five-minute conversation in the ladies' room.

The sun assaulted me as I stepped outside, searing every inch of skin it touched. I hurried to Bluebell, hopped in, and blasted the AC. The hot air from the vents struggled to cool as I edged into traffic. My mind was still locked on Jennifer Weston. I had to ask myself—what would I do if Jax's memory of the murder was of Mark Richardson attacking Jennifer and her shooting him in self-defense?

Would I tell the cops? Would I tell anyone?

The muted sound of "Witchy Woman" drew my attention from the moral quandary. I pawed around in my purse till I found my cell phone. It was my sister.

"Hey, Em, what's up?"

"Guess again, honey!"

I knew the voice instantly and grinned. "Wes? Hey, you're in town!"

"I am—and guess what we're doing tonight?" I felt my smile falter.

I loved Wes. I had since the moment we met on the playground in the fourth grade and he told me my hair was the prettiest he'd ever seen. I have a thing about my hair. Hey, every girl has a favorite feature. Of course, his compliment was not of the romantic nature. Even at nine, I knew that Wes didn't like girls all that much.

This fact never bothered me. I loved him. I loved seeing him when he came back into town. But the fact that he was already with Emma meant they had plotted against me. There was a dress in my future—I could feel it in my bones.

"Emma told me you didn't have any plans, so I made some arrangements."

I winced and tried to think of something, an excuse, to get me out of doing whatever they had planned, but Wes knew me way too well. Just as I began sputtering about having to stay home, Wes said, "You know, it just won't be the same celebrating my birthday if you aren't there."

"Your birthday? Wes, your birthday was in June."

"You know we Geminis can't just celebrate once. And tonight will be my birthday with my girls."

I couldn't say no, and he knew it. "Okay, but I have one condition."

"Oh?" I could almost hear him grinning over the phone.

"You have to change the ring tone on my cell to something else." The sneak had hijacked it and reprogrammed it a month ago. I still hadn't figured out how to change it back to a normal ring.

He laughed. "But nothing else fits so well, my raven-haired, psychic beauty."

I rolled my eyes. Since Wes was the only person outside of my family that knew about my ability, he was also the only person who could get away with calling me things like Witchy Woman, and Gracelicious, without getting run over by a vintage blue Suburban.

I sighed and promised I'd be there. Oh, joy of joys.

CHAPTER 4

Treat? Moss punctuated the thought with a wavering whine.

I ignored him, took another bite of my lunch—a grilled triple-cheese sandwich on thick white bread. As I chewed the melted deliciousness, I pondered what I had learned that morning with Kai. He liked to surf, was quick to suspect ulterior motives in others, and at the moment, was not liking the odds of wrapping up the case quickly. He also had a mountain of evidence to sift through and was clearly missing something important, hence having to head back to the crime scene.

Moss licked his chops loudly and sniffed the grilled cheese–perfumed air. I shot him a look. *Get out of this kitchen and behave.*

Jax clicked-clacked in from the living room, looked from me to Moss, and promptly assumed the same position as his companion.

"See, you're teaching him bad habits." I motioned to Jax, who had also begun to sniff the air.

I turned my back on the dual quivering noses, and chewed pensively as I sorted through my messages. I'd decided that rather than thinking about Sergeant Kai Duncan's clear inquisitive eyes, libido-stoking grin, and the fact that the cops were nowhere near solving the case, I would concentrate on returning the phone calls I'd been neglecting the past couple of days.

I sighed when I saw just how big a pile it was. Between searching for a new place to live and dealing with a wayward murder witness, I had ignored my duties.

Six of the messages were from dog owners with house-training problems; one was from a woman with a destructive potbellied pig.

Best to start with the weirdest first, I decided, and called the owner of the problem pig.

"I just don't understand," lamented the woman who answered the phone. "Daisy has been such a sweet pig, and now we'll have to replace the carpet, and she's pulled up and chewed on the vinyl!"

I bit my lip, forcing back the laugh that danced in the back of my throat. "Uh, how old is Daisy?" I asked, thankful that the woman couldn't see my expression.

"She just had her first birthday. I've had her since she was a baby. This whole time she's been so good," the woman promised, as if I might think Daisy had always been a bad pig.

I sighed inwardly. "I'm sure Daisy's a very sweet pig. Does she have a fenced yard to play in?"

"Yes, but I hate to put her out there in all that dirt."

"I see," I said, though I didn't. People's utter misunderstanding of animal nature would never cease to bewilder me. "Ma'am, I'm going to make a few suggestions. I'd like you to try them, and if Daisy isn't behaving any better in a few days, call me back and we'll set up an appointment."

The woman agreed, and I outlined some suggestions for creating a pig-topia.

Starting with plenty of time outside in the dirt.

I hung up the phone and allowed myself the chuckle I had been holding in. Still grinning, I divided the last bite of my sandwich into two equal portions and tossed them to the dogs. They both snapped up the pieces midair and inhaled them.

I shook my head as I watched them sniff around the floor for stray crumbs. "You guys are pitiful. You act like you're starving." Brushing off my fingers with a napkin, I grabbed my glass of water and went into the room my sister used as an office.

Like the rest of the condo, the space was artfully decorated with colors I'd never imagined would work together. In this room Emma had gone with soothing hues of light aqua-blue and silver, paired with large black-and-white framed prints, and a dark ebony-stained desk and chair.

Quiet glamour—Emma all the way.

I sat on the surprisingly comfortable padded chair and turned on the sleek flat-screen computer. Though I'm about as good with computers as I am with people, I have learned how to do some basic stuff. I quickly checked my e-mail— junk, junk, and more junk. And then I began searching the Internet for property.

"We need something with a lot of room, don't we, boy?" I spoke to Moss, who had followed me into the office and laid his head on my lap.

Ever since my old landlady had decided that large dogs, especially ones that looked like wild animals, were a liability, I'd been desperately searching for a new place to live. Thankfully, my consultation business had been a success. I'd been saving for over a year, and already had enough for a down payment. Now I just had to find the right place. Emma had insisted that I stay with her until I found something suitable.

"You are *not* going to stay in some scummy motel," Emma had ordered. "We'd have to hose your room down with bleach."

I'd resisted, but arguing with Emma was like arguing with a fence post.

Staying here had certainly been helpful. But now that Jax was in the picture, I felt even more pressure to get out of her hair. My sister's place was roomy, overlooked the ocean, and was in an exclusive area. It was not a place for a wolf-dog and his sidekick, the huge Doberman.

So I started what had become a daily ritual and scrolled through online real estate listings, jotting down phone numbers and brief descriptions of the houses I was interested in.

Thirty minutes into my search, I arched my back and rolled my shoulders. *How do people sit in front of these things all day?* I pushed away from the desk.

Moss lifted his head to watch me. He stood and slowly dipped down into a long stretch. *Walk?*

"That sounds like a wonderful idea. What do you say, Jax? Care to take an afternoon stroll?" Jax, who had been lying by the entry to the office, was already on his feet and heading to the foyer closet where the leashes were kept. I grabbed my old Auburn ball cap off the hall table and looped my ponytail through the back. I gathered the dogs' leashes and a tennis ball out of the closet. A few minutes later, we were following a sea oat–lined path to the beach.

The wind had picked up, and the sky was dark and threatening. I watched a distant thunderhead press toward the beach. The blustery wind was thick and heavy with moisture.

There was a big storm brewing offshore. The surf was up. I could see a cluster of surfers bobbing around on their boards, waiting for a good set. I figured Kai wouldn't be able to take advantage of the waves this time.

I hoped like heck that he and Jake would catch Mark Richardson's murderer soon. Part of me felt guilty that I hoped the case would wrap up quickly for purely personal reasons. Not that I was opposed to justice being served; I just didn't want to be the waitress.

I closed my eyes to make the wish official and tried to relax. Breathing in the warm and wonderful scent of the stormy sea, I lingered and listened to the waves crash and rumble as they dove at the sand.

Even though I knew I needed acreage, I was going to miss the beach.

I opened my eyes and scanned the shoreline. No one out

walking but me and the dogs. *Good,* I thought. I would be able to let Jax and Moss frolic free of their leashes for a minute.

I pulled the tennis ball out of my pocket and threw it down the beach. Jax tore after it, kicking up sprays of sand in his eagerness to reclaim the ball. He loped back to me, pranced in a victory circle, and plopped the sand and slobber–covered ball at my feet.

Unlike Moss, who had no interest in such games, Jax never tired of it. He fetched over and over with joyous canine abandon, always ready for the next pitch.

After several minutes of the volley, I felt my arm wearing out. "Let's take a break, buddy. You're killing me." I smiled as I knelt down and stroked the dog's sleek neck.

Jax pawed at the tennis ball, then picked it up and placed it in my hand. *Ball?* He pleaded with me to throw it again.

"Okay, but then we've got to head in."

I hurled the ball as far as I could into the surf and smiled as Jax paused, uncertain, near the water's edge. After a tentative shuffle, he plunged clumsily in after it.

I looked for a sign of Moss and spied him about fifty feet away, sniffing at something on the ground. I watched him for a moment and then closed my eyes and concentrated on calling him to me. *Moss, come, Moss!*

After a few seconds, I opened my eyes. He hadn't even turned to look.

"Oh, well." I didn't know why my ability didn't work at long range. I had tried many times in the past, with the same result. Apparently my brain waves were limited to about a dozen feet.

Shrugging off that humbling thought, I placed my thumb and forefinger into my mouth and whistled. Moss instantly turned his attention to me and, after a second whistle—for some reason it always took two—he trotted toward me.

Jax, also summoned by my whistle, ran up alongside.

"Come on, boys, let's go." I stood, brushed the sand off my shorts, and started toward the condo.

A low rumble sounded from the Doberman's chest. *Danger.*

I could feel the anxiety coursing from the dog. I turned to look for the source of his alarm.

A young black man was walking down the beach toward them. He wore the red swim trunks of a life guard.

I quickly reached down and leashed the two dogs. I could feel Jax's anxiety building. I tried to calm him. "Easy, it's okay."

Jax began to snarl, and I was flooded with an image of Mark being attacked by a black man. I felt instantly that the man was familiar to me. I blinked and tried to focus on the man's face. Did I know him? The moment came and went so quickly in Jax's mind I wasn't sure.

The young lifeguard eyed Jax warily and altered his path to give me and the dogs a wide berth.

I watched as he walked past us and wondered. Was the image a memory of the murder? Or could it be some earlier event? I strained to remember. I had gotten the feeling that there were other people around. Could it have been the night of the party? The night Mark Richardson was killed?

A sudden rumble of thunder pulled me from my thoughts. A cool wind pressed my clothes against me and coaxed goose bumps to rise on my arms. An ominous shiver raced up my spine. Jax was remembering the murder. And I was running out of time.

CHAPTER 5

"Em, this is ridiculous. It's too tight." The bodice of the dress squeezed me like an anaconda. I could barely wheeze out the words.

"That's because your boobs are too big. Here, try this one, it's lower cut . . ." Emma handed me a shimmering aquamarine dress.

I turned to let her unzip me, sucking in an enormous breath as I shimmied out of the black ensemble. "Wes told me it was just us three getting together. Why can't I wear my clothes?"

Emma's only response was to chuckle.

Grumbling, I pulled on the other dress. It fit perfectly. Damn.

"You promised Wes you'd come to dinner and you are going to do so dressed properly." Emma handed me a pair of oversized, silver, dangly earrings.

I reluctantly put them on. "Why can't we go to Cruiser's?" A local hole in the wall, Cruiser's had the best fries on the planet and great homemade ranch dressing. Emma's one weak spot was their cheddar fries.

"Nice try. We are going to Madure. Wes knows the owner, and he's got a special table for us. Besides, I need to talk to him about an event I would like him to cater."

"Hey, if you have to work, then I should just meet you later—"

"Don't even try it." Emma cut me off and held up a pair of strappy high-heeled sandals. "These will be perfect. They may be a little too big, but with the ankle strap, they'll work." Emma eyed me and, finding me lacking somehow, frowned.

"Hmm . . . close, but not quite." Digging in her purse, Emma produced a plump cosmetic bag.

"Oh no"—I held up my hand in self-defense—"no way, no makeup."

My sister arched a flawlessly tweezed brow. "You brought a *Doberman* into my house."

I sighed. "All right, just lipstick."

"And a little eye shadow." Emma held up a swab dusted with citrine-colored powder.

I blew out a breath, crossed my arms, and glared at my sister. "You have got to stop. No war paint."

"It's M.A.C. and this color will bring out the blue of your eyes." She grinned. "With that dress, your eyes will really pop."

There was no point in arguing. Emma was in "make Grace pretty" mode. It happened on occasion. Especially when she had a good excuse like she had tonight. Wes was a successful lawyer in Savannah. He only made it into town a few times a year, and we were celebrating his birthday. I knew resistance was futile, so I closed my eyes and tilted my head back to allow the application.

Emma quickly began brushing on the shadow. "Perfect. Now I just need to add a touch of mascara . . ."

I opened my eyes to see her coming at me with some sort of metal implement. Eyelash curlers. I backed away and shook my head. "No way, Em. I'm drawing the line at torture devices."

"Oh, come on. You tame lions and you can't take eyelash curlers?"

I shook my head. "Nope. No way."

She held up the little metal clampy thing and squeezed the ends together. In her best German accent, she sneered, "Ve haf vays of making you talk, Dr. Jones."

Laughing like a lunatic, I squealed loud enough to set the dogs into a state. Moss barked and Jax surged to his feet with a low, confused growl.

I'm okay, we're just playing. I noticed it took Jax a while to relax after that. "I shouldn't even be going out. I should stay with Jax."

"You said he needed time, right? Give him some," Emma said. "Besides, you might actually have fun if you'd talk to people. Mingle a little."

"And say what? 'Hi, I'm Grace, I communicate with animals psychically. What do you do?'"

"You could just learn to chat, not be so prickly, for God's sake. Hold still." She finished by painting a layer of gloss on my lips and beamed. "You look gorgeous."

I was just getting ready to say something about looking more like a hooker, when the doorbell rang. Jax and Moss, who now eyed us with only mild interest, both sprang to the ready.

"Moss . . . Jax . . . stay."

"I'll get it. Put on those shoes," Emma commanded and sauntered out of the room.

I did as she asked and teetered out of the bedroom. "Emma how do you walk in—" I broke off mid-sentence when I stepped out of the hall into the main living area.

Kai Duncan was following my sister into the condo. He stopped dead when he saw me. His lips parted as he took in my appearance. The sexy heels. The sinfully cut aqua dress that flowed over my curves like water. His eyes didn't seem to know where to look first. Finally, his gaze settled on my cleavage before he managed to yank it up to my face.

I crossed my arms. "It isn't polite to stare, Mr. Duncan."

He seemed to be struggling to find his vocal cords. I've been known to leave men speechless on occasion. Usually, because I've cut them off at the knees. I handle machismo, unwanted advances, and jackassery in a very precise and cold manner. For some reason, the Ice Queen glower didn't seem to work on Kai.

Maybe with the sexpot dress, it didn't have the same effect.

"Sorry, you look . . . different with your hair down. And it's Kai, remember?"

If I was vain about anything, it was my hair. Freed from its typical ponytail and bushed into a fall of shimmering jet, it was easily my best feature. Thanks to my grandmother's Cherokee blood, my hair has always been thick and long and perfectly straight. But somehow, I didn't think it was my locks he'd been admiring.

"What are you doing here, Kai?"

"Oh, I . . ." He started to hand me a few loose sheets of paper when he became aware of the dogs that had entered the room to stand on either side of me.

He seemed to recognize Jax from the crime scene. But Moss soon commanded Kai's undivided attention. He blinked a few times, almost like he thought he was seeing things. "Ah, is that a *wolf*?"

I absently placed my hand on my dog's enormous white head. It was easy, as it came to my waist even in heels. "Moss is a hybrid; he's only half wolf."

"Really? Only half? 'Cause judging by the way he's looking at me . . ."

"Moss won't eat you." I just couldn't help myself. I let my lips curve up slightly and added, "Unless I tell him to." Right on cue, Moss let out a low growl.

Kai's eyes widened, but he stood his ground. A big point for him.

Emma placed her hands on her hips. "Grace, that isn't very polite, is it?"

I glared at Emma for a moment. "Oh, all right." *Go on, boys.* I flicked my wrist and my two canine sentinels turned and disappeared down the hall. "What can I help you with, Kai?"

He relaxed a little, now that he knew he wasn't going to be eaten. "I told you to read what you sign." He smiled, holding out a sheet of paper.

"Excuse me?"

"The papers you signed this morning were for reclaiming an impounded vehicle. I figured I'd save you a trip and bring you the right ones."

I took the papers. "You came all the way out here just to give me these?"

"No. I was on my way back to work. I live in Atlantic Beach. I ran home to get some sleep and feed my cat, Dusty."

"Well, that was nice of him, wasn't it, Grace?" Emma smiled coaxingly at me.

It *was* nice, damn it. And he had a cat. A cute surfer who liked cats and apparently, from the way he had been staring, liked me.

Wait, amend that, I thought. Kai is a cute *cop*. A cop who I might have to tell about my ability. Then we'd see if he still liked me . . .

I started to thank him for bringing the papers just as his cell phone rang. He flipped it open. "Duncan." Turning, he walked back into the foyer.

As soon as his back was turned, I felt myself being pulled into the kitchen. Emma whispered intensely as Kai talked on the phone. "What are you doing? Ask him to meet us after he gets off."

I rejected the idea at first, but then thought about it. Kai was clearly . . . impressed with the way I looked in my outfit. Maybe he'd be distracted enough to give me a little more information on the case. After a drink or two, I might even be able to flirt, if I tried.

"You're right, Em, I should."

Emma gasped and clapped her hand over her mouth like I'd just cursed in church.

She started to say something, but I held up my hand. "Shhh."

It sounded like there had been a break in the case. I heard the word *suspect*, which seemed like a good thing. I inched into the foyer to eavesdrop.

Kai's voice echoed in the small space. "What? Why wasn't it in its cage? Was anyone hurt?" I felt a twinge of unease. Something was wrong. I walked out of the kitchen and toward the front door just as Kai was opening it. As he turned away from me, I heard him say, "LaBryce Walker's in serious shit for this. I'm on my way." He hung up and I felt a sudden twist of fear.

"I've got to go, Grace," he said, and started out the door.

"Wait, Kai." I snagged his sleeve. "Is LaBryce Walker a suspect?"

"Yes. And he evidently left a little surprise for our team that went over to search his house. His pet jaguar was out of its cage."

"Charm."

"What?"

My heart began to hammer in my chest. "Did they hurt her?"

"Who?"

"The jaguar."

"Not yet, but if it gets outside—"

"Em—" I spun toward her.

Emma was already handing me my purse. "We'll go out some other time. I'll tell Wes you had an emergency."

"Thanks." I grabbed my keys and cell phone off the hall table and walked out the door. "Let's go. I'll handle the jaguar. Call your people back and tell them not to go into the house." I glanced back at Kai, who was looking at me as if I'd just proclaimed I was the messiah.

"Wait a second, Grace, that thing isn't in a cage—it's loose in the house. It could break through a window or—"

"Kai, call them back, please." He followed me as I hurried down the stairs to the parking lot. "If she's being aggressive, it's only because she's confused and scared. She's half-blind."

"And you know this because . . ." Kai stopped next to a small silver pickup.

I walked around and pulled open the passenger door. "I'll explain on the way."

Kai hesitated a moment and then, cursing, opened his door and slid in behind the wheel. He dialed the phone and relayed my message as he drove.

"Tell them to get away from the house and turn any lights or sirens off." I rifled through my purse in search of a pony-tail holder.

Kai did as I asked and hung up.

We sped along Beach Boulevard, Kai's dashboard light flashing silently. "Okay, Grace, explain to me why I just put the guys on the scene in danger by telling them not to kill that animal."

I paused in my search for a hair tie. "Remember about three years ago, there was a guy breeding exotic animals up in Georgia?"

"Yeah, he got mauled to death by a tiger, or something."

"It was a jaguar." I quickly looped my hair up away from my face and twisted it into a haphazard bun. "When the breeder got word that the authorities were onto him, he panicked. He tried to take the healthiest animals with him. Somehow the male jag got a hold of him—he'd been dead two days when we got there."

"We? You were involved in this?"

"Along with handlers and investigators from the ASPCA and the Humane Society." I shuddered, remembering the appalling scene. The half-eaten man, the stench of disease and decay. "It was terrible. The animals were all in such bad condition, most were starving, or dead."

I felt a lump rise to my throat. I paused and swallowed hard. God, the poor things had all been so scared and in so much pain. And of course, I'd felt all of it.

When I spoke again, I wasn't surprised to hear that my voice was barely more than a whisper. "There wasn't much we could do."

"What happened to the survivors?"

I glanced at him and saw true compassion in his face. It made it easier to tell the story, knowing he cared, and didn't just want to know out of morbid curiosity.

"The male jaguar was taken to a rescue facility in Kentucky. The female had been dead for at least three weeks, as were two of her cubs. The only other animals that made it where a couple of male dogs, a female timber wolf, two of her pups, and a jaguar cub." I looked over at Kai, watched as he pieced it together. I shouldn't have been surprised. After all, he was an investigator.

"So that's where you got Moss."

"And that is where LaBryce got Charm."

Kai looked at me with raised brows. "Charm? As in Lucky?"

"Hugh Murray, the zoo vet, came up with the name because she was lucky to be alive. Somehow, she'd managed to squeeze through a gap in her cage and had gotten out to where the timber wolf had been tied to a tree and had been nursing with the wolf pups, but she was still very sick. She had a severe respiratory infection and was blind in one eye. Zoos wouldn't take her, and the rescue centers couldn't take a cub with so many problems. A group of volunteers took turns looking after her."

"I don't get it. How did Walker end up with her?"

"The local news ran a story on her. LaBryce saw it. He called and asked if he could adopt her."

"You've got to be kidding me," he muttered.

"Why would you go into LaBryce's house anyway?"

"We have a search warrant."

"You think LaBryce had something to do with Mark Richardson's murder?" It was hard to imagine. I'd known LaBryce for years; he'd never shown even an ounce of temper, especially to his friends.

"You look shocked," Kai said.

"I am."

"Can't picture LaBryce as a killer?"

A yes or no would be too simple. I thought for a moment and asked, "Why do you think LaBryce wanted a jaguar? Aside from it being his team's mascot."

Kai lifted a shoulder. "Because he's a macho football player who wanted a cool status symbol?"

I shook my head. "I thought the same thing when I heard he wanted her, but no."

"To get chicks?"

That made me smile. "Maybe some. But truth is, he cares."

"Are we talking about the same guy?" Kai's voice was dripping with skepticism. "The LaBryce Walker who stars in gangsta rap videos and hangs out with thugs?"

"That's just publicity stuff. He sells a lot of merchandise based on an image that isn't real."

Kai scoffed. I ignored it. "The first time he came to see Charm, I knew his thug persona was just an act. You should have seen him." I smiled, remembering how enamored the giant running back had been with the sickly cub. "He didn't want to make a big deal of it. Didn't want a lot of people to know he had adopted her. LaBryce wasn't just thinking about how cool it would be to own a pet jaguar. He was moved by the whole situation, donated thousands to the ASPCA. He went to extra lengths to make sure Charm had an enclosure that mimicked her natural habitat. He spent months learning how to handle her. If you own an exotic pet, the USDA has the right to inspect your home. It's not like having a big tabby cat. Not even close."

Kai pulled onto J. Turner Butler Boulevard, where several billion-dollar subdivisions had popped up during the building boom. He seemed to be mulling over this new information as he drove.

He looked at me. "Okay, so if LaBryce is so enamored with this animal, why would he leave her out? He must have known that there would be a chance one of the officers would shoot her."

I frowned and shook my head. He wouldn't. There was no way. "It must have been an accident. I think you should find out who was supposed to be taking care of Charm tonight. I know you believe that LaBryce left her out on purpose, but I don't think so. "

Kai scoffed. "Right."

"I'm serious. LaBryce has to have someone care for her when he's out of town."

"We have people who will be looking into it. Believe me, we're investigating everyone who might have been involved in the murder. But right now, we have to concentrate on our most viable suspect."

We turned off JTB and sped toward the end of a cul-de-sac, finally pulling up to a long drive. Kai turned off his light and held up his badge as we slowly passed two officers in a squad car. We rolled to a stop about fifty feet from the front of the house.

I slid out of the truck and my sister's high-heeled sandals sank into the grass. I noticed Jake Nocera eyeing the front windows of the house as he talked on his cell phone. "Yeah, we got someone on the way. No one was hurt. I opened the door, nearly shit my pants, and closed it." He noticed me and Kai and walked toward us. "You make sure Walker stays in custody until I get back. We're gonna have a little talk. I've gotta run." He slapped the cell phone closed and paused to look me up and down. "Not quite dressed for big-cat wrangling."

I felt heat creep into my cheeks and noticed more than a few pair of eyes focusing on my cleavage. Inwardly, I cursed Emma's fashion sense and sent Jake a frigid glare. The rest of the oglers didn't warrant a glance.

I held up my cell phone and turned to Kai. "What's your number?" He told me, and I programmed it into my phone. "I'll call you when I get her secured."

I hurried quietly toward the large, ultramodern house. It was angular and sleek with a lot of glass and dramatic lighting. Of course, I'd been there plenty of times. I'd made it my personal mission to make sure LaBryce was living up to his promise to learn how to handle a big cat. I was the person who'd taught him those techniques. At first, I hadn't liked anything about the big, cocky football player. Except that he clearly wanted to care for an animal that might have had to be euthanized otherwise.

But much to my surprise, and I'm sure his, LaBryce and I had become friends. We didn't agree on everything. I refused to help him with photo shoots where he wanted to use Charm as a prop, and he couldn't understand why I was such a hard-ass when it came to not feeding her people food. Ever. But we both cared about Charm, and when she was still a cub, I'd bring Moss over and they would play.

During those visits, LaBryce and I would chat. I learned he wasn't the brainless football player I'd thought, and he really did love his jaguar. There was no way he'd endanger her by allowing her out of her enclosure unsupervised. He wouldn't just set her loose, though she clearly was.

Through the massive front window, I could see movement, a hint of gold, speckled with black. Charm was in the living room to the right of the front door.

I heard Kai's quiet footsteps in the grass. I looked at him—he didn't look happy.

"Is the door unlocked?" I whispered.

"Yes."

I nodded and tried to come up with a plan. It had been a while since Charm had seen me. Though I couldn't tell from this distance, she might be highly upset about all the commotion. Or she might not.

Only one way to find out. "Okay, I'm going to go in. If she jumps me, shoot through the glass window. It might distract her, scare her off."

I knew instantly that I shouldn't have said that.

"If she *jumps* you?" Kai whispered as we crept up the front steps. "I thought you helped raise her."

"Well . . ." I paused, feeling a sudden twinge of nerves. "She might not remember me."

Kai followed close behind me as we made our way onto the porch. "But you walked up to a snarling Doberman without batting an eye."

"This is different. Dogs have been domesticated for thousands of years." I inched up to the huge picture window and peered inside. "It may be hard to believe, but *that* is a wild animal."

We both gazed into the room. The jaguar lounged benignly on a black leather sofa. Her tail flicked up and down, and her attention was fixed on the entryway to the room.

I could hear Kai's breath next to my ear. "Grace, I can't let you do this."

I turned and asked, "You have a better idea?"

"Yes, we get someone from the zoo to dart it and you don't risk your life."

I reached up on impulse and patted his cheek. "You're cute when you're worried."

His eyes hardened. "You won't think I'm so cute when I toss you over my shoulder and haul your ass away from here."

From the look in his eyes, he meant it. If he really thought I was in danger and I resisted, he would fireman-carry me back to his truck. Usually, I'd be irritated by the caveman machismo, but coming from Kai it was . . . sweet.

"Look, I'm sure she'll remember me, okay? And if someone from the zoo came to tranq her, they'd have to go inside. I have a much better chance of ending this peacefully. Trust me."

Kai seemed to think about it for a long time. Finally, he nodded. "So what are you going to do?"

I shrugged and moved quietly to the riveted metal front door. "Talk to her."

I began to turn the handle. The cat tensed on the other side of the door.

My stomach tightened nervously in response. I focused on remaining calm. *It's okay, Charm. It's me, Grace.* I opened the door slowly and stepped inside. The living room was to my right. I tried to conjure up as many memories of the jaguar as I possibly could. Starting from the time I had cared for Charm for those weeks as a cub. She had been so small and bony. I always worried she'd get cold. So I'd piled blankets around her, just in case. She loved for me to cover her with them, with just the tip of her spotted tail sticking out. With those images firmly in place, I walked cautiously into the room.

Charm had abandoned her perch on the sofa and was now standing, facing me.

I kept my voice level and quiet. "Hey, pretty girl, remember me?"

The jaguar let out a low growl. Her pupils dilated and she lowered her head, focusing intently on me.

I knew what Charm was doing; she was getting ready to pounce. I felt her pulse quicken. I took a deep breath to steady myself and concentrated on strengthening my memories of her, and bringing them to the front of my mind.

No fear, just thoughts of the jaguar's time with me as a cub—sleeping on the rug under all those blankets, wrestling around the house with Moss, the way she would beg for bottles of milk even when she wasn't hungry.

The growling slowly subsided. Charm's head and tail lifted in recognition. She sniffed the air. *Bottle?*

Relief flooded through me, and I let out the shaky breath I hadn't even realized I'd been holding. I grinned at the big cat. "Oh, so you remember your bottle, huh?"

Charm loped forward and wound her sinewy body around my knees in indisputable feline welcome. *Bottle!*

I knelt and took hold of the big cat's round head in both hands. I looked into the green-rimmed golden eyes, one slightly clouded. "I don't have a bottle for you right now."

Charm butted my head with hers. *No bottle?*

I laughed. *Maybe later.* I remained on the floor, stroking the cat. I glanced at the window. Kai stood outside, gun drawn, watching intently. I nodded to him, and he slowly holstered the gun.

I turned my attention back to Charm, who had stretched out on the floor so she could lick the scented lotion off my leg. "Ouch! Sandpaper Tongue." *Quit that!*

Charm looked up at me and plopped a giant paw on my bended knee.

"Quit begging. Haven't you been fed tonight?"

In answer, Charm sprang up and loped across the room. I followed. The big cat led me into LaBryce's spacious stainless-clad kitchen. Charm pawed at the refrigerator door that I knew was reserved just for her food. *Fish.*

"Tonight is fish, huh?" I opened the wide fridge. Charm paced in anticipation as I searched the shelves.

No fish. In fact, except for a small container of ground beef, there wasn't much in the fridge at all.

I glanced at Charm.

"Who's supposed to be feeding you?"

Fish!

Something wasn't right. If the police had brought LaBryce in for questioning and he hadn't warned them she was out of her enclosure, he must have thought she was being fed and cared for. Which wasn't the case.

Charm rubbed her head against the back of my knee, making me stumble forward. She pawed at my ankle and began licking my calf. *Hungry.*

Okay, I could ponder the hows and whys later. I needed to offer the jaguar something other than my leg to munch on.

Opening the freezer, I found a bag of whole herring—but it would take too long to thaw.

"No fish tonight, girl. We're moving on to plan B."

Charm followed me around as I rummaged through the cabinets.

Finally, I came up with an acceptable amount of canned tuna, added it to the ground beef, and mixed the two together to make a lumpy, fishy meat loaf.

I dumped the concoction onto a stainless tray and said, "Okay, you can eat in your enclosure, let's go."

Charm padded beside me looking up at the tray like, well, like a hungry jaguar. *Go on.* I shooed her forward with my mind. I was sure Kai was wondering what was taking so long, and I wanted to get her secured as quickly as possible.

She bounded past me out of the kitchen. I hurried behind. The house was dark, and I had to flip on lights as I went. It had been a while since I'd seen the addition LaBryce had commissioned to be Charm's room, and I'd never been there in the evening.

It was a bit eerie at night. In the day, the room appeared to be part sitting area, part jungle. In dim light, all I could make out was the large couch and exotic stone coffee table. The far side of the room seemed to be swallowed by the blackness of a thick tropical forest.

I took a step toward the thicket of trees to my right, looking for a light switch. After a moment I found one and clicked it on. A gentle glow lit the room. And somehow didn't take away from the wild feel. Though I knew the sitting area was separated from the jungle by a wall of thick glass, it didn't look like it. The room just melted into forest. The illusion was aided by several large potted trees and ferns that were grouped in front of the glass and along the perimeter of the room.

Charm stood at the far end of the room near a clump of banana trees and grumbled impatiently.

I walked toward her. "Who let you out?"

Open. Charm slinked behind the giant banana tree and vanished.

I moved to where the large guillotine door was tucked behind the thick foliage of the trees. The rope holding it open was wrapped tightly around a metal cleat. I ducked inside and hunch-backed through a short tunnel.

When I emerged on the other side, I straightened and drew in a deep breath. The air was humid and thick with the scent of moist earth and exotic plants.

A waterfall trickled into a shallow pool. Through the thick canopy, stars sparkled down through the glass ceiling. Moss-covered logs and orchid-draped trees surrounded us. I smelled the sweet scent of a night-blooming cirrus and saw a giant one in one corner. LaBryce had added some great touches since I'd been there last. "I need to come see you more often."

But Charm was interested in one thing. She butted her head against my thigh. *Fish!*

"Here you go." I chuckled. "We should have named you Piglet." I set the pan of fish-meat down and Charm grumbled contentedly.

"Oh, shit." In my admiration for the enormous enclosure's improvements, I had forgotten that Kai and the others were waiting out front. I walked to the second guillotine door on the inside wall of the tunnel. I freed its ropes from the cleat, allowing the door to slide down into place.

I dialed the stored number to give everyone the green light.

Kai answered on the first ring. "Are you okay?"

"I'm fine."

"Are we clear?"

"Come on in. We're in the enclosure in the back of the house. It looks like someone left the door open."

"Walker?"

"No. LaBryce wouldn't be that careless. Whoever should have been taking care of Charm screwed up. She wasn't fed."

I glanced down at the jaguar, who slurped happily at her dinner.

"Maybe he wanted her to be hungry."

"I know you don't believe it, but LaBryce wouldn't do that." I looked up and saw Kai enter the sitting room, still holding the cell phone to his ear. He walked over to the glass partition and said, "We're going to be here awhile . . ."

I shrugged. "That's all right. I'll stay in here with Charm."

Kai looked over at the crouching feline, who hardly responded to the men clambering into the sitting room. "I guess she remembered you."

"Luckily."

"You sure you'll be all right?"

"I will, though I'm not sure my sister's shoes will survive." I glanced down at the dirt-caked sandals and shook my head. "Emma's going to flip."

"Are you actually more afraid of your sister than of being mauled by a three-hundred-pound cat?"

"Cats I can handle." I looked down at Charm, who had finished her meal and was looking up at me hopefully. When I glanced back at Kai, he caught my gaze and held it.

"I'm beginning to think you could handle just about anything," he said.

I flushed at the compliment and the intensity of his gaze. Could I handle loose jaguars? Yes. Wild horses? No problem. Hot cops? Not so much. Thankful that Kai had turned his attention to Jake, who had just entered the room, I focused on forcing the blush out of my cheeks. Kai spoke to Jake for a moment then turned back to me.

"I'll call you when we finish up." He was all business now. "Don't touch anything in the enclosure. We'll have to search it, too."

I nodded and then flipped the cell phone closed. I watched as Kai joined the other investigators. Damn it, despite my best efforts, I was beginning to like him.

And that scared the hell out of me.

If I liked him, that meant I cared. If I cared, I could get hurt.

I shoved away the thought. I would be able to freeze Kai out. I'd done it before.

I was grateful that, for the moment, I had a distraction. And it would serve as a reminder why I couldn't care about Sergeant Kai Duncan. My friend LaBryce Walker was suspected of not only endangering the lives of police officers by leaving his jaguar out, but murder. I didn't believe he was guilty of either.

As luck would have it, I knew someone I could ask.

"Come here, Charm." I led the cat away from the glass. I picked up the steel tray, flipped it over, and set it on a log to use as my seat. At least it kept Emma's dress from getting any more grime on it.

I took the cat's head in my hands and looked straight into her large, intelligent eyes. "Now, tell me what happened last night."

CHAPTER 6

I watched Kai from where I sat on the large damp log. He snapped off his latex gloves, his face lined with frustration. The cops had come up empty. It had taken them four hours to figure out what I already knew. There was no murder weapon in the house.

I'd been sitting on that log for a long time wondering how I was going to convince Kai, or Jake, or any cop, for that matter, that the reason they hadn't found the gun that killed Mark Richardson was very simple. LaBryce didn't shoot him. He had spent the night snoring on the couch with a jaguar pillow.

I still hadn't come up with a way to explain this to the police. I couldn't tell them the truth—that the *cat* had told me what had happened the night before.

From what I could gather, LaBryce had come home earlier than normal and let her out of her enclosure. He'd made himself several drinks and passed out on the couch, resting his head on her side.

Apparently, this morning LaBryce had been hungover and irritated that the person who was supposed to be preparing meals for Charm and taking care of her when he left was not there. She called him "Foodman," for obvious reasons. Charm showed me his face, which was no help because I had never seen him before.

In Foodman's absence, LaBryce had fed her something she had never had before—from the description, I thought it had probably been pizza.

After that, he had left and hadn't come home.

Charm was LaBryce's alibi. Not exactly something I could tell the cops. The truth did not always set you free.

I saw Kai walk to a cop who seemed to have been stationed in the room to keep an eye on me. I guess they wanted to be sure that I didn't tamper with anything. I understood the reasoning. But it still wounded my sense of pride to have a babysitter. Maybe the cops just wanted to be ready if Charm decided she didn't like me anymore. I looked down at where she dozed peacefully at my bare feet. With my fancy dress and shoes, I probably looked like a shipwreck survivor on some tropical island. Except most people would be eaten alive by the cat that was drooling on my toes.

I heard a light tap on the glass. Looking up, I saw Kai pointing to his cell. I guess he didn't want to call me and startle the sleeping jaguar. I picked up my phone and called him.

He answered as soon as it rang. "Hey, you ready to get out of there?" he asked.

"If she'll let me leave." Charm looked up and I leaned over to stroke the huge spotted head. "Let me say my goodbyes and I'll be right out."

I hung up and was aware that Kai was watching me as I petted and talked to the jaguar. I leaned in close to the big cat's ear and promised to be back soon. I slowly massaged her neck and allowed myself to feel her utter satisfaction.

I placed my forehead against the jaguar's and closed my eyes. "I'm going to make sure you are fed and have someone to look after you until this whole mess is sorted out, okay?"

At the thought of food, Charm plopped a paw on my knee.

"No." *It's not time to eat again yet, Miss Piggy.*

I stood, ignoring the hopeful look and gentle grumble and walked to the passageway. I turned to Charm, who had stood up to follow.

"Stay," I ordered with both my voice and my mind.

I felt ridiculous standing there in the clingy dress pointing my finger at a jaguar like someone would a misbehaving poodle. But hey, it worked.

I tugged on the ropes and slid the guillotine door open and secured them to the cleat. I crouched through the passageway, released the ropes on the other side, and lowered the second door into place.

Kai watched me thoughtfully. "The double doors are obviously a security precaution. Were both of these doors open when you came in?" he asked.

"Yes."

"So, chances are, the person who opened them was familiar with both the cat and how to operate the doors."

I nodded. "It would be stupid to open the enclosure and free a jaguar you had no control over."

Kai picked up a stainless case I assumed contained a bunch of crime-solving paraphernalia, and we started through the house. As we moved past the loitering police officers who were standing around the living room, I tried to catch snippets of conversation. Hearing a familiar gruff curse, I caught sight of Jake standing near the foyer. He was talking on the phone, and he was not a happy Yankee.

In fact, I'm sure he was muttering a curse in Italian, or a North Americanized version, at least.

He saw us approach and said, "Look, *sir*, I know you want this case closed and I'm doing—" Jake pressed his lips together tightly. He started turning an unhealthy shade of red. "How about next time there's a warrant to search someone's house with a *lion* in it, I'll let you do the honors?" He slapped the phone closed so hard I wondered if it was still in one piece. "Chief wants to hand this thing to the governor wrapped up in a pretty little bow."

"We can't just wave a magic wand and make evidence appear," Kai said.

Jake's gaze settled on me. "We've still got one more place to look before we have to cut Walker loose. Grace, can you come back tomorrow and make sure no one gets mauled?"

I nodded, and Jake's phone rang. Guess it wasn't broken after all.

Jake moved back into the house. Before he was out of range, I heard him say, "Yeah, but I'm still going to nail Walker's ass for reckless endangerment."

Kai and I walked through the foyer and stopped at the front door to let two uniformed officers past. Through the open doorway, I saw half a dozen or more news vans crowding the street.

I was glad Kai had parked his truck inside the perimeter. The last thing I wanted to do was fight my way through a crowd of reporters.

"How'd the media know to come here?" I asked.

"Scanners. I'm sure someone overheard what was going on with Charm. A wild jaguar on the loose. A famous football player suspected in the murder of the governor's son. It's a reporter's dream."

I folded my arms and glared at the crowd. This was not good. LaBryce would be put on trial by the media before he was even charged. I had to think of a way to explain that he was innocent. But how? I'd thought myself around in this circle all night and was starting to feel like a hamster. Running, running, running on the wheel . . . never getting anywhere.

I was so caught up in the merry-go-round in my mind that I barely noticed Kai pulling on a new pair of latex gloves. Then I felt something brush my backside.

"What the—" I spun to face him. "What are you doing?"

"Collecting evidence."

I stared at him doubtfully. "From my . . ."

He held up the hairs he'd pulled from my dress. "We collected hairs very similar to these from Mark's body. Hold still."

Kai placed his case on the ground, opened it, and grabbed a bag. He knelt down beside me and carefully began brushing more hairs off into the bag. I felt myself tense in response to the way his hand seemed to linger longer than it needed to. Normally this sort of liberty would infuriate me. I waited for the glacial calm to descend, for the biting comment to come to my lips, but instead, I felt a stir of heat where he had touched me.

"Sorry. I just need enough to do a comparison." He was still kneeling at my hip, and when he grinned up at me, his eyes held just enough glimmer to tell me he'd gotten more than enough hairs but not nearly enough touching.

I tried my best to give him an arch look. "Did you enjoy that?"

He stood, holding my gaze. "Yes. It's always nice to find evidence in unexpected places."

There was a rumble overhead, and I remembered the line of storms I'd seen earlier.

"Come on, before it starts to rain."

We hurried out of the house toward the driveway, quickening our steps as the first raindrops began to fall. Florida thunderstorms are not known for their gentle rain and light breezes. It only took an instant for the sparse, fat drops to become a deluge. The gusting winds made us stagger on our race to the truck.

We leapt inside, slamming the doors closed. I could feel rainwater trickling in little rivulets all over me. It dripped from my hair, which had come loose and was plastered like a wet cape to my shoulders.

The thin material of the aqua dress clung to my breasts and upper thighs. In the movies this would be sexy. I felt like a drowned ferret.

"Great." I shivered, goose bumps marching over my skin.

"Here." Kai reached over and opened the glove box. His arm brushed over my thigh as he did and he froze for a moment. "Napkins," he said, finally seeming to remember what he was doing. "I always keep some in here."

I took the paper napkin and wiped the rain off my face and arms.

I noticed Kai watching me as I dabbed at the hollow of

my neck, then my upper chest. Apparently he didn't think I looked so bad.

Glancing at him, I asked, "What?" My voice was a little breathy and I can honestly say that shocked me.

"I've never wanted to be a piece of tissue paper before, but at the moment, it seems like a great idea."

I didn't know what to say to that. But I felt heat rush to my face.

Kai seemed to shake himself mentally and turned away. He started the truck and backed out of the driveway. Winding through the swarm of reporters, who were apparently undeterred by the rain, he turned away from the house and headed back into town.

After a few minutes of awkward silence marked only by the swish of windshield wipers and driving rain, I decided to try to break the tension that had settled like fog in the small cab.

"Beside the hairs, did you find anything?"

"Not yet." Kai seemed to relax. Maybe he was glad I hadn't commented on his tissue paper remark.

"But you think you will?"

"We still have one place in the house we haven't covered."

"Charm's enclosure."

Kai nodded and glanced at me. "Do you think you can meet me at the house tomorrow morning at nine?"

I lifted a shoulder. "Sure, but you'll just be wasting your time." I had to tread lightly here.

"You seem to be pretty certain of that."

"I am. I know LaBryce. And I'm telling you, whatever information you have that made you think he's involved is faulty."

"LaBryce Walker and Mark Richardson got into a fight the night of the murder."

I thought of the man Jax had remembered when we had been at the beach that morning. LaBryce.

"So? People get in fights all the time. Especially at parties when drinking is involved."

"LaBryce threatened to kill Mark."

I found this utterly shocking. "LaBryce and Mark were friends."

"Not according to the latest issue of *Sports Illustrated*. Mark was quoted in an interview saying he thought LaBryce was done. That he had lost his edge and hoped the team could survive another year with him as running back."

Ouch. "I don't get it. LaBryce told me he was the one who talked the coaches into signing Mark in the first place."

"You don't think people toss each other under the bus all the time, even if they're supposed to be friends?"

I knew they did. One more reason to stick with animals. Animals are much more civilized. The thought made me laugh out loud.

At Kai's questioning glance, I said, "That just reminds me of why I love my dog."

We drove for a while in silence. Though this time, it was more companionable. I worried about the person responsible for taking care of Charm's meals. I'd barely been able to scrape up enough to feed her dinner; she'd be hungry again in the morning.

"Kai, would it be possible for me to talk to LaBryce?"

"Why?"

"I need to talk to him about Charm. If I'm going to take care of her in the morning."

Kai seemed to think about it for a long time. I'm not sure if he was becoming suspicious of me again or if he just didn't want to go through the trouble.

"A hungry jaguar is a dangerous jaguar. I need—"

"Okay. I'll run you by the JSO." He didn't seem happy.

I felt a twinge of temper. What did he think I was planning? To slip LaBryce a file so he could saw through his bars? They could and, I'm sure, would listen to everything I said to LaBryce. I started to point that out when Kai's phone rang.

He answered, "Duncan." There was a long pause. "Let me guess, jaguar hair?"

He flicked a glance at me. "I collected some tonight for comparison. I'd be willing to bet they're a match."

He said a few other things that were so cryptic and technical I had no idea what he was talking about. But I knew this was not good news for LaBryce.

Kai flipped his phone closed and said, "You might need to make long-term arrangements for the cat."

• • •

Kai led me out of the elevators and down a nondescript hallway. The overhead lights were bright and buzzing. The floors either industrial carpet or industrial tile. It was nothing like the cop shows on television where the lights are dim and there are sleek glass partitions everywhere.

This was a bit more humdrum than I had envisioned.

Kai opened a door and motioned for me to go inside. I saw LaBryce seated at a table, his eyes hooded, massive ebony arms crossed over his chest. Whoever he was expecting to walk through the door, it wasn't me. His expression didn't change that much, but I saw a flash of confusion in his eyes, then he looked me up and down and his whole body tensed.

I knew I looked a mess. The dress had dried some, but it was a disaster, smeared with dirt and clumps of jaguar hair. I'd tried to finger-comb my damp hair, but it was still tangled from the brief but violent encounter with the driving rain. I was sure the makeup my sister had so carefully applied was gone or had moved to where it shouldn't be.

The harsh lights didn't help.

LaBryce began to shake. He looked past me at Kai, and his face twisted into a horrible mask of rage.

"Bastard!" More suddenly that I thought possible, he launched himself out of the chair and slammed Kai against the wall. The next few seconds passed so fast I was hardly able to process them.

Kai, who must have been as stunned as I was, was slow on the uptake. LaBryce, a man who had based his ten-year career in the NFL on speed and power, held Kai easily against the wall. Then pivoted, trying to slam Kai to the ground.

At some point I screamed. Or at least yelled, "No!" Kai managed to keep his feet and they both staggered into the table. It scooted over the floor, and I heard LaBryce yell, "What did you do to her?"

I jumped forward and grabbed one of LaBryce's immense shoulders. Like I was going to pull him off. It was like trying to wrestle an elephant. "LaBryce, stop!"

Though leaning back over the table, Kai managed to get enough leverage to swing an elbow. It landed with a thud against LaBryce's cheek.

There was shouting and commotion behind me. I was shoved away and against the wall while a swarm of cops filled the small room. I saw the oversized shape of a Taser gun in someone's hand, and in an instant, LaBryce was on the ground, stunned, and Kai was standing in front of me. His face was cold and stony, but his eyes burned with anger.

He grabbed my arm and half walked, half dragged me back to the elevators. I wanted to ask him where we were going, but I was still a little shocked over what had just happened.

LaBryce had taken one look at my disheveled appearance and leapt on Kai. It made no sense. If Kai was going to ask me to explain, he was out of luck.

"I don't know why he jumped on you."

Silence. The elevator opened and he pulled me down to an office marked DUNCAN. Once we were inside, he slammed the door.

"Talk." It was an order and not a nice one.

I felt my back go rigid. "I just said I don't know."

He shook his head. "Walker took one look at you and assumed I had done something to you."

"So?"

"So, he didn't react like a *friend*."

I didn't like the implication. I might not tell the whole truth when it came to my ability, but I wasn't a damn liar. "I don't know why he did what he did. Why don't you ask him?"

"I'm asking you."

"I answered your question."

There was a knock at the door. Kai took another moment to glower at me and pulled the door open.

Jake stepped into the office. "I heard LaBryce jumped you. You two okay?"

"Fine," Kai snapped.

Jake gave Kai a quizzical look before turning to me. "You?"

"Sergeant Duncan seems to think I orchestrated it somehow."

"Did you?"

"No."

He nodded. "Come with me, Grace."

I stalked out of Kai's office.

Once more, I was in the elevator. After a second or two, Jake said, "Kai's been under a lot of stress. I'm sure he meant to question you more . . . professionally."

At the moment, I really didn't care. He had dragged me into his office and acted like I was responsible for LaBryce leaping over the table at him.

"And he seems"—Jake paused as if he was searching for the right word—"distracted by you."

I huffed out a breath. But I had to admit I was curious. I had to ask. "What do you mean?"

"Kai is a very steady guy. He's laid-back, professional, and focused. Usually he's focused. You seem to have . . . blurred his vision some."

I wasn't sure what to make of that. Had Kai asked Jake about me? The sudden adolescent thought caught me off guard. Why did I care? I looked into Jake's face. His gaze shifted around, looking anywhere but directly at me. He was a jowly guy to start with, so his frown was a *frown*. Everything about his features said he was uncomfortable with talking to me about this.

He lifted his shoulders and said, "Look, I'm just askin' ya to cut him some slack. I think he was, you know, kinda upset that you and LaBryce are a thing."

"Jealous? Are you telling me Kai is jealous?" I was aware

that my voice had risen enough to be quite loud in the cramped elevator.

" 'Disappointed' might be a better word."

"I met Kai *yesterday*. Don't you have to be in a relationship with someone for them to be jealous over you?"

Clearly Jake realized he'd opened a can of worms and regretted it. "I'm just sayin' . . . cut the guy some slack."

I could hear music suddenly. My phone. I don't know how I managed to keep up with my purse through the scuffle, but somehow, it was still slung over my shoulder. I pulled the phone out.

"Hello?"

"Grace. I wanted to call and check on you. You didn't answer your text." My sister sounded worried and I was sorry about that, but half the time I didn't hear the little chime that told me I had a text message.

"Sorry, Em, I'm fine, aside from almost being arrested a few seconds ago."

"Arrested?"

I knew I shouldn't have said it the second it was out of my mouth. "Never mind—"

"Grace." Wes's voice replaced my sister's. He sounded very serious. You would never know the two of them had been out all evening drinking martinis and celebrating. "Tell me what happened."

The doors slid open and I asked Jake to point me to the nearest ladies' room. Once I was inside, I said, "Look, it was just a misunderstanding. This altercation happened and the cops, one stupid cop, thought I was involved, but I think it's cleared up now."

"You think or you know?"

"Um . . ." I actually wasn't sure. Jake had just told me Kai was upset because he thought I was involved with LaBryce. Like I was his girlfriend or something. Which I wasn't. But if they thought that, they would stick me in one of those rooms and start asking me all kinds of questions.

"Grace?"

"I'm not sure what's going on. Let me call you back." I

hung up and caught a glimpse of myself in the mirror. Wow. Not good. But not terrible either. I didn't look beaten or roughed up. My hair was a tangled mess and the mascara had run down my cheeks. I looked like I'd been crying. But it wasn't bad enough to drive LaBryce to attack a cop, even if he were my boyfriend.

Which he wasn't.

I pushed the door open, deciding to straighten this out once and for all. Jake was stationed outside the door waiting for me.

"Listen. I'm not LaBryce's girlfriend. I wanted to see him so I could talk to him about Charm. The jaguar. I'll have to feed her in the morning."

Jake was nodding, but I could feel his skepticism. Damn cops and their trust issues.

Cops get lied to all the time. I'm sure he—and Kai—were used to thinking "liar liar pants on fire" half the time they talked to people. But I knew Jake. I thought he'd believe me with a little reasoning.

"LaBryce and I are friends, nothing more. I haven't seen him in months. Check my phone, his phone, e-mails . . . whatever. We are not involved. And I have no clue why he attacked Kai. I really don't."

I saw Jake's eyes focus behind me and I turned. Kai had walked up, still looking irritated, though he'd toned it down a bit. He didn't apologize to me, but he suggested we all go talk to LaBryce, who was conscious and asking to speak to me.

I was baffled. Really and truly. But I went along and walked back into the same room we had been in before. This time LaBryce was hunched over the table. He was crying.

I rushed forward. "LaBryce! Are you okay?" I thought maybe the cops had beaten him up after Kai had dragged me from the room. But when he looked up, he seemed unharmed, aside from a lump under his eye from Kai's elbow. Tears trailed down his cheeks and snot bubbled out of his nose. Blubbering. My friend, the super badass football player, was blubbering.

LaBryce did not blubber. I stared at him, mouth agape.

"Tell me it was quick, Grace." His voice was low and quavering.

"What?"

He sniffled. Not a pretty sound, or sight for that matter. "She didn't suffer, right?"

I had no idea what he was talking about. I started to ask him to clarify when it hit me. Charm. He thought something had happened to *her*. And I had shown up to break the news.

"Oh, LaBryce, she's fine. I fed her and we sat and visited and . . . she's fine."

Relief crumpled his face like an aluminum can. He leaned back and cried harder. He was making noises foreign to human ears. Moose in Canada awoke and began to migrate toward Florida.

I looked over my shoulder at Jake. He and Kai shared the same expression. Eyebrows raised, lips parted. Stunned. I wondered how often that happened—two seasoned investigators shocked into silence.

LaBryce struggled to speak, heaved in a sigh, and finally managed, "First Mark . . . then Charm. It was too much." He looked right at Kai. "I'm sorry, man. I saw Grace and thought . . ." He trailed off and started crying again.

"You have your answer, Sergeant Duncan." My voice was a tad more waspish than I'd intended. Kai blinked at me, then looked back at LaBryce.

"You attacked me because you thought I had done something to Charm?"

LaBryce nodded. "Why else would you be here, Grace? I heard the commotion here a few hours ago. Everyone was talking about a big cat on the loose. Sayin' they was gonna shoot her. I saw you, like that, and thought . . ."

His huge body was wracked with sobs again.

"LaBryce, why was Charm out of her enclosure?" I asked.

His face became hard. "I don't know. Alex should have fed her and put her up tonight. I'm gonna kill that little shit."

I tried not to wince at the threat. The last thing LaBryce needed to do was talk about killing someone.

"Alex was scheduled to take care of the cat?" Kai asked.

"Yeah. Alex Burke. He was supposed to come this morning, but he didn't show. I called him. He texted me back and said he was on his way, but he was running late. I had an appointment I was late for, so I left." He turned to me. "I never leave her out like that, Grace. I don't know what I was thinking."

I patted his arm and nodded. Though part of me wanted to smack him upside the head. Alex Burke was Foodman. I now had a name with the face. Whatever—he was going to get an earful from me. I started to ask LaBryce for his number when Jake stepped closer to the table.

"No matter who did or didn't show up for work, you're responsible for that animal."

LaBryce nodded.

"I could arrest you for attempted assault with a deadly weapon. I could have been killed. One of my guys could have been killed." Jake's voice was low and filled with disgust.

I wanted to say something, defend LaBryce. But Jake was right. LaBryce was accountable. Jake had worked in K9 and understood what it meant to be in charge of an animal that was capable of killing. Control is important. No—it's paramount.

LaBryce knew this, too. He just sat, silent and miserable.

"Miss Wilde has agreed to take care of the cat tomorrow morning. Your ass is staying here."

"Thanks, Grace." LaBryce looked over at me. "She usually gets meat in the morning."

"I'll pick up a beef shank for her. Is she on meds?" I wanted to make sure she didn't miss any doses.

"Just vitamins. They're on the counter." He looked away from me, staring off at a blank spot on the wall.

I glanced at Kai and Jake, hoping they would come to see the truth.

LaBryce wasn't acting guilty. He was acting like a guy who had learned his friend was dead, that he was the prime suspect, and thought his beloved pet had been killed—all in one day. Maybe the fact that I knew he was innocent made it easier for me to look at this tough, hulking man and see that he was scared and sad and completely shell-shocked.

I looked back at LaBryce and said softly, "It's going to be okay." I hoped I was right.

There was a long pause. Jake motioned to someone outside the room, and a uniformed officer walked in. "You're under arrest for assaulting a law enforcement officer."

"Okay," LaBryce said.

"LaBryce, don't you want to call your lawyer?" I asked.

Silence. Everyone looked at me. LaBryce seemed to be trying to wrap his head around the idea. All three cops gave me blank looks that barely masked the undercurrent of annoyance.

"Yeah, I guess I need to do that."

And with that, he was cuffed and ushered from the room.

CHAPTER 7

Kai offered to take me home, and even though I was still miffed at him, I agreed. Mainly because I wanted to talk to him more about finding Burke. And because I wanted to give him a chance to apologize.

We stood waiting by the elevators. When they slid open, a small, trim man stepped out. He glanced at me and then silently turned to scan Kai's face with deep-set, sharp blue eyes. Though I had no idea who he was, everything about him said "head honcho."

"I need a word with you, Sergeant."

"Yes, sir."

I excused myself and walked away, stopping as soon as I rounded the corner that led to the bathrooms so I could hear what was said.

"Any more on Walker?" the man asked Kai.

"Not yet, sir."

"I know you're aware of the pressure surrounding this case."

"Yes, sir."

"Don't let it affect your work. No matter who crawls up to bite you on the ass. You can't rush the evidence, Kai."

There was a pause and I wondered if that was all the man had to say. I peeked around the corner—he was staring up at Kai, his gaze as sharp as a laser. "Now having said that, I want to hear you tell me that you are on this like white on rice."

"I'm all over it, Chief."

"Notify me when you get something." The chief dismissed him with a nod, turned, and walked way.

I watched Kai blow out a breath and look up at the ceiling. It was obvious that the pressure was mounting. I felt a pang of sympathy for him. How was he supposed to do a good job under this much stress? No wonder he was hoping to find something on LaBryce that would cinch the case.

He looked over and saw me. "Sorry." I came around the corner and walked up to him. "I guess that was your boss?"

"Yeah."

The elevator dinged and we got on. I moved to face him once the doors closed. "Your boss is right, you know." No point in denying that I was listening to their conversation. "If you rush to a conclusion, you could be ruining the life of an innocent man."

Kai shook his head. "You are so certain LaBryce is innocent. Why?"

I thought about it for a moment, taking time to study his face. His brows were knit together, his green eyes dark and serious. Gone was the half grin and surfer boy nonchalance. Oh, hell, now I was really in for it. Not only did I want to make sure the cops dropped LaBryce as a suspect, I really wanted Kai to solve the case. I wanted to see the playful cockiness return to his manner. I had no idea why. Well, maybe an inkling of an idea.

"What would you say if I told you I knew—for a fact— that LaBryce is innocent?"

"You *know* he's innocent? Are you telling me you can provide LaBryce Walker with an alibi?"

"Not exactly."

"Then what are you telling me, *exactly*?"

I took a deep breath, and let it out slowly. "Just trust me, okay? Pretend like this is an anonymous tip or something."

"Trust works both ways, Grace. You need to tell me everything you know."

"Jesus, this is crazy," I muttered.

Kai waited for me to elaborate.

I looked away. What was I supposed to say? "I'm sorry. I can't."

"Grace, are you in some sort of trouble?" He grabbed my arm and gently turned me to face him. The concern I saw in his face made me feel like an ass. Kai was worried about me. And all I was doing was keeping secrets. But what choice did I have?

The doors of the elevator opened. Neither of us moved until we heard, "Take your hand off my sister. Now."

I glanced over. Emma and Wes stood looking at us. Emma's face was cool and expressionless. Not good.

I started to explain that everything was fine when Wes said, "If you have anything else to say to my client, you will do it through me."

Kai dropped his hand as if my skin suddenly burned. "Fine by me. Though your *client* has agreed to assist us tomorrow. Should I make other arrangements?"

"No. I'll be there." The doors began to close and Wes caught them, forcing them to bump back open.

"Let's go, Grace," Emma said, though her eyes were still on Kai.

With a last backward glance, I walked out of the elevator and into a hailstorm of questions and admonishments. What happened? Why didn't I call? I should know better than to let the cops ask me questions without counsel.

I was suddenly too tired to talk. I wanted out of the dress. I wanted to forget about Kai and Mark Richardson and Alex Burke. The knowledge that LaBryce had been arrested and the fact that I would have to dive back into the case in the morning only made me want to forget more.

We walked out of the sheriff's office and to the limo waiting for us. I wasn't surprised to see it. Wes traveled in style. I knew I'd ruined his birthday celebrations.

"I'm sorry about tonight, Wes," I said when we'd all settled into the soft leather seats.

He waved a hand, and smiled. Wes was handsome in a chic, meticulously groomed way. His dark hair was styled, his clothes tailored and elegant. He and Emma sat across from me. If I didn't know he was gay, I'd say he and my sister were the perfect couple. Two peas in a pod.

To prove my point, Wes nudged Emma and said, "I think you were right—the cop is into her."

"I told you. I thought he was going to trip over his tongue when he saw her in that dress. Though it's seen better moments." Emma skimmed her gaze over the grimy outfit.

"I'll pay for the dry cleaning."

"I know."

"He seemed very intense, your cop." Wes grinned and lifted his brows, waiting for me to dish out some detail.

"He is not my cop."

"Maybe too intense," Emma said. "What was going on in that elevator?"

I shook my head. "I don't know, he thinks I know something."

"Do you?"

I leaned my head back onto the soft headrest. My temples had started throbbing. "I know that LaBryce is innocent."

"How do you know that?" Wes asked.

"Because his pet jaguar told me."

"Oh . . ."

"Did you tell Kai? Is that what the whole severe look was about?" Emma asked.

I snorted out a laugh. "No. I didn't tell him." I raised my head off the seatback to look at my sister. "What could I possibly say? He already knows I'm hiding something from him. If I told him what I knew, which, by the way, I have no proof of other than from the cat, then what? How could he possibly believe me?"

"What do they have on LaBryce?" Wes asked.

I told them about the hairs, the fight, and LaBryce threatening to kill Mark.

"Circumstantial. If he has a good lawyer, he'll probably get off," Wes said.

"But the cops aren't even looking at anyone else. Someone killed Mark Richardson. And it wasn't LaBryce. They're totally barking up the wrong tree."

"What are you going to do?" Wes asked.

"I have no idea. I've got to go to LaBryce's house in the morning to feed Charm and make sure the cops can search her enclosure safely. Maybe I'll talk to Kai then."

"And tell him about your ability?" Emma asked.

"No! I just . . . maybe I can convince him that LaBryce is innocent."

"Sweetie, how are you going to do that if you don't tell him the truth?" Wes reached over and patted my knee.

"I don't know."

"Have you tried seducing him yet?" Emma grinned wickedly.

"Be serious, Emma!"

"I am being serious. I saw the way he was looking at you earlier." Her smile widened. "You may be clueless when it comes to men, little sister, but I'm not. He wanted to suck your toenail polish off."

"I'm not wearing any toenail polish."

"Details. My point is this—the man is totally into you. You need to use that to your advantage. Tomorrow morning, get him alone and flirt a little bit."

"Use your womanly wiles," Wes added.

"I don't have any womanly wiles!"

They rolled their eyes in tandem.

"Grace, you are beautiful," Wes said with a smile. "Even in this state, you've got a whole wild temptress thing going on."

"Like Raquel Welch in that cavewoman bikini."

Now it was my turn to roll my eyes. "Please. There's no way I can just flirt LaBryce out of jail."

"You underestimate yourself," Wes said.

"And the power of cleavage," Emma added.

"Right."

"Listen, sweetie," Wes said. "You need to understand this. Kai will be more interested in listening to what you have to say if you work him over a little first."

"Distract him," Emma said. "Pull his strings. Bat your eyes and smile. If you're not going to tell him the truth, which, for the record, I think you should, at least you'll be able to influence him."

I laughed even though what she said wasn't funny. It was preposterous. Even though Jake had blamed Kai's lack of focus on me, I still didn't buy it. Normally, I distracted a man no longer than it took him to drag his eyes from my C-cups. The idea that I could manipulate Kai with a few well-timed giggles and a tight shirt was ridiculous.

"Emma, you can't really think he's dumb enough to fall for something that base and contrived."

"Would it be contrived?" Emma asked.

I looked from my sister to Wes and back. "What? You think I like him?"

"I know you like him."

"Don't pretend, sweetie. Not with us."

I had to admit, I liked him a little bit. "I feel bad for him. He's dealing with some pressure."

"Some!" Wes scoffed. "Are you kidding? The governor's son has been murdered. A fellow Jaguar player is a suspect. Turn on the news and it's all you hear. By tomorrow, the press will have spun it eight different ways. If they arrest LaBryce and then have to release him with no alternative suspect, the cops will look like idiots."

I hadn't thought of that.

We eased to a stop in front of the condo. I knew, although it was almost midnight, the night was still young for the martini twins. So I hauled myself out of the limo and walked toward the condo alone.

Blissfully alone. I let my mind drift along with the quiet ocean breeze as I climbed the stairs. If I hadn't been so tired,

I'd have been tempted to take a moonlit stroll along the shore. Let the rumbling murmur of the sea scour my mind and soothe my soul.

"'I must go down to the seas again, for the call of the running tide . . . is a wild call and a clear call that may not be denied.'" I recited the words of a poem memorized so long ago for an English class I could hardly believe I remembered any of it.

The line was fitting, though. I'd lived near the ocean as long as I could remember. Leaving the beach, its salty air, and sandy soil may very well give me sea fever. For a moment, I thought about staying awhile longer with Emma, until I'd saved enough to pay the inflated price of a house on the beach. The idea had almost taken hold when I reached the door.

Three sticky notes were affixed to it.

Moss must have farted too loud.

With a sigh, I stripped the notes off the door. "The country life it is."

I opened the door and the dogs trotted into the foyer to greet me. Moss recognized the jaguar's scent and began busily sniffing my toes.

Charm! He was expressing overwhelming excitement over *eau de jaguare*, and I was bombarded with his memories.

I squinted and tried to block out the zooming slide show. "Yes, I saw Charm."

Jax was sniffing my legs and also seemed to recognize the scent. Though he wasn't as excited as Moss. I figured Jax had been around LaBryce enough times to remember it.

Shivering in the crisp air-conditioning, I padded barefoot through the condo and into the bathroom. Moss's nose was still glued to my leg. I peeled off the dress and tossed it out of the room.

"There, go nuts." He loped after it and continued sniffing. I took a quick, steaming shower to banish the chill and rinse the grime off my hands and feet.

When I stepped out and wrapped myself in a thick towel,

Moss still had his nose buried in the dress. Jax had taken up his position at the door and watched as I squeezed the water from my hair with a smaller towel. I combed it out—thanks to Emma's selection of fine hair-care products, it was a fairly easy chore. By the time I started pulling on my pajamas, Jax had reclined all the way to the floor, his eyes half-closed, his head resting calmly on the cool marble.

I wondered if he might dream of the murder again tonight. I hoped vehemently that he wouldn't, then chastised myself for such a selfish thought. If Jax did have a dream that detailed the murder—guess that would be a nightmare, really—it was my duty to watch and take in every detail I could.

No, I didn't want to see Mark Richardson get shot. But if I saw the whole thing, in all its horrible goriness, maybe something . . .

I had a sudden thought and realized I'd been going about this all wrong. I had told Kai to act as if the information I gave him was from an anonymous tip. What if I could do exactly that? Call the hotline and give the cops the identity of the real killer?

I looked at Jax, who now slept peacefully across the doorway. If I saw the murder through Jax's memory, I could tell the cops but never reveal myself. Even if they didn't totally believe me, they'd have to look into it, right?

I had been to the crime scene. I had details in my head already; surely we could come up with something.

Easing over to Jax, I bent and stroked a hand down his smooth body. He blinked up at me, but I pressed his mind to relax. He did, letting out a long sigh. After a minute, I carefully planted the seed of what I hoped would stir his memory.

Flipping off the light, I crawled into bed. Moss's mind was still occupied with thoughts of Charm. The last thing I remembered before falling asleep was the garbled image of a young jaguar.

My dreams were anything but what I'd expected.

CHAPTER 8

The next morning, I stumbled groggily toward the kitchen. It was early. Not even six yet. Normally, I was still drooling on my pillow at this time of the morning, but I needed to think. I needed a plan. I needed coffee.

I attempted to blink away the grit that seemed to coat the insides of my eyelids and focus on the blur that was my sister.

Emma was perched at the dining room table, wearing her usual martial arts *Gi* and sipping what I knew to be a cup of green tea. She looked up at me and beamed. "Good morning, Sunshine!"

I shot her a baleful glare. How my sister managed to be chipper and fresh after staying out half the night drinking martinis I would never know.

Still smiling, Emma got up and followed me into the kitchen. "The kettle is still hot if you want some tea. I also made coffee."

"Bless you." Sighing gratefully, I managed to offer her a feeble smile before pouring myself a cup of coffee. I took a moment to breathe in the wonderful scent carried out of the mug on spiraling waves of steam. I felt my brain waves begin to awaken. Synapses stirred.

"I take it you didn't sleep well?"

"I don't think I slept at all." I yawned, dumping an unhealthy amount of cream and sugar into my mug. I took the first sip. Good and strong. Thank you, Emma.

"Want to tell me about it?"

I took another sip of the steaming coffee. I had woken up during the night a dozen times. Thanks to the dogs, my head had been filled with a tsunami of memories and thoughts that weren't mine. And some that I was afraid were—like the dream I had about Kai. I felt a flutter of embarrassment and pushed those thoughts away.

There had been other flashes. Images I hadn't completely worked through yet and didn't understand, but nothing at all about the murder.

I rubbed a hand over my tired eyes, "Weird dreams and disturbing thoughts."

"Did these thoughts concern Kai?"

I nodded. "I have no idea what I'm going to say to him."

"Yes, you do."

"Don't start this again." Frustrated, I clunked my mug down on the counter, sending coffee sloshing onto my hand. "If I tell him the truth, he'll think I'm nuts."

"You should have figured out how to reveal your gift to people a long time ago." Emma handed me a paper towel. "Then you wouldn't be in this position, all stressed out about what to do."

"You're saying that this is my fault?" I wiped my hand and tossed the paper towel on the counter. It had always been so easy for Emma. People loved her. If she claimed to be Elvis reincarnated, they would still love her.

"I'm saying you should have the courage to accept yourself for who you are."

"Courage? Accept—" I sputtered the words like a five-year-old.

"You're special, Grace." Emma poured out the rest of her tea and set the cup in the sink. "You need to accept that. Be honest. With everyone. I'm not just talking about Kai. I'm talking about the people you work with at the zoo, and at the Humane Society. I'm talking about your clients. Have you ever considered that you're being selfish?"

"Selfish? I bend over backward for animals that need me. I get up in the middle of the night to find missing parakeets!"

"But you never tell anyone how you manage to do it. Have you ever thought that there are people that love animals just as much as you who feel terrible and foolish because they failed to understand why their dog suddenly won't walk on a leash, or professionals who doubt themselves because they aren't as good as you? You waltz into their lives and, *voilà*, problem solved."

"So, I should subject myself to ridicule to make people feel better?"

"Ridicule . . ." Emma said the word slowly, like it was foreign. "You, dear Sister, are not afraid of being laughed at."

"It's easy to say when you've never *been* laughed at."

Emma smiled. But it wasn't a good smile, or even her wicked, Emma grin. It was a smile filled with pity. "I know it's safer to never let anyone get close, but you're going to have to someday."

I felt my temper reach its flashpoint. "What the hell is that supposed to mean?"

Emma crossed her arms and tilted her head, the way she'd always done when ready to cut to the quick. "What are you really afraid of, Grace? If you tell Kai the truth, are you afraid he won't believe you, or more afraid that he will?"

"What?"

I watched as Emma turned and walked toward the front door. "Think about it. I'll meet you down in the dojo in fifteen minutes. There's a *Gi* in the bathroom for you." She glanced over her shoulder at me. "You can work some of that anger out on the mat."

• • •

Thirty minutes later, I lay sprawled on the padded training mat, glaring up at my sister. "Tell me again—" I gasped, attempting to suck air back into my lungs. "Why am I doing this?"

"Because you promised you would. And it's a great way to get your mind off all this stuff with Kai and Jax and LaBryce. In chaos there is clarity."

"What?"

Emma bent down to grab my hand and hoisted me back onto my feet. "If you don't worry about what you're going to do, maybe you'll figure out you already know."

I half expected her to tag a *Grasshoppa* on the end of the sentence.

"Do you always get all Zen when you come down here?" Emma had turned part of her garage area into her personal dojo. It was decked out with a wall of wooden staffs and practice swords called *shinai*. Which, I had been told, were made with split bamboo so 911 was not called when you struck your opponent on the head. A shrine on the wall to the right of the training mat was decorated with a real sword and a picture of an old Japanese guy Emma called *O Sensei*. On the far side of the mat, she had placed an array of boxing gym–type equipment.

Emma patted me as I caught my breath. "Being Zen is kind of the point, Sister."

"I thought it was learning to kick ass."

"That, too. Now, almost ninety percent of attacks on women come from behind. So, turn around, and this time, I'll attack you. Just try to move like I showed you."

I turned my back. "When? While you were planting me into the floor?"

"Exactly. Okay, remember to use my momentum—"

Emma hurled herself forward and made to grab me around the neck. I took hold of her arm and tried to imitate the movement I'd seen her do. To my amazement, I felt her slide past me.

Emma stumbled then turned, grinning. "That was better. Last time you couldn't even get your feet in the right position. Try again, and put your hips into the movement."

I turned around and Emma launched her attack.

We continued practicing until finally, with almost no effort, I slammed my sister onto the mat.

Stunned, I stared down at Emma. "I did it!"

"Yes, you did." She smiled up at me proudly and hopped to her feet in a move straight out of the last Charlie's Angels movie.

"You're really amazing, Em."

Emma beamed and brushed a feathering of stray hairs away from her face. "If I had a dollar for every time I heard that."

"I mean it." I felt all my lingering anger melt away. I thought about the reason Emma had trained in self-defense and martial arts for the past six years. I thought about Jennifer Weston and the bruises on her arms.

"I think Mark Richardson's ex is being abused."

Emma's smile flickered, then died. I told her about my meeting with Jennifer in the bathroom. And about the way she tried to brush me off when I saw the marks on her arms.

"Do you think she killed him?"

"I don't know. If she did, it would be self-defense, right?"

"Grace, that's not for you to decide. If Jax remembers the murderer was Jennifer, you have to tell the police."

I shook my head. "I think about you and that bastard Anthony." I gritted my teeth at the thought of the man who had almost beaten my sister to death. I could still remember walking into the hospital and seeing her lying like a battered doll in that bed.

"If it hadn't been for Anthony, I wouldn't be who I am." Emma forced a smile. "I'm stronger and wiser. Not to mention a hell of a lot richer."

The details of my sister's divorce from real estate mogul Anthony Ortega had been kept low profile. In return, Emma had gotten a huge settlement.

"No price is high enough for what he did to you."

"On the contrary, I got everything I wanted. My life," Emma said lightly.

I could feel anger boiling up again. "He's lucky I didn't have Moss back then. He would have made a great snack."

Emma laughed. "Look who's getting all fired up again. Come on, let's go take that aggression out on the heavy bag."

I followed her to the other side of the dojo. Thinking about Anthony Ortega had pissed me off. I marveled at how well my sister always handled the subject. Leave it to Emma to find the positive in every situation.

Emma handed me a pair of boxing gloves. "Now just do what I do. Picture Anthony's face right here in the center of the bag . . . and go to town."

• • •

An hour later, I stood on the beach with the dogs, watching the rhythmic flow of the Atlantic. Emma had been right. Working out with her had given me more than just sore muscles. I had come to a decision.

I can count my close friends, human ones anyway, on one hand. I had to help LaBryce. But that did not involve telling Kai the truth. At least not the "I'm an animal empath" part of the truth—I wasn't ready for that. As Emma had suggested, I planned to get Kai alone and see if I could work some magic. I only had a few minutes before I had to head in and go to LaBryce's to meet him. Apprehension flooded through me.

What are you really afraid of? Are you afraid Kai won't believe you—or that he will? My sister's words bounced though my head.

So, what was the answer? It was true that I had been hurt before. The first man I had ever fallen for had rejected me because of my abilities. I hadn't fully realized until today just how much I had been hiding behind that one incident. In reality, that wasn't why I never opened up to anyone. It had been at first. But I'd gotten over Dane Harrington years ago.

I thought about Hugh Murray, the zoo vet. Emma was right, I hadn't ever given him a chance. Why? What did I really dislike about Hugh? That he had hung all over some girl *after* I had made it clear I would never go out with him? That he was hunky and rugged and knew it? Take away the idea that he might just pick up on my telepathic ability if he were around Moss and me for any amount of time, and I had to say, there wasn't much about him not to like.

I had used my experience with Dane as an excuse for a long time. A sort of litmus test to show how rotten people could be.

I breathed in the warm, salt-laced air and sighed slowly, turning away from the rolling waves.

If I was honest with myself, I had to admit, deep down, I wasn't really afraid of rejection. I was afraid of acceptance, and all the vulnerability that came with it.

I didn't like the realization that I was being a coward. Cowardice was pretty high on my list of things I did not want to be afflicted with. Right up there with the stomach flu and thong underwear.

As the dogs and I made our way back from our romp on the beach, I had to wonder: What if I told Kai the whole truth and he *believed* me? The door I had kept locked would be wide open then. I would have nothing to hide behind. No reason to play Ice Queen and push him away.

Thinking about it made me feel queasy.

Moss, who had been watching me with a mixture of concern and protectiveness, nudged under my hand. *Sick?*

"I'm okay, big boy." I gave his head a reassuring pat.

He whined softly, unconvinced.

I knelt down and looked into his eyes. Not doggie eyes. Moss's were the almond, black-rimmed gold of his mother's. I'd seen his gaze transform burly men into blubbering boys. Many who've looked at Moss see a rapacious beast. I only see my friend.

I wrapped my arms around his thick, furry neck. His coat smelled like a mixture of sand, sea, and the earthy, wild scent of wolf. I breathed in deeply. And felt my anxiety melting away. Not wanting to be left out, Jax nudged under my other arm.

Laughing, I wrapped it over his back. I could feel his contentment—he was relaxed and happy.

I turned and focused my attention on Jax.

Maybe if I tried, he would open up.

I looked into his eyes and took a deep, relaxing breath.

"Okay, boy, give me something. Something I can call in to the hotline that will get LaBryce out of jail." *And keep me from having to dig myself any deeper into this mess.* I didn't push it. I stayed gentle and calm as I brought what little I'd learned about the murder to the front of my mind.

Jax had been outside looking in. It was dark.

For a moment, I sensed his memory stirring. I could feel his anticipation, wanting Mark to open the back door so he could greet the person. But in an instant the memory was gone. Jax began to whimper and quake.

I immediately backed off. "All right, Jax, you're okay." I felt a pang of guilt. Forcing Jax to remember was cruel and wrong. I would just have to make do with what I had.

Scolding myself, I decided to make amends by throwing the tennis ball for him a few times. I pulled the ball out of my shorts pocket. "Okay, boy, you want it? Go get it!" I hurled the ball down the beach.

Jax flew joyfully after the ball, scooped it up mid-bounce, and bounded back.

Moss, wanting no part in the game, started to wander off, nose to the ground.

"You have some nerve!"

Startled, I turned toward the shrill accusing voice. It was our neighbor, Mr. Cavanaugh. The old man had a perfect potbelly and skin the color and texture of a World War II bomber jacket. He held a metal detector in one hand and something that looked like a large cat litter scooper in the other. Glaring, he gestured with both as he spoke.

"Those animals do not belong on this beach!"

I reached out and secured Jax by his collar. I forced a smile. "Hello, Mr. Cavanaugh—"

"Don't you 'hello' me." He advanced toward us.

Moss, who had been inquisitively sniffing at a crab hole a few feet away, turned his wolflike eyes toward the complaining man. I sensed his unease and moved toward him. I bade both the dogs to stay calm. *Easy. It's okay.*

Jax reacted to my request and sat obediently. Moss, on the other hand, reserved judgment.

Mr. Cavanaugh, clearly incensed, took another step in our direction. "Filthy. Leave their droppings for me to find."

I had a feeling there would be a sticky note on the door for Emma today.

"It's an outrage!" He swung the metal detector to point at Moss, and it emitted a long high-pitched *weeeeeeer!* Barely audible to me, I knew it was like a foghorn to the dogs.

Moss let out a deep disapproving growl. Jax followed his lead. The old man didn't seem to notice and continued toward us, punctuating his censure by thrusting at them with the squeaking metal detector.

By now I could feel the *weeeeeer!* ringing in my head.

"Moss . . ." He had taken all he could. I reached for his collar and had barely wrapped my fingers around it when he lunged at the metal detector.

Mr. Cavanaugh tumbled back onto the ground. His bony, liver-spotted legs kicked at the air and his arms flailed in the sand. He looked like an animated rotisserie chicken.

It took all of my strength, but I managed to bring the dogs under control. I pulled them away from the piercing noise of the metal detector.

"I should have you arrested! Those animals are a menace!" he shrieked, scrambling to get to his feet.

"I'm sorry. They don't understand the metal detector. It hurts their ears. They weren't after you—"

"Explain that to animal control!" With that last barb, the old man stomped furiously away.

"Great." Now Emma would *really* be hearing from the old goat. The door would probably be covered with sticky notes. I needed to find time to go house hunting before the condo association started hassling my sister. Frowning, I led the two dogs back to the condo. I brushed them both off with an old towel before letting them inside.

I had just hung the leashes in the foyer closet when I heard the ring tone of my cell. Hurrying into the kitchen, I plucked the phone off the counter and flipped it open.

I started to say hello, but realized I had missed the call. I looked at the number; it wasn't one I recognized.

I listened to my messages. The first was from Preston White, who identified himself as LaBryce's attorney. Mr. White spoke in short, clipped sentences. He informed me that LaBryce would not be bonded out until the judge had "more information" and asked, on his client's behalf, that I look after Charm until further notice.

I let out a sigh. Not because I minded looking after Charm, but because I hated that LaBryce was stuck in jail, sitting in a cell while the cops looked for evidence that would keep him there.

The second message was from a man named Bo Bishop. He said he was Mark Richardson's brother and was hoping to adopt Jax. I wondered why he and Mark didn't share the same last name, but let the thought go. As long as he was willing and able to give Jax a good home after the mandatory quarantine, I didn't care. The guy sounded a little country—lots of *ma'am*s and few *ain't*s—but at least he seemed genuinely concerned about the dog.

I smiled and decided to call him back and set up a time to meet with him.

I hung up and started to hit Redial, but the phone rang before I could press the Send button.

This time it was Kai.

I hesitated a moment before answering. "Hello?"

"Hi, Grace, it's Kai Duncan. I'm on my way out to LaBryce Walker's house. There's already a lot of media there. Just ignore them and come up to the front of the house. I'll wait for you."

The sound of his voice gave me a jolt of apprehension. "I'm on my way."

"See you soon," was all he said before hanging up.

I stood for a moment, tapping my finger thoughtfully on the counter, and then walked into the hall bath. I yanked my hair out of the wind-whipped ponytail and carefully twisted it into a perfect bun. I ran my fingers over my hair, checking for lumps. Satisfied that I looked professional, I grabbed my keys, dropped my phone into my purse, and bade farewell to the dogs.

"Here we go," I muttered and walked out the door.

• • •

I elbowed through the reporters and ducked under the yellow police tape that marked the crime scene perimeter in front of LaBryce's house. An officer whose obvious duty was to keep people from breaching the line walked importantly toward me.

"Ma'am, I'm sorry, you can't be here."

Spotting Kai, I waved. He motioned for me to step forward, making sure that the officer saw him.

My heart pounded a little harder as I walked over the lush lawn toward the house. I forced a slow, calming breath before looking up at Kai. He was standing next to a young Asian man who, judging from the matching field case, was also a member of the crime scene unit.

Kai turned to speak to me. "Thanks for coming."

"Sure." Though my nerves were humming like a bee, I refused to let it show. I clamped down on the little ripple of anxiety I felt and focused on Kai's introductions.

"Grace," Kai said. "This is Charlie Yamada. He's with the Crime Lab."

"I assumed as much." I nodded at Charlie then looked back at Kai. "Ready?"

"We've been waiting for you." He looked at the grocery bag I was carrying. "Breakfast?"

"Beef—for Charm, not me."

He nodded and motioned inside.

We walked through the open front door and made our way to the kitchen.

"I'll just get her fed. Then I can call you and you can come on in."

I glanced at Charlie and decided I didn't necessarily want anyone else to hear the conversation I was going to have with Kai. Plus, I had to remember to flirt, and there was no way I could pull that off with an audience. Heck, I wasn't sure I could pull it off without one.

"Um, it would probably be best if just one person searched the enclosure. Too many people might make her a little nervous."

Charlie grinned at me in obvious relief. "Fine by me. I'll go over the perimeter again. I might find something in the daylight."

Kai nodded. "Thanks, Charlie."

I opened the grocery bag and pulled out the beef shank. It was vacuum sealed in heavy-duty cellophane. "I need some scissors."

We both started opening drawers until Kai found a pair and handed them to me.

I cut open the wrapper and placed the shank on a cookie sheet. I saw a bottle on the counter. It looked like a large vitamin bottle except that there was a homemade label wrapped around it. The words were written with a marker. They read: *X-mix*, followed by *one tbls in AM*. I opened the bottle, and saw that the tablespoon scoop was inside. There was barely one scoop left. Sighing, I sprinkled it on the meat. "Have you talked to Alex Burke yet?"

"No. I think Jake has called him. We haven't heard back."

"I'm going to need to talk to him." I rubbed the powder into the beef, the way someone would work in a special marinade for a barbeque. "This vitamin mix is gone. It looks like something he made up himself. Charm has had a lot of health problems—it might be something she needs."

"I'll make sure he calls you after we talk to him."

"Don't you think it's weird that he just stopped coming to work?"

"He wouldn't be the first guy who Houdini-ed on a job."

"Pretty irresponsible."

"Yes."

To me this meant he didn't care about Charm. Something about that didn't seem right. Most trainers and handlers I knew were loyal to the animals they cared for. I had to assume he was no different. Maybe I'd call Alex Burke myself, see what was going on.

I noticed that Kai was watching me carefully. Probably

looking for clues to my big secret. Well, he wasn't going to get that. Not today anyway.

I picked up the cookie sheet. "Okay. Let's go."

By the light of day, the separation of the two rooms was more obvious.

Charm was stretched out in the morning sun on a platform made to look like a large rock. She spotted me and nimbly leapt off her perch.

I pointed to the rope wrapped around the cleat next to the guillotine door. "Go ahead and pull open this door and close it behind me."

"Got it." He pulled on the rope, and I bent over to step inside.

"I'll call you and let you know it's okay to come in," I said over my shoulder.

He nodded and slipped the door back into place.

I waited a moment while Kai closed the first door behind me before opening the second leading into the enclosure. Charm was waiting anxiously on the other side. She let out a happy growl as I moved inside. *Bottle?*

"Don't start that again. Here." I set the shank down in front of her.

The big cat collapsed onto her belly and began munching.

I looked over to see Kai standing by the glass wall, looking in at us. I tried to read his expression but couldn't. He just seemed to be watching. Suddenly, I was self-conscious. This was what it was like to be a goldfish. No. I didn't think goldfish could feel awkward. And I was feeling awkward as hell.

I tried to remember the tips my sister had given me before she left that morning. Make eye contact. Pay him some compliments. Smile. I tried a casual smile. It felt thin and fake.

Charm crunched on the shank bone and growled with possessive pleasure. I turned and watched her licking the bone clean. She wouldn't need to eat again until tomorrow. Maybe LaBryce would be back by then. I was starting to think that I might be able to talk Kai into believing that

LaBryce was innocent. I had come up with a convincing speech. At least I thought it was convincing. I'd find out.

In an alarmingly short amount of time, Charm finished off the shank, crunching down to the tasty marrow. I've worked with all kinds of big cats, but it's always a bit disturbing to be reminded of how quickly they can devour meat and bone. She lifted her head. *Bottle?*

"No. Come over here, pretty girl, you need to sit with me." Grinning, I led the cat over to the same log I had sat on last night. Unconcerned with dirt and grime this time, I plopped myself down on the damp log. "You're going to have a visitor."

Charm looked to where Kai stood on the other side of the glass.

"Yep, that's him." I focused on expressing friendship and trust. The jaguar needed to know that Kai was not a threat, and he wasn't food. Thankfully, Charm accepted my assessment of Kai and went back to begging for a bottle by butting her head persistently against my knee.

I nodded at Kai, who opened the guillotine door and stooped, moving cautiously into the enclosure.

I felt sudden tension from the big cat. Charm growled in warning.

"Stop, Kai."

He froze.

I concentrated on identifying the object of Charm's aversion. After a moment I was successful. "She doesn't like that case. Set it down and back away from it."

Kai did as I asked.

I released the cat and Charm stalked up to the case and sniffed it for a few moments. Then she turned her interest to Kai.

I watched, amused, as Kai flinched at the inspection. "Don't move, just let her smell you."

"Oh, don't worry. I'm not going to move."

I couldn't help but smile as I watched. Charm examined Kai thoroughly, even licking at the back of one of his hands. "She likes you."

"Likes me as a friend or as food?" He remained stock-still.

I managed to swallow the laugh that threatened to scamper out of my throat and called the cat off. *All right, that's enough.* "Come here, Charm."

Charm waited a beat and then slunk back to me.

Kai let out a long breath. "Can I move now?"

"Sure." The jaguar watched with interest as Kai pulled a flashlight from his case, turned it on, and started walking back and forth across the width of the enclosure.

Taking a calming breath, I asked, "What are you looking for?"

He glanced up. A smile played at his lips. "Clues."

I rolled my eyes. "Come on. Really."

"His gun would be nice." He muttered as he scanned the earth and pine bark–covered floor.

I knew LaBryce had a gun. It was a super-duper custom deal. He'd shown it to me on one of my visits. "You're looking for the shiny one?"

Kai's gaze leapt up to latch onto mine. "You've seen it?"

My knee-jerk reaction was to deny it. But I thought about Kai's assumption the night before that I was involved with LaBryce and reconsidered. I'd have to earn Kai's trust if I was going to have any hope of swaying his opinion.

I nodded, hoping I looked eager to help. "LaBryce showed it to me just after he got it. He told me the gun was customized by some guy in Arizona, or maybe it was Texas—I don't remember. It was actually kind of pretty, for a pistol. Big. Polished chrome with a jaguar on each side of the handle."

Kai nodded and went back to his search. "Arizona. We have a copy of the receipt."

Passed that test. Hoping to keep the goodwill flowing, I added, "He kept it in a case."

"It's not in the case."

I felt a jolt of confusion. Where else would it be? "You think he used it to kill Mark and hid it in here?"

"I have to look. LaBryce says he doesn't know where the gun is. He locked it in its case and put it in a drawer."

It was obvious that Kai didn't believe this story.

I sat and pondered the missing gun for a while. LaBryce hung out with some folks that ran afoul of the law. He had parties. He had domestic help and an animal trainer. All of them had access to the house and, presumably, his gun.

"Maybe someone stole it."

"Yeah, that's what he said." Kai paused in his search and looked at me. "We've been checking with pawn shops and Jake has talked to his informant. No one's seen a custom, chrome-plated, semiautomatic pistol."

"Oh," was all I managed to say. This was not good news. I knew LaBryce was innocent, so I was not infected with the doubt that plagued Kai. But I had to admit the AWOL firearm looked bad. It would make it doubly hard to talk Kai into accepting the idea that LaBryce was not the gangster his PR firm wanted everyone to imagine he was.

The real LaBryce was a kindhearted man who loved his mama and had a soft spot for animals.

I couldn't think of a way to express this without sounding antagonistic, so I changed the subject. "How long have you been doing this? Been a crime scene investigator?"

Kai answered without stopping his examination of the enclosure. "I started with the CSU about ten years ago, as a grad student."

He didn't expound like people tend to do, and I couldn't think of a follow-up question. I suddenly wished I had paid more attention to Emma's social techniques. *Think of something to say, genius.*

As I cast about for a more fruitful subject, I reached out to place my hand on Charm. She sat with her back against the log, leaning her upper body against my legs. Not totally relaxed, she kept an eye on her new guest.

I began massaging her sleek, supple neck, as much to comfort her as me. Within moments, feline contentment poured into me. Riding the gentle wave of blissful calm, I turned my attention back to Kai.

He stopped, knelt, and leaned forward, gently flipping

over a bit of bark for scrutiny. As he worked, I spotted something that sparked an idea.

"Are you from Hawaii?"

This time, he stopped his search and looked up at me. "Why would you think that?"

"Your necklace." I pointed to the swirl of carved bone that dangled on a woven cord. "It's a fishhook, right?"

"A *makau*." He tucked the pendant back into his shirt. "A lot of surfers wear them."

"But not a lot of surfers have a name like Kai."

He laughed. The sound was so unexpected and appealing I found myself grinning back at him like a fool.

"What? I'm that far off?"

"No. You're right on." His laugh settled into the devastating grin I remembered with embarrassing clarity. "For someone who claims to have issues with humans, your anthropologic skills are pretty good."

"So, you *are* Hawaiian?"

He nodded and stood, beginning his scan of the enclosure again. "Half. My father's family is Scottish-American."

The mix explained the exotic tilt of his intense green eyes. "How did your father end up in Hawaii?"

"He was in the Navy. Stationed at Barbers Point when he met my mom. We moved to Jacksonville when I was fourteen."

"Out to Mayport?"

"Yep." Kai bent down again to examine something, only to disregard it as unimportant. "What about you? Are you from here originally?"

"I grew up on the beach. So did my parents."

"Do they still live out there?" He glanced at me but didn't stop the search.

"No, they sold their house and took off in a Winnebago about a year ago." I stroked Charm absentmindedly and thought about how excited they had been. "The great American adventure. We get postcards from all over now."

"Nice." His voice was soft, and there seemed at be an undercurrent of emotion in the word.

"Are your parents still here, or did they move back to Hawaii?"

"My mom did. My dad's dead." He paused to look at me. "He was murdered."

"Oh God, I'm sorry."

"They never found out who did it. The case is still open." He shook his head and smiled, but it wasn't his usual heart-stopping grin. This smile was stiff and tainted with bitterness. "And once again, I find myself telling you more than I intended to. You'd be a good cop. You have a way of making people open up."

It didn't sound like a compliment.

"I didn't mean to pry."

After a long pause, he blew out a slow breath and shook his head. "You weren't."

Flustered, I looked at Charm, who stretched out and rolled over to expose her white belly for me to scratch. I leaned over and ran my fingernails over the cat. As I touched her, her satisfaction and pleasure rippled through me. The emotions soothed, blanketing my anxiety with an odd sort of euphoria.

Along with the sensation came the thought that this was a quid pro quo situation. Kai had shared something personal; I should return the favor. For the life of me, I couldn't think of anything. *My favorite color is green* didn't seem to cut it.

Maybe a change of subject was in order. "I had a lemur on my head Sunday when Jake called me."

Kai's brows arched.

"He thought I was his mother," I clarified.

"That happen a lot?"

"Yep. My days are filled with the unexpected. What about you? You've seen some weird stuff, I'm sure."

"Aside from you taming a Doberman and a jaguar with nothing more than few words?" His grin was back, though not as wide.

"Not just words. I have a winning personality."

Kai seemed to relax back into the rhythm of his search. The awkwardness of his confession passed. As he moved,

I tried to think of an admiring comment. But all I could think of was that he had nice eyes and a hot bod. Not smooth. Not smooth at all.

Well, at least I had gotten him alone, aside from Charm. Now I was supposed to flirt. Get him hot and bothered so I could mold him like clay.

Yeah, right.

I looked up and watched Kai tapping on the faux rock face that made up the far wall. He nimbly climbed onto it and started looking through the thick banana leaves and palm fronds that served as the canopy of the mini forest.

Charm rolled onto her feet. Ears pricked—eyes wide.

"Hold on, Kai."

He stopped. "What?"

"Charm is not cool with you climbing around up there." I honed in on her mind. Her senses had focused to a fine point. *Hunt.*

The rustling noise Kai was making as he searched though the canopy had triggered her drive to stalk and kill.

"Don't move. You sound like an animal rummaging through the forest."

"Like food?" he asked softly.

"Yeah, like food."

Easy, girl. I reminded Charm that Kai was a friend. But her predatory instinct had kicked in, and she wanted to track what she had heard.

"Kai, listen. Without turning your back, very slowly get down. Do not make any more noise."

Keeping his eyes on the cat, he silently sat on the rock and moved back down to the ground.

Charm's head was lowered, and she watched him with an intensity I knew he could feel. There really wasn't anything like being stared down by a big cat. A cat with hunger in its eyes.

"Easy, girl. Kai's a friend," I murmured. I knew I couldn't physically stop her if she decided to spring. But I could alter her attitude. I blanketed her mind with my own. Smothering her burning predatory need like I would a fire. I breathed slowly, pressing the calming hiss of nothing in to drive out her brain's fixation. Slowly, she lost interest in Kai and looked back at me. *Bottle?*

Disaster averted. I pressed my lips together to hide my smile. Charm and her bottle obsession. *Sorry, girl. No bottle.* She sniffed at the pocket of my shorts, where I had stowed a few dog treats, and a thought occurred to me. Even though Kai was the cop, I was in control here. This was my turf. Why wasn't I acting like it?

"All right. I think we need to reiterate that you are a friend. Come here, sit next to me, and give her a treat."

"Okay." Moving cautiously, Kai eased himself down onto the log next to me.

I reached into my pocket and handed him a dog biscuit. *Gently, Charm.* I wanted to make sure Kai didn't lose any of his fingers.

Charm gingerly took the biscuit from Kai's hand.

"Should I pet her?"

"Sure."

He reached out and stroked Charm's shining spotted fur. The jaguar, now totally reformed, butted her head against his chest to beg for another treat.

"She likes it when you scratch her head right here." I placed my hand in between the cat's ears. Kai followed my hand and raked his fingers back and forth.

Charm let out a contented growl and closed her eyes. I could feel pure bliss radiating from the big cat. It sent pleasant chills up my spine. My fingertips brushed against Kai's and a surge of heat that had nothing to do with the cat rushed through me. I pulled away and glanced at Kai. He was so absorbed in petting Charm he hadn't seemed to notice the contact. I wasn't sure if I was relieved or disappointed. Wasn't I supposed to be flirting?

Kai looked up, his face alight with excitement. He looked like a kid who'd just walked into Disney World. "This is something I never expected to be doing."

"Keep it up and I think you'll have a new girlfriend. I'm pretty sure she's in love."

He looked down at the big cat, who had practically melted into his lap, and chuckled. The sound was a low, sensual rumble. I felt my mouth go dry.

Wait a second. Wasn't I supposed to be the one who was working *my* wiles? Drawing him into my carefully spun web?

"Is it typical for a jaguar to go from hunt mode to this?" he asked.

Shrugging, I reached out and ruffed Charm's coat. "She trusts me."

Kai glanced up at me. "I've never met anyone quite like you, Grace."

Oh, you have no idea.

Kai's hand moved along the cat's body until his fingers brushed over mine again. This time, when the flash of heat came, I didn't pull back.

Now or never, Grace. Do something. Slowly, deliberately, I moved to thread my fingers over his, sweeping over the back of his hand with featherlight strokes. Kai stilled. My pulse thrummed in my ears as I stared at our hands.

I felt his gaze on my face and wanted to look at him. But I couldn't. He turned his hand over and I drew my fingers along his rough palm, tracing them along the inside of his wrist then back again.

Kai stopped my plundering fingers by clasping my hand. I looked up into his face. His eyes were riveted on mine. The heat in them would have made most women spontaneously combust.

"You're not like most guys I know either." My voice was so husky I almost didn't recognize it.

"Really, why's that?"

I tried to remember the speech I had come up with. Nope. Nothing. Now he was the one stroking his fingers along my arm. My thoughts became jumbled as his hand brushed up past my elbow.

"The Ice Queen."

"What?" His grin flashed and I felt myself lean into him.

"I'm good at being cold. But not with you." What was I saying? Was this flirting? I didn't know anymore. All I could see was the heat in his eyes and the way he looked at my mouth.

"I'm not very objective with you either." His voice was almost too low and rough to hear. Clearing his throat, he seemed to remember himself.

He stood abruptly and said, "I only have one other place to check."

Charm grumbled at his sudden departure and shifted to lean against the log with her head in my lap. As she settled in for more petting, I struggled to get my heart rate under control. I could still feel where Kai had touched me.

Get a grip, Grace.

It wasn't like we had kissed, or ripped off each other's clothes or anything. I squeezed my eyes shut. Why had I thought about that? I would not think about ripping off Kai's clothes!

I concentrated on counting the spots on Charm's head, marking each one off with my finger. When I reached ninety-seven, I looked over at Kai. He was packing his case. His shoulders seemed tense. Damn. I'd blown my chance.

Wait, no, I hadn't. We were still alone. There was still time.

I stood and stepped forward, until I was looking up into his face. "Kai, I was hoping to talk to you about LaBryce."

I saw his back go rigid and winced inwardly. "I owe you an apology. I jumped to conclusions last night. Like I said, I'm not terribly objective when it comes to you."

He didn't look happy about it. So much for using my "influence" to my advantage. The fact that Kai was attracted to me only seemed to irritate him. "That wasn't what I wanted to talk about." It was time for Grace to act like Grace and cut the crap. No more buttering up. No more BS.

"You remember what I said yesterday in the elevator? That I know, for a fact, that LaBryce is innocent?"

He nodded but said nothing, waiting for me to continue.

"LaBryce was here. He came home after the party, got drunk, and slept it off on that couch." I pointed through the glass.

Kai's eyes didn't follow my finger; they stayed fixed on

me. "Are you telling me you know this because you were with him?"

"No. But I know someone who was." She just couldn't talk—not to Kai anyway. Charm was talking to me, however. Asking me about a bottle and wondering if there were more dog biscuits in my pocket. I ignored the persistent hum of the cat's brain.

"I need to know who. Give me a name."

"I can't."

"You are withholding information in a murder investigation."

"No. I'm not. I'm giving you information. LaBryce is not the killer. He was here." I spoke calmly, thankful that Charm was ignoring Kai's irritation, preferring to sniff my pockets.

"You're really not going to tell me anything else, are you?"

I shook my head. "I'm really not."

"I could take you in. Arrest you for interfering with a police investigation."

As soon as he said it, I knew he wouldn't. Maybe my flirting had done some good after all. But something about the way he had listened when I described what LaBryce had done the night of the murder made me think Kai had heard the story before. From LaBryce.

"You know I'm telling the truth. Because it matches LaBryce's story, doesn't it?"

Kai didn't answer immediately. When he finally spoke, it was almost to himself. "He told us that he slept on the couch, and not in his bed."

Kai's cell phone vibrated audibly in its holster. He flipped it open. "Duncan." He paused to listen. "Okay. I'm almost finished here."

He closed the phone. "I've got to head back to the lab. There's a security camera at the entrance to Mark's neighborhood. The guard booth is only manned until midnight, but the camera runs twenty-four-seven."

This was a good thing. "I guess you'll see that LaBryce left Mark's and didn't come back."

"Maybe."

I had to smile. Even if Kai was not yet convinced, that was okay. I reminded myself that it was his job to be skeptical. I assumed Kai was a show-me-the-proof kind of guy.

He would get it soon enough. I felt a strange little whoosh in my heart. What would happen if they identified the killer from the tapes? LaBryce would be cleared.

I'd be off the hook. I felt a surge of relief and then a stab of disappointment because at some point in the last few minutes I'd realized . . .

I might actually want to get caught.

CHAPTER 9

I left Charm with promises that I'd be back soon. Though I hoped it was under less stressful circumstances. I needed to run home and pick up Jax and Moss. The appointment I had made to have Jax evaluated at the Humane Society wasn't until later, but after my lovely encounter with Mr. Cavanaugh that morning, I didn't want to keep the dogs cooped up inside too long.

Moss howls for me after a while. Though I've told him time and again that I can't hear him after I drive away, he refuses to believe it. I was sure there would already be one complaint waiting for Emma. No need to add another.

By the time I'd ushered the two canines into Bluebell and vaguely pointed us toward town on Beach Boulevard, I'd decided to track down Alex Burke. I needed to get some more vitamin powder. I also planned on giving him a nice dose of what for. I didn't mind looking after Charm. But after the call this morning from Mark's brother, I needed to remember that Jax required my attention, too. I had to make sure he would be safe to adopt out.

I could do both, of course, but it wasn't my job.

Even though Kai seemed to think that Alex had blown off work because LaBryce was in jail, I didn't think that was much of an excuse.

I called the only person I could think of who might know Burke—who wasn't in jail. Dr. Hugh Murray, the zoo vet, was busy, or so I assumed when he didn't answer his phone.

I sat at the light at University, drumming my fingers on the steering wheel. So, how could I find Burke's number? I called Information, and lo and behold, there was a listing for A. Burke off Kings Road.

Who knew people still had listed phone numbers? I called; the phone rang and rang. No machine picked up. No answering service either. This had to be his home phone since it was listed with an address.

Kings Road wasn't too far away if I hopped on 95. I had plenty of time before I had to get Jax to his evaluation.

Burke's neighborhood had seen better days. Like, in the 1950s when the small concrete block homes were a perfect starter for John, the salesman, and his new wife, Betty. Back then, you would have seen Johnny Jr. playing catch on the neatly trimmed grass of the tidy front yard. Now the yards were cordoned off with chain link and guarded by pit bulls. Junk littered the front porches and was strewn over weedy lawns. The flotsam and jetsam of poverty.

Burke's house was no exception. Though the yard was devoid of broken toys and tattered couches, I was willing to bet the squat, square cube was not going to be featured in *Southern Living* anytime soon. I parked Bluebell on the street, and ignoring the dogs' requests to come with me, I left them in the 'Burb and hopped to the ground.

The gate barring the way to the front walk was leaning awkwardly on its hinges, and though it was technically closed, there was no latch. I pushed it open and walked to the front door.

I knocked, and peeling paint flaked off the door and drifted to the ground. I tried to peek inside, but the jalousie windows didn't appear to have been cleaned in the last thirty years.

I thought about going around the house, but that seemed to be overstepping a bit. Finally, I decided to try Hugh again.

Voice mail. Damn. I thought about running to the zoo and tracking him down, but rejected the idea as soon as it popped into my head. Even though I went to the zoo fairly often to enjoy the soothing white noise of the multitude of animal brains after a long day, I always avoided Hugh. I'd told myself his flirtations made me uncomfortable, and though that was somewhat true, I knew it was an excuse.

A reminder of my cowardice.

"Unacceptable, Grace."

I needed to find Alex Burke, tell him Charm was out of his special vitamin mix, and find out if he could come back to work. If that meant I had to deal with Hugh's charisma, so be it.

I climbed back into Bluebell, pulled out of the depressed little 'hood, and a short ten minutes later, I was parking at the zoo.

Moss being a better theft deterrent than any alarm, I decided to leave the engine running with the AC on while I ran my errand. Walking under the tiki hut–inspired thatched entryway, I nodded to the ticket taker, who recognized me, and headed toward the animal hospital.

"Hey, beautiful."

Hugh's voice stopped me in front of the Black Bear exhibit in the Wild Florida section of the zoo. Hugh trudged through a thicket of palmettos and hopped a short wooden fence with the ease of a panther. *Wild Florida indeed*.

"Hugh, do you have a minute?"

"For you? As many as you need." Those warm honey eyes roamed my face as he stepped closer.

I had to fight the urge to step back. "I was wondering if you know Alex Burke. He works for LaBryce Walker."

Hugh's eyebrows shot up. "LaBryce is in deep shit."

"I know."

"You think he did it? Do you think he killed Mighty Mark?"

Why did some athletes have such stupid nicknames? "No. I don't think he did it."

I was glad that Hugh didn't ask me to expound on my belief. He just nodded and asked, "Alex Burke. Like, Alexander Burke?"

I shrugged. "LaBryce just called him Alex. But that makes sense."

"I remember a guy named Burke. He applied here a few years ago, I think. I remember because there was some issue with him."

"What do you mean?"

"I don't remember exactly. There were rumors."

"What kind?"

"I bet Lucy Ann will remember."

Lucy Ann was the informational hub of the zoo employees. If someone was getting married, divorced, was allergic to strawberries, whatever, somehow Lucy Ann knew about it. She was a volunteer who came in a few times a week to do little educational talks to kids. I estimated her age to be approximately one hundred and seventeen, though she was as healthy and hale as any sixty-year-old.

Lucy Ann's omnipotence always made me a little nervous. She reminded me of my grandmother. Not that I was scared of my grandma. I wasn't. Well, maybe a little. In the way that kids are afraid of adults that seemed to be able to pluck ideas right out of their brains. My grandma could take one look at me and know if I was lying, if I'd washed my hands before dinner, or if I was mad at Emma.

When I was a kid, I thought it was some sort of weird grandma-power. I still think that's possible. Lucy Ann had it, too. Maybe there was a club.

Lucy Ann was usually near the Kid Zone, an area that functioned exactly as it was titled. I walked with Hugh through winding paths past gorillas and chimps. I could feel the buzz of their brains, but no one was close enough for me to talk to. Which was good. I wasn't there to chat. Chimps could be very chatty once they got going.

I spotted Lucy Ann as we rounded the same corner I had navigated two days ago with a lemur on my head. I glanced into the lemur exhibit and spotted Kiki right away. He gave me a friendly whistle and I called out a greeting before turning to Lucy Ann.

"I heard you had to get a little ringtail back in there the other morning," Lucy Ann said.

"Yes, ma'am." Of course she knew; she knew everything, which was why I was standing in front of her.

Lucy Ann eyed Hugh and then looked back at me. "What are you two up to today?" The way she said it sounded more like she was talking to a married couple she'd run into as she strolled down her street. I shifted away from Hugh, just to make a point.

"Lucy Ann, do you remember a man named Alexander Burke?" Hugh asked. "He applied for a job here a while ago, but I remember there were some objections about him, and he didn't get the job."

Lucy Ann's eyes stayed fixed on me. "You should stay away from that man."

I felt my eyes widen. I hadn't expected this. "Why?"

"Because he's trouble, that's why."

This was where Lucy Ann and my grandmother began to meld into the same person. I knew, sure as my eyes are blue, that if I asked her why, she would not elaborate. She had spoken, and that was that. Thankfully, Hugh intervened.

"Grace needs to talk to him. Business. But if he's trouble, we need to know what kind."

I glanced at him—when had this become a *we*?

Lucy Ann seemed to think about that for a second. "Well, I'll tell you what I know. We didn't hire him because he has a criminal record. Drugs. Among other things."

"Other things as in . . ."

"As in he's a violent man."

"What do you mean 'violent'? Did he assault someone?" Hugh asked. We both knew Lucy Ann would know the answer to this question, but at that moment, a bevy of preschoolers were herded up the path toward us by a teacher and several other adults. Lucy Ann turned toward them, beaming.

She glanced over her shoulder at us before wading into the sea of little bodies. The meaning of her look was clear. I should steer clear of Alexander Burke. And Hugh should make sure I did.

I glanced at Hugh, who lifted a shoulder and said, "If Burke was convicted of a crime, it's public record. We can check."

We headed toward Hugh's office, which was in the hospital. As we walked into the building, I pulled in a deep breath. The cool air was infused with the scent of antiseptic and animal. I felt a pang, knowing I could never work in a veterinary hospital again. I missed it. I had experienced an overwhelming amount of terror and pain in a place like this, but I had good memories, too, of the ones I helped save, despite my ability.

Hugh led me into his office. He sat at his computer, and I hovered over his shoulder as he tried to find Alexander Burke's criminal record. I knew such things were possible, theoretically, but I was still impressed when after a few keystrokes and mouse clicks, we were reading Alexander Burke's rap sheet.

"It looks like Burke was charged with possession at the same time he was arrested for aggravated assault."

"What's the difference between aggravated assault and regular assault?"

Hugh swiveled in his chair to look up at me. "I don't know. Got any lawyers you can ask? Or a cop?"

I had both. But I knew I'd be calling Wes. "I have a good friend that's a lawyer. I'll call and ask him."

Hugh flashed a sudden, brilliant smile. "This is nice."

"What?"

"Talking to you."

I angled my head, felt my brows knit. I talked to Hugh fairly often.

"I mean about something other than the animals."

"Oh." The warm glow in his eyes seemed to reach out and brush against my skin. I started to move back but discovered that I didn't really want to. What was wrong with me? One flirting session and I was in heat or something.

Or maybe I had let some part of my defenses collapse with the idea of coming clean about my ability.

The thought made me want to bolt, and when Hugh stood, I *did* step back.

"Are you going to try and find Burke?"

"Maybe."

"If you wait for me to get off work, I'll help you. I think Lucy Ann is right, you shouldn't go hunting this guy."

I felt a reflexive burst of temper at the comment. If I wanted to talk to Burke, I would do it. I didn't need a man to protect me. I wanted to snap at Hugh, but I couldn't bring myself to do it. He was trying to help. Yes, I was aware that this change in my policy was sudden. The inner feminazi I had nurtured for years was screaming that I should put Hugh in his place and stomp out of his office.

But I couldn't, not with him standing in front of me with real concern in his eyes. How could I snap and snarl and brush off such sincerity? How had I done it for so many years?

I smiled, and it was a real, open smile that I wasn't sure Hugh had ever seen on my face. "Come on, Hugh, I tame dragons. Don't worry about me."

He seemed a bit off balance then. I didn't know if it was my comment or that I didn't react like he'd expected. I had the sudden image of a dog that had been hit over and over and didn't understand kindness. I felt a hot rush of guilt. God, I'd been a total bitch.

All because I was afraid.

On an impulse that shocked me as much as it did him, I leaned into Hugh, stretched up onto my toes, and bussed a kiss on his cheek. "Thanks for caring."

I stepped back and watched his stunned look morph into a slow grin. It dawned on me that I might have given him the wrong impression.

Crap!

Without comment, I turned away and walked out of the room.

• • •

I didn't have time to drive back to Burke's house before Jax's appointment. But I planned on stopping by later if I could. With or without Hugh. Thinking about him made me want to bang my head against a wall.

Why couldn't I have a fraction of insight when it came to people? I'd wanted to apologize for how unfair I'd acted—instead I'd managed to come on to him.

"Brilliant, Grace," I said to myself as I climbed into Bluebell.

The dogs greeted me with curiosity as I slid behind the wheel. They could smell every animal Hugh had been near during the day and sniffed and snuffled with interest at my shoulder—the only part of me available from where they stood in the backseat.

"Okay, okay, enough."

Bird . . . bear . . . musk . . . The thoughts zipped from one to the other.

"Sit. Go." I waved my hand and tried to disregard the excited buzz of their minds. It can be distracting to drive with so much noise. I could shield my mind when I had to, but it took so much concentration I was nearly incapable of doing anything else.

Emma had tried to get me to sit in when her *Sensei* taught meditation and focusing techniques, but I didn't think I'd be into it. Every time I tried to meditate, I just kept thinking of things I could be doing instead.

Oh, well, I had to rely on my own methods. Like a mother with rowdy kids, I just tuned out Moss and Jax as I headed down Main Street.

When we finally pulled into the shady parking lot of the Humane Society, I was feeling a little worn out. Too many things going on at the same time. Not that I wasn't used to running around a lot with my job. But the personal revelations were starting to wear on me. I was tired mentally. It was only three o'clock, and I was ready to call it a day. Usually, I went for a good book to escape, but right then I wanted to watch TV with a bag of Zapp's chips and a beer. Let my mind check out for a while.

But that was not to be. I had to get Jax evaluated and then go take care of a client with a peeved Persian. I led the dogs to the back of the large brick building. I knocked hard on the metal door with the toe of my tennis shoe and stepped back. Jax and Moss sat obediently as they waited for the door to open.

The afternoon sun was relentlessly strong, even in the shade. The dogs panted loudly, and I could feel a sheen of sweat begin to form under my clothes. Finally, the door was pushed open, and we were greeted by cool air-conditioning and a tall, smiling black woman.

Sonja Brown, blessed with high cheekbones, burnished ebony skin, and a build that was somehow both willowy and strong, was striking. And that was before you added the gigantic gold disk earrings and alarmingly turquoise scrubs. An animal behaviorist with the Humane Society, Sonja was down to earth, solid, upbeat, and dependable. She was one of my few friends, and had a knack for evaluating aggression in dogs.

"Hey, girl!" Sonja's smile was wide and toothy, with a gap in the front that lent her a youthful, mischievous air. She ushered us inside and knelt down to allow Moss to nudge under her chin affectionately. "*Monsieur* Moss, I guess you're expecting a treat?"

"Only because every time he sees you, he gets fed." I shook my head but couldn't help grinning. "It doesn't help to spoil him. He's hard enough to live with."

Sonja stroked Moss's head, her hand a dark contrast to his snowy fur. "Anytime you get tired of him, he can always come home with me." She reached into her scrub pocket and pulled out a dog bone. Moss took it gently and then trotted off to the corner of the room to enjoy his snack.

Sonja's gaze slid over and came to rest on Jax. He

returned her gaze with mild curiosity. "Is this your newest refugee?"

I grinned and patted the dog's head. "Yeah, I think he's going to be fine; at least he is with me. I was hoping you could run a few tests on him. See how he reacts to a stranger."

"Has he shown signs of aggression?"

"Only when I first got him. I'm not sure if his hostility is a passing thing, but I need to find out what his weaknesses are so I can work on them."

Sonja nodded and walked over to the counter and started opening a can of moist dog food. "So, how's the consulting business?"

"Good. The number of people out there who need help understanding their pets is huge. I'm always shocked at people's ignorance." I leaned against the counter to watch Sonja scoop a couple of spoonfuls of wet food into a red plastic bowl.

"Well, we can't all have your talent."

I shrugged. "At least it pays well." Not wanting to talk about my talents, I changed the subject. "I've saved enough for a down payment on a house."

"That's good. Soon you'll be able to keep all the strays you find."

I huffed out a laugh. "I hope you're wrong. Or I'll end up with a zoo."

"Oh, you will, believe me. I keep adding to my crew, and my place only has two bedrooms. Evan says he'll divorce me if I bring any more critters home." Sonja chuckled as she moved to set the bowl in the middle of the room.

"He gets just as attached as you do." I knew her husband, Evan, had as big a soft spot for animals as Sonja.

"He just likes to talk big. I brought a kitten home last week that needed to be fed every few hours. Guess who got up at two in the morning to feed it?" Sonja glanced at me as she walked over to a cupboard.

I watched her rummage around in the cabinet and found myself wondering what it would be like to have someone like Evan to share my life with. Someone who understood.

My mind jumped to thoughts of Kai and Hugh. Could one of them be that person for me? The notion of *that special someone* had been missing from my life for so long . . . I hardly knew what to do with it.

"Here we go." Sonja's voice snapped me out of my thoughts. She had found what she was looking for—a fake human hand on the end of a stick. "Ready?"

I nodded. I knew this test well. Sonja was going to see how Jax reacted to the fake hand trying to take away the food.

When Sonja signaled, I unclipped his leash and stepped to the other side of the room. Jax watched me for a moment and then went to investigate the bowl of food.

I was careful to keep my mind blank.

As Jax began to eat the moist dog food, Sonja reached in with the hand on the stick and pulled the bowl away. Jax followed the bowl, trying to eat and walk at the same time.

I let out a relieved sigh. He didn't snap at the fake hand or even growl.

Sonja praised the dog and looked up at me. "Passed that one better than my dachshund. Do you want to try an aggression test?"

"That would be great."

I pulled up a metal chair and sat holding Jax's collar firmly with one hand. I knew the faux attack she was about to launch might jog the memory of Mark's murder loose. I had to prepare for that. I pressed all thought that could influence him out of my head, and left the gates open to receive even the slightest recall.

When I was ready, I nodded at Sonja.

Sonja stood a few feet away and began yelling at me and the dog. "You're an ugly stupid woman and so is your mutt dog!"

Jax whined softly and looked up to me for guidance. I was careful to stay as neutral as possible.

Sonja took a step forward and started yelling again, this time adding erratic arm movements. "Ugly, ugly mutt dog!"

This time Jax reacted with a low warning growl.

It was no less than I had expected. After all, Jax was a trained guard dog.

Sonja shrugged. "I wouldn't say that's too bad, especially for a Dobie. Where're you going to try to place him?"

"I'm not sure yet. There's a family member who's expressed interest, a man, but I haven't talked to him yet." I needed to. I made a mental note to call Bo Bishop as soon as I could.

"Kids?"

"I don't know. I'll call him later today and find out if there are any other animals or children in the home."

"I really don't think Jax will be any trouble." Sonja folded her arms and lapsed into a thoughtful silence. "While you're here, you mind taking a look at one of my problem cases?"

"Sure." I leashed Jax and led him to where Moss was licking minuscule crumbs off the floor.

I tied the ends of their leashes together loosely and looked pointedly first at one, then the other.

"Stay."

Jax immediately sat, ready to comply. Moss cocked his head and began negotiations. *Treat?*

No.

Treat?

If you don't move a single inch. I turned to follow Sonja, who had started toward the door that led to the rest of the clinic. I shot a quick glance over my shoulder before leaving the room. "I mean it, Moss. Stay."

Sonja chuckled. "You know he always listens to you."

"Yeah, right." I followed Sonja until we reached an area filled with a number of narrow concrete runs. We stopped in front of one occupied by a large mastiff-type dog.

"This is Demon." Sonja raised both her hands before I could comment on the name. "That's what was on his tags. And he answers to it."

"That'll help with adopting him out." People came up with the dumbest names.

Sonja turned her attention to the dog. "He was abandoned in an empty house. He was really aggressive in the beginning but started improving quickly and passed all the evaluations. Then yesterday, he tried to bite my hand off when I went to take him for a walk."

I looked down at the hulking brown dog. He returned my stare with an almost imperceptible growl. It was hard to interpret his thoughts. He seemed afraid. But there was something else . . . pain?

"Was he injured when you brought him in?"

Sonja shook her head. "He was emaciated and weak. But the vet didn't find anything other than that."

Nodding, I reached for the latch on the chain-link gate. "I don't think he's going to be aggressive—"

No sooner had the words passed my lips than the dog lunged, snarling at us. I snatched my hand away from the latch.

"See, it's weird." Sonja shook her head. "Even you can't get him."

It *was* weird. It served as a reminder that I was not always right about animals—an unsettling thought considering the situation with Jax.

"You sure he's not injured?" My phone rang. I glanced at the display; the number was blocked.

"Hello?"

"Grace Wilde?" a man asked.

"Yes?"

"My name is Aaron Stein. I represent the governor and his family. Do you have a moment?"

The Richardsons' lawyer? "Sure."

"I'm actually calling on behalf of Mrs. Richardson. She would like to meet with you, today, if that's possible."

Meet with me? "Does she have some questions about Jax? I'm happy to call—"

"She'd like to speak to you in person."

I wasn't sure what to say. I couldn't turn down a grieving mother just because I was busy and tired and really wanted this day to be over.

"I can come by now. But I can't bring Jax, he's in quarantine."

"Of course." He gave me directions to the family hunting lodge, which was at least a thirty-minute drive south.

I scribbled down the information and turned to Sonja. "Hey, I've got to ask a favor. Can you keep these guys here for a while? I've got to go down to Mandarin and I don't want to drag them with me." Technically, I wasn't supposed to let Jax out of my control but rules are made to be broken, and Sonja was more than capable of handling him.

"I can put them both in my office."

"Thanks."

We started toward her office and she paused in the main kennel area. Puppies yipped. Dogs of various sizes barked or whined with wagging tails.

"Oh—and don't forget about Bark and Bowl tonight."

"Bark and Bowl?"

"You know, like rock and roll? Bark and Bowl."

"Uh-huh."

Sonja was always coming up with new themes to try out for adoption events. Sometimes they worked—other times . . .

"So, what's the gimmick? You're giving away dog bowls with every adoptee?"

Sonja shoved her hands on her hips. "Who cares about getting a dog bowl? I'm talking about bowl-*ing*."

"Like at a bowling alley—and you expect me to come to this?"

"Of course." She flashed a grin, which caused the gap in her teeth to wink at me. "You match people with pets better than anyone. It's like you're psychic or something."

Or something, I thought.

"But why bowling?" I narrowed my eyes as a thought occurred. "Have you been brainstorming with Emma?"

"Please. We can't afford to hire your sister." Sonja waved away the idea then turned and continued toward her office.

"When has that stopped you?" I muttered as I followed.

Emma had counseled Sonja on the ins and outs of event planning in the past. I dreaded the day they finally managed to coordinate a real function. There would be costumes and glitter and, quite possibly, a dunking booth.

"You better get going. Bark and Bowl starts at five."

I opened my mouth to protest but the words died in my throat as I watched her lead Jax and Moss into her office.

"Okay, but I'm not wearing those shoes."

CHAPTER 10

The drive to Mandarin was quiet. Without the dual canine brains humming in my head, I could relax and think.

As I cruised along winding roads, past new subdivisions and old farmsteads, I let my mind drift. Despite the number of things I had tap dancing around in my brain—like, what the governor's wife could want to ask me that required that I drive halfway to St. Augustine—one issue kept resurfacing.

The mastiff, Demon. I played the incident over and over. "What did I miss?"

Something. Why would a dog who was progressing so quickly make a one eighty? I'd felt no aggression from him. Wariness, a tinge of pain, but nothing to make me think he'd launch an attack. It nagged at me.

Because I'd been wrong.

I relied on my interpretation of an animal's thoughts and feelings, and from time to time, I was off. It happened. Not often, but enough to make me wonder what else I could be wrong about.

I thought about Charm. The jaguar had told me clearly what had happened the night of the murder, but what if I was misinterpreting the timeline? What if LaBryce had come home drunk and passed out two nights before Mark Richardson was killed? Animals don't see time as a linear thing, past is past, now is now. My interpretation labeled how far back the memories went. Usually chronology wasn't really important.

This time it was.

I balked at the idea that LaBryce had killed Mark. Because he was my friend. I tried to remove my bias and look at the possibilities.

I imagined LaBryce, angry over the magazine article, returning to Mark's house. To coldly murder his best friend after threatening to kill him? No. Even in his drunken state, I didn't think LaBryce would be that stupid.

Maybe he wasn't there to fight; maybe he just wanted to talk. Things got heated, and without others there to break things up . . . But then there was the issue of the missing gun. If he'd gone to Mark's just to talk, he wouldn't have carried his pistol.

I was so distracted by my musings that I almost missed the turn. I would have if it hadn't been for the news vans clustered along the narrow road. I eased past the crowd with their sprouting satellite dishes and antenna and pulled to a stop at the gate.

A young male reporter sat in his car with his door open, ready to spring into action at the first sign of the bereaved governor. He watched as I cranked down my window and spoke to the security guard.

The gate opened, and I pulled through it. I glanced in my rearview mirror and saw the reporter scribbling on his notepad. Was he taking my license number?

A sense of unease settled over me as I guided Bluebell down the long shady lane and around a stand of gargantuan moss-draped live oaks. I didn't like the idea of a reporter checking up on me. I didn't have anything to hide—nothing newsworthy anyway—but it made me nervous all the same.

I rounded a turn and braked to a sudden stop. My anxiety amplified as I looked at the house. No, not house—*estate*.

"*This* is a *hunting* lodge?" When the Richardsons' lawyer had said it, like an idiot, I'd thought about my uncle's hunting camp. I had expected a large cabin. Something rustic, a place for the guys to get together and pound a few beers.

I should have known better.

The antebellum mansion was a white titan. Sitting regally in front of the oaks, like a queen holding court, her towering two-story columns glowed copper in the late afternoon sun.

The landscaping around the house was just as grand. Pink shrub roses lined the front of the porch, and large crape myrtles, heavy in bloom, dusted the driveway with tiny fuchsia petals.

I swept my gaze over the sprawling grounds. The rolling lawn and ancient oaks whispered *old money*.

Then it hit me.

As someone who spends more time with animals than people, I tend to ignore things like politics. But I remembered, in that moment, that though Governor Buck Richardson touted himself as a self-made man—a hardworking boy from a middle-class family—he had one major connection.

Mrs. Gardenia Clarke Richardson.

The Clarke family name graced libraries, parks, and bridges. They had more than enough money and contacts to win campaigns.

I parked and walked up the azalea and crape myrtle–lined brick path. When I reached the heavy front door, it swung in before I could knock.

An elderly housekeeper stood square shouldered in front of me. The crisp white collar of her uniform contrasted like a blade against her caramel-colored skin. I told her my name, and she motioned me inside.

"Miss Gardenia will be with you in a minute." She said *Miss* like *Miz*. Her voice was as rich and warm as freshly made fudge. "Wait here, please." Her rubber-soled black shoes squeaked on the polished white marble floor as she turned and walked down the large entrance hall.

The ceiling in the foyer was at least twenty feet high. Large stained wooden pocket doors flanked me on either side. At the end of the hall, a grand sweeping staircase arced upward. I half expected to see Rhett Butler leaning against the smooth oak banister. As a child, Emma and I would snuggle against our mother and watch *Gone with the Wind,* one of her favorite epics. She would have loved to see this place.

The soft hum of a feline brain caught my attention. So the Richardsons had a cat somewhere. I looked around the foyer but didn't see one.

"Kitty-kitty." *Where are you?*

The answer came from just inside the room to my right. I moved toward the heavy pocket doors and they rumbled open. The housekeeper ushered me into a formal sitting room. It was just as grand in scale as the foyer but infinitely more ornate. Everything in the room seemed to be bathed in gilt. *Froufrou* was the word that popped into my head.

Mrs. Richardson sat on an antique damask settee. The hand in her lap grasped a dainty white handkerchief; the other ran along the body of a beautiful silver Maine coon cat, who was stretched out beside her. The animal watched me with cool intelligence, and its long, plume-like tail flicked with curiosity. It had felt my mind reach out to it a minute ago and now had the urge to come investigate. The only thing keeping the cat on the settee was the constant stroke of his owner's hand.

I shifted my attention back to Mrs. Richardson. Despite the shadows under her eyes, she was still an attractive woman. Petite and slender, with expertly coiffed blond hair that barely brushed the shoulders of her black satin blouse.

Standing behind her was a tall man in a dark, expensive-looking suit. The lawyer, I assumed.

"Thank you for coming on such short notice." Her soft voice was the epitome of Southern gentility. She motioned to a set of chairs opposite her. "Please have a seat."

I eased down onto the dainty gilded chair.

"Would you like something to drink? Tea?"

"No, thank you, ma'am."

The housekeeper, who had been hovering unobtrusively, took that as her cue to exit, sliding the pocket doors closed behind her with a soft thump.

Quiet settled around us like a funeral shroud. As I sat in the hush of the overdecorated room, across from Mrs. Richardson, I started feeling more and more uncomfortable. Neither she nor the lawyer spoke; they both just looked at me. His expression was blank. Hers held a mixture of interest and something else I couldn't read.

"So, what can I do for you, Mrs. Richardson?"

"Please, call me Gardenia."

"Okay."

"Do you mind if I call you Grace? It's a lovely name."

"No, ma'am, that's fine. Thank you."

"This is Atticus." She patted the Maine coon; his tufted ears twitched at the sound of his name.

"He's beautiful." This was getting weird. She wanted me to meet her cat?

The little clock on the mantle dinged, announcing the time with a merry jingle. Three o'clock. I'd already been there for almost ten minutes, and I still had no idea why I'd been asked to come.

As I looked into Mrs. Richardson's red-rimmed eyes, I knew I couldn't demand that she tell me. The woman had lost her son. Compassion and my Southern upbringing would not allow me to press her. So I sat quietly and waited, clasping my hands together so I wouldn't fidget.

The longer the seconds ticked by, the more out of my element I felt. I didn't drive down here to sit and be scrutinized in silence. If there was a reason for my summons, *Miz* Gardenia needed to get to it.

"Did you want me to come here because you need help with Atticus?" I doubted that was the case. The cat was the picture of feline bliss. Purring like an outboard motor. The thrumming, rhythmic serenity was so strong it had started to make me want to doze.

"Atticus is fine. As far as I know."

"Then you must have some questions about Jax. I'm happy to say he's progressing very well."

"Good." She turned her head toward the lawyer. "Aaron, would you give us a moment?"

The lawyer seemed to hesitate before leaving. For some reason, being alone with this delicate, quiet woman was unsettling. I didn't know what she wanted from me, but she was after something.

"What do you call yourself, Grace?"

"I'm not sure what you mean."

"The term you use for what you are."

I felt my senses sharpen, and my pulse quicken. My instincts warned that an attack was coming. I agreed completely.

"What I am?"

"Dane Harrington told me you claimed that you have a psychic ability. But from how he described it, I would think the word *telepathic* would be a better fit."

I don't think I ever really understood the term *blindsided* until that moment. The room seemed to tilt. I felt my fingers reach to curl around the arms of the chair. "Excuse me?"

"I realize this is a bit of a surprise, and I regret bringing it up." The cool indifference in her voice contradicted the claim. She had no problem dropping a bombshell in my lap. "I have to know. Did Jax see who killed my son?"

"I don't . . ." My mind was suddenly filled with a whirl of questions and confusion. She knew about Jax? Dane Harrington had told the governor's wife about my ability? Why? One question seemed to press forward, though it was irrelevant. For some reason I had to ask.

"How did you know about me and Dane?"

She didn't answer, waving her hand as if to wave off the question the way a person brushed away a fly. I realized I was insignificant to this woman. My questions, my feelings, meant nothing to her.

"When the police came and told us about Mark's murder, one of my first questions was about Jax. I'm sure you understand why. Mark loved that dog. The thought of Jax being killed, too . . ." She stopped and dabbed at the corner of her eye. The shift from callous to lachrymose was sudden and baffling.

Sniffing, she managed to say, "I was beside myself when the police told me Jax was in quarantine."

"I'm taking good care of him." It was a stupid thing to say. But really, I wasn't exactly thinking straight.

"Yes. I learned quickly that you are the best. But that wasn't enough. If Jax is not considered safe, he'll be euthanized. I can't let that happen." The superiority was back, but now it was tinged with hostility. Her bloodshot eyes glinted. Her soft, genteel voice sharp as a razor. "I thought the best way to ensure his protection would be to offer some payment to you."

I let that sink in. "A bribe?" Was this really happening? My brain was having a hard time getting a grasp on the situation. The ping-ponging between steel magnolia and moray eel was wigging me out.

"An incentive," she corrected coldly. "Naturally, I had to learn as much about you as I could. As I read your file, it became obvious that there was more to your way with animals."

File? I had a file? A flare of temper shot through me, cutting though the chaos of my spinning thoughts.

"Seeing Dane's name was a surprise. But I was glad to have someone to contact. Someone who wouldn't merely give you a glowing recommendation."

"You've contacted my clients?"

"They all love you. Dane was not so . . . enthusiastic. I don't think he would have spoken to me at all about you if our families hadn't been so close."

That was it. I couldn't stand to listen to one more word. I stood so abruptly that the cat and his mistress both started. "I don't know what you've been told, but you're wrong. I'll show myself out, *Gardenia*."

I turned on my heel to leave, but her next words stopped me.

"Your sister is planning my niece's wedding in the spring. Emma is also handling a gala for the Junior League—of which I am now president. I spoke to my niece today, and asked her if she had considered another event planner . . . just in case there was a problem."

I turned back toward her. I'd never seen a more ruthless creature in such a lovely package.

"There won't be, will there?"

I lowered myself into the chair and pulled in a slow, even breath. I let my anger settle like an icy pool in my gut. As a rule, I don't hiss and spit like an alley cat. My temper flares and burns cold. This bitch was using my sister to push me. She would find out just how bitter cold could be.

"Answer my question," she snapped. "Did Jax see what happened to Mark?"

I had no intention of even acknowledging the question, or that she knew about my ability. "Don't you trust the police to solve your son's murder?"

"LaBryce Walker's a friend of yours, isn't he?"

"Why ask? I'm sure it's in my file." As angry as the thought made me, LaBryce's name being mentioned made me remember that he was in jail. As much as I wanted to freeze this woman out, sit in uncooperative silence, and shrug as she asked me questions, I wanted to help him more. I realized that there might be an opportunity sitting in front of me. If I worked it right, I might be able to learn something.

"The police haven't arrested LaBryce for Mark's murder. If they could, they would have. Did he do it? Are you protecting your friend?"

Was I? I really wasn't a hundred percent sure anymore, but I wasn't about to let Miss Gardenia know that. "LaBryce didn't kill Mark."

"Does that mean you know who did?"

"No."

"But Jax saw what happened, didn't he?"

"I'm not sure." She arched a brow in such a haughty way, that I was tempted to keep up the vague responses, just to piss her off. But that wouldn't help anyone. I was so impressed with my restraint I wondered why my mother hadn't named me Temperance.

"Listen, I don't know what to tell you. Jax is confused."

"What do you mean? The police said Jax was there. How could he be confused?"

"I mean there is a lot going on in his head. Images I don't understand."

She leaned forward and I knew I had her. "What images?"

"They are hard to describe. I don't know Jax, or Mark, so it's hard to interpret what I see."

"But you saw the killer?"

"No. I don't think so. I can tell you some things, and you could tell me what you think they mean." She didn't agree, and I didn't give her time to think about it. "I remember Jax showing me a young woman, pretty, blond. She and Mark were fighting." Not exactly true, but maybe if I brought up Jennifer Weston, I'd learn more about her relationship with Mark.

"Jennifer? I don't believe she . . ." Gardenia shook her head. "No. Jennifer would never hurt Mark. She would never hurt anyone."

"When I look into an animal's mind, I can't always tell when things are happening." That was true enough. "But I do know that the argument was a bad one. Are you sure this Jennifer is so nice?"

"Of course. We've known Jennifer for years. She is still a part of this family. Now more than ever."

That surprised me, but I couldn't think of a way to push further. "Mark opened the door for his attacker."

"Yes, the police told me." Something in her expression changed. I couldn't quite place it, but the idea that Mark opened his door in the middle of the night to someone seemed to disturb her. What about that would make a mother frown? Then it hit me. Had he been seeing someone new? Someone Mommy didn't approve of?

If that were the case, she would have given the police the woman's name. Or maybe not. What if Mark was dating a stripper or something? I had no doubt that the Richardsons would want to save face; maybe that was the real reason I was here. The family wanted to know who killed Mark, not just for justice, but for damage control.

"Do you have some idea who he would be expecting that late?"

Her eyes locked onto mine then looked away. "Certainly not," she snapped. She was lying, everything about her body language told me.

"Okay, well, do you know what I should be looking for with Jax?" It was a real question that I hoped she had a real answer to.

"I know that my son had not been himself for weeks. Mark sometimes trusted people he shouldn't."

"So you think he might have opened the door to a stranger?" If that was the case, I was screwed. I could just imagine Jax remembering the murder and not having a name to work with. Or calling him something like Tall Man or Garlic Breath. How would I explain my sudden need to work with a composite artist? *Did I mention that I happened to be in the neighborhood the night of the murder and I saw this guy . . .*

"No, not a stranger. But Mark could be very gullible at times." There was such sadness in the way she said it that I almost forgot to dislike her . . . almost. I might feel sorry for Gardenia Richardson, but I would never like her. She'd threatened my sister.

The door the lawyer had left through earlier swung open, and the housekeeper stepped in. "Miss Gardenia, the gov'ner is on the phone."

"Thank you, Evelyn. I'll take the call in my office." She stood, and the cat hopped off the couch and walked away. I watched him go and wished I had some time to talk to the animal. "Grace, thank you for coming." She had once again morphed into the demure lady most people thought she was. "I'll be in touch. If you think of anything, please call."

I nodded but didn't comment. After she left the room, I sought out the cat, hoping to gain some information from it. But the Maine coon had slunk out of range. I opened my mind, trying to stretch it as far as possible. If I had been at my sister's, I might have been able find the cat, but this place was way too big. I blew out a breath and gave up. Really, what was I expecting to find? A memory of Gardenia digging a shallow grave in the rose garden? Maybe a vision of her dancing with the devil as she cackled over a boiling caldron?

I glanced up at a portrait that dominated one wall. I'd had my back to it until then. The painting was of Gardenia and her two sons. Her eyes were cast slightly to the side, as if she was looking over the artist's shoulder. Her lips curved up in a half smile. Most people would see it as a sweet, somewhat whimsical expression. To me, she looked calculating. The two teenagers were more animated. Grinning as they stood behind her throne-like chair.

I wondered again why Bo Bishop would have a different last name. Was he a child from a previous marriage? In the portrait, he looked to be the same age as Mark.

"Can I show you out?"

The old housekeeper had somehow snuck up on me. "Oh, sorry. I just noticed this portrait. What a beautiful painting."

The woman sighed. "Breaks my heart to look at it."

"I'm sure it does." I was trying to think of something I could ask her that would yield some dirt on her employer, but I got the feeling the woman had been working there for a long time. I was sure she knew every skeleton in every closet. I was equally sure she dutifully dusted each one of them.

Maybe if I pretended to be in the know . . . "Bo called me the other day. He wants to adopt Mark's dog. It's my responsibility to make sure he's going to be taken care of. Is Bo good with dogs?"

"No one better. Bo's real good with the huntin' dogs." She motioned toward the rear of the house.

"He lives here?" I didn't hide my surprise.

"Always has, eve' since he was a boy. Bo lives at the cottage down by the quarry pond."

"Why?"

"Bo's daddy and the gov'ner was best friends. When Bo was five, his parents died in an accident. The gov'ner and Miss Gardenia took him in." She smiled sadly. "He and Mark came up together, like brothers. Now, he takes care of the huntin' dogs and watches over the grounds. You need to talk to him, just drive around the main house and follow the road. You cain't miss it." She walked me to the front door and pointed to the road wrapping around to the back of the house. "Good day, ma'am."

With that, Evelyn stepped back into the house and quietly shut the door. It was clear she had said all she was going to. If I wanted to learn more about Bo Bishop, I'd have to find out for myself.

CHAPTER 11

I cranked Bluebell and headed along the dirt road. After several minutes I reached the pond, which was closer to the size of a small lake.

A rustic wood cabin sat at the water's edge under a towering magnolia. A short dock jutted out from the rear of the cabin into the still waters. Past the cabin, on a small rise, was an old barn. It had a rust-streaked tin roof, and the red paint had faded to a dusty crimson. I pulled to a stop behind an old pickup. When I opened the door, I could hear the excited yapping of several hounds.

I slid out of the seat and slammed the door. It was almost four in the afternoon, and thanks to the storms the day before, the air was muggy. Insects buzzed about slowly as if the humidity sapped them of strength.

I knew how they felt. After my restless night, long drive, and chat with the wicked witch of the South, I was beat. Alexander Burke was safe from my ire until the next day.

Leathery magnolia leaves crunched underfoot as I moved toward the cabin. I swept my gaze over the area. A fiberglass canoe sat upside-down against one wall of the cabin. A cane pole, cast net, and other fishing paraphernalia littered the area. I had to wonder how it would feel to be "adopted" by one of the richest families in the area and end up in the back forty next to the barn.

I had only walked halfway to the cabin when a man called out from behind me.

"Can I help you?"

I turned to see a lanky young man in a soiled white T-shirt and grimy faded jeans walking toward me. His eyes burned at me from under a sweat-stained Jaguars baseball cap. He carried an ax handle like he knew how to swing it. No ax head, just the wood—not as scary as the whole tool, but scary enough.

I wondered if Kai or Jake had talked to this guy. Going on first impressions, I'd say he fit the murderer bill pretty much to a T.

"If you're a reporter, you need to get the hell off this property—now." He motioned back toward the main road with the ax handle.

"I'm not a reporter." I held my hands up. "Are you Bo Bishop?"

He narrowed his eyes. "If I am?"

"I'm Grace Wilde." I met and held his wary gaze.

"You're the lady that has Jax." He eased his grip on the ax handle.

"I'm sorry to stop by without calling, but I was here and thought I might talk to you about Jax?"

"Yeah. Come on inside." He pushed his cap up and wiped his brow with the back of his hand. Though his demeanor had changed when he realized I wasn't a reporter, I was still a tad reluctant to go into the cabin. So far, what I knew of this family was not giving me warm fuzzies. Maybe it was the ax handle or the fact that his adoptive mother reminded me of a trapdoor spider.

"It's hotter than six shades of hell out here." He moved past me and leaned the ax handle next to the door. I hesitated but followed him inside.

The cabin was cool. I could hear a window air conditioner

rattling and humming somewhere. I'd characterize the décor as classic redneck. Mounted deer heads were hung next to Nocona boots and LET'S RODEO posters. A well-stocked gun cabinet dominated one wall. There was even a big wooden eagle spreading his wings triumphantly on the mantle. The whole place smelled vaguely of stale Budweiser and cigarettes.

Bo closed the door behind me. "Sorry about that." He motioned outside. "Damn reporters haven't left us alone—helicopters, people sneaking through the woods—no damn respect." He walked into the small efficiency kitchen and opened the fridge. "You want a Coke or somethin'?"

"No, thank you."

Bo grabbed a soft drink and slammed the fridge closed with a grimy boot heel. I noticed a couple of photographs attached to the door with magnets. The first was similar to the one I'd seen at Mark's house. Jennifer Weston holding a floppy-eared Jax. But in this snapshot, Bo was at her side, grinning at the camera. The second photo was faded, the edges worn. It was of Bo and Governor Richardson. Both were dressed in camo, holding up the head of a dead deer by the antlers.

I cringed inwardly. Hunting is popular with a lot of people—obviously I'm not one of them. If everyone could have a conversation with the animal in the crosshairs and feel its pain after being shot, there'd be a lot fewer hunters.

I know it's good for the health of the deer population, blah, blah. And I know most hunters are, in their own way, nature lovers, but there are some that aren't. I'd seen plenty of wounded tortoises, foxes, and beavers that some jackass decided to shoot just to be mean. I wondered which category of hunter Bo Bishop fell into.

I also wondered why there were no photographs of Mark.

"How's Jax doin'?" Bo popped open the drink and took a long swig.

"After the murder, he was highly aggressive and dangerous. But he's getting better every day."

"I can't picture it, him being dangerous. Jax is a pussy-cat." Bo's brows drew together, and he looked slightly confused at the idea that the dog he knew had been aggressive. "He was a present for Mark's twenty-first birthday. From me and Jennifer."

"If I can rehabilitate him fully, I can turn him over to family. You said you wanted to take him?"

"Yeah, I'd like to have him."

"That's great." I smiled but didn't commit to anything. If Jax was going to be given to someone, I had to be sure it was a good fit. And I wanted to see what I could learn from Bo. Not just about the murder. I still wanted to rip Gardenia out of her cocoon of entitlement. "Mr. Bishop, since you are looking at adopting Jax, I need to ask a few questions."

"It's Bo, and you can ask whatever you need to."

"Do you have children?"

"No, ma'am."

"Jax is nicely socialized to other dogs. Do you have any other animals? A cat? Rabbits?"

"No, ma'am. Just the huntin' dogs."

"I assume you understand the responsibility of handling a dog of Jax's breed and training."

"I sure do. I'm real good with dogs."

I nodded. "I heard the hounds. Are they kept by the barn? Do you mind if I go see them?" Seeing how well he cared for the hunting dogs would tell me a lot. But if I really wanted to know about Bo Bishop, why not get some inside information? Nothing's more earnest than a hound. If they liked him, it would be a big mark in his favor, redneck hunter or not. Plus, if you get a guy talking about his dogs, he might just let a family secret slip.

"Sure. I guess you must know a lot about animals. You heard of a bluetick?"

"I have. You have coonhounds?"

"Well, they ain't mine, but I train 'um."

I had been around blueticks before, but only a few times. They were smart, good problem solvers, but needed skilled and consistent training. I slid a sidelong glance at Bo as we headed outside. If the hounds turned out to be happy and well behaved, it would be another point for him.

The late afternoon sun felt like a steam iron hovering next to my face, and the distance up the hill to the barn seemed to stretch the longer we walked. Who needs a sauna when you have Florida in July?

As we approached the open door, I could feel the hounds' excitement. Though they had been exercised today, they were hopeful that the arrival of another human might mean they would get to do some training. My hunting lingo being rusty, I had a hard time interpreting the thoughts of the yapping dogs.

Words like *open* and *ike* kept being repeated. Along with the phrase *hunt'um up!* In fact, it was being repeated so much and with such enthusiasm, I had a hard time hearing what Bo was saying aloud.

"Don't think I'll be keepin' Jax out here . . ."

Hunt'um up! Hunt'um up!

". . . too far from the cabin . . ."

Hunt'um up! Ike, ike, ike!

"Don't you?"

I literally had to force the connection to the hounds shut. Something I rarely had to do. Usually, I was reaching out, trying to link my mind to an animal's. But this was overwhelming. There were at least ten hounds within my "range," and each of them seemed to be screaming in my head.

Maybe meditation wasn't such a bad idea after all.

"Miss Wilde?" Bo was frowning at me.

"Sorry, what did you say?"

"I was just sayin' that Jax would stay in the cabin with me."

"That's good." I nodded and thought about trying to reconnect to one of the hounds. Just one. I wasn't sure I had that kind of control, but nothing ventured . . .

Before I tried, I needed to distract Bo, so he wouldn't notice that I was ignoring him, and I needed to pick a hound.

I looked around the interior. Though it was plain and utilitarian, it was neat. The stalls were clean. It smelled like dog, old wood, and earth. The back of the old horse stalls opened, via large dog doors, to what I assumed were outside runs.

"How many hounds do you have?"

"Right now, seven and a half couples. Four dogs and three and a half bitches." He was using hound lingo that I wasn't quite following, but I knew by a quick head count that there were over a dozen dogs in the kennel.

I could still feel the excitement rolling off the canines, and my heart rate seemed to be trying to match theirs. If I was going to pick a brain, I needed to do it fast or I might become possessed, start baying and take off after the next squirrel I came across.

I skimmed over the hounds. All of them were sturdy, with the speckled steel-blue coat that gave them their name. But without putting my feelers out, I couldn't tell who was the lead dog, so I asked Bo.

"That there is Marcus. He's a great hunter, and he knows how to carry a line. Next to him is Sadie. She's his backup, and the fastest of all of 'um." He continued to name off the dogs, but I had my leader.

Focusing as hard as I could, I tried to separate Marcus's brain from the rest of the pack. It wasn't as hard as I thought. His energy was calmer and more stable than the others. He was more interested in me, my scent, and my intentions than the chance of getting a training session. Good alpha.

I extended my thoughts to his. As soon as I fully connected to the low buzz of his brain, I offered my friendship. I wanted to meet him and his pack. I didn't want anything else.

Marcus was smart enough to realize that I was a strange human.

Different.

You could say that. Yes, I'm different. Do you like living here, with Bo?

I sent images to Marcus. Bo's face. The feeling of contentment. The feeling of safety. But I left the ideas open-ended. That was the only way I'd ever been able to ask a question as abstract as the one I was attempting.

Yes. Good. Fair. A mingling of other impressions flowed from the dog. And I had my answer. Bo was responsible and hardworking. Organized and firm.

I could have pushed for more, but I felt like I had a good idea of who Bo was. A dog person, from his soiled cap to his steel-reinforced boots. The knowledge made me feel instantly more at ease.

Thanking Marcus, I turned to Bo. He was pointing at a hound in the farthest run.

"And I'm still working with him. Might not be able to keep him if he doesn't learn to stay on the line and quit skirtin' off and goin' after trash game."

I was nodding, though I only had a vague idea of what he was talking about.

We left the barn, and I let out a sigh as soon as I could drop the shield I'd had to hold up in order to keep so many excited animals out of my head.

"You sure you're all right?"

"It's been a long couple of days." I regretted the words as soon as I said them. "Oh God, I'm sorry. You've had it much worse than me."

Bo lifted a shoulder. "It ain't easy. I just keep thinking I should have known."

"Bo, there's nothing you could have done."

"Maybe." His face took on a hard edge. Having someone you love murdered was bound to piss you off. But the intensity of his sudden anger was startling.

"Um . . . if you want, I can bring Jax down here for a visit."

Bo's features softened. "Yeah?"

"Sure. I need to see how he does in a new place. But if all goes well with the visit, it'll be a done deal. You'll just have to sign some paperwork."

"It would be nice to have Jax. Mark was like a brother."

"I noticed you don't have the same last name." I'd heard the story from the housekeeper, but I wanted to know Bo's take on it.

"Buck and Gardenia took me in when my parents died. I owe 'um everything."

I glanced around the little cabin. It wasn't much. Most people would look at the battered truck and grimy yard and feel sorry for Bo. An orphan who'd been given the short end of the stick compared to his famous, wealthy "brother."

But people were different. Not everyone wanted fame and fortune—some people wanted a quiet life with their dogs. I understood that.

"I'm supposed to go talk to the cops," Bo said. "But I don't know what I can say. I left the party early."

"You were at Mark's house the night of the murder?" I'm not sure why it surprised me, but it did. The two men seemed to lead such separate lives.

"Yeah. I saw LaBryce jump Mark, but I don't think it was him."

We reached the Suburban, and I turned to look Bo in the eye. "Why not?"

"He was mad. But he wasn't killin' mad. He was just drunk."

"If you believe that, you need to tell the police." It would be nice to have someone else join my chorus. "You knew Mark and his friends—you might know more than you think you do."

Bo seemed to mull that idea over for a while. "There is one thing. Mark told me about a guy that was following him a lot."

"Following him. You mean like stalking him?"

Bo wrinkled his brow. "I don't know. He was always showin' up and asking for Mark's autograph. Mark said that the guy was fruity or somethin'."

"Fruity?" I frowned at the term. "You think the man was gay?"

"Yeah, you know."

I didn't, but I'd thought of another, more important question. "Do you know his name?"

Bo shook his head. "Don't think Mark ever told me."

"Bo, if Mark was being stalked by an obsessed fan, the police definitely need to know." I turned and pulled open my door. Leaning across the seat, I fished my cell out of my purse. I tried Kai's number, but my phone let out a slow, forlorn beep.

No signal.

"When are you supposed to meet with the police?"

"Tomorrow. After I take care of the dogs."

Which probably meant midmorning. "I really think you should go in now. Let me give you a number." I opened the car door and, after rummaging around on the floorboard, came up with a pen and crinkled Whataburger receipt.

I flattened out the paper and scribbled the number I'd stored in my phone. "Ask for Sergeant Duncan. He'll want to know what you just told me."

I felt a rush of excitement. For a moment, I understood the appeal of being a detective. Searching for clues, tracking leads, and then finally, after prowling through information and evidence, moving in for the kill.

Solving a mystery would be a heady, seductive thing.

CHAPTER 12

Bark and Bowl, though not a complete failure, was not the success Sonja had hoped for. The dim lighting and echoing crash of the pins frightened some of the dogs. I tried to calm them down, but my mind can only link to so many brains at a time.

Still, we were able to adopt out a litter of puppies and even an adult Labrador mix. Sonja and I helped the other volunteers load the vans, and as we watched them head back to the ASPCA, she let out a slow sigh. I turned, expecting to find her downtrodden, and was surprised when she grinned.

"All in all, not bad, right?" she said. "Let's celebrate with a drink and some nachos."

"The nachos here are made with cheese that comes in a two-gallon can."

"I know! They put jalapeño juice in it, too. You can't get that everywhere."

I made a face but followed her back into the bowling alley. The bar was separated from the rest of the building by a set of saloon doors and was even more dimly lit than the alley itself.

The place was fairly busy, and the bartender, a rail-thin woman with lank, dark hair, could only acknowledge us with a nod as she waited on a cluster of elderly men in identical blue bowling shirts.

We found seats at the bar and sat on cracked, pleather-clad stool cushions.

The bartender scurried over to us and took our order. True to her word, Sonja went with the nachos. I decided to play it safe with a bag of Doritos. We each ordered a Corona, which the bartender supplied at lightning speed before handing me my chips and zipping into the back to prepare Sonja's "meal." We chatted as we sipped our beers, and I gave Sonja the short version of the fiasco with Charm and LaBryce and, apparently, mentioned Kai a few too many times, because she eyed me slyly and asked, "So who's this investigator you keep talking about?"

I shrugged but she wasn't about to let it go that easily. "Come on, give an old married lady something juicy to think about."

"You're not old."

She raised her brows and waited.

"It's complicated."

"How's it complicated?"

I couldn't explain the situation. I'd never told Sonja about my ability and I wasn't about to confess in a crowded bowling alley bar.

The bartender plopped the plate of nachos in front of Sonja and I took advantage of the momentary distraction and tried to come up with a way to change the subject.

"Emma gives me a hard time because I don't give anyone a chance—she thinks I should've gone out with Hugh."

"Hugh? Please, girl, that boy ain't nothin' but a flirt."

"So you don't think he was serious when he asked me out?"

"I didn't say that." She took moment to lick a glob of cheese off her finger. "I'm sure he could get serious about someone, but most of the time, he's just a flirt."

"I'm not following you."

"He can't help it. It's the way he communicates."

I took a sip of beer and thought about it. I had never really considered the idea that Hugh hadn't been as serious about pursuing me as I had assumed. The thought was humbling, but more important, it was a relief.

"Why are you smiling?" Sonja asked.

"Because I'm an idiot." I told her about the encounter Hugh and I'd had in his office earlier. "I was worried I gave him the wrong impression when I kissed his cheek, but maybe not."

Sonja shook her head. "Girl, you really do need to spend more time with people."

"That's debatable. I screw up with people, Sonja. If I'm not getting the wrong impression about someone, I'm giving it. It's like my one party trick."

"Come on—you're not that bad. You just need more practice."

When I shot her a doubtful look, she pointed down the bar and said, "See that nice young man over there? Why don't you go over and sit next to him—I bet he'll say hello. All you have to do is say hello back."

I swiveled in my seat to see who she was talking about and had to grip the bar to stop from falling off my stool. The guy was wearing a bowling shirt so spangled with sequins I almost had to shade my eyes in the glare. He looked like a bad Elvis impersonator.

"Is that a pompadour toupee?"

"Looks like it."

I swiveled back to face her. "Why would I—"

"Practice. Who else at this bar gives as strong a first impression? You'll have to look past the exterior and really listen to what he says." Her eyes sparkled with humor. "Think of it as an experiment."

"You're nuttier than squirrel poo if you think I'm going to go hit on that guy."

"I never said anything about hitting on anyone. Just go talk to him. Come on, girl. Why not? You know there's a story that goes with that outfit—go find out what it is."

• • •

As it turned out, the bedazzled bowler did have a story. Hound Dog Jim, or just Hound Dog, as he liked to be called, was a genuine bowling alley karaoke star.

He'd performed all over the world. When I asked if he was big in Japan, he chucked and nodded, saying, "I even have a T-shirt to prove it."

All in all, talking to him wasn't a terribly painful experience. I even considered staying to hear him sing until he invited Sonja and me to sing backup.

At that point, I came up with an excuse to leave and hauled Sonja out of there.

"I think we would have been great," Sonja said as we walked out of the bowling alley into the muggy night. "We could have done choreography."

She did a side shuffle step and began snapping her fingers.

"Trust me, you don't want me to try to dance and sing at the same time," I told her. "I'm not that coordinated."

" 'I'm not good with people. I'm not coordinated.' You've got to stop being so negative."

"I'm being honest."

"You're being stubborn." She used her key fob to unlock her car door with a tweet.

"Hey, I talked to Hound Dog Jim, didn't I?"

"Exactly! You met a famous karaoke singer—you never know what life has in store."

She grinned and we said our good-byes. As I drove back to the condo, I had a feeling I knew all too well what life had planned for me, and after my meeting with Gardenia Richardson, I was sure it wasn't good.

The dogs greeted me enthusiastically and I gave them each a pat on my way into the kitchen to fill their bowls with kibble. Emma had left me a note saying she would be out late and had collected ten sticky notes from Mr. Cavanaugh. A new record.

My stomach grumbled and I threw a bunch of salad

greens into a bowl, chopped up a small tomato, topped the whole deal with ranch, and sat at the peninsula that separated the kitchen and the living room. I stabbed at the lettuce and thought.

I didn't want to tell Emma about Gardenia's threat, or that she knew about my ability. That would mean telling Emma about Dane, and I really didn't feel like going there. The fact that I had dated a Harrington and had not told her would be a problem in and of itself.

The fact that I had been thrown out like so much trash by said Harrington would be a bigger problem. It would tick Emma right off to think I'd been hurt and hadn't confided in her.

The buzz of canine brain and the sound of licking chops made me glance down at Moss. Finished with his meal, he was now thinking he needed some of mine.

Bite.

"It's a salad. You don't want any." This tactic never worked. I don't know why I tried.

Bite.

No.

Bite.

I shook my head and pulled my mental shield into place. At least I didn't have to listen to the begging. Proving me wrong, Moss whined loudly, then licked his chops.

Jax click-clacked into the room and watched us. I ignored them and finished my salad. Both dogs followed me as I walked into the kitchen, gazing up at me with wide, hopeful eyes. No animal did the "I haven't eaten for months" look like a dog. It's in their genes. Sometime way back, a wild dog gave a caveman that look and it was all over.

Man's best friend—created from one part kindness and two parts leftovers.

I reached into my shorts pocket and pulled out a surplus treat from my visit with Charm.

I tossed the treat to Jax and set the bowl down for Moss to prerinse for me. It was something I never did in front of Emma. She would go ballistic at the thought of a dish being licked by a dog, even though her commercial-grade dishwasher got hot enough to sanitize medical instruments.

Thinking of Emma brought me back around to Gardenia Richardson. I was already looking into her son's murder because one of my friends was being implicated. LaBryce would be cleared soon . . . I hoped. Bo Bishop's claim that Mark was being stalked should be enough to help the police take off their blinders.

So in truth, Gardenia wasn't really asking me to do anything I hadn't already been doing. I just hated the way she'd done it. No one likes to be bullied and threatened.

As immature as it was, I wanted to find her weakness like she'd found mine. I wanted to locate a sore spot and poke it—hard.

Bitchy? Yes. But hey, the woman had threatened my sister.

I called the only person I knew who might actually have some dirt on the Richardson family.

"Hello, beauty. What's up?" Wes shouted over loud music and the din of people in a large group.

"Hey, can you hear me?"

"Sort of, hang on." The music and noise began to fade. "Hey, sorry, what's up?"

"Are you still in town?"

"I am. I'm at La Vida Loca. It's a new salsa place your sister took me to last night."

I wanted to ask about Gardenia Richardson, but didn't think it was a good idea to have Wes screaming about the governor's wife in a public place. I was being paranoid, but for all I knew, the woman had bugged my phone.

"How long are you going to be there?"

"You're coming out?"

I grimaced. "Yeah, I think so. For a little while."

"To make it up to me for missing last night? You are so sweet! I'm sending my car; it will be there to pick you up in twenty. Wear something sexy. I'm teaching you to Merengue!"

Crap. "Uh, Wes?"

He'd already hung up.

I took a moment to curse myself and what a crappy friend I was, then went into Emma's bedroom to hunt up something to wear. I couldn't let Wes know that the reason I wanted to see him was to find some dirt on the Richardson family.

Moss and Jax followed me. "I am a bad friend," I told the dogs. "And you know what I get for being a bad friend? I get to drag my tired ass out. And I get to put on something sexy, and learn to cha-cha."

I let out a sigh, flipped on the closet light, and took a step over the threshold.

This was Emma's inner sanctum. The source of all her happiness lined one wall in neat pairs. Jimmy Choo, Manolo Blahnik, Christian Louboutin. These were the real men in Emma's life. I couldn't wear my sister's shoes; most were too big, thank God. Her jeans were too long and her tops too tight. Unfortunately, the too tight part was what I was going for.

I found a scoop neck red top that had a lot of stretch and was edged with a kind of ruffle. I'd seen Emma wear it before. She'd looked daring and flirty. I knew it wouldn't look quite the same on me but whatever . . .

I went into her bathroom and let my hair out of the drooping bun. Keeping it tied like that all day made it wavy. I brushed my hair, and just to go the extra mile to ease my guilt, I swiped some eye shadow over my lids and dug around in Emma's makeup till I found a lipstick called Diablo Red.

I learned a lesson very quickly. Precision is important when applying red lipstick. Who knew that coloring inside the lines as a little girl had been vital training? Each time I tried to correct the application by tracing a little farther past the edge of my lips, the worse it got. I tried to wipe the lipstick off, but it must have been one of those long-wear super lipsticks.

Giving up, I headed back to my room to throw on some jeans and ballet flats.

My cell rang. It was the driver letting me know he was waiting.

I told the dogs to be good and grabbed my purse. When

I passed the hall mirror, I jumped. Holy Cow! Skanky the Clown had broken into the condo! No wait . . . that was just me.

Chuckling to myself all the way to the limo, it took all my restraint not to burst out laughing when the driver opened the door and said, "Good evening, Ms. Wilde. You look lovely."

A short time later, we rolled to a stop in front of La Vida Loca. I climbed out of the limo and the driver handed me a little plastic bracelet that had LVL VIP printed on it. He helped snap it on my wrist, and I started for the door.

It was a Tuesday night, but the club was packed. I asked a beefy bouncer where the VIP section was, and he pointed up a staircase to my right. I weaved through the crowd and showed the second beefy bouncer at the bottom of the stairs my nifty bracelet and was allowed to pass. At the top, the vibe was a bit different.

Fewer people, more cocktail waitresses, lots more bottles of champagne.

I spotted Wes. He was chatting up a guy who was so feminine I only knew he was a guy because of his Adam's apple. They were sitting at a round banquette, and I suddenly felt doubly bad about crashing Wes's night.

Wes saw me before I could bolt. He smiled and waved.

Crap.

I made my way to them. Wes introduced me to his friend, Eric, who he'd just met. Well, at least I wasn't going to be a total third wheel.

"You look like a little hot tamale!" Wes said as he kissed my cheek.

"Thanks."

"Love the lipstick," he said with a grin. "Gives you that just-kissed look."

"Like you been smooching in a dark corner," Eric added.

A cocktail waitress set a margarita in front of me. I lifted it and took several gulps. It was strong—plenty of tequila and orange liqueur. I felt a warmth settle in my belly and took another sip.

Twenty minutes later, I was smiling and chatting. I even laughed a few times.

Wes leaned toward me. "Having fun?"

"I am, actually." It was true. Thanks to my measly salad dinner, the tequila was giving me a buzz. The music was upbeat but not so loud that I couldn't hear.

"Eric seems nice," I said in Wes's ear.

"He's got to go soon. Meeting some friends. But I think we might go out tomorrow." Wes wiggled his eyebrows.

I hoped they hit it off. Wes hadn't had a boyfriend in a while. Eric had an exuberant personality that might have been annoying in another setting. But he was quick witted and funny.

Just as Wes predicted, Eric soon got a call on his cell and said his good-byes.

We watched him leave and Wes turned to me and smiled. "Now, why don't you tell me why you really wanted to come out and meet me?"

Leave it to Wes. He and my sister seemed to share the ability to see through my crap.

I sighed and decided to start with the less pressing question. Alexander Burke had been arrested for aggravated assault. I needed to know what that meant.

Wes shot me an amused look when I asked. "Do I need to be worried about someone?"

I smiled. "No." I told him about Burke's record.

"Basically, assault is defined as a plausible, unlawful threat to do violence to another person. *Aggravated* assault can be one of two things—assault with intent to commit a felony, or assault with a deadly weapon."

"Seriously?" And I had been banging on this guy's door?

Wes lifted his finger. "But that doesn't mean anyone was hurt."

"What do you mean?"

"You could be arrested for aggravated assault if you threaten someone with a baseball bat. Even if you don't use it. Was he convicted?"

"I don't know."

"I'll look into it. I should be able to get a hold of his file."

The word *file* made me think of the real reason I'd hunted Wes down. But I'd thought of another question. "LaBryce was supposed to be out today. Why would a judge hold off?"

"Pressure is high. I've heard some scuttlebutt that demands are being made . . . by powerful people."

Gardenia Richardson. "People like the governor, you mean."

He dipped his head in consent. "Among others. I'd be surprised if LaBryce's lawyer manages to get a bond hearing at all."

"What can you tell me about the Richardson family? Under-the-rug-type stuff."

"You want dirt?"

"I want muck."

His brows shot up. "Ooooh, can I ask why?"

"Let's just say I don't really like the governor's wife."

"Hummmm, that's some big guns, sweetie. The Clarke family. Old money."

"Old money means old secrets. You know any?"

"A few." Wes took a sip of his margarita and leaned against the back of the banquette. "Grace, you know that woman is a snake. Poking at her will just piss her off."

"Calling her a snake is inaccurate and insulting to ophidians everywhere."

Wes leveled me with a look that said, *You know what I mean.*

I did.

"I guess the most recent scandal is over Jennifer Weston."

"What about her?"

"Well, according to a tenacious young reporter at the *Times Union*, she wasn't always the nice girl. Recently, he did a story that revealed Miss Weston grew up in Emerson."

"Emerson? Like, Emerson Arms?"

Emerson Arms was the projects—the for-real, big-time projects. It was last place in the world I pictured sweet, angel-faced Jennifer growing up.

Wes nodded. "Her mother was an addict who, rumor has it, recruited her daughter to do everything from stealing to prostitution. Though her juvenile records are sealed, of course. And the governor has been paying her college tuition. In fact, it seems that he's paid for everything, including her housing."

"Why?"

"When the story leaked, they claimed that after dating their son for almost four years, Jennifer had become like a member of the family. She had struggled out of the ghetto and made it into college, so being the benevolent people they are, the Richardsons decided to be sure she got a good education."

"What's the real story?"

"Who knows? Maybe Jennifer and Mark broke up because Jennifer set her sights higher in the Richardson household."

"You think she's sleeping with the governor?"

"That's one of the rumors." Wes took a sip of margarita and his eyebrows wiggled in a delighted gossip-fueled dance. "But that's nothing compared to some of the stuff the Clarkes have gotten away with. That family has more lawyers on retainer than the Iditarod has huskies." He leaned forward. "I heard from a friend who used to work at one of the firms that, back in the fifties, the patriarch, Thurman Clarke, killed his first wife."

I tried to remember if I'd ever heard of Thurman Clarke; I came up empty. "What happened to her?"

"Officially, she died in a car accident. Unofficially, the story is that Old Mr. Clarke lost his temper and tossed her out of a limo while they were on 95."

"Holy shit! How do you cover up something like that?"

"Money. Lawyers. And more money."

"Jeez." I sucked down the last sip of my margarita. "Did you ever work for them when you lived here?"

He laughed. "Lord, no. I'm far too gay. No self-respecting, card-carrying bigot would hire a gay lawyer."

"So the Clarkes are murderous bigots, and the

Richardsons are slimy philanderers? Must make for an interesting Thanksgiving."

Wes laughed. "Makes me glad all I have to endure is my Uncle Arty's bad jokes." He grabbed my hand and tugged me to my feet. "Come on, let's salsa."

•   •   •

There were no nasty notes stuck to the door, so I assumed Moss had been quiet. It was just shy of eleven o'clock, and Emma wasn't home yet. The dogs greeted me and I gave them both a quick hello pet before I staggered into my room and dropped into bed. I was too tired to shower or even wash my face.

Unfortunately, I wasn't too tired to wonder what to make of everything Wes had told me. I thought about Jennifer Weston, who obviously was not as innocent as she seemed. Had she kept ties with people from her old life? Were the bruises on her arm from a run-in with some past contact? Or could they be from the governor? Or even Gardenia?

I wouldn't put it past the woman. Though she probably had someone else do her dirty work.

Jennifer was getting her tuition and expenses paid. After meeting Gardenia, I didn't believe the philanthropist shtick. Taking Jennifer's past into consideration, there was the possibility that she was blackmailing the family because she had something on them.

I imagined her going to Gardenia Richardson with a manila envelope filled with damning evidence. The scene in my head was just like in the movies—Jennifer demanding payment and then saying the line, "If anything happens to me, copies will be mailed to the press *and* the cops."

I have to admit, I kind of liked that scenario.

But what about Mark? According to Wes—and my own astute observations—both sides of the family bred hypocritical despots who believed they were above the law. So, did the apple fall far from the tree?

Everyone had said Mark was a nice guy. Even though he hung out with LaBryce, who most people thought was a thug. I knew LaBryce was nothing like his image. Maybe Mark wasn't either.

Believing the person who killed Mark was a friend of his could be a big mistake. Mark could have opened the door for a drug dealer, a hooker, or a candlestick maker.

I squeezed my eyes shut. My head was overflowing with theories and ideas that circled around and around but never went anywhere. Like a clogged toilet.

Maybe detective work wasn't so great after all. I reached over and placed my hand on Moss. He was dozing. No dreams, just a mind filled with peaceful, soothing white noise. I locked onto his brain waves, wrapped them around me like a down blanket, and was lulled to sleep.

• • •

Mind melding with a half wolf is not always the best idea.

I'd spent part of the night racing through snowy woods and calling out to my pack. When I finally opened my eyes, Emma was looking down at me.

"Umm . . . good morning?" She was staring at me the way you look at a two-headed tortoise at the interstate fair.

I tried to speak, but my throat was raw and my tongue felt cemented to the roof of my mouth.

Emma handed me a glass of water. "I walked the dogs. Mr. Cavan-ass gave me the stink-eye when he saw me."

I guzzled the water. It took me a second, but I was finally able to force my lips to work. "Was I howling?"

"Umm. . . . nooo. Why?" Her expression shifted from *freak* to *mental freak*.

I rubbed my fingers over my eyes. "Then why are you looking at me like I'm a carnie reject?"

"Well . . . you look like you fell asleep eating a red Magic Marker."

I pressed my lips together and glanced down at the pillowcase. It was smeared with Diablo Red. "Your makeup sucks."

"Uh-huh."

"Margaritas suck, too."

"Dare I ask?" Emma eyed me as I slowly dragged myself out of bed.

"Wes."

"You went out last night! Why didn't you call me?"

I grunted and shuffled toward the bathroom. I needed to brush the fur off my teeth. And I still didn't want to tell Emma about Miz Gardenia's threats. She would find out from Wes that I was asking questions about the family, but I would deal with that later.

I began evasive maneuvers. "Wes met a cute guy last night."

"Oh?"

I knew this would perk her up.

"Eric. He was funny and seemed—" I stopped as soon as I turned on the light in the bath and saw my reflection.

"Oh. My. God." Skanky the Clown had a bad night. "Get me a washcloth and a blowtorch."

Emma hooted with laughter. I could hear her hysterics all the way to and from her room. When she returned, she handed me a container of moist towelettes. I gave them a dubious once-over. I mean how was a thin wet tissue supposed to combat napalm?

"They'll take it off, I promise." She patted me on the shoulder and sighed. "I'll go make you some coffee."

Though vigorous scrubbing had left my lips pink and puffy, after a shower and a cup of coffee, I felt ready to tackle the day. I had only one stand-by appointment: a man who was introducing a new cat into his pride of five had me on speed-dial. If the suggestions I gave him didn't do the trick, I'd have to swing by and play kitty ambassador. Not always easy, cats being cats.

Thinking of cats reminded me that I also needed to check on Charm. She shouldn't be hungry. The supersized meal I'd fed her would hold her over till later in the afternoon, but it would also mean there would be supersized jaguar poo to contend with. LaBryce was going to owe me big time for this one. Not only was I taking care of his pet, I was trying to help the cops solve Mark's murder. Well, in a roundabout way.

Honestly, I was hoping to get a call any minute from LaBryce telling me he had seen the judge and was on his way home. But I had to consider Wes's scuttlebutt and warning that LaBryce wouldn't be going anywhere anytime soon.

Left with a fairly free morning, I decided to make a run to Alexander Burke's house. Maybe I would find the truant handler and drag him back to work or, at the very least, get Charm's vitamin mix.

In a vain attempt to stem the flow of complaints and insulting sticky notes from Mr. Cavan-ass, I'd promised Emma I'd take the dogs with me. Squinting, I shoved my sunglasses on and ushered them out the door.

The morning sun beamed as we all climbed into Bluebell. It was half past eight, and it was already hot enough to bake a turkey in the passenger seat.

Both dogs were panting loudly. I made sure their water container was full, gave them both a quick pat, and cranked up the AC.

I'd barely made it onto Beach Boulevard before my phone rang.

"Ms. Wilde, this is Aaron Stein." The Richardsons' lawyer. Great.

"Yes?"

"I was asked, by my client, to check in with you. Regarding the matter you spoke about yesterday."

"Well, it's nice to know Gardenia is as patient as she is kind."

If he picked up on my thinly veiled sarcasm, he didn't let on, commenting with only a mild "Indeed."

"Here's an idea. Maybe your boss should keep her garters on and stop pushing people. I'll call her when I have something to say." I flipped my phone closed and spent the next few minutes impugning Gardenia Richardson under my breath.

By the time I reached Burke's house, I had calmed down,

but not so much to make me think twice about pounding on his door extra hard with the toe of my shoe when he didn't answer.

Irritated, I marched back to Bluebell. I climbed in and rifled around for a pen. Finally finding a discarded envelope in my door's side pocket, I started to write Burke a nice but firm note requesting he contact me. As I scribbled, I noticed a group of young gangster wannabes watching me from the yard across the street.

I've been around predators long enough to know when I was being sized up as prey. The tallest thug—a tall, muscled, black guy wearing a wife-beater and pants so baggy he had to grasp the front of them to keep them from collapsing to his ankles—ogled me with a hostile smirk. A second, smaller, hoodlum took a slow drag from his cigarette and muttered something to the rest. They all glanced at him, and I knew who was alpha of the hostile little pack.

He flicked his cigarette and started forward.

Crap.

The driver's door to Bluebell was still open. The dogs, sensing my unease, stood at attention in the backseat. Of course, I could have just shut the door and driven away. But I'm not easily intimidated and I tend to be foolishly stubborn when it comes to standing my ground.

Oh, and I had two lethal weapons at my command.

Never turning my back to the thugs, I slid out of the seat, shut my door, and opened the back.

Moss. Jax. Come.

I hadn't really needed to summon them. Both canines readily leapt from the truck and moved to flank me.

With my sunglasses shading my eyes, I was able to watch the thugs' reaction without locking anyone in a stare-down. Not only was there a stop in forward motion, but the lead thug muttered an expletive as his eyes widened.

Lead Hoodlum's gaze never left Moss as he slipped backward through the gate and eased it closed. Maybe his animal instinct was still acute enough to know when he was on the wrong end of the evolutionary chain, or maybe he just didn't think one white girl was worth the trouble I obviously brought with me, but he backed off.

Moss moved a step forward, lowered his head a fraction, and I knew he was giving the hoodlums his "go ahead . . . make my day" stare.

As if they were trying to harmonize, both canines uttered deep growls.

The thugs coolly retreated and didn't look at me again.

I clipped the leashes on the dogs and led them around Bluebell toward Burke's house.

Guard. Jax didn't like turning away from the obvious threat, but I wanted to stuff the note in the door and get out of there, so I pulled him with me, with both the lead and my mind.

It's okay. Leave it. I tried to calm him, but he was uneasy. I decided to leave my note in the side door that led into the house from the carport. I figured Burke used that entrance more—and was it closer.

With part one of my brain telling Jax we'd be leaving soon and another asking Moss to keep an eye on the thugs, I was having a hard time sliding the folded note into the crack of the door.

If only I had sticky notes like Mr. Cavan-ass.

I tried the door handle, thinking there might be some give if I pushed it . . .

Unlocked.

In this neighborhood?

I stood staring as the door swung in.

"Mr. Burke?"

Moss, stay. For once, he did as I asked. My wolf-dog sat, gaze directed across the street, his eyes locked on the thugs. I kept Jax with me as I stepped inside.

Oddly, Jax's anxiety seemed to fade as he sniffed around the tiny kitchen.

Mine didn't.

The cabinet doors hung open, revealing sparse, if any, contents. The counters were littered with newspapers, cups, plates, and other kitchen gadgets. At first, I thought that

Burke had been robbed—which would explain the door being unlocked, but then I noticed the cardboard box. It had KITCHEN written on the side in bold, block letters.

Alexander Burke was moving.

I took another few steps into the kitchen. "Hello?"

There was no answer, no movement or noise at all. My heart started to thud hard in my chest. The feeling of wrongness and disquiet pressed down like a lead cloak.

Jax agreed. *Guard.*

Maybe he was just picking up on my unease, but his mind had suddenly become a tangle of agitation. He wanted to go farther into the house to investigate. He wanted to stay to protect me. He was troubled by the sudden uncertainty I felt.

"Shit." I didn't like sneaking around in someone else's house. I really didn't like the feeling of dread that clutched my chest like the talons of a raptor.

Without meaning to, I had crossed the kitchen. My hand sat ready to push open the swinging door that led to the rest of the house. I hesitated and started to back up, but Jax had become focused on moving forward through the door. The desire was so intense, I felt my arm react before I could stop it from shoving the door open.

The smell hit me first, stealing what was left of my breath.

Death.

I started to take a step back, get the hell out of Dodge, and call the cops, when I saw him.

"Oh God."

Alexander Burke was seated at a small, wooden desk. Part of his head was gone. His remaining eye was rolled back. Cast up as if he was looking to heaven.

The window next to the desk was splattered with blood. In a part of my mind that had, in self-defense, separated from reality, I noticed the bright light streaming in cast an odd-patterned red tint to the room, like stained glass. On the floor near Burke's feet, a gun was spotlighted by the macabre beam.

Jax's low whimper snatched me back from my stunned detachment. The dog's dismay hit me like a charging bull. My stomach clenched and roiled. Bile clogged my throat. I was swamped by a wave of nausea.

Moss must have heard or felt the shocked cry that slipped from my throat, because he was at my side ready to defend or assist. I slapped my hand over my mouth, turned, and stumbled through the kitchen.

I'd barely made it outside before doubling over and upchucking all over Detective Jake Nocera's brown loafers.

"Jesus H. Christ!" He lurched back several steps.

Eyes watering, shaking and dizzy I struggled to breathe.

"Grace?" I heard Kai's voice, felt a steady hand clasp my upper arm. My eyes still closed, I focused on that one point—letting Kai's firm hand be my anchor.

Slowly, I straightened and opened my eyes. I glanced at Jake, then turned to Kai. His face was set and nearly unreadable. The only signs of worry, the slight pinch between his brow and the question in his intense gaze.

"Alexander Burke has been murdered."

CHAPTER 13

I should have known dropping the M-word was a bad idea.
After I said it, I realized my mistake. I should have said,
"Alexander Burke is dead." Instead, I had said "murdered,"
which is very different—especially to cops.

"How do you know he was murdered?" Kai asked for the
second time. He was sitting on the passenger side of Bluebell's bench seat. I'd told him if he wanted to ask me questions, he could do so just as easily out of the heat. So there
we sat, me looking out at the ever-increasing activity in and
around Alexander Burke's house, and Kai staring at me the
way a cat watches a mouse hole. Focused. Patient. Com-
posed. Knowing his prey would eventually emerge. Then
he would have what he was after.

The air conditioner rattled as it struggled to pump out
cool air. The dogs sat in the backseat panting quietly.

It was actually Jax's fault that I had announced Burke's
murder the way I did. After all, it was his canine sense of
smell and understanding of things humans cannot that led
me to that conclusion.

Death leaves a mark. Murder leaves a stain. An indelible

tear in the fabric of a place that is violent and raw. Dogs can sense it. I knew Burke had been murdered because Jax knew. But I wasn't about to tell Kai that.

I shrugged. "I don't know. He was murdered, wasn't he?"

Answering a question with a question doesn't work with law enforcement. My attempted deflection had the opposite effect. Kai's face, already a blank mask, took on a harder edge. He pinned me with his gaze but said nothing. The silence stretched out to fill the space between us as thick and solid as Hadrian's Wall.

I weighed my options. Kai knew I was holding out on him. He was clearly prepared to pursue me like a bloodhound to get answers. I could either keep being vague and cagey, which would probably only pique his interest, or I could come up with an explanation.

Well, when you can't beat'um . . . lie.

"Okay. I'll tell you why I think he was murdered. But you won't believe me."

Kai straightened. "I'm listening."

"Jax knew Burke was murdered."

"Jax." That single word held a mountain of doubt.

"Just hear me out. There's a theory out there that dogs can pick up on things that linger after death."

"You mean pheromones?"

"Pheromones and . . . other things."

"Like what?"

"I don't know . . . stuff." I felt a twinge of insecurity, but banished it with a deep breath. I had to express this idea, but had to be careful not to say too much. I couldn't explain the feeling of violent wrongness that lingered after someone's life was ripped from them. I'd felt it only because Jax had. Science was something Kai understood. So I tried to think of a scientific example.

"You can hear my voice and understand me. Why?"

Kai gazed at me, baffled, for a few moments then he finally said, "The vibrations of your vocal cords produce sound waves, which are picked up by my inner ear."

"And?"

"And your mouth forms words in a language that I understand."

"But *why* does it work?"

He paused. "Because my brain has the ability to decipher the raw material that is speech." I watched as understanding slowly crept into his eyes. "So you're saying a dog's brain can interpret some sort of lingering aura? The same way that we understand voices as language?"

"That's the idea."

"But how?"

"I haven't got a clue."

Kai studied me for a moment, the way I'd come to understand meant he was dissecting every word I said. Frowning, he asked, "But how did you know? Jax didn't tell you, 'Hey, that dead guy was murdered,' right?"

Wrong. "He did actually. His behavior told me." Now I had to layer a pinch of extra BS into my little story. "I've seen it before, with bloodhounds. They freak. Dead is dead. But violent death . . . it affects dogs. So I saw the body, and because of Jax's reaction, I made the assumption."

"Your conclusion was based on a different set of factors," Kai muttered.

I didn't follow that. I thought my factors couldn't be that different from his. I mean, Burke was dead. Part of his head was blown off. It seemed obvious to me.

"But there's only one problem with that."

"What?"

"If you're right, then we're wrong."

"What do you mean?"

"There was a suicide note next to the body."

"What?"

"Preliminary findings suggest Alexander Burke shot himself."

"No." I was shaking my head. It wasn't possible. Burke had been murdered.

"The evidence disagrees."

"Just because there's a note?"

"A note. And gunshot residue on his hand."

"So he fired the gun?"

"It looks like it."

"That doesn't make sense."

"Maybe your theory is wrong. Or you misinterpreted Jax's reaction."

I didn't believe that. Nothing else feels like murder. At least nothing I'd ever experienced. A thought cut into my confusion. "Why were you and Jake here? Did someone call the cops?"

"No." His succinct answer and the way he glanced away from me spoke volumes. He and Jake had come to Burke's house for a specific purpose.

Now it was my turn to wait in silence.

He turned back toward me, and locked his gaze with mine. "We came here to search the house."

"For what?"

"Financial records. And LaBryce Walker's gun."

I remembered the glint of metal on the floor next to Burke's body. Shining like a jewel—LaBryce's gun. "You found it."

"We did."

I closed my eyes and leaned my head back on the seat. LaBryce's gun was next to the body. And I, in all my stupidity, was insisting Burke was murdered. A thought occurred to me. "Wait. You can't think LaBryce did anything. He's been in jail."

"I can't be sure of anything at this point. But I know the ME estimates time of death to be between three and four days ago."

"The same night Mark was killed?" Did he think LaBryce had killed Burke? "I see. So when I tell you Burke was murdered, you consider it. But when I tell you LaBryce is innocent, you ignore it. Convenient. Do you always manipulate the evidence to suit your theories, or is this a special case?"

He stared at me as if I'd slapped him.

"I need to talk to LaBryce," I said.

"About?"

"His pet jaguar is now my responsibility. I need to talk to him about Charm." Kai's face was unreadable but his silence grated on my nerves. "Can I see him or not?"

"He's being taken back to custody right now. I'll go with you."

"Don't you need to stay here and look for clues?" I really wanted him out of my car.

"Burke's not going anywhere." He settled in and, by buckling his seat belt, all but said I was not getting rid of him.

I stared at him for a moment and tried to figure out what he thought he could possibly gain by keeping an eye on me. Did Kai think I had something to do with Burke's death? Was he hoping I'd fold under his scrutiny?

I put Bluebell in gear. "I have to drop off the dogs. Unless you want me to leave them in your office."

I'd meant the last as a sarcastic barb. Kai didn't seem to get it. "Fine with me. Let's go."

• • •

The Police Memorial Building was busier in the middle of the day. Phones rang. People walked around with fast-food bags and coffee mugs. My canine escorts and I received some questioning looks, but we quickly deposited the dogs in Kai's office.

"Lock the door," I instructed as we walked out. Kai didn't ask why, proving he was smart.

He walked me to an interview room and asked me to wait. I sat at the table and drummed my fingers on its smooth top. Time seemed to crawl by.

I looked around the small room and noticed a bubble on the ceiling. It held a camera, I assumed. I realized, as I looked at it, why Kai had not objected to my request to see LaBryce. The police couldn't question him without his lawyer. But I could.

Kai was hoping LaBryce would let something slip while he was talking to me. Great.

I heard the door open, but I kept my gaze on the bubble for a second longer. "I hope you're paying attention," I said to the camera.

My friend shuffled into the room. LaBryce is a big guy, but he seemed diminished somehow. His face brightened some when he saw me and folded into a smile. "Hey, Grace."

"Hey. How you doing?" I asked as he lowered himself into the chair across from me.

"Okay, I guess. My lawyer says the state attorney is messing with me. Stalling. They charged me with endangerment or somethin'. 'Cuz Charm was out the other night. The judge keeps blowing me off. Won't let me ask for bond."

I had a feeling I knew who was pulling that string. "You're up against some power players."

"Yeah. The governor."

I was thinking of his wife but, six of one . . . "I found Alexander."

"Good. What'd that little shit have to say for himself?"

"Not much."

LaBryce shook his head in disgust. "As soon as I can find someone else to take care of Charm, I'm going to fire his ass."

"He's dead."

LaBryce blinked at me as the words traveled from ear to brain. "What?"

"The cops think you killed him."

"What?" He shook his head. "Nuh-uh. No way."

"I know you didn't do it."

"What the . . . These jokers think I killed Mark *and* Alex?" He gaped at me, shocked. "I've been here. This is bullshit. I didn't kill anybody."

"I know that. You're not a murderer." I reached across the table and covered one beefy hand with both of mine.

After a long pause, I asked, "LaBryce, what happened to your gun?"

He lowered his eyes and shook his head.

"It wasn't stolen, was it? Who'd you give it to?"

"Mark."

"Why?"

"He said he needed it."

"For what? Was he afraid of someone?" I squeezed his hand, though what I really wanted to do was reach across the table and strangle him for not telling the cops the truth. But who was I to throw stones?

After a few slow breaths, he looked up. "He said he was getting his own gun, but he had to deal with the waiting period."

"Why did he need a gun?" This seemed very significant to me and I shot a quick *are you getting this?* glance at the camera bubble.

"He said something about getting phone calls at night. Hang-ups."

"No threats? Just hang-ups?"

"He just said they'd call and hang up. At, like, three in the morning."

I thought about what Bo had said about a stalker and asked LaBryce what he knew.

"Mark never said anything about that. All he said was that he got calls, and one time, something had spooked his dog, Jax. Someone outside sneaking around." LaBryce let out a loud snort, like a Grizzly. "I thought he wanted the gun to flash, you know, to scare 'um off if they came back. It's a big gun."

"Why didn't you tell the police?"

"I don't know. I was afraid whoever killed Mark might have used my gun. How would that look?"

"Bad. It all looks really bad, LaBryce."

"I know. I'm stupid."

"Not all the time." I smiled. "But it's not as if the police are looking at anyone else."

"No alibi. Except Charm. Makes me an easy target."

I felt a pang. Guilt poking its accusatory finger right into my chest. "It doesn't help that you threatened to kill Mark in a room full of people the same night he was murdered."

A look passed over my friend's smooth, dark face. Guilt? Shame? Did he feel bad that his last words to his friend were filled with malice?

"It was a setup."

"What was a setup?"

"The interview, the argument, all of it. For the hype."

I had to let that sink in. "You mean you pretended to be mad and fight with Mark because you wanted publicity?"

"Well, no. Yes. I mean, it was planned. I knew Mark was going to be interviewed. He told me he was going to make it sound like we were rivals. Enemies. Then after a while, we were going to come together and make up. But when I read the article, I'd been drinking and I got mad for real. I wasn't supposed to get in a fight with him until the night of this charity thing that's coming up. That was going to kick it off."

"Who came up with this? Some idiot at your PR firm?"

"It was Mark's idea. He said we needed to shake things up. Get people talking. He had some endorsement deals lined up if we could get enough press."

I didn't get it. Not even a little. "Why would you get endorsements for acting like the Hatfields and McCoys?"

"Mark had it all worked out. You know he studied marketing in college? He was pretty smart." LaBryce's eyes got glassy and he took a second to squeeze them shut before continuing. "Look, I can't play ball forever, Grace. I need something to fall back on. For when I retire."

"Retire?"

"This is going to be my last season." He leaned forward and whispered, "I think it was going to be Mark's, too."

"Why?"

"Something was going on with him."

"Like what?"

"Couple times he hinted that he was going to be quitting. When I asked him, he just shook his head. Told me, 'You never know, until you know.'"

"What does that mean?"

"No idea." He leaned even closer, keeping his voice soft. "I think whatever he was up to, that's what got him killed. Maybe it was his new girl."

"What new girl?"

"He was on the phone a lot. Arguing with someone. Whoever it was, he called her 'baby.' "

"A new girlfriend already? He and Jennifer just broke up."

LaBryce shrugged his massive shoulders. "Not like there aren't girls lined up for guys like us."

"Nice humility. No wonder you're not married." I gave him a dramatic eye-roll.

That got a smile out of him. "Every girl I've started dating thinks I should get rid of Charm. Just 'cause she gets a little possessive. You know. She doesn't like it if I'm on the couch with anyone else. Till I find someone who Charm takes to, I'll be single."

I understood the sentiment, though I could only imagine how terrifying it would be to have a jealous jaguar giving you the eye from across the room. "I'll help with introductions when you find someone you really like."

"If I get out of here."

"You will. Don't worry." Just as I uttered the words, a cop poked his head in the door and I was asked to step out of the room. Kai was waiting for me in the hall, and I walked up to him and said as civilly as I could, "I'd like to get my dogs. Now."

He nodded, and we made our way back to his office.

The dogs rolled to their feet as we entered. I started over to where I'd left the leashes draped over the back of a chair when I heard the office door close with a fatalistic click. Apparently, Kai felt we had something to talk about. I didn't. But I turned to face him anyway. Though I couldn't read his expression, I was pretty sure he could read mine.

I was mad. I wasn't sure who I was more ticked off at— myself for still being afraid to claim my psychic ability or Kai for being so single-minded in his pursuit of my friend. But the result was that I was ready to rumble.

"If you still think LaBryce had anything to do with Mark's murder, then you're not very good at your job."

"You were whispering. What did LaBryce tell you?"

"It doesn't matter. It's clear that you won't believe anything LaBryce says. Unless it's 'I did it!' "

Anger colored Kai's voice as he stepped toward me. "You're saying I'm biased?"

"I'm saying you've got blinders on. What evidence do you have against him?"

"He threatened to kill Mark."

"You heard what LaBryce said. He and Mark were plotting some big media hoopla."

Kai gave me a dubious look. "He lied about his gun being stolen."

"And only the guilty lie?"

"According to everyone but you, he has no alibi. Even LaBryce claims he was home alone that night. Either he's telling the truth and you're lying or he's lying to protect someone." The way he said "someone" clearly meant me.

"You're right. He's protecting me. I conspired with LaBryce to kill Mark because I wanted Jax." I motioned toward the dogs. They had inched closer, disturbed by our raised voices. It took a good deal of concentration to keep reassuring them *and* argue with Kai. My head was going to be pounding later.

"If that was a joke, it's not funny."

"No. It's ridiculous." I pulled in a breath and tried to force my voice down an octave or two.

"We have the security tapes from the entrance to Mark's neighborhood. If LaBryce came back, we'll see him."

"There are other people who could have wanted Mark dead. Think about it, Kai." My argument in LaBryce's defense was cut off before it really got started.

"I can't! I can't think. It's like you walk into the room and my brain short-circuits." He raked his fingers through his hair and paced away. The dogs watched him with a mixture of wariness and all-out aggression. "I've been working this case for what seems like forever. I'm tired. I'm ready to have something solid to work with. A fiber. A palm print. Anything." He turned back to face me, and I felt a spike of panic. Not because I thought he would hurt me. But because I knew I was going to regret what I was about to do.

He moved forward. I stepped back, bumping into the bookcase.

"But all I have is you." He braced his hand on one of the shelves, penning me in.

The dogs growled in tandem.

He ignored the canine warning and leaned in. Only inches away from my face he said, "Come on, Grace, just tell me the truth. All you have to do is give me the name of LaBryce's alibi. If it checks out, LaBryce is out of here. Who was with him, Grace? Why won't you tell me?"

I hesitated, but only for an instant. "Okay."

He eased back a fraction and waited.

"Charm."

"What?"

"The reason I know LaBryce is innocent is because Charm told me he was home the night of the murder. I have the ability to communicate with animals. Telepathically." I couldn't believe I'd actually said it. I thought I would feel foolish or even anxious, but what I felt was . . . freedom. Open, soaring freedom.

"What?" Kai said the word as if he literally had not understood what I said.

"I can talk to animals. With my mind."

Kai blinked at me for several seconds. "You mean psychically? You're saying you have a psychic power?"

"Yes. That's what I'm saying."

Kai's lips, which had been drawn into a thin line, slowly turned up into a smirk. "And you're telling me Charm, the *jaguar*, is LaBryce's alibi?"

My newfound wings buckled under the weight of his stinging sarcasm. I ignored the plummeting feeling. "Yes. And there's something else you should know."

"And what's that?"

"Jax witnessed Mark Richardson's murder."

"Uh-huh. So, who did it?"

"He hasn't told me yet. He's too traumatized."

"Riiight."

"I'm telling the truth. Think what you want." It was pretty clear he was thinking I was a big fat liar. His obvious disdain affected me in a way I hadn't anticipated. I felt tears press against the backs of my eyes. I managed to blink them away, but the dogs felt my sudden flutter of distress, and Moss went from growling to letting out a trio of barks. The sound was nearly deafening in the small office.

"Okay, if you really are psychic, tell your dogs to back off. Telepathically, of course." Kai was studying me again. I wondered if he was really giving me a chance.

I felt hope flutter to life in my chest. "Okay." *Jax, Moss, leave it!*

Jax hesitated but sat. Moss didn't. *Guard.*

No, Moss, leave it. Go.

Guard. His growl continued, deep and low.

Kai arched his brows with a look of such utter smugness I wanted to slap him. "Problem?"

"Moss doesn't like you."

"I can tell. And I'm not even psychic."

"No. You're an ass." I pushed past him and gathered the dogs, trying all the while not to let my feelings get the better of me. "If you really want to find out who killed those two men, you need to open your mind. And that means considering that there are some things you just have to take on faith."

"You really expected me to believe you?"

I turned before opening the door and looked him in the eye. I wanted him to see that he had hurt me. "No, Kai. I didn't."

CHAPTER 14

I sped over the Matthews Bridge at a pace that made Bluebell shudder in protest. I gripped the steering wheel and
muttered under my breath.

Damn it!

I'd been prepared for Kai's disbelief, had even expected
it, but the hurt that flowed in its wake had been startling.

"That's what I get." Choosing to tell a man who worships
at the Altar of Tangible Evidence that I was psychic. Never
mind that if he bothered to open his eyes long enough to see
past his microscope, he would realize I was what I claimed
to be. Just because my gift couldn't be dissected and analyzed in a laboratory didn't make it any less real.

Maybe I should have taken Emma's advice and stopped
hiding my ability years ago. If I had, I would have refer-
ences. People who would back me up. A website with success stories and testimonials.

The idea was so silly it made me smile. I took a deep
breath and eased off the gas.

"I could have told Sonja at least," I said to myself. And

maybe even Hugh. After working with me so many times, he might have believed it.

"I should call him right now," I said, my thoughts as reckless as my driving. Just come out with it. Why the hell not?

My cell phone rang. I looked at the number and wondered if Hugh Murray wasn't a bit of a psychic himself.

"Hey, Hugh. What's up?"

"We have a situation with the giraffe. You have time to lend us your . . . talent?"

I had to pull onto an access road to make a U-turn, but after backtracking over the bridge and onto Twentieth Street, it only took fifteen minutes to get to the zoo. By the time I'd zipped into the lot and parked in the stingy shade of a palm, I'd decided it would be best to keep my head on straight and focus on what needed to be done. There would be no more soul-baring confessions from me.

"I'll be as quick as I can, guys." I hated leaving the dogs in the car, but the AC was on and I had put a bowl of water in the back for them.

I hurried down the zoo's winding paths, and as I neared the giraffe enclosure, I spotted Hugh and a couple of keepers standing in a huddled group next to a John Deere Gator. Leaning against the cargo box of the small utility vehicle was Karen Leach. I muttered a curse.

My day just kept getting better and better.

Karen was one of the uppy-ups at the zoo. She had a plethora of degrees and over fifteen years of experience.

And she hated me.

I was an enigma to most of the zoo employees. When it came to using my "talent," I demanded they stay out of my way and do as I asked. I was not understood, but I was respected.

By everyone but Karen.

I got it. Really and truly, I did. Karen had been supplanted by me on numerous occasions. I questioned her authority. Ignored her orders. If the shoe were on the other foot, I'd hate me, too.

"Hey. What happened?" I asked with a forced smile.

Karen didn't bother to be polite and return it.

"Grace, someone called you."

She shot Hugh a censorious glare. He returned it with a dashing smile. "I figured we could use the extra hand. Grace was in the area . . ." He allowed the rest to be left to interpretation.

Karen narrowed her small eyes. She was not a beautiful woman to start with. She had a weak chin and a long, Roman nose. Her hair, a mass of thick curls, was always piled high on her crown in a frizzy blob. Anger did not improve her looks.

Hugh's voice wrenched my mind into focus. "Like I told you on the phone, the male giraffe has some wire tangled around his left rear hoof. We think one of the maintenance guys left the wire in the pen yesterday. We're afraid he's going to trip, or it might be cutting into him. I tried to get close enough to see, but he gets really worked up and runs around the enclosure when anybody goes inside."

I knew I had only one option. Tranquilizing the giraffe could kill it. Animals that big do not take anesthesia well.

"I'll have to try to get close to him."

"That's not going to happen," Karen snapped. "He almost killed Hugh when he went in."

Hugh nodded gravely. "He tried to kick my head off. Flipped out totally."

This was bad. The giraffe knew Hugh—who had to inoculate him on a yearly basis. No wild animal is ever truly tame, but if he was ready to defend himself against people he was familiar with . . . yep, the day just kept getting better. "Well, it's the only option."

The silence that followed my statement shocked me. "You're not thinking of darting him?"

"We're going to have to." Karen turned her back on me, reached into the back of the John Deere, and pulled out the tranquilizer gun.

"Karen, this is ridiculous. You know there's a chance he won't survive."

"It's a chance we're going to have to take."

"The hell it is." I straightened, turned, and walked to the giraffe pen.

"Grace—" Hugh hurried to catch me.

"Give me five minutes in the enclosure. After that, if I'm not dead, I'll let you tranq him."

"Wait—"

"No." I knew if I waited, I'd be too late. The dart gun didn't take long to load.

At the rear entrance to the enclosure, I paused. I had to sacrifice a few moments to quiet my thoughts before entering the large, landscaped pen. One kick from an adult giraffe was strong enough to kill a lion. The giraffe was spooked. He wouldn't hesitate to defend himself against a new threat. Ignorant of my noble intentions, he would view me as the enemy.

Unless I could get close enough to reach into his fear and replace it with assurance and calm.

I eased through the chain-link gate and glanced around. A young female giraffe stood a few feet away to my right. She watched me with a mixture of curiosity and wariness. I took a moment to ease her suspicions, focusing my thoughts on calming, friendly feelings. After brief consideration, the giraffe accepted me and resumed her grazing, stretching up to munch on the leaves of a nearby branch.

One possible disaster avoided. If the female giraffe had been startled or given away my presence, my chances of getting anywhere near the male giraffe would be nonexistent.

I shifted my attention to my target. The male stood directly in front of me. He was looking away, toward the opposite side of the pen. I focused on stretching my mind forward, reaching out to his. Nothing.

Too far away.

I had to get closer. Which meant getting within range of his powerful back legs. On silent, careful feet, I crept toward the lanky giant.

I advanced measure by measure, breaths shallow, hands

hovering slightly out to my sides like a tightrope walker. I could see the coil of wire glinting in the afternoon sun. It was snarled around his ankle like the tendrils of a predacious vine.

Sweat beaded on my forehead and trickled down my back. Even though it was hotter than all get-out, I was thankful there wasn't a breeze. Giraffes have an outstanding sense of smell.

The closer I got, the taller the animal seemed. His hindquarters loomed before me, a mosaic mountain of buff and brown set on knobby legs and hooves the size of dinner plates. The giraffe flicked his black-tasseled tail. I could hear the whistling rush of air and got a whiff of the pungent, musky smell that accompanies male giraffes. *Eau de funk*. I was almost close enough . . .

An explosion of emotions rocketed through my head. I flinched, sucking in an audible gasp.

A mistake I would pay for.

The giraffe kicked. I spun to the side but was too slow. Jolting pain shot through my upper arm as the rigid edge of his hoof connected with my soft muscles and tendons.

In an instant, I found myself lying flat on the dusty ground. Slightly dazed, I lay motionless, trying to catch my breath.

"Grace!" Hugh called out to me from the gate.

I didn't move. "I'm okay."

"That's it!" I heard Karen's voice. "Give me the gun."

"No!" I shouted. "I just need a minute. Please."

There was some muttering and I could tell Karen was bitching up a storm. But finally Hugh said, "Hurry up, Grace. She's gone to get the spare gun."

Which meant Hugh hadn't given in to her. He believed in me. Better prove him right. I did a quick assessment. My shoulder didn't hurt. Thank you, adrenaline. I knew it was temporary, but I'd take what I could get. I needed to finish my task, and to do that, I needed to think.

Ignoring my pounding heart and trembling breaths, I tried to figure out what just happened. Instead of kicking me and then running away, the giraffe had stopped and was now watching me from about twenty feet away.

He must have sensed my thoughts as I had sensed his. If I lay still, he might eventually decide I wasn't a threat and come over to investigate.

I used the time to center my thoughts. I closed my eyes and took in deep, measured breaths. After a few moments, I heard the giraffe begin to shuffle closer.

I opened my eyes and watched him. In three tentative steps, he covered half the distance between us.

And then I had what I needed.

His mind was a tangle of thoughts and emotions. The burn of lingering panic scraped through the inside of my skull. *Snared.*

Hunted.

Run.

Fight.

I could feel my heart rate rise to an almost painful level. I forced my breathing to remain calm. I couldn't allow myself to be overwhelmed.

Easy there, boy. I willed him to feel my calmness. Offered him my friendship. *I'm going to help you.*

He had come very close now. He stood over me, head angled to the side to look down with one huge, liquid eye.

I squinted up at him. The pulse of his mind had become less frantic. He was still wary but was much calmer, more trusting. I shifted my focus and tried to send him an image of my hands on his leg. Freeing him of the painful wire.

Let me help you.

Help. Understanding rose up and banished his lingering fear.

That's right. I'm going to help you. Gradually, I sat up. He took a cautious step backward. *Easy, you're okay.*

I rolled carefully onto my feet, ignoring the pain that bit into my shoulder. Soon, it would be throbbing like a bitch. But that was irrelevant.

I walked around to the giraffe's back leg. He arched his long neck around to watch me. I laid my hand on his leg—just a gentle touch. As always, physical contact strengthened my connection. I could feel the heavy throb of his giant heart—the relief as I began to gingerly untangle the wire.

He lifted his foot to assist me in my task. Then he was free.

Gratitude billowed around me like a warm embrace.

I smiled up at the leggy giant. *You're very welcome.*

• • •

The kudos was short-lived.

I stepped out of a wild animal enclosure and came face-to-face with a far more savage creature. Karen Leach stood next to the Gator, holding the second dart gun. For a few insane moments, I actually thought she'd shoot me with it. Instead, she set the weapon back in its case, turned to me, and said, "You have five minutes to vacate zoo grounds."

Normally, after I "helped out," Karen was mollified. She'd give me a curt nod, or more often, just bark at anyone within hearing range to get back to work. I was ignored and, therefore, dismissed.

Today, the woman was sporting for a fight. As luck would have it, I was ready to rise to the occasion.

"Wow, Karen, I'm touched." I stretched my lips into a wide, overzealous smile. "And to answer your question, the giraffe is fine. Just a scrape or two. Probably won't even need antibiotics."

Her eyes narrowed to slits. "We'll handle it."

"Like you were going to handle it by darting him?" Karen's hostility toward me had been an irritation, but I wouldn't excuse her for endangering the giraffe. "You were willing to risk that animal's life? For what?"

Karen took two quick steps toward me. An attempt at intimidation. Though petite—if you don't count the chia pet on her head—Karen's one of those small people who can seem large, just by sheer force of will. Being a member of the same club, I was not impressed. She had to pull up short when I didn't flinch away.

"Don't question me." She thrust a skeletal finger in my face, then aimed it like a spear at the handful of zookeepers who had gathered on the sideline to watch the drama. They edged away, as if she were casting a hex. "Just because these bozos hang on your every movement doesn't give you the authority to question me. In fact, you shouldn't even be here." She made a big show of looking at her watch. "You're down to four minutes. Then, I'm calling the police."

"Come on, Karen . . ." Hugh moved toward her and she spun to face him.

"Shut up! You—you're worse than anyone!" Her voice was a strangled, serpentine hiss. "You follow her around like a fool as soon as she sashays in here."

Hugh was stunned. His jaw was literally hanging open as he stared at Karen. Her eyes glistened with the sheen of unshed tears. I was tempted to be embarrassed for her, but at that moment I was too offended.

Sashay? I do not sashay.

"Karen, stop." I kept my voice as cool and quiet as possible. "You're being irrational, and you're making a scene."

She turned to me, and if she grasped any truth in my words, she wasn't ready to admit it. "If I ever see you here again, I'll have you arrested."

"Do what you have to. But if someone asks for my help, I'll be here. I don't care who you call." I turned and walked away.

"Grace. Hang on." I was halfway through one of the zoo's botanical gardens when I heard Hugh's voice.

I ignored it and kept walking.

"Grace."

I turned. "What?"

The word had snapped out. But I couldn't help it. My shoulder was throbbing, my fingers had gone numb, and the scene Karen had instigated had made me mad enough to spit nails.

"She can't ban you from coming back. I'll talk to the board—"

"Drop it, Hugh. I mean it."

He raised his hands in a gesture of surrender. "Okay. Just . . . let me look at your shoulder."

"I'm fine." It was a lie. He knew it as well as I did.

"It's not fine. You should let me take a picture of it."

I didn't want to linger long enough for x-rays. "No."

"Come on, it could be dislocated." He reached out, cupped my elbow, and then, with the caution he would use on some wild creature, ran his hand up to my shoulder.

As he began his evaluation, I looked out over the garden. It reminded me of a little oasis. The pond in the center was rimmed with mounds of grassy foliage. Water lilies dotted the surface of the dark pool like stars. The feathery leaves of the date palms fluttered and rustled in a sudden breeze.

I focused on these things to distract me from Hugh's efficient and soothing fingers. I knew my shoulder wasn't dislocated. But I stood there anyway and let Hugh palpate and assess. I had to admit it was nice to be fussed over a little.

Hugh leaned in and glanced at me. "How's this?"

"Sore, but it's okay."

"What do you have for it?"

I knew he meant what kind of painkillers. "I'll take some ibuprofen."

He gave me doubtful look. "You'll need more than that if you want to sleep."

I did want to sleep. I hadn't gotten much rest lately. "Ketamine? I'm sure I have a vial locked up somewhere."

He chuckled. "Come to the hospital with me. I'll get you something."

I knew this was a ploy to do a more thorough examination. "I've got to go. Thanks."

I eased away from him and headed toward the exit. I'd almost reached Bluebell when Hugh caught up to me again.

"Here." He handed me a small bottle of pills. "Codeine."

I thanked him and turned back to where I'd parked. Moss and Jax were eyeing Hugh wearily. When he continued to follow me, Jax began to growl.

"Grace . . ." Hugh reached out at the same time I started

to turn to face him. The awkward movement jostled my shoulder and I hissed in pain.

Jax lunged forward with an explosive snarl, his face ramming against the window.

The clap of gunfire made my ears ring. Everything was suddenly dark, a bend of shadows and rage and fear. I could smell blood. I was blind and choking.

"Grace!" Hugh's voice seemed tinny and distant. "Grace! What's wrong?"

I blinked up at his shocked face and realized I was in his arms. We were on the ground. I was draped over his lap like a reverse *Pietà*.

"I—I don't know." Of course I did know. But I couldn't tell him the truth—that I'd just seen Mark Richardson's murder.

CHAPTER 15

Having extracognitive ability is not always fun. Yes, I make my living using my "skill," and most days I actually enjoy what I do. But the strings attached are often long and tangled. And there is no one—no one that I've met yet anyway—with experience to guide me through the cat's cradle without being snared.

I'd done a few Internet searches just out of curiosity. I can't be the only person out there with a psychic connection to animals, right? But mostly I'd found websites for animal communicators that seemed hokey and bogus.

At that moment, I'd have given my right arm to have someone to call for advice.

Frustrated, my head and shoulder pounding in unison, I let out a long breath and wearily guided Bluebell onto Beach Boulevard. Driving like a zombie, I finally gave up trying to make sense of what I'd experienced.

The images of Mark's murder had burst through my mind with the speed and ferocity of a train wreck. Flashes of disjointed shapes and shadows.

On the flipside, the emotions Jax had felt were sharp and cutting as a razor blade; everything else was clear as mud.

Aching and moving like a geriatric tin man, I led the dogs up the walk to the condo. The bottle of painkillers Hugh had given me rattled in my hand, beckoning me with every step.

I took a moment to send Hugh a text as he'd asked me to do, and hoped that soon I would be soaking in a tub, adrift on a narcotic cloud. I was so focused on reaching the condo and drawing a hot bath, I barely nodded to the maintenance man as we passed on the stairs.

Vaguely, I wondered what had required his services, but I let the thought go as soon as it popped into my head.

"Hey!" Emma stood at the open door, smiling. Her voice was eager and filled with cheer.

Crap. Emma was up to something. I was too tired and too sore to be up for whatever had sparked her enthusiasm. "Hey. What's up?"

"I have a surprise for you."

I thought about trying to smile but I just didn't have it in me. "Okay."

"Close your eyes."

"Em, I'm not really—"

"Just close them. It will only take a second."

I closed my eyes and allowed her to lead me into the condo. I shuffled through the foyer, grumbling to myself. Why couldn't Emma be going out? Or working an event?

We stopped in what I thought was the living room. "Okay, look!"

I opened my eyes and immediately felt like a total ass. The sliding glass doors that led to the balcony now had an addition.

I stared, blinking at the sudden sting of tears and swallowing back the hard lump that clogged my throat.

A dog door. Emma had had a dog door installed.

"What do you think? I got the extra large."

I turned to Emma—my sister and friend—and saw that her eyes had teared up, too. Her chin came up. "Mr.

Cavan-ass has threatened me with a lawsuit. If you don't leave by the end of the month."

"Oh crap, Em—"

She held up her hand. "You, and all your critters, will stay until you find the perfect place. No one runs my sister off but me."

It was such an adolescent comment that reminded me so much of our childhood, I had to smile.

Emma looked back to the new door. "Will they use it?"

Moss, smelling salt air, was already investigating. As he sniffed around the flap, I urged him to step through. "Go on. You can do it."

But in the end it was Jax who hopped through to the balcony first. Moss poked his head out and, finally, lurching forward with the grace of a drunkard, made it outside.

Emma and I laughed. "This is great. They are going to love being able to go in and out." Even though there was no way down from the second story, the balcony was large. Partly shaded by an overhang and dotted with potted palms, it was already one of Moss's favorite lounging areas. Now he could use it at his leisure.

"They have to wear these once we turn the lock on." Emma handed me two bell-shaped doohickies that attached to the dogs' collars. "They send out an infrared signal that unlocks the door. That way, only the dogs can go through. Cool, right?"

"Very cool." And expensive. I knew Emma well enough not to ask how much the door cost, so I walked to the sliding door and pushed it open. The dog door, being a solid addition, didn't prevent the slider from working. I affixed the transmitters onto the dogs' collars and wiped a few stray tears from my eyes before turning back to my sister.

"Thank you."

"You're welcome. Oh, and one more thing." She went to the counter and picked up a long box. "Got you these."

"Business cards?" I asked as I pulled the top off the box.

"Well, you have a business, don't you? You need cards."

I'd never thought about it before.

"Don't worry. I resisted putting 'Animal Psychic' under your name." She slid a card out and handed it to me.

I read aloud, " 'Call of the Wilde. Expert solutions for any species.' " The words were printed in bold ink on a subtle, foiled animal print background. Somehow, the cards managed to look professional and elegant. I swallowed back another knot of tears that burned in my chest. "These are awesome, Em."

"Maybe you'll remember to use them instead of writing your number on whatever happens to be floating around in Bluebell."

She had a point. I grabbed a section of cards and went to stuff them in the side pocket of my purse.

"We're doing spaghetti tonight," Emma said as I walked into the kitchen.

"Sounds good." Actually, it sounded great. I had barely eaten all day, and the thought of food made my stomach grumble awake like a starving bear.

Suddenly, I was ravenous. Even my shoulder pain was overshadowed, outdone by visions of garlic bread and grated parmesan sprinkled over a mountain of spaghetti.

Emma already had a sauce pot on the stove. I tossed some kibble into the dogs' bowls and moved gingerly back into the kitchen. I popped a pill with a slurp from the faucet and turned my attention to the stove, watching Emma add spices to the pan the way a hawk watches a prairie dog mound.

"Here." Emma handed me a clove of garlic. "Mince it. But wash first. You look a little . . . dusty. What happened?"

Where to begin? "I screwed up."

"I need a little more to go on." Emma stirred the sauce, and placed a baguette on a cutting board. I watched as she sawed the bread into even slices.

"I told Kai about my ability."

Emma's hands stilled. She set the knife down and turned to me, eyes wide.

"And I screwed up." I gave her the abridged version of my day. Her mouth dropped open when I reached the part about finding Burke and my trip to the sheriff's office to talk to LaBryce.

"I was so mad, Em. I mean, if you could have seen LaBryce's face when I told him Burke was dead. He was shocked. But when I pointed that out to Kai, he just blows it off. Like it didn't matter. He tells me he can't think around me. Like somehow it's my fault he hasn't figured out who killed Mark."

"Oh?" She gave me an odd look.

"Yeah. And then he starts asking who LaBryce's alibi is. He was like a damn terrier in a rabbit hole—nothing else mattered."

"So you told him."

I nodded. "He asked me to prove it." I shot a heated glare at Moss, who chose that moment to wander into the kitchen in search of a handout. "But I couldn't. Moss wouldn't listen to me. He wanted to show his teeth and be all protective. I'm pretty sure I did more harm than good for LaBryce today. Kai either thinks I'm lying to cover my involvement or that I'm delusional."

"It wasn't fair of Kai to test you like that."

"Why not? It should have been easy. I should have been able to call the damn dogs off. But noooo! Mr. Wolf-butt over there decides he's not okay with that. He doesn't believe I'm safe. So even when I tell him to *leave it*, he keeps growling like the mongrel he is, and I look like a lunatic."

"You've told me a hundred times that you can't control an animal like a puppet. They have free will."

"Yes, but I still screwed up. I couldn't calm down enough to really focus. Moss wanted to bite a chunk out of Kai's leg. The more I thought about it, the more I liked the idea."

Emma's sudden laughter brought an end to my rant. I laughed with her, so long and hard my shoulder started throbbing again.

I winced and walked over to open the freezer. "Isn't there an icepack in here somewhere?"

"In the door. What's wrong?"

"I got kicked in the shoulder."

"By . . ."

"A giraffe."

"What?"

"I'm fine."

"Are you crazy? Did you have anyone look at it?"

"Hugh. He said it was probably just a bad bruise."

"Probably?"

"He wanted to x-ray it but I wasn't in the mood."

As I said it, I felt an idea begin to form. Emma was talking. Saying words like *stubborn* and *idiot*, but I'd stopped listening. I played back the last thing that happened before Jax had his momentary recall. Hugh had touched me. I was hurt. Jax lost it. At the time, I thought the trigger was Hugh grabbing me and my pain. But now, I realized that wasn't it.

"Bluebell."

"What?"

"Jax was in the car. He couldn't get to me. That's what made him remember."

"Remember . . . ohmygod! He remembers the murder?"

"It was just a flash. Like when you fast forward the DVR. Too quick to really see anything."

"So you're saying the reason he remembered the murder was because he was locked away from you when you needed him."

"He thought I did. And like at Mark's house, Jax could see everything. He was looking through the glass door."

"Helpless to do more than watch," Emma said.

We both looked at the big Doberman. He was stretched out like a sphinx between the kitchen and the living room watching us. Intelligence sparkled in his brown eyes. I like all dogs, but Jax was exceptional. Under the shining coat and rippling sinew was the heart of a knight. Calm and noble and capable of fierce and deadly action.

"Why was he outside?" I wondered.

"You mean when Mark was killed?"

"Jax was in the backyard. Locked out. He's not an outside

dog." I could tell from the way he positioned himself at entrances and from his ease with condo living. Plus, trained protection dogs stayed close to their owners.

"Maybe Mark let him out to go potty?"

"At the exact same time the murderer knocks on the door?"

"Mark could have put Jax outside for the party. And forgot to let him in?"

It was a possibility. But it didn't seem to fit for some reason. "LaBryce said Mark had gotten hang-up calls and had heard someone messing around outside the house."

"So . . . Mark could have gotten a phone call, woke up, and let Jax out to investigate," Emma said as she checked the bread and the spaghetti.

"Or the killer calls, hangs up, and waits. If he was watching the house, maybe he knew the dog would have to be out of the picture to get to Mark." We stood mulling the ideas over as the sauce simmered and the pasta boiled.

"Why not just shoot him? I mean, you're going to shoot a human, why not a dog?"

It was a good question. I would wait until the dog was safely out of the way, so I wouldn't have to hurt him. But I'm not like most people. Unless . . . "If I'm the killer, I know Jax, and like him, I might go to the effort."

"You said the killer knew Mark. He might have known Jax, too."

"He or she. Jennifer Weston certainly knew Jax."

"Or . . ." Emma set her large stainless colander in the sink and turned to me. "The killer doesn't want to risk getting bitten. Right? You knock on the door. Mark opens it, lets you in. You pull out a gun and bam! Jax is pretty fast, he might have time to attack."

I nodded. "Same goes for the opposite. Shoot the dog first—Mark might have time to fight back or run."

"Too many variables with the dog inside."

"So the killer wanted Jax out of the way." Logical. But not very helpful in discerning an identity.

Emma drained the steaming pasta while I retrieved the bread from the oven. The warm scent of garlic butter merged with the savory aroma of tomato, basil, and onion, and I was powerless to resist.

I snagged a piece of bread and stuffed it into my mouth like a squirrel hoarding for winter.

I groaned. My stomach did a triumphant back flip. The painkillers must have been working their magic because, at that moment, I felt no pain. My world was constructed entirely of garlic bread.

"Hey! Save some for me, horker."

I looked down at the baguette. Roughly half of it was missing. I tried to chew enough so that speech was possible. "Sa-wee."

Emma nodded, understanding the grumbled apology. "Here. Go sit down." She handed me a plate. "Do you want some wine?"

I swallowed the chunk of bread. "Better not." I was already feeling a bit loopy. Hugh must have given me gorilla-strength codeine.

I tried to think through the fog that was rapidly robbing me of coherent thought. Jax had expressed overwhelming emotions along with the memory, which was why I blacked out. The strongest had been rage and . . .

"Betrayal."

"Do what?" Emma glanced at me from where she sat across the table. Her fork twirled in the mound of spaghetti on her plate.

"Jax knew the murderer. Well enough to feel betrayed by what happened."

"Okay, so . . . who was close to Mark Richardson, and was also someone Jax would trust?"

"Jennifer Weston. LaBryce. The UPS guy, for all I know."

I couldn't help but think of Mark's mother. It was true that she had asked me to report back to her. Maybe she wanted to know what Jax had seen to make sure he hadn't told me Mark was killed by his own mother.

As much as I wanted to believe Miz Gardenia was guilty of more than being an entitled bitch, I couldn't come up with the why. Why would she kill her own son?

LaBryce's motive was now in question as far as I was concerned. And I wasn't sure about Alexander Burke. Did he know Mark well enough to be trusted by Jax?

Jennifer Weston had a motive, too. If losing Mark meant getting booted off the money train, that would be motivation, on top of the possibility of him abusing her.

And what about a new girlfriend? Would Jax have taken to someone he'd only just met? Round and round my thoughts went. I blinked down at my plate and realized I hadn't eaten anything. But I felt full. Must have been all the bread. As I stared at the plate, I got the odd feeling of weightlessness. The plate seemed to float away from me, or maybe I was floating away from it, like a balloon.

I heard Jax's nails click click click on floor and Moss's dog tags jingle. The sounds were muted yet amplified.

Emma was talking.

I didn't understand her. My eyes wouldn't work right. The last thing I remember was trying to speak. I'd thought of something important. I could remember. I had to remember . . .

CHAPTER 16

I'd had a rough morning. Aside from having to roust myself from a drug-induced stupor, I'd also spent over an hour trying to persuade a ferret named Boudreaux to show me where he'd hidden his owner's diamond ring. Boudreaux, who was fond of pilfering anything shiny, did not want to give up his stash. Finally, I negotiated a trade. The ring in exchange for a ball of tinfoil.

Believe it or not, the strangest part of my morning hadn't been my parley with a domestic weasel. It was the cryptic note Emma had left me. It read:

G, you made me write this down. Jaguar tag xo Em

I had called to ask her what the hell it meant, but she hadn't answered. Emma was doing a big shindig that night and was always super busy on event day, or E-Day, as she called it.

My stomach grumbled. I checked my phone to see if she'd called back as I pulled Bluebell into the long line at the Wendy's drive-through. I'd missed two calls, neither from Emma. The first was from Sonja. I glanced at the creeping line of cars ahead of me. I had plenty of time to call her back.

"Well, you were right about Demon," she said.

"He was injured?"

"No, but he was in pain. Abscessed tooth."

That would explain his sudden change in temperament. "You guys extract it?"

"This morning. And he's already back to being everyone's friend."

I felt an unexpected wave of relief. I believed in my heart that LaBryce was innocent, but knowing that I was right about the mastiff did a lot to boost my confidence. "That's great, Sonja."

"You saved his life." Her words made me smile.

"Just doing what I do."

After we'd made plans to do lunch the next week and said our good-byes, I indulged in a little back-patting. I'd saved a dog. My interpretation that he had been hurting was correct. Ha! I blew a mental raspberry at the niggling doubt regarding the timeline with Charm and LaBryce.

The only other call I had to return was to Bo Bishop. When I got his voice mail, I let him know that Jax was doing well. I hung up and reminded myself that he should be added to the list of suspects. Jax would have trusted him, too.

I finally placed my order and inched forward in line. Thinking back to the night before, I went over my list of suspects. So far, it was pretty short. Jennifer Weston, Bo Bishop, and my favorite, Gardenia Richardson. Who else would have Jax's trust? The governor, Buck Richardson, most likely.

"Who else?" I drummed my fingers on the steering wheel. Most people were murdered by those close to them. Had Mark been seeing someone new like LaBryce had thought?

I was idling in line, contemplating this idea, wondering

what the heck *jaguar tag* meant, and waiting on my order of biggie fries, when my phone rang. I glanced at the number. Hugh.

"I was in a stupor 'til eleven this morning, thanks to you," I said.

"You should have broken the pill in half." Hugh's easy laugh seemed to reach though the phone, coaxing my lips into a smile.

"That would have been nice to know last night," I said as the kid at the window handed me my order.

"I was going to mention it, but I became distracted by your sudden loss of consciousness."

I winced at the reminder. Nothing says self-sufficient like fainting into a man's arms. The embarrassment and confusion I'd felt had made me a teensy bit irritable. I had climbed into Bluebell with a few harsh *I'm fine*'s and hadn't bothered to thank him for keeping me from cracking my head on the pavement. Ah, well, better late . . .

"I appreciate you being there, Hugh, and not making a fuss." He'd let me leave, grudgingly, with a promise to text him, instead of trying to drag me to the hospital.

"I've been around you enough to know—when you're set on a course, there's no point in trying to alter it. I was calling to see if you might want to catch some lunch."

"Too late. I'm hardening my arteries as we speak." I tacked a *sorry* onto the end, because I was.

"Another time."

"Sure. How's the giraffe?" I asked as I turned toward the condo.

"Good. He won't walk over the spot where the wire was left, though. It's funny what animals remember."

As Hugh said the words, I felt an idea begin to take hold. "I've got to run, Hugh. Traffic."

He said something else before saying good-bye, but my mind had already shifted gears. I knew what I needed to do, and I wasn't sure why I hadn't thought of it before.

I had to take Jax back to his house. Back to the crime scene.

• • •

By the time I'd gone to the condo to grab Jax and doubled back into town, it was past two o'clock. I pulled to a stop at the gated entrance to Mark Richardson's neighborhood. The elderly rent-a-cop at the little guard booth eyed me and my less-than-sleek Suburban with open disparagement.

Sunday, I had been here as a police consultant. Now . . . not so much. I would just have to wing it.

Clearing my throat as I cranked down my window, I smiled at the portly man. "Hi, I'm Grace Wilde. I'm a volunteer with the Doberman for a Day program." I handed him one of my new spiffy business cards.

Frowning, the guard glanced at the business card and then at Jax. "Who are you visiting?"

Good question. "Let me check . . ." I beamed him what I hoped was an Emma-worthy schmooze-smile, and started to riffle through the papers in the seat next to me. I had heard the reporters talking to a neighbor the day I had come to the crime scene. What was his name? It was something Hispanic. Martinez? I picked up a piece of paper and squinted at it. I let out a little self-deprecating chuckle. "I can never read my own handwriting. Uh . . . I think it says Hernandez? On Saint Johns Street?"

"Menendez?" he asked helpfully.

I smiled again. "That must be it. I wrote the code for the gate down, too, but I can't make it out either." I shrugged sheepishly.

"They expecting you?"

"They're expecting *him*." I hooked a thumb toward Jax. The man glanced toward the backseat.

Don't call to check. Please don't call.

Finally, he nodded and handed my card back. I rolled forward and stopped, waiting for the gate to slowly begin to swing open. Just a few feet ahead was the keypad Kai had mentioned. It was mounted on its own little brick pillar, a simple number pad with a perforated circle below it. A speaker. Kai had said the entrance was only manned until midnight. After that, anyone coming in had to use the keypad. So the killer had either called and was buzzed in or had a code.

I didn't see a camera anywhere near the keypad. I looked back over my shoulder toward the booth. High in the eaves a small camera was mounted, aimed right at me.

Fighting the urge to smile and wave, I faced forward and watched the gate shudder and bounce its way open.

As I guided Bluebell down the curving street, I lamented the fact that the camera wasn't mounted near the keypad so the driver's face would be visible. If it had been, LaBryce would be cleared.

I figured the camera must be aimed to capture evidence such as the license plate and the make of the vehicle.

A realization hit me.

If I had any chance of helping LaBryce, Jax would have to show me more than the killer's face. I couldn't go to Kai, or Jake even, just to point a finger. I'd have to have evidence of some kind.

The idea was so daunting I actually thought about turning around. Tucking my tail and running away. It wasn't my fault LaBryce had made himself look guilty. And why should I do the police's jobs for them? I had tried to tell Kai the truth. Moss was the one who'd messed that up.

Okay, I was being pathetic.

"Why not make it official, Grace, and get an ice cream cake that has 'Poor You' written on it? Get some balloons, too, and make it a proper pity party."

I straightened as we rounded the corner and caught sight of Mark Richardson's place. Time to grow a backbone.

Jax had come to attention, staring out over the lawn at his old house. He wanted to get out and go inside. *Home.*

I parked in the driveway and stared at the faux villa.

Home. He let out a high, brief whine.

"I know, boy. Give me a second." Though I'd recovered from my bout of self-pity, I still didn't have a plan. Sitting in the driveway thinking, "Now what?" wasn't going to get me anywhere, so I opened my door and hopped out.

Midday in midsummer. Even though clouds had rolled in to blot out the sun, I could still feel heat radiating off the concrete under my feet.

Sweating, I surveyed the house—the wrought iron gate, the arched front door beyond, the stained wooden garage doors—all appeared to be locked up tight. Of course.

I knew there was a backyard. There had to be a way into it. Not that I expected a back door to be unlocked, but at least I could get Jax to where he'd been the night of the murder. "Okay, the backyard it is."

I let Jax out of Bluebell, secured his leash, and started toward the house.

Jax wanted to go straight through the front courtyard. I knew from the stir of his memories that this was the way Mark had taken him in and out for walks.

After letting him sniff around for a second, I guided him past the entry, onto the lawn. We walked over the thick carpet of grass, past some sort of large-leafed greenery, and finally rounded the corner of the house.

A stucco wall, the same dusty cream color as the house, stretched across our path to the neighbor's yard. Right in the center was a smaller version of the front gate. I strolled toward it, trying to look natural as I jiggled the latch.

Locked. *Damn.*

I thought about trying to scale the six-foot wall. I could probably manage it, using the gate as a ladder. But then what? I needed Jax with me.

"Okay, plan B." I led Jax back around the side of the house. Just as we rounded the corner, a van with the sheriff's office logo and CRIME SCENE UNIT written down the side pulled into the driveway.

Crap.

Kai would know I was here. Bluebell might as well have been a beacon blinking my name. All I could do was play the hand I was dealt.

The driver's door to the van swung open, and a compact man with a round face and spiky black hair stepped out.

I let out the breath I'd been holding and smiled.

When he saw me walking toward him with Jax, he paused. His expression was blank. I couldn't see his eyes behind his sunglasses, so I wasn't sure what had stopped him, me or the dog.

I smiled and tried to act casual. "Hey. Charlie, right?"

"Yeah. Charlie Yamada. And you're the animal lady." He finally smiled. "I knew I'd seen this car before."

He hadn't called for backup, or made the sign of the cross, so I assumed Kai hadn't spread the word about me yet.

"Grace Wilde. This is Jax. I was hoping to pick up a couple of his things." I motioned to the dog. "I didn't realize there wouldn't be anyone here."

"Nah. We released the scene earlier today. I just had to come check one last thing." He turned his attention to Jax. "So you're Richardson's Dobie, huh? I've heard about you." He looked back at me. "Can I pet him?"

"Sure." Jax was relaxed and receptive. I gave him the mental thumbs-up to let him know this guy was okay. After a few pats, Jax started wagging his back end and smiling. His inner doggy radar was going off. Charlie Yamada was a dog person.

I had a feeling my luck with the CSU was about to change.

Jax was leaning against Charlie's knees, and the man was petting him saying things like, "Aren't you a handsome guy?" and "Bet you like to play, huh?"

Jax's tongue lolled out of his mouth as he tilted his head to look back at me. *Jax, good boy.*

Yeah, you're amazing. I shook my head and grinned. "Do you have a dog?" I asked Charlie.

He sighed. "Nah. My wife's allergic."

"Too bad."

Straightening reluctantly, he said, "It is. I love dogs." He turned his attention back to me. "So what kind of stuff do you need?"

And just like that, the way was cleared. Never underestimate the power of puppy-dog eyes.

Charlie retrieved his metal CSU case and we walked to

the house. As we entered the courtyard, I felt a sudden wave of anxiety from Jax. He was no longer just anxious to be inside his old home. He was nervous.

I tried to reassure him. *It's okay, boy. I'm here. Everything is okay.*

As Charlie unlocked the door, he turned to me with a thoughtful smile. "Hey, I've heard there are some dogs that people aren't allergic to. Is that true?"

"Some breeds shed less. So, they aren't as bad."

"We always had Labs growing up. They shed like crazy."

We paused in the foyer, and I smiled and nodded as Charlie talked. I had to get rid of him to have any chance of accomplishing my task. There was no way I'd be able to guide Jax through his memories with Charlie chattering at me like an excited squirrel.

"I had this one dog, Zeus, a chocolate, and he was the biggest, craziest Lab. He would climb over our fence like it was nothing. I had to have him pull me on my skateboard around the neighborhood just to wear him out."

He shook his head, remembering the hyper Zeus.

"Labs can be energetic," I said, praying he'd get a phone call or a sudden urge to use the restroom.

"My wife would never want a Lab. Even if she didn't have allergies."

I moved toward the kitchen, Charlie shadowing me like one of the faithful Labs from his youth. The room was large, well appointed, and dirty. Though some of the party stuff was gone—taken to the Crime Lab, I assumed—there seemed to be a layer of dust on everything. I spotted two large stainless bowls on the floor and walked over to pick them up. They gave me an idea. Maybe if I gave Charlie a job, I could shake him for a few minutes.

"So what breed do you recommend?" he asked me.

We were back to hypoallergenic dogs. "Poodle, or schnauzer," I said as I opened the pantry door. "Both shed less and are smart and trainable. And they come in a variety of sizes."

"Cool."

It only took a second to find what I was looking for. A giant bag of dog food. I grabbed it and tugged with my good arm, sliding it out into the kitchen with difficulty. Jax started sniffing the bag with interest. This was his favorite flavor.

Dinner.

"If I can get it in the car, you can have a big bowl later," I told Jax.

"Oh, here," Charlie said. "I'll get it."

Bingo. "Thank you so much."

He hoisted the bag onto his shoulder, and I followed him to the foyer to open the front door. I shut it quietly behind him. I thought about locking him out but that wouldn't help—he had a key.

"Okay, down to business." I wouldn't have long. But all I needed was the killer's face. With that, I could work backward to find evidence. One step at a time. *Focus.* I steadied myself, blanking my mind the way I had the first time I'd been here. No Technicolor expectoration for me today.

We walked toward the living room. Jax began to whine quietly.

"It's okay, boy," I whispered.

Just as it had at Burke's house, the violence of murder lingered like a dark, rank phantom.

I tried to push the uneasy feeling away, filling my head with a vast, white calm. But as we entered the room, my stomach roiled. Swallowing hard, I paused and tried to combat the sudden dizziness. It was too much, too fast.

I was going to need more time. Charlie would be back any minute. Presumably to resume his cheerful babbling. There was no way I could stay focused and steer Jax's thoughts with Sir Chats-a-Lot around. Not through such a violent, emotional memory.

We'd have to come back. Which meant I needed a way in.

I pulled Jax back around to the kitchen. Dark granite topped the rustic-chic cabinets. I scanned the countertops for a set of keys or a garage door opener. Napkins, a few paper plates, the odd bit of confetti. I saw a flat, shallow bowl sitting near the fridge and rifled through it. Junk mail, a pen, notepaper, random bits of unidentifiable stuff. No keys.

I started opening drawers systematically. I'd only gotten through two when I heard the front door open.

Crap. I grabbed the dog food bowls and pulled the pen and notepad out of the catchall. I started scribbling a list. Food. Bowls. Toys. Bed. I put big checks next to Food and Bowls. Yep, that's me. Miss Organization. I turned to Charlie, hoping he wouldn't suspect I'd been rifling through drawers.

"I figured I'd make a list." I tore off the paper and held it up. As if he needed a visual to go with the word *list*.

He was looking at me in an odd way. Not suspicious, but not as friendly as he'd been. Probably wondering why I hadn't followed him to Bluebell. This would have been a good time to make my exit, but I still needed a way back into the house. I'd have to find a key or unlock a window.

"Have you seen a dog bed anywhere?"

"Yeah, there's one in the bedroom. I'll show you."

I set the bowls down in the foyer to pick up on the way out. They clattered loudly against the marble floor.

Jax and I followed Charlie down the hall and into the master suite. And it was a suite. The room was huge. The décor was oversized and masculine. Hemingway-esque tropical. Rich earth tones dominated the palette of the large area rug and draperies. A king-size bed, the headboard of which almost touched the ceiling, dominated the wall in front of me. It looked like a fine antique, with large columns and heavy carving. On the far right wall, potted palms accented a set of French doors. They led outside. Maybe, if I could get Charlie to turn his back for a minute, I could unlock one.

As I tried to think of a way to manage that, Jax pulled at his leash. He wanted to go in the opposite direction. Through an archway to my left, there was a small, private study. One wall was lined with bookshelves, the other with football trophies. A desk and chair sat in the center.

"A library?"

"I know." Charlie's voice had regained its lighthearted air. "Who would have thought a football player could read."

Jax was dragging me into the study—sniffing the floor and the air with anticipation. There was something in this room he wanted. "What is it, boy?"

We walked around the desk and Jax found his prize. A well-used length of knotted rope. Jax picked it up and pressed it into my hand. *Tug! Get it!*

"You want to play tug-of-war?" I grabbed the toy to indulge him for a second. As he growled and shook the toy, I saw into his memories.

Bringing the toy to Mark while he was at the desk working at the computer. Mark saying, *"Aus!"* Jax dropping the toy. Mark tossing the toy into the bedroom. Jax bringing it back to start the game again.

"Aus!" I said the German command. Jax let go immediately.

"Cool," Charlie said from behind me. "I've heard some of these guard dogs are trained in German, like the K9s."

"A lot of them come from the same kennels overseas." I wasn't sure what to make of this knowledge. If Jax was trained in German, why had he been listening to me? Because of our mental connection? I filed the subject away to be examined later. There was a more pressing question on my mind.

"Where's Mark's computer? Did you guys take it?"

Charlie gave me a startled look. "Yeah, how did you know?"

I looked back at the desk. Hoping there would be a telltale dust outline or other evidence to point out. Nope. Then I remembered seeing something when I'd bent to get the rope for Jax.

"I noticed a power backup and connection cords under the desk," I said casually. "Can you guys really look at everything on his computer? Even the erased stuff?"

"Yeah. Most of the time. You wouldn't believe the stuff people keep on their computers. They don't even encrypt it. Not that it would matter."

"Really?"

"It might take longer to get into, but our computer guy would decode it eventually. One time, we were going after this pedophile. He was really careful, never had anything on his PC. We went over the computer a thousand times. It turns out he kept everything on an online server. I went back to the guy's house just to look around the office one last time. I found a bill for the server; he'd written his user name and password on it."

"So you caught him?"

"We did. Gotta love stupid criminals." He was back in the groove, chatting away. And I wondered if I could use it to my advantage.

"Kai said you didn't have much physical evidence. That's got to be frustrating."

"We have a pile of physical evidence. None of it's relevant."

"Because of the party?"

Charlie set his case on the floor of the study. "Yeah. But we did get a break last night."

"With the computer?"

"We glue-fumed the keyboard and it was wiped clean."

I nodded. Though I had no idea what glue-fuming was. Charlie was working on the assumption I was in the know—I didn't want to blow the illusion by asking too many questions. I assumed he meant that there were no fingerprints on the keyboard.

"So, the killer touched the computer and wiped his prints off. And you came back to see if he was as careful everywhere in here?"

"Yep. I'm going to go over the desk again."

"I hope you find something." I was really hoping he'd get started working and I'd have my chance to covertly unlock the door. But that was not to be.

Charlie pointed into the bedroom. "The dog bed is over there." We walked back into the main part of the suite and I spotted a round, fleece-covered dog bed in the far corner near the French doors. "Hey look. There's your bed, Jax."

Jax walked toward it, and I wondered if I could get Charlie to carry it to Bluebell for me. Probably not, unless he was sure I followed him.

To get to the dog bed, I had to pass the doors leading outside. The handles were wrought iron levers. I didn't see a lock. All around the handles, black smudges and dust coated the door. I'd seen the same thing in the kitchen. I paused to scrutinize the dust.

Fingerprint powder. "Man, this stuff is messy."

"Yeah. It gets everywhere."

I looked down at the floor. There was a small pile of dark dust on the light stone. But of more interest to me was the little latch anchoring the bottom of the door to the tile. I could reach down and pull it up, unlocking the door, if Charlie weren't standing over my shoulder.

I needed a diversion.

Like Westley in *The Princess Bride*, I made a quick list of my assets. I still held the rope toy. The dog bed was only a few feet away. And I had Jax.

No holocaust cloak, damn.

I turned my back to the door and saw that Jax had plopped onto the dog bed. Perfect.

"Awww. Look at him," I said. "Poor baby. He thinks he's staying."

Charlie's attention was on Jax.

Jax, stay. I urged him not to move with my mind while I said aloud, "Come on, Jax. We've got to go." *Stay!*

Confused, he wiggled a little in the bed. *Stay?*

Yes! Stay! "Let's go, buddy." *Stay!* I tried to remember the German command. *Platz!* I wasn't sure if that meant "down" or "stay," but it worked. Jax was no longer unsure. He had an order.

I pulled on the leash, thinking, *Platz! Platz! Platz!* Jax didn't move. *Good boy!*

I looked at Charlie. "This is so sad. I don't want to yell at him."

Charlie took the bait and squatted down. "Come on, big guy!" He clapped his hands. "Come see Charlie."

Jax didn't budge.

Good boy! You are so smart! I joined Charlie on the floor, positioning myself as close to the door as possible. The latch was within reach. I turned to Charlie.

"I have an idea. Here." I held out the rope toy. "You pull that end and shake it. I'll keep hold of this one. Maybe if he sees us having fun, he'll want to play, too."

It was silly. But Charlie was a dog lover, and bless his heart, he was game. He even made growling noises, God love him.

Thankfully, I knew the German command for "come." *Jax, hier! Tug! Get it!* He launched himself off the bed like it had caught fire. I shifted out of the way and let go of the toy. Jax barreled into Charlie, bowling him over.

I scooted to the door and popped the latch with a quick flick.

Charlie was laughing and wrestling with Jax. Not even a little upset that he'd been flattened. I smiled. Dog people are awesome.

CHAPTER 17

I was being followed.

I'd gotten the feeling as I left Mark's subdivision. That prickling uneasiness that puts the senses on alert. After glancing in the rearview mirror a few times, I managed to shake the feeling, telling myself I had imagined it. Now, I knew my instincts had been right.

I had been caught up worrying about my impending breaking-and-entering venture—going over all the ways to get busted—and almost missed my turn. I had to shoot over two lanes of traffic, much to the irritation of my fellow motorists. One man I'd cut off shot me a rude hand gesture, and I had turned to give him a vapid smile and pageant wave when I spotted the dark sedan.

It had been behind me at the Wendy's drive-through.

Being unschooled in counterspy tactics, I had no idea how to lose a tail. Though judging from the way the sedan had also nearly missed the turn, making sudden changes in direction seemed to be a good idea.

One thing I didn't want to do was lead whoever it was to my sister's.

"Okay, so now what?" I could see the sedan in my mirror. It had dropped back a couple of cars. I thought about driving over the median; after all, Bluebell could handle it. But I had to remember Jax was lying in the backseat. I wasn't going to risk hurting him by trying some stupid evasive maneuver.

My heart had started pumping hard and fast. Who would be following me? Why? The longer I drove knowing I was being tailed, the more my adrenaline urged me to act. Traffic stopped at a red light. I took the chance to turn in the seat and stare at the sedan, which was three cars behind me. The driver was too far away to see.

Jax let out a low growling bark. *Guard.*

I looked at Jax. "It's okay. In fact, you know what? Screw it." I shifted Bluebell into Park and got out. The light had turned green, and there were a few honks of protest. I ignored them. I walked straight toward the sedan.

I'd only made it to my rear bumper when I heard the squeal of tires. The driver had decided it was time to leave. The sedan lurched into traffic and rocketed past.

I glared at it as it sped away. Tinted windows.

I couldn't tell if the driver was a man or a woman. Black, white, or purple.

Shaking, as much with anger as fear, I walked back to Bluebell. Checking my mirrors every other second, I headed home.

By the time I parked in front of the condo, paranoia had taken hold. I stuffed the rope toy in my purse and climbed out of Bluebell slowly, scanning the area around me like a commando on recon. I ordered Jax to stay with me, grabbed the dog bed, and left the bag of food for later.

My hyperawareness continued even after we entered the condo. I was ready for anything. If there was someone lurking in a corner, they were toast. I would kung fu them without hesitation.

Only the sight of Moss sitting outside, blithely watching the seagulls from the balcony, made me realize how far up the crazy tree I'd climbed.

I let out a shaky half laugh. Who could be lurking with Moss around?

I got Jax's bed situated in my room, and after I took a couple of ibuprofen, I sat on the sofa in the living room and tried to relax.

I glanced at Moss. Though he was out of my "range," I knew he'd heard us come home and had decided to stay outside—probably enjoying the way the dying sun seemed to spotlight the gulls. Their white undersides glowed pink, sparking like embers as they swooped down to settle by the shore.

Jax flopped onto the far corner of the rug and let out a deep sigh. He was tired.

"Me, too, buddy. But our night isn't over yet." I watched him close his eyes and wished I could do the same. But my nerves were too frazzled. So much so that when Moss clambered through the dog door with the grace and stealth of a drunken wildebeest, I nearly jumped out of my skin.

I pressed my hand over my pounding heart and sucked in a breath.

Moss walked to where I sat and sniffed my face. *Scared?*

"Yes, boy, I was scared. But I'm okay." I slid down to the floor and wrapped my arm around his back. "Someone followed me today. It upset me."

In Moss's solid presence, I could think a little more rationally. I leaned my head on his side and replayed the event. My dog picked up on the emotions I'd experienced. I had felt as if I was being tracked. Hunted. He didn't like it.

Moss growled. So low, it was little more than a rumbling exhale. Jax sat up, instantly alert. *It's okay.* I forced a slow breath, and Jax settled back to nap. Moss stayed on guard.

Where? Moss always wanted to know the identity and location of the enemy.

"I don't know who it was or what they wanted," I said. It helped to sort through my thoughts out loud, and Moss was a good listener.

"Maybe they wanted to find out where I live." I tried to

figure out the reason. To keep tabs on me? Know when I was coming or going? Again, the question was why?

I lifted my head and looked at Moss. "What have I got that anyone cares about?"

I glanced over at Jax and understanding swept over me. "The frigging reporter."

When I had gone to meet with Gardenia Richardson, I'd seen a young man in a sedan watching me as I'd gone through the gate. And hadn't Wes said something about a reporter at the *Times* digging into the Richardsons' past?

Oddly, this made me feel much better. Sooner or later, he'd see that I was just caring for Mark's dog and move on to juicer scoops. At least, I hoped he would. What if he started asking around and came to the same conclusion Gardenia had? What if a reporter knew about my ability?

That terrifying idea was cut off by my cell phone's sudden eruption into song. It was Emma.

"Hey, Grace. Sorry it's taken so long to call you back." In the background, I could hear people talking and what sounded like glasses and plates clinking as tables were set.

"I know you have a lot to do."

"I've hit a lull. The calm before the storm." She sounded happy and energized. My sister, the true extrovert, loved the action and controlled chaos of her job. I would never understand it, but then again, I can't even plan dinner.

"Em, I got your note. *Jaguar tag?*"

"I have no idea what it means. You made me promise to write it down."

"Did I say why?"

"You were speaking in tongues. But I think it was something Jax saw."

"Huh." Dogs don't see well. Or rather, they don't see like people. I have to interpret some visual cues and translate them. Maybe my drugged brain had made a connection I'd missed. "Okay. I'll see if I can't figure it out."

"How's the shoulder?"

"Better. It twinges every once in a while. I'm going to ice it in a minute."

"Hey, I almost forgot. I saw Gardenia Richardson a few minutes ago. She asked me to be sure I told you hello." There was a pause. "Do you know her?"

"I met her yesterday." I felt myself cringing, waiting for the barrage of questions.

"Where?"

"At her house in Mandarin. She wanted an update on Jax."

"In person?"

"Look, it's a long story. I'll tell you when you get home. Okay?"

"Okay," she said slowly. "Grace, listen, Gardenia Richardson is . . . she's not as nice as she seems."

No kidding. I tried to change the subject. "So what's the event tonight anyway?"

"A bachelor auction."

"Like in *Indecent Proposal*?" I never really got that movie. Woody Harrelson . . . Robert Redford . . . and a million bucks? What was the big dilemma?

"Yep. Mark was supposed to be one of the bachelors. So was LaBryce."

This must have been the "charity thing" LaBryce had talked about, where he and Mark had planned to have their first argument. "Is that why Mrs. Richardson was there?"

"She wanted me to understand that just because Mark was not here—it didn't mean we could skip his charity. I had to scramble to find a substitute."

"Who's taking his place?"

"One of the other Jaguars—Eric Ruby. He and Mark were pretty close, according to Mrs. Richardson."

"Really?" I understood what Emma was saying. Eric Ruby might make the list of suspects.

"I'm going to talk to him later. See what I can find out. I'll let you know if he has anything interesting to say."

"See if he knew anything about Mark's new girlfriend." I had no doubt that Emma would get him talking. Knowing Emma, she'd come home with more inside scoop than the cops would find out in a month.

I heard Emma say, "Alec! Get these boxes out of the way. We have all the linens we need."

"I'll let you go, Em."

"Okay. It's going to be a late one. There's plenty of left-over spaghetti in the fridge. If you decide to take another one of those pills, do it after you're in bed."

"Yes, Mommy." I said the sarcastic retort the same way I'd done for most of my life. And true to tradition, Emma answered with, "Don't you take that tone with me, young lady."

After I hung up, I thought about the note. *"Jaguar tag,"* I said aloud.

I must have decided something about it was important to make Emma write it down. But what?

I closed my eyes and tried to think. *Jaguar tag.* Like a vanity license plate? I'd seen them around. But Jax wouldn't have been able to see the killer's car tags.

I heated up some spaghetti, and with Moss and Jax both trailing behind me like I was the pied piper, I settled into the chair in front of the computer.

Tech stuff is not my forte, but I know the basics. I Googled *jaguar tag* and got over five million results. Mostly websites about the car.

"Okay, maybe in images?" I tried but fared worse. Aside from an adorable photo of a black jaguar cub that made me smile, I got nothing useful.

I looked at Jax who, predictably, had stretched out by the doorway. "What the hell does *jaguar tag* mean?"

He blinked, without so much as a flicker of recognition. I closed my eyes and pictured the Jaguars logo. I offered the image to Jax mentally. Nothing.

"Well, you're a big help."

I continued futzing around on the computer for what seemed like days but came up with zip.

On a whim I did a search for German K9 commands and found a list with pronunciations. I remembered some of them, but couldn't resist trying a few out.

"Jax. *Sitz!*" He sat.

"Steh." He stood—eyes locked on me as if I were the only being in the universe.

I looked back at the screen and picked another command. *"Sprechen!"*

He let out a chorus of barks.

"Cool." I squinted at the screen. *"Zie Brav."*

Jax, good boy. He panted happily.

"And bilingual, too." I guess he was trilingual, if you counted canine. I printed the webpage with the commands and looked at Moss.

"Now what?"

He offered no suggestions—too busy staring at my empty spaghetti bowl with a longing I can only describe as desperate.

"Here." I set the bowl on the floor so he could cleanse it of every remaining molecule of food.

I stared at the computer and sighed. Not the most productive endeavor.

I thought about redoubling my efforts but knew I was just stalling. The little clock at the bottom of the screen showed it was nearing 9 p.m. Time to pull out the ninja suit and grab a flashlight.

Before I got up, I did one last search. It was easy to find a photo of Mark's teammate, Eric Ruby.

I studied his headshot. Brown hair and eyes, handsome chiseled features, slightly crooked nose. If Jax came through and showed me the killer, at least I'd be able to recognize everyone on my list.

I went into my bedroom and changed into dark jeans and a navy blue T-shirt. In the kitchen, I found a tiny flashlight in the junk drawer and turned it on. Dim, but that was good. I wanted to be as stealthy as possible, and the Maglite I kept in Bluebell was too big and too bright.

"Okay, Jax. Showtime."

By the time we pulled up to the guard booth, I had moved past feeling nervous and had reached a strange state of detached calm.

The paunchy guard remembered me and motioned me

through with a nod. He didn't even glance in the backseat, where Jax was lying on the floorboard. I smiled and waved and then waited patiently for the gate to open.

Jax sat up and whined as we neared his old home.

"I know, boy. But we can't go in yet."

I had decided that parking in Mark's driveway would be too conspicuous, so I cruised past his house, hoping to find a spot between two houses, with the theory that each resident would assume I was visiting their neighbor.

The problem was that the lots in this upscale 'hood were spacious. Walkways leading from the sidewalk to the front door were positioned hundreds of feet apart. There was no way to park Bluebell in an ambiguous spot. I'd gone a couple of blocks up and turned when I saw a solution.

A huge white house on the corner was shining like a beacon. Lights blazed inside and out. Cars lined the street on both sides. A party.

"God loves me." I parked as far from the streetlight as I could and realized I had hit a snag.

Not wanting to leave Jax tied up in the front yard while I went around—I was afraid he'd start barking or be seen—I had planned to park close to Mark's, quickly walk to the side gate, hop over, zip through the house, open the front door, and stroll out casually to walk back and get Jax.

But now I had driven two blocks up and one away from where I needed to be. It would take a while to get to Mark's and back. Longer out in the open where I could be seen.

"Damn." I sat and weighed the pros and cons of parking close, making for a quick entrance and, more important, a quick getaway, or concealed with other cars. The longer I sat, the more the decision eluded me.

"Come on, Grace. You gonna fish or cut bait?" My grandmother would ask me this whenever I was dragging my feet.

I turned to Jax. "I'll be back in a minute, okay? Be good."

Jax, good boy.

Yes, you are. I left the shelter of Bluebell with that jovial thought and strolled toward Mark's house. The air was thick and quiet. Katydids hummed their summer symphony. I tried not to look suspicious, just a girl out for a walk on a warm evening.

In blue jeans.

By the time I reached Mark's, the jeans were damp and sticking to my legs like cling wrap. I walked straight to the side gate and, pausing only a moment to choose my toeholds in the swirls of wrought iron, began my climb.

It was not as easy as I had hoped. My jeans, which were on the tight side to begin with, did not yield to my knees—or my hips, for that matter. Grunting and puffing like a pregnant rhino, I struggled to scramble quietly to the top of the gate.

Muttering profanities and insulting Mark Richardson's taste in fencing products, I grimaced as a decorative spike threatened to skewer me in my moneymaker

Vlad the Impaler was your inspiration, huh, Mark?

Proving, once again, that my mother should have chosen another name for me, I finally managed to tumble over in one sweaty piece. I guess Queen-of-All-Stupid-Ideas Wilde didn't have the same ring.

Breathing hard, I tiptoed to the French doors and prayed Charlie had not decided to do a security check before leaving earlier. I grasped the handle, pressed the lever, and pushed. The door swung in.

I stood for a moment at the threshold. Compared to the moonlit backyard, the interior of the house seemed like a black hole. Vast, lightless, and enigmatic. Forcing myself to move, I stepped inside and pulled the penlight out of my pocket.

Clicking it on, I did a quick sweep to get my bearings. I pulled the door closed behind me and, because I wasn't going back out that way, crouched down and engaged the lock. At some point in the last few seconds, I'd lost the grip I had on my nerves. Maybe it was being locked in, or the odd shadows brought to life by my tiny light, but as I straightened, I had a very real sense that I wasn't alone.

I stood completely still and listened. Nothing. I reached out with my other sense and found the source of the "presence." I breathed out a sigh. Birds. Right outside. Either roosting in the shrubs or maybe nesting in a birdhouse.

"Get a grip, Grace." If I was so wired I was honing in on every critter within my bubble, I was going to drive myself crazy. With a straighter spine and renewed hold on my nerves, I started toward the door that led to the hall. Once there, I turned off the light. I didn't need it, and I was afraid someone might notice the beam as it danced around.

I reached the end of the hall and froze. My heart lurched. I held my breath, straining to hear over its erratic thrum. Just when I was about to berate myself again for being a gutless ninny, I heard it.

The creek of a gate—outside in the courtyard. I started to peek around the corner when I heard a click and the sound of the front door swinging open.

Crap.

I scuttled backward, turned, and slunk back down the hallway. There wasn't enough time for me to make it all the way across the bedroom and out the door so I ducked into the office. I pressed my back against the wall and held my breath.

Someone entered the bedroom. Whoever it was didn't flip on the overhead light. I could hear rustling and a click. Dim, golden light poured into the study from the bedroom.

I blinked, trying to banish my night vision. I could feel my heart hammering hard against my ribs. My breaths were quick and irregular. One of the lamps on the bedside table had been turned on. At that moment, I realized that the person in the other room had to know Mark and his house very well to accomplish this in the complete darkness.

My suspect list flashed through my mind. I reached out with my left hand and grasped the central column of one of the many trophies on the shelf next to me. Lifting it silently, I took great pleasure in feeling the solid weight of it in my hand. Facing off against a possible killer had not been on my agenda. But at least I was no longer unarmed.

Hyperalert, I could hear each whisper of movement in the other room. Each footstep. A sigh.

There were a few moments of stillness. Then footsteps coming closer.

A figure passed under the archway, walking right past my meager hiding place without even breaking stride. I had a hold of the trophy, even though I now recognized the figure moving to stand on the other side of the desk. A drawer was opened. Then another. Each was searched with quick, frantic movements.

I could hear hushed curses.

I had been pressed against the wall that held a light switch. I crouched slightly, ready to leap out of the way if there happened to be a reason. Like a gun. With the back of my hand, I flipped on the light and said, "Jennifer."

She shrieked. Her eyes were wide as a screech owl's. She blinked at me in stunned silence. The switch I had hit had turned on the bookcase light. The rest of the room was still in shadows. I could only see one of Jennifer's hands. I divided my focus between her obscured hand and her face. One of them would tell me her intentions.

"What are you looking for?" I was glad to hear my voice sounded calm—casual, even.

"I—I was . . ." She trailed off. Her brows came together. "You're the woman from the bathroom. At the sheriff's office."

"I have Jax."

"Jax?" She looked completely thrown by this comment, which was good. If Jennifer had killed Mark, she was capable of killing me. Keeping her off balance could help me get away.

Not that I had an exit strategy.

The crackle of a police radio solved my problem. Or at least one problem.

"Sheriff's office!" a man's voice announced from the foyer.

Looks like I'm going to jail. I glanced at Jennifer; it was clear she was thinking the same thing.

"We're back here!" I called out, like a hostess inviting a

late guest to join the rest of the party. I hoped that by sounding cheerful I also sounded innocent.

I set the trophy back on the shelf and, like a fool, stepped out into the bedroom. The young patrolman jerked his gun out of its holster and pointed it right at my chest.

"Hands! Let me see your hands!" he yelled.

My hands were already up. I didn't move. I didn't breathe. I was pretty sure my heart had stopped.

The officer maneuvered around so that Jennifer was also in his line of sight. But the gun remained aimed at me.

His eyes were so wide, I thought they might actually pop out of his head. His gaze jumped from me to Jennifer and around the room randomly. He looked more than a little crazy. Crazy people with guns scare me. When I'm scared, I do stupid things.

I lowered my hands and smiled. "Hey. I remember you!" I did. He was the officer who had led me into the crime scene. "I'm Grace. I came to get the Dobie, remember?"

"Don't move! Do you hear me?"

He was screaming, so I was pretty sure the whole neighborhood could hear him.

I froze. So much for the hail-fellow-well-met technique.

His radio sputtered to life, and he seemed to relax a fraction. He grabbed the radio with his left hand and spoke in the police jargon I could never understand.

The light in the foyer flipped on and I saw the silhouette of a man approach. "Parsons, holster your weapon. Now."

My heart sank, not because I wanted a gun pointed at me, but because I recognized the voice. Kai stepped into the room, his eyes piercing me like two lasers.

Crap.

CHAPTER 18

Kai crossed his arms over his chest and looked from me to Jennifer and then back at Officer Parsons. For some reason, he seemed as irritated with the patrolman as he was with me.

"What's going on, Parsons?"

"I got a call that there was suspicious activity at this address."

"Where is your partner?"

Parsons swallowed hard and looked a little flushed. "This is a side job, sir. I was hired by the community association to patrol the neighborhood from eleven thirty to three thirty."

"And you decided to investigate the call without waiting for backup?"

"I . . ." The young patrolman had started shifting his weight from one foot to the other, as if the movement would help him evade Kai's laser-like glare.

"Do you like being a cop, Parsons?"

"Yes, sir."

"You like being a living, breathing cop? With no bullet holes?"

Parsons just stood there shifting back and forth. I actually felt sorry for the guy. Until I remembered he'd pointed his gun at me. Maybe he needed to learn a lesson.

Kai said, "That was a question."

"Yes. Yes, sir."

"Then you make sure someone has your back. Always."

"I didn't think there'd be anyone in the area, sir."

Good point. What was Kai doing here?

"Parsons, don't think. Just do. Call for backup every time."

"Yes, sir. I will, sir."

Kai shifted his ire to me and Jennifer. "Ms. Wilde, Ms. Weston. I'm sure you have an explanation for being here."

Because he assumed we were together, I decided to run with that. I only hoped Jennifer's self-preservation instinct would jump on board. "We came to try and find Jax's papers."

"Papers?"

"His records of sale and registration. I have to have them before I can finalize the adoption."

"And you needed to get them at . . ." He glanced at his watch. "Midnight?"

"That's my fault," Jennifer said. "My study group ran late. I told Grace I had the papers, but after we looked, I remembered they were here. I still have a key, so we decided to run over and get them."

I glanced at my new ally. She motioned to the drawer she'd been rifling through. "I think they're in here somewhere."

"You might be able to find them if you turned on a few more lights," Kai said.

Good point. Though I'd flipped on the bookcase light, the room was still very dim. The rest of the house was also suspiciously dark.

"I didn't want to see the . . ." Jennifer trailed off and seemed genuinely horrified at the idea of having to look at the gore splashed on the living room wall. Either she wasn't the murderer, or she was a really good actress. Maybe she just didn't want to be reminded of what she'd done.

"We left the lights off in the rest of the house. I was

getting ready to flip on a couple more when this officer burst in the front door and decided to point his gun at me. Which, by the way, I did not appreciate."

When in doubt, go on the offensive.

Kai gave me a hard look. He didn't buy it. But then again, he'd probably never believe anything I said.

No one spoke for several seconds. Finally Jennifer said, "Now that I think about it, I remember Mark saying he kept all of Jax's stuff in the file cabinet." She turned and opened a drawer to the left of the desk and began flipping through the contents. "Here. Did you need all his veterinary records, too?"

"Yeah. Thanks."

She walked around the desk and handed me the file. I guess Jennifer's plan was to just assume we were off the hook. She looked at Kai expectantly. "Would you like me to lock up and set the alarm?"

She shoots . . . she scores! Reminding Kai she had a key was the clincher.

Kai shook his head. "We'll handle it."

We made a hasty but casual exit. Just two gals ready to head home after a long day. Once we were outside, Jennifer quietly asked, "Where's your car?"

"River Way. Two streets over."

She nodded. "We'll have to leave, then double back."

"Miss Wilde?" I froze at the sound of Kai's voice. My fingers had just reached out to cup the door handle of Jennifer's sporty BMW. I glanced back toward the house. Kai stood at the open gate to the courtyard. "Can I have a quick word?"

I looked over the roof at Jennifer. "I'll just be a minute."

It wasn't a long walk, but by the time I reached where Kai stood waiting, I was drained. I wasn't sure my brain could handle another round of questions. Or more accurately, handle coming up with plausible answers.

Kai led me a few steps into the courtyard. I could see past him through the glass of the front door. Officer Parsons was moving around inside, checking doors and windows to be sure they were secure. I was glad I'd taken the time to relock the door in the bedroom.

"Grace, please tell me the truth."

So I was Grace again, instead of Miss Wilde. Okay, was this the good-cop part? If so, he'd have to do better. Especially if he was going to ask me for the truth. We'd been down that road. I hadn't enjoyed the ride.

"Sorry, but you'll have to be more specific."

For several seconds, he didn't say anything. He looked like he was trying to decide what approach to take. "Jake has told me you're a straight arrow. You have no connections to the thugs LaBryce hangs out with. No drugs. Not even any traffic citations. But then I find out you've gone to the Clarke estate, and now you're running around with Mark's ex in the middle of the night. What's going on, Grace?"

I felt my eyebrows arc up in disbelief. "Wait a second. You've been investigating me? You really think you'll be able to solve this murder by looking to see if I have parking tickets?" I realized something in that moment that hadn't occurred to me before. "Have you been following me?"

He didn't reply so I assumed the answer was yes. But if that was true, he would know my story about coming to Mark's house with Jennifer was bogus.

"I'm not following you." His voice had dropped to a low rumble. "I needed to talk to you. I called your cell and didn't get an answer."

"How did you know where I was?"

"I'm an investigator."

I waited, but it was clear he wasn't going to elaborate. "Okay, so talk."

"Why did you go to the Clarke estate?"

"Gardenia Richardson wanted me to promise I'd let Bo Bishop adopt Jax."

"And she didn't ask you to do anything else?"

"Like?" I wasn't about to bring up Gardenia's demand that I find out what Jax knew about the murder. Or her offer of payment.

"I don't know, Grace—like helping Jennifer do whatever

you're really doing here tonight? Maybe lie to the police. Suggest you go find a dead body . . ."

"You think Gardenia Richardson is involved in her son's murder?" I hoped the eagerness in my voice could be interpreted as shock.

Kai gazed into my eyes as if he was literally trying to see into my soul. "It's difficult to investigate a family with so much power. Buck Richardson is almost untouchable."

"But you're looking into the possibility that one of them is involved?"

"There have been some developments with the case. We finished going over the security tapes. LaBryce's car was only seen entering the neighborhood once. So unless he came back in another car, he's in the clear. We still have to run all the tags."

I felt an immense wave of relief, and I let out a long sigh. LaBryce was going to get out of jail. I didn't have to try and extract anything else from Jax. I smiled at Kai. It was the real Grace smile, the one that comes from deep inside and is reserved for friends and family. I was so relieved, I didn't even say, "I told you so!"

Kai's expression shifted from scrutiny to expectation. I didn't understand what he wanted from me. "What?"

"I thought you might tell me . . ." He let the rest hang, and suddenly, I got it. I knew what this little talk had been about. Kai wanted me to admit I'd lied about having a psychic ability. He was hoping that giving me the news that my friend was on his way to freedom would inspire me to recant.

I felt the smile flicker. The idea of rewinding to the moment before I had so clumsily confessed the truth was tempting. But now that I'd taken the step, I wasn't going to backtrack. No one ever got very far doing that.

For some unknown reason, the idea that Kai preferred Grace the Liar to Grace the Psychic hit me in the gut like a mule kick. It made me angry and sad at the same time. Unaccustomed to those mixed feelings, I chose to simply turn and walk away from the source.

"Grace."

I stopped and did an about-face. My jumbled emotions hadn't taken long to polarize. I was pissed. "Is this why you hunted me down in the middle of the night? To ask me to admit I lied about my ability?"

"Your phone pinged off a tower near here. I knew if I showed up, I'd find you."

"Find me doing something nefarious, you mean?"

"I want to know the truth." He looked like he was almost desperate to understand me. Like I was the only puzzle piece left and none of my edges were shaped right.

The thought rankled. "I've told you the truth. You don't get to ask me to lie to you so you can stuff me into some pigeonhole. I am not a piece of evidence to be analyzed and categorized and filed away. If that bothers you, tough."

I turned and walked back to Jennifer's car. She had cranked up the engine, and the AC was blasting. As I slid into the leather seats, I let out a slow breath, turned to her, and said, "Let's get out of here."

• • •

Women know things. Intuition, or whatever you want to call it, is stamped into our double X chromosomes.

Jennifer shot me a sideways look as she drove out of the neighborhood. We parked less than a mile away in a dark construction site to wait. Within sight of the main road but with the headlights out, no one would notice us.

After a respectable amount of time, she shifted in her seat and asked, "Is he your ex or something?"

I sighed. "No. That plane was grounded before takeoff."

"Because he's a cop?"

"Because he's an idiot." Not charitable, but I wasn't in the mood to give Kai a pass. I glanced at Jennifer; her lips were turned up in a wry grin.

"Guys can be clueless."

"And yet we're surprised by it every time."

"So, maybe we're the clueless jerks?" She was smiling

in earnest now, and I was struck by how young she looked. At the most, I was only five years older, but tonight I felt like I was pushing eighty. Worn out physically and mentally from lack of sleep, battling inner demons and midnight excursions, I wanted to close my eyes and sleep for a week.

The only bright spot was the knowledge that LaBryce was soon to be cleared. I no longer had to scale fences and creep into canine dreams in an attempt to identify a murderer.

I thought about what Kai had said about the governor and his wife and wondered if Jennifer knew they had come under suspicion. Wes had said she was being supported by them. Had she been at Mark's, riffling through drawers looking to destroy some sort of evidence? Trying to make sure her bread was buttered?

Only one way to find out.

"So, what were you really looking for?" I asked.

Her smile morphed into a closed-lip line. She shook her head.

"Were you looking for some scrap of proof you missed when you killed Mark?"

"What? No!" She looked truly shocked. "I loved Mark."

"But you weren't *in* love with him." I knew it was true from the way she said it. That intuition thing again.

She sat for a long time looking at me. Then I saw a flicker of some decision in her eyes. "You first."

"Me first what?"

"Tell me why you were in Mark's house."

I had already come up with an excuse, in case I got busted. I just hadn't expected to get caught with someone else. My well-crafted lie was still in my pocket. I took it out and presented it to Jennifer.

"I lost my phone. I was at Mark's house earlier today to get some of Jax's things. I figured maybe I dropped it while I was in the backyard picking up tennis balls. So I came to look for it."

Jennifer gave me a dubious look.

Okay, so maybe it wasn't so well crafted. I tried embellishing a bit. "I could have waited, but my phone is how I run my business. I was afraid it might rain. I can't afford to lose all my contacts."

"Then what were you doing inside?"

"I couldn't see in the backyard. It was too dark. I started looking around for a way inside to turn on some lights. One of the back doors was open."

"The lights weren't on."

Clever little thing. "I got inside and decided it would be easier if I just called my phone. I went into the office and you came in the door."

"Why didn't you tell the cops that and let me fend for myself?"

Now we were getting into unrehearsed territory. "I kind of panicked. After having a gun aimed at me and seeing Kai . . . well, my brain wasn't working right."

"Kai, that's the guy who's into you?"

"I don't know about that."

She looked at me as if I was beyond dense. "He is. I met him the other day. He didn't seem nearly as"—she paused, looking for the right word—"passionate."

That was a surprise to me. Kai always seemed animated by an inner fire when I'd seen him. "You met him at the sheriff's office?"

She nodded. "He was there when they questioned me. He's pretty cute. Like that hot carpenter guy who models for Nautica."

I had no idea who she was talking about, but I agreed that Kai was cute and he probably could model for Nautica. Or maybe Rip Curl. "He's a surfer."

"Really? Then he's double-hot." She grinned, and I found myself returning it. There was something in the way she tilted her head, in the curve of her lips, that felt familiar. She shifted toward me in the seat and asked, "So, what happened?"

"I made a bad choice, for a good reason." Telling Kai the truth about my ability had been a rash attempt to help LaBryce. "And it didn't matter in the end."

"That sucks."

I shrugged. "That's life."

"Yeah. You're right about that."

"So—your turn. What were you doing going through Mark's things?"

Jennifer nibbled at her bottom lip and looked away. "I know who killed Mark . . ."

There was a moment of suspense where I thought she might whip out a gun and finish her sentence with "me." But instead she let out a deep sigh. I could see the tension leaving her shoulders, as if knowing that she was about to tell her secret was lifting a physical weight.

"His name is Alexander. Alexander Burke."

To say I was shocked would be an understatement. "How do you know that?"

"He was stalking Mark."

I wondered if Jennifer knew Burke was dead. Had it been on the news? It seemed like a week had passed, but I had found his body only the day before. Maybe the police hadn't released his name.

"How do you know Burke was the person stalking Mark?" So far, all anyone knew was that Mark had gotten hang-up calls.

I could see she was considering how far to go with our conversation. I waited.

"If I tell you, you have to promise not to let it get out. I mean, you can't talk to the press or anything."

"Okay. I promise."

"He would listen to you, right? Kai? If you told him something?"

"Right," I lied. Mostly because she'd made me so curious I didn't think I could take much more suspense.

"Mark and I weren't really together."

"Okay." The confession was not exactly newsworthy.

"Mark was gay."

That, however, was.

"Gay?" I stared at her, disbelieving.

"Mark and Alexander Burke had been seeing each other for a few months. I think Alexander killed Mark. No, I'm sure of it."

I blinked at her in the dim moonlight, trying to get a grip on what she'd just told me. "Why didn't you tell the police this?"

"I haven't had the chance. I needed to talk to someone privately, and Mr. Stein has always been with me when the police have wanted to speak to me."

Stein, the Richardsons' lawyer.

"Besides," Jennifer continued, "I grew up in Emerson. I know cops. If I'd told them the whole story, they wouldn't have believed me. Mark Richardson, the football player, gay?" She huffed out a short, derisive breath.

I understood her point. "It would have been a hard sell." I agreed. "But there has to be evidence. Macho guy crap or not, that should have spoken for itself."

She shook her head. "Mark was always really careful. No guys were allowed to come to the house. Mark would always meet them out someplace. Or I would drop him off."

"So you went along with it? Mark said, 'Hey Jennifer, want to pretend to be my girlfriend?' and you didn't have anything better to do?"

To my surprise, she didn't seem offended by my sarcasm. "Close. We met at a male revue. I was still in high school. But I had a fake ID. Mark and his frat brothers had decided it was the best place to pick up girls."

"You met Mark at a male strip show?"

"Some of the dancers are gay. One of the hottest guys kept looking at Mark. But Mark kept hitting on me. Overdoing it. The tension was so high between him and the dancer I was surprised no one else noticed. Finally, Mark dragged me out of there. We got in his car and I said, 'Must suck being in the closet.'"

"And he confided in you?"

"We'd been drinking. Maybe that's why. We talked for a while. I told him about living with my junkie mom; he told me about his life. How hard it was to go out with girls. Pretend he was someone else.

"We sat in the parking lot 'til long after the show was over. When I saw the dancer who was so into Mark walking to his car, I dared Mark to drive over and talk to him. I told him if anyone saw us, he could tell them I wanted the guy's autograph. The guy ended up giving Mark his number. And that was that."

"So you became his girlfriend publicly."

"I know what you're thinking—a girl from the projects saw an opportunity and took advantage. But that's not what happened. It was a fair trade. I got out of the ghetto and got an education. He got to be himself with me and sometimes find a guy he liked. I'd go with him, drop him off, or pick him up after a date."

She was right, the cops wouldn't believe her. "So what changed? Why the big breakup?"

"We'd always agreed that we would break up during my final semester of school. But I think the bigger reason was Alexander. He was jealous to the extreme. Even though Mark told him we were never physical aside from the expected hugs and hand-holding in public, Alexander couldn't stand it."

She was quiet for a while. "I should have known. When you live in a place like Emerson, you have to learn to read people. If you can tell who is mean, strung out, or crazy, you can stay out of trouble. Some people try to hide who they are, some don't bother, but if you know, it's better. Safer." In the last few moments her face had changed—aged. The skin around her eyes tightened, her lips thinning as they pressed into a frown. Yes, Jennifer Weston was younger than me, but her life experience had shown her things I never wanted to learn.

She looked at me, and her face held a shocking amount of anger. "I met Alexander and I knew what he was like. He had that way about him. Open and friendly, except for his eyes. His eyes said he could do terrible things if you crossed him." A single, fat tear slid down her cheek. "I should have seen it coming."

"You can't blame yourself." It was useless to say things like that. But it was all I could think of.

She brushed the tear away. "You wanted to know how I got the bruises? Alexander gave them to me."

"What happened?"

"A few days before the murder, Mark called me. He was

really upset. He asked me to come over. He told me that things had gone too far with Alexander. They had talked about living together and planned ways for Mark to be honest about his life, maybe even leave the team if necessary. But to Mark, it had all just been talk. He had gone to Alexander's place that day and saw that he was packing."

"So Mark realized he wasn't ready."

"He realized a lot of things. He wanted to be himself. He wanted to be happy. But football was a part of him. He didn't want to give that up, and he didn't want to hurt his family."

"You mean Buck Richardson? Why, because he's a Republican?"

"Having an openly gay son would've complicated things. But I think Mark wanted to come out in his own time. When he was ready and not for someone else. Especially someone he didn't love. I told him he didn't have to do anything he didn't want to. He could break up with Alexander and move on. Neither of us realized that Alexander had let himself in and was listening to the conversation. He was furious. He grabbed me and tried to throw me out."

"And Mark didn't stop him?" It was hard to imagine Mark, a man built of well over six feet of lean muscle, would allow Jennifer to be roughed up. I also wondered where Jax was during this altercation.

"He did." She smiled. "Mark ended up telling Alexander to leave. That it was over. But Alexander lost it. He started begging Mark to reconsider. He said he'd do anything. That he couldn't live without him."

"Did Mark take him back?"

"No. But he didn't make him leave. Mark promised Alexander they would talk about it. I left, but when I called Mark the next day, he said he was trying to let Alexander down easy. He shouldn't have. It only made things worse."

"Because it gave Burke hope?"

She nodded. "Alexander had written Mark a bunch of letters after the fight. At least one a day. That's why I was there tonight. Mark's desk has a hidden drawer, I thought I might find a letter, but the drawer was empty."

"You wanted proof that Mark was gay?"

"I wanted to be able to show the police that Alexander was obsessed. Erotomanic delusion." Pride had her straightening, lifting her chin slightly. "That's the clinical name for a stalker who believes a stranger or acquaintance is in love with them. I'm getting my degree in psychology. Ironic, right? A girl with my background wanting to be a shrink?"

"I think you'd be better at it than some spoiled, sheltered brat whose most difficult life lesson has been remembering which fork to use first."

She laughed, and I realized why I felt so comfortable with her. Jennifer Weston reminded me of my sister. It wasn't their looks, but their mannerisms. And maybe more important, Emma and Jennifer shared that *je ne sais quoi*. They both possessed the same magnetic charm.

The realization made me wary instantly. People with that kind of charisma can use it to get what they want. Sometimes without even realizing it. I was somewhat immune to Emma. But I'd have to make sure I was on guard with Jennifer. So far, I didn't think she was trying to manipulate me, but the best puppet masters never let you feel the strings.

"So what do you want me to do? Tell Kai I think Alexander Burke killed Mark?" I decided to hold off informing her of Burke's death until I knew what she wanted.

She seemed to think about it for a while. "Tell him you talked to me and I mentioned the name. Maybe suggest the police go look at his house? Get a search warrant or something? I'm sure if they did, they'd find some proof of his obsession. Even if he tells them the truth, that he and Mark were lovers, they'll just think he's crazy." She shrugged and looked at me, waiting for my thoughts.

"Jennifer, I don't think you have to worry about Burke. He's dead."

Her eyes went wide. "How do you know that?"

"Kai told me it was a suicide." No need to add the drama of my big discovery.

"Suicide." She whispered the word slowly, as if it was a

new concept. "Of course. It makes sense. Mark rejected him and that was the catalyst."

I could see the budding therapist in her as she reasoned it out.

"Obsessive love follows a pattern. I know Alexander was controlling. When he realized Mark was never going to take him back, he jumped from the obsessive phase to the destructive phase. Denial, rage, revenge, self-loathing, depression."

"If I can't have you, no one can, and if you're gone, I don't want to live?" I summarized.

She nodded. "Alex killed Mark and then experienced self-hatred so strong, he took his own life." She closed her eyes for a moment. "Thank God."

I thought that was a bit cold. Jennifer must have read my mind because she said, "I was afraid he'd get away with it."

Something else motivated her relief. Feeling that justice had been served? Revenge meted out? I was going to ask when Jennifer flipped on the dashboard lights.

"God! It's almost one in the morning!" Turning on the headlights, she put the car in gear. "They're gone by now, don't you think?"

"Not the rent-a-cop. He's on 'til after three."

"It's a big subdivision. If he's patrolling, we probably won't run into him. Do you want to try and find your phone?"

"Too risky. Parsons seemed a little trigger happy. I'll make arrangements to come back in the morning."

Jennifer nodded and we drove back into Mark's neighborhood. I pointed to the hulking form that was my SUV and she pulled in behind Bluebell and stopped. I thanked her and was about to get out when I heard her suck in a breath.

"Is that Jax?"

I looked up. Spotlighted by the Beemer's headlights, Jax stared at us through one of my back windows. For some reason, he'd decided to climb all the way into the back. I remembered the bag of dog food.

"Yes, that's him. He better not have torn into that bag of food."

"Can I see him?" The request sounded so full of hope, I knew I couldn't deny her. She'd known Jax for years. I'm sure she missed him. He probably missed her, too.

Unless . . .

I sat staring at her for what seemed like an hour as I got a grip on my sudden idea.

"Grace? Would that be okay?"

"Yeah. It's fine. Let me just . . . grab his leash." I took my time getting out. It wouldn't do to freak if things took a turn. I had to be ready. I yanked up my mental shield and moved slowly. When I felt centered, I opened the driver's door, put the file she'd given me on the seat, and grabbed Jax's leash. I could hear him stumbling over the objects I kept in the very back. Then he started scrambling over the seats. I shut the door and took one last look at Jennifer; she was waiting near the bumper.

I opened the back door and clipped on Jax's leash. He leapt to the ground and immediately began straining forward to get to Jennifer. Even shielding against his mind, I could feel the intensity of his emotions.

The question was, did he feel joy at the thought of greeting a beloved friend? Or rage in the face of his master's murderer?

CHAPTER 19

I braced myself, and let my shield drop. The feeling slammed into me.

Joy.

Pure and unrestrained. The kind of delirious elation only canines possess. Jax's thoughts were filled with such excitement and love I had to pull the shield back into place just to be able to think.

Jennifer knelt to accept his doggie hello. Laughing and cooing to him. I felt warmth spread through my chest at the sight. Jax loved Jennifer with an honesty most humans would never share.

Feeling a little like an intruder, I moved around them to open the rear double doors and check the condition of the dog food bag. To my surprise, it was still intact. If Moss had been left with such a temptation, the results would not have been the same.

I straightened the things Jax had knocked about as he explored the interior. He had overturned a box I kept for extra nylon leads, toys, hand wipes, and other stuff. I remembered that I'd confiscated a homemade stun gun from a kid who thought it would be a good way to motivate his Great Dane to pull him on his skateboard. Carefully feeling around, I found it next to the bag of food.

Glad Jax hadn't stepped on it and accidentally zapped himself, I tucked the foot-long cylinder on the other side of the box. Reminding myself to toss the stupid thing, I closed the doors. When I turned to Jennifer, she was crying.

"What's wrong?"

"I just miss him." She had draped her arms around him and was patting his side.

"Well, you can adopt him. I haven't promised anyone anything." Not exactly true. But it was clear they loved each other.

She sniffed. "I can't. I'm going to study abroad next semester. I'm leaving next week."

I lowered myself to sit next to her on the curb. "Where are you going?"

"Florence."

"Is there a big psychology school in Italy?"

She smiled. "Art. I held off a bunch of credits so I could go."

"You could get Jax when you come home. Maybe work something out with Bo?"

"Maybe. We'll see."

I was suddenly ready for a shower and a bed. Not only was I tired, I didn't want to run into the gun-happy Officer Parsons.

Just as I was about to say something, Jennifer sighed and hugged the big dog. "Gotta go, buddy."

I picked up his leash and said good-bye. Thankful the night was winding to a close.

The condo was dim and quiet by the time Jax and I made it back.

Emma was still at her event. The tale of my adventure would have to wait until morning. Emma, who knew everyone, and every bit of gossip floating around in the *crème de la crème,* was going to have a conniption when I told her about Mark Richardson. Grinning, I tossed my keys, Jax's file, and my purse on the little hall table and whistled for Moss.

I listened for the familiar jingle of his tags. Moss was probably overdue for a walk by now, which meant he was ignoring me in protest.

"Moss?" I flipped on the kitchen light.

The bright glow flooded the kitchen and illuminated the living room. Moss wasn't curled up on the couch snubbing me as I'd expected.

In fact, I didn't sense him at all.

Jax trotted in front of me as I made my way to the guest room. No Moss. I called out again, probing out as far as I could with my mind.

Nothing.

I began to feel a twinge of worry.

I hurried out to the living room again, and remembered the dog door with a flood of relief. I stepped to the door and turned on the balcony light.

I whistled, cupped my hand on the glass, and peered out to the balcony. I caught sight of something small and rectangular near the edge of the banister, and I squinted, trying to make out what it was. Lying on its side, green liquid pooling around it, was an open bottle of antifreeze.

Poison.

Panic pierced my chest. For a moment I couldn't move. Someone had poisoned Moss. *No. No no no no.* I spun around and flew back through the house.

Confused and alarmed, Jax scrambled out of the way and then quickly followed as I sped through the condo.

I searched each room with crazed purpose, finally finding Moss in my sister's bathroom, slipping and wobbling on the slick tile. "Moss! Oh God."

Flinging myself down to the floor, I cupped his head in my hands. *Thirsty. Sick.* He leaned toward me. His dizziness swooped into me and the room spun. My stomach clenched. This was bad. Fear clouded my mind. How much had he ingested? When?

I tried to push the panic away and focus. "It's going to

be okay, boy." Tears stung my eyes. My hands shook so violently I wasn't sure I would be able to use them. "Shit! Pull it together, Grace."

Crushing down my fear with an iron fist, I dragged myself up and ran into the kitchen.

Mentally, I ordered Jax to stay out of the way. I couldn't afford to be tripping over him. Time was running out for Moss. The longer the antifreeze coursed through his system, the greater the chance he would not recover. I needed to think. I was a veterinarian, I had to act like one.

I wrenched open the door to the liquor cabinet, searched the shelves, and snatched out a bottle of vodka. Now all I needed was an IV. I hurried into the guest room, where I kept my second kit. Clawing through its contents, I grabbed what I needed and rushed back to Emma's bathroom. If I could get enough alcohol into him, there might be a chance.

"Grace?" Emma walked into the bathroom, where I knelt next to Moss. She was still holding her keys and clutch purse. "What the hell . . ."

I looked up at Emma and a fresh wave of emotion washed over me. "Someone poisoned him—" A sob cut off the explanation.

"Oh my God, is he okay?"

"I've got to give him this IV." I held up the needle with a trembling hand. "Here, hold off his vein for me."

Emma only hesitated for a split second before dropping to the floor and reaching out to do as I asked. I showed her how to grip his front leg, and though my fingers shook wildly, was able to administer the IV.

Emma's eyes followed the IV line up to where it ended in the opened vodka bottle.

I answered her before she could ask. "The ethylene glycol won't be metabolized by the liver and processed by his kidneys if there's enough alcohol in his system."

"Really?"

I nodded.

"Saved by Stoli." Emma offered me a weak smile. "He will be okay, won't he?"

"I don't know. It depends on how much antifreeze he ingested."

"Antifreeze?"

I nodded. "It's toxic. Someone left an open bottle on the balcony."

"You mean someone put a bottle of antifreeze on our balcony to kill Moss?" The look on Emma's face had turned from concern to blazing anger.

"Antifreeze is sweet. Animals drink it because it tastes good. It's an easy way to get rid of a dog or cat you don't like."

"Fucking Bert Cavanaugh." Emma's eyes had narrowed and her mouth was set in a thin, angry line. "That bastard. I never imagined he would do something like this."

Mr. Cavanaugh. Of course. I looked down at Moss and whispered, "If he did this to you . . ." I let the thought go. *Don't you worry about that. Just get better. Please.*

"Oh my God, Grace. The door. Moss could get on the balcony because of the dog door." Emma's eyes were wide and filled with horror.

"No, Em. Listen to me." I reached out and grabbed her hand. "This is not your fault. Mr. Cavan-ass is going to pay for this."

She nodded slowly. "It's a crime, isn't it? Poisoning someone's dog?"

"Yes."

"Good. I'm going to put the evidence in a bag. You need me to do anything else? Pillows? This floor isn't comfortable."

I glanced at Jax. The Doberman had been standing nervously in the doorway to the bathroom. He knew something was very wrong with Moss. "Jax needs to be walked."

"Got it." Emma hopped up and began to flit around. I knew my sister was at her best when she could focus her energy on getting things organized and done. Emma brought me a blanket and some pillows. She walked Jax and warmed up some spaghetti for me, even though I'd told her I wasn't hungry.

It had to have been well into the wee hours by the time I agreed to let Emma help me get Moss into a more comfortable spot in the bedroom.

Emma had made a huge pallet on the floor out of piles of blankets and throw pillows.

"He's better, isn't he?" she asked.

"I think so. It's hard to tell. The vodka makes him sick and woozy and so does the poison. I won't know 'til tomorrow."

Emma nodded. "Don't worry. He's too stubborn to die, Gracie."

"Thanks, Em. You're the best sister in the world."

"I know." She shot me a cocky grin. I was probably the only person in the world who could see the undercurrent of worry and anger that came with it. Emma was pissed. If Cavanaugh thought he could drop the gauntlet on Emma's balcony and get away unscathed, he had underestimated her.

He had underestimated both of us.

• • •

For the next few hours I lay on the floor with Moss. Jax had stretched out in front of the bedroom door and regularly got up to check on us, first sniffing Moss then looking at me. He was worried, knowing that his friend was sick and that I was upset.

My emotions had run the gamut from grief to worry and had finally settled into a fierce and chilling anger.

Jax let out a low growl in his sleep. He was picking up on my emotions. I immediately felt guilty. Jax had been through enough without having to deal with my baggage.

Sighing, I checked Moss's IV and got up to go into the kitchen. Jax rolled onto his feet as I approached the doorway, looking up questioningly.

"He's going to be okay, Jax." I forced myself to believe it.

Jax glanced down at Moss, who was breathing more steadily now. *Okay?*

Don't worry. "Come on, let's get you some breakfast."

Jax hesitated a moment before trotting into the kitchen

behind me. I poured some food into the bowl and was reminded that I hadn't eaten more than a few bites of spaghetti.

My stomach grumbled at the thought of food, and I walked across the kitchen to grab a banana from the fruit bowl. I caught sight of a Ziploc bag on the counter, and stopped, hand extended mid-reach. My sister had put the bottle of antifreeze in the bag as evidence. Its blue-and-red logo clashed with the vibrant green smeared on the inside of the bag.

Seeing it made my stomach turn. With the vicious speed of a viper, I struck out, slapping the bottle to the floor. It hit with a hollow thud and skidded across the marble, landing at my sister's slippered feet.

I watched Emma pick up the bag carefully by the corner and walk into the kitchen. Her face was calm. "Are you going to call Kai?"

"I should just find a way to pour that into Bert Cavanaugh's morning coffee."

Emma set the bag back on the counter. "I had considered that myself. Or an accidental tumble down the stairs . . ."

"Or a nice visit to the zoo. I'm sure I could talk one of the lions into eating him." I felt the whisper of a smile play across my lips before I felt another surge of anger wipe it away. "Em, how can people be so . . . so . . ."

"Mean? Evil?" Emma moved around the counter and clasped both my hands. "They just are sometimes, sweetie. You know that."

I did know. I'd seen it countless times in countless ways. Kittens tossed into a river, dogs with collars so tight they cut into the skin. But this time it was my dog, my *friend*.

Emma smoothed a hair from my rumpled ponytail back into place. "The only thing you can do is make sure he doesn't get away with this."

"I screwed it up, Em. How can I go to Kai and ask him to do me a favor when he thinks I'm a nut?"

"He doesn't think you're nuts, he thinks you're a liar. Which gives you an advantage."

"Right. I'm holding all the cards."

"You are." Emma flipped on the coffeemaker and turned back to me. "You have the advantage because you still have something he wants."

I rolled my eyes. "Em . . ."

"Not that. Well, not *just* that." She smiled. "Kai thinks you're lying. So in his mind, you can still tell him the truth."

"He's not going to listen—"

She held up a finger. "No, you're not listening." She paused to make sure I was paying attention. "The truth, in Kai's opinion, isn't that you're telepathic. It's something else. Go to him and make a deal. He looks over the bottle for proof of who poisoned Moss, and you'll tell him everything you know."

I thought about what he'd said last night. He wanted the truth. "Just make something up?"

"I might be able to give you some scoop." She handed me a mug of coffee and pulled the cream out of the fridge. I watched as she made herself a cup and realized how tired she must be to shun her usual tea. "I talked to Eric Ruby. He plays tight end. And for good reason." She grinned. "Anyway, he seemed to think whoever Mark was dating was a big secret. But I got a name. Alex. Eric overheard Mark on the phone and he called the new girl Alex. Pretty good, huh?"

I felt my mouth drop open, but not because this was a revelation. I knew who Alex was. I was shocked at myself. I couldn't believe I hadn't told Emma about my conversation with Jennifer Weston.

"I forgot to tell you."

"What?"

"I know who Mark was seeing. Alexander Burke. Mark was gay."

Emma's eyebrows shot up toward her hairline. I told her the short version of my night. Breaking into Mark's house. Running into Jennifer Weston. Her story that Mark and Burke had been dating.

"So Burke was the stalker. Well, that explains the jaguar thing." At my blank look, she added, "The note. You made me write down *jaguar*, like it was the key to something."

"What about the *tag* part?"

"Tag. Jag. Who knows what you were saying? I was lucky to figure *jaguar* out. But it makes sense. Burke would have smelled like a jaguar."

"I'm still having a hard time with the idea of Burke as the murderer. If Jennifer's right and Burke killed Mark and then killed himself, why would Jax have told me Alex was murdered?"

Emma looked thoughtful as she sipped her coffee. "Have you ever been to a suicide with a dog before? Maybe the feeling is the same."

"Maybe." Something still didn't seem right.

"Or maybe Jax was also thinking about Mark's murder. He sees, or smells, Mark's killer and his thoughts get all mixed together."

"That makes more sense."

"Well, it looks like you've got something to tell Kai after all."

"I promised Jennifer I wouldn't tell anyone about Mark."

"Well, you'll have to break that promise."

I nodded, but I really hoped I could come up with something else to tell him. I glanced at the clock; it wasn't even five yet. Too early to go to Kai's office, and I needed to take care of Moss before I did anything else.

"I'm going to grab a quick shower and then take Moss to get some blood tests," I told Emma.

"You'll call Hugh?"

"No, there's one other person in the world who loves Moss enough to get up at this hour." I poured my cooled coffee into the sink and called Sonja.

CHAPTER 20

Just before dawn, I pulled into the ASPCA parking lot. Sonja had gone from half-asleep to wide awake when I had called her and told her what happened. She had insisted I bring Moss in as soon as possible.

I'd decided to leave Jax at the condo with Emma. His big meeting with Bo was later—he needed some calm and quiet.

Sliding out of Bluebell, I started toward the building, but only made it a few steps before Sonja pushed open the front door and rushed out to meet me. Worry lines creased her smooth ebony face. "How is he?"

"He seems a bit better."

"Should we carry him in?"

I nodded. "He's pretty out of it."

We walked back to Bluebell, and I opened the door to the backseat. Moss blinked up blearily at Sonja.

"Well, hello, handsome. Let's get you fixed up." I was eternally thankful that her voice was calm and held no trace of tears. I wouldn't have been able to handle it if Sonja had started crying at the sight of him.

Moss thumped his tail sluggishly against the seat at the sound of her voice.

Sonja gave him a quick pat and then grabbed the sides of the blanket. She and I used it as a stretcher to haul him into the clinic. My shoulder twinged a few times, reminding me that it was still injured.

"As many times as I've seen these things, it never fails to piss me off." Sonja puffed, struggling a little with the weight of the giant wolf-dog. "Take him to my office. No reason to lug him all over the place."

We maneuvered Moss into Sonja's office and placed him gently on the cool tile floor by her desk.

"He can stay in here with me today."

I knelt beside him and felt a wave of dizziness flow from the dog. I tried to ease his unsteadiness by taking a slow, focused breath. *Easy, boy. You're okay.*

I looked up at my friend. "Who'd you call in?"

"Dr. Patrick. He should be here any minute." Sonja glanced at the clock and joined me on the floor and began gently stroking Moss's head. "He's going to fix you up, sweet boy."

I knew, if anyone could, it was Dr. Patrick. He had been a vet longer than I had been alive, had countless hours of experience, and even more important, he had great instincts. I was grateful to Sonja for calling him.

"Any idea who did it?" She lifted her gaze to me.

"We have a neighbor who's been complaining about Moss. He's the most likely candidate."

"I can get a couple of our investigators to question him if you want."

"That would be great." Having an official record of the poisoning would be the key to bringing him down. If I failed to persuade Kai to check for evidence on the antifreeze bottle, the ASPCA investigation would be all I had.

Thankfully, Dr. Patrick arrived to distract me from my thoughts. He always reminded me of a beardless Santa, with his rotund belly and half-moon glasses. Speaking in a low, calming monotone, he quickly performed his examination of Moss. He asked me several questions, and I was relieved to see he seemed somewhat optimistic about Moss's recovery.

He peered at me over his glasses and gave me a gentle smile. "We'll keep him drunk, and I'll run some tests to try to determine the extent of the damage to his kidneys and such. It may just make the difference that you were able to treat him quickly. We'll have to wait and see. I'd like to keep him here."

Sonja said, "I'll keep him in here with me. I've got paperwork I've been putting off."

"Thanks." I knew there was nothing more I could do. But I was reluctant to leave, so I lowered myself to sit next to Moss. It was hard to tell if he was better or not. The vodka was making him as loopy as the antifreeze. I still felt wave after wave of dizziness from him and had to swallow back the urge to be sick over and over.

"Why don't you go on and do what you need to do today. I'll watch him." Sonja had joined me on the floor and sat on the other side of Moss. When I didn't answer, she added, "Don't put yourself through this, Grace. You're making yourself sick."

I looked over at my friend. Her voice was gentle, but it carried an edge. "What?"

Sonja sat, quietly studying me for a long moment. She shook her head and sighed, like I was the dunce of the class. "You remember the first week you came to volunteer here? When you were off for the summer during college?"

I nodded, not sure where she was going with this.

"One day, we got a call about some abandoned horses."

"Out near Kent. I remember."

"So do I. We're all out in this muddy field in the pouring rain, and the stallion breaks out of his stall and comes charging across the corral. Right at you."

I remembered it vividly. I had been standing between him and the other horses. The stallion had viewed me as a threat to the herd. It had taken every ounce of my courage to stand my ground and stay calm. My lack of reaction as he reared had confused him. Was I friend or foe?

The stallion stopped and stared. Nostrils flaring, mind racing, he attempted to assess the situation. I had taken advantage of his hesitation and used my ability to reach out with my mind. I managed to smother his blinding panic with a blanket of calm. I'd soothed him. Reassured him. And eventually, to everyone's amazement, led him quietly into the transportation trailer.

"I'll never forget it," Sonja said. Her voice was hushed. Her dark eyes seemed as depthless as the ocean. "You turned and faced that horse, and I knew you were different. I watched you. Over and over you did things, knew things, *felt* things no one else did. And now you're sitting here torturing yourself." She tsked.

"You know?" I was shocked. I shouldn't have been. Sonja was wise. An old soul, my grandmother would have called her.

"Of course I know," she said, indignant. "Anyone who's seen you work would know, if they wanted to see it."

"Really?"

"Please, girl. You'd have to be blind. Or stupid."

I thought about it. Kai was neither of those things. "I don't know. I think some people's brains just aren't wired to accept it. Me."

"Maybe." Sonja's shrewd gaze swept over my face. "If that's the case, it's not on you. If these people don't want to accept you, they're doing it for their own reasons. We can all choose what we'll believe and what we won't."

"I didn't think *you'd* believe me."

"Do I look stupid to you?"

I shook my head and smiled. "Honestly, I wasn't only afraid you wouldn't believe me, but if you did, you'd think I was some sort of freak or something." I thought about the instigator of that fear. Dane Harrington. "My first year of college, I fell madly in love with this guy. When he saw what I could do, he dropped me like I was on fire."

"What happened?" Sonja asked.

I sighed. "We were in the Bahamas. A small pod of bottle-nosed dolphins beached themselves in a lagoon near our hotel. I went down to see if I could help. The inlet was really shallow with a lot of sandbars; it made their sonar all screwy. Every time the rescuers got them in the water, they'd beach again."

"What did you do? Even you can't fix that. Can you?"

"No. I didn't try to fix it. We got them pointed in the right direction at high tide, and I swam them out past the sand bars into open water."

"You did what?" Sonja asked, eyes wide.

I chuckled at her astonishment. "It sounds a lot more heroic than it was. I've been a swimmer all my life, plus I had on fins and snorkel gear. Anyway, once they were out deep enough, they swam away. I came back to shore and Dane asked me how I managed to get the dolphins to follow me."

"And you told him the truth?"

"I did. I thought he'd find it interesting. After all, we were in love; nothing could come between us, right?"

Sonja shook her head, knowing that wasn't how the story ended. "Ugh, I'm sorry."

I shrugged. "I used Dane as an excuse for a long time. I've always hated people who wallow in self-pity."

"Feeling sorry for yourself is something everyone does at some point in their lives. The real test of character comes when it's time to stand up, dust off, and get back on the horse. It doesn't matter how long it takes to do it. As long as you can mount up and go for another ride."

On impulse, I reached over and hugged my friend. I started laughing. Sonja joined in. The movement nudged Moss and he stirred.

Sonja leaned back and gave Moss a gentle pat. "What is it? Is he okay?"

"I hope so. It's hard to tell." I softly stroked his head, willing him to get better, professing my love and promising all the people food he could ever want.

"Okay, that's enough." Sonja gave my arm a little squeeze.

"You're making yourself sick again. You need to get out of here. I'll call as soon as I know something."

I puffed my cheeks and blew out a breath. "Okay."

Pulling herself to her feet, Sonja started toward the door then stopped. "Oh! I know. I've got something I want to give you." She turned and opened one of her desk drawers. She handed me a small, worn, white cardboard box. "I've had it for years, thought I'd lost it. I came across it a few weeks ago and planned to give it to you for your birthday. I think today is better."

I stood and slowly opened the box. Inside, tucked in cotton, was a silver medallion on a delicate chain. I peered closely at the figure on the pendant. It was a monk, flanked by several creatures and holding a bird in one hand. Even though I had been raised a heathen, only attending church when my grandmother dragged us to the tiny Baptist chapel where she lived, I still recognized the icon. "Saint Francis." I was touched. Saint Francis of Assisi, the patron saint of animals. "It's beautiful."

"I had it engraved." She lifted the necklace out of the box and flipped the medal over.

JOB 12:7 was inscribed in bold text. "A Bible verse?"

"It makes me think of you every time I read it. 'But ask now the beasts, and they shall teach thee; And the birds of the heavens, and they shall tell thee.' " She opened the clasp, and I turned to let her fasten it around my neck. "God blessed you with an ability. Don't take it for granted."

I turned back to face my friend, hugged her, and whispered, "I'll remember. Thank you."

She patted me. "I'll call about Moss as soon as we know something."

I nodded and sent Moss several mental reassurances before I left.

It was time to call in a favor.

• • •

It was still insanely early. Not even six. Some industrious folks were out for morning walks, but mostly Dolphin Street was quiet. Glancing at the address I'd scrawled on the paper, I found the right number and pulled into the driveway.

So this is Kai Duncan's house. Cute.

A giant magenta bougainvillea engulfed one side of the house and draped gracefully over a trellis. Its beautiful flowering limbs swayed and shuddered in the breeze. The rest of the landscaping followed the bold flowering vine's lead—island-style rustic with clusters of banana trees, hibiscus, and beach morning glory.

The house itself was small, dating from the early sixties, when just about anyone could afford to live on the beach. It had been skillfully updated with stucco and cheerful coral paint.

The overall impression was that of a secluded tropical bungalow.

Kai the surfer lived here, not Kai the cop. Part of me regretted that I'd never get a chance to know the surfer better.

The thought brought on a rush of anger, which quickly devolved into a flutter of nerves. I glanced up and down the street and distracted myself by wondering how much the real estate in this neighborhood went for. I'd seen FOR SALE signs in a number of yards. Maybe I'd widen my house-hunting search to include Atlantic Beach. These homes seemed to be on deep enough lots. Moss needed a yard.

My heart squeezed. The thought of my dog elicited a painful spasm in my chest. I refused to imagine he would not recover from the attack. *Moss will get better,* I told myself sternly. *And he will need a yard.* I promised to grab a few real estate flyers when I left. But first things first.

I sat for a moment and considered my next move. It surprised me how easy it had been to find Kai's home address. Just a quick Google search and *voilà.* I was afraid convincing him to do what I asked might not be so easy.

"You are going to plainly and calmly tell him what you learned from Jennifer Weston and ask that he look over the bottle for evidence."

And you will not let him turn you down.

Taking a deep breath, I grabbed the bag with the anti-freeze bottle and slid out of Bluebell. Squaring my shoulders, I walked to the front door.

I knocked and then, giving in to impatience, rang the bell. The anxiety I held so adamantly in check came roaring back when I heard the click of the dead bolt.

I swallowed hard as the front door swung open. "Hi." I forced a smile that felt more like a grimace.

It was returned with a puzzled frown. "Grace, what are you doing here?" Kai stood barefoot, his hair still wet from a shower. He was dressed in a collared shirt with the JSO logo embroidered on the breast, and khaki pants.

I forced my voice to be utterly cool. "I need to talk to you."

Still frowning, he studied me for a moment, "What happened?"

"Can I come in?"

After several seconds of consideration, he moved to the side.

I stepped into the foyer and then followed him into an open living room with parquet floors. The room was tidy and comfortable—lived-in without being cluttered.

Kai propped one hip on the back of a wicker and rattan couch and crossed his arms. "What's going on?" His keen gaze had assessed me as soon as he'd opened the door. I'd seen my reflection when I'd gone back to the condo to get the antifreeze bottle and hunt down Kai's address. Eyes red and puffy. Lines of fear, sorrow, and anger scored my face. I knew I looked like death with a hangover. I didn't care.

"I need a favor. I know I have no right to ask, but it's important." I paused and took a steadying breath. I held out the grocery bag. "I know it's probably against the rules, but I was wondering if you could get fingerprints off something for me."

"Grace, tell me what happened."

"Someone poisoned my dog, Moss."

Kai's eyes flicked over the bag. "The wolf?"

I nodded. "Last night."

Kai opened the grocery bag and pulled out the bottle

Emma had sealed in a Ziploc. "Antifreeze. Jesus. Is he all right?"

"I don't know. He might have severe kidney damage." My eyes grew hot. But the sting of tears didn't come. I'd cried myself empty.

"I'm sorry, Grace." Kai's voice was filled with sympathy. For a moment, it seemed he might reach out to me. I stepped back. I didn't think I could stand to be comforted right then. I might not have any tears left, but that didn't mean I wouldn't completely unravel in the strength of his embrace.

I forced myself to refocus. "Jennifer told me something last night." I paused, hating to betray a confidence. But as I watched Kai set the antifreeze bottle on the side table, I knew it was my only bargaining chip. "I'll tell you, if you promise to look at the bottle."

"So this isn't really a favor. You want to make a deal." All compassion had vanished from Kai's face, replaced with hard lines of suspicion.

"Call it what you want. I know who poisoned Moss. My next-door neighbor, Burt Cavanaugh. I just need proof."

"Okay. I'll check the bottle for prints. But if this guy isn't in the system, it won't do much good."

"Thank you."

Kai waited. It was time for me to hold up my end of the bargain. "Jennifer said Mark was being stalked by Alexander Burke."

Kai raised his brows, but not in surprise. It was more of a "This is your big news?" look. When I didn't continue, he said, "And . . ."

I tried to think of a way around telling him about Mark and Burke's relationship. I had promised not to, after all. "Jennifer said Burke was crazy. He had sent Mark several letters. That's what she was doing at Mark's last night. Looking for a letter to show you, so you'd go question Burke."

"And what about you, Grace? What were you doing there?"

So he hadn't bought our story. Not surprising. I thought about trying the phone excuse, but just then, I felt a whisper of an animal mind. The presence of a feline brain hummed just inside my periphery. "You have a cat."

"Yes. I told you about him."

I had forgotten that he'd mentioned having a cat. An idea began to form. I looked in the direction of the buzz. A few feet away, a sliding glass door led outside. I stepped toward it and spotted my target. A gray cat crouched behind the thick monkey grass that edged the patio. He was captivated by something moving in the long leaves.

Hunting.

So intent was the animal's focus that he started when I tapped on the glass, staring up at me with round, chartreuse eyes.

I glanced over my shoulder at Kai. "What's his name?"

Kai raised his eyebrows and cocked his head. "Why don't you ask him?"

"I will."

I unlatched the door and slid it open. The cat trotted in, meowing a greeting. I knelt down and began speaking to him softly. "Hello, kitty." I ran my hand gently from head to tail. *Let's show Daddy that I'm not a whack job. What do you say?*

The cat pushed into my hand. I cupped my fingers and scratched under his chin. Pure pleasure radiated from him in warm waves. *Good. Yes. There.*

It would be tricky. If the cat wasn't talkative, and you never knew with cats, it might not get me much. But it was worth a try. I focused on drawing the cat's name out of his contented brain.

Dusty. As soon as I gleaned that tidbit, I remembered Kai had told me when he'd come to the condo. I couldn't use it as proof of my ability. And that was exactly what I was planning to do. Prove I could do what I'd claimed.

I thought about Sonja, the beautiful Saint Francis medal, and knew that this was my chance. I would lay it all on the table. *What's it going to be, Grace, half-ass or badass?* Last time, I'd done a half-assed job of showing Kai what I could do. Not this time.

Pressing every distraction out of my mind, I reached for Dusty's. The cat spun under my hand and looked up with a questioning squeak.

Gotcha.

It took a while. Dusty was very chatty, and that was a good thing. I beamed down at the cat—he was just full of interesting stories. I laughed and glanced up at Kai. "I'll be sure to tell him." Smiling, I stood and turned to face him.

With a look of supreme skepticism, Kai leaned back on the couch. "A message from Dusty?"

I stood in front of him and said, "Your cat wants you to know that he doesn't want you to take showers anymore."

"Excuse me?"

I couldn't suppress my grin. "He's afraid you'll drown. That's why he stands on the back of the toilet and cries while you're in the shower."

"What?"

"Oh, and he wants you to change the doorknob on your bedroom door back to what it was."

Kai stared at me, stunned. "The doorknob?"

I nodded. "I have to admit, I'm not really sure what that means."

Lips parted in shock, he looked from me to the cat. "Dusty could open the door," Kai murmured, almost to himself. "He would reach up and pull down on the lever with his paw and open my bedroom door in the middle of the night. It used to scare the shit out of me. I almost shot him twice." Kai focused on me. "I changed it to a regular turn-style knob. How did you know that?"

"You're really asking me?"

"But. You can't really talk to animals. That's just . . . impossible."

"He disagrees." I motioned to Dusty, who had begun weaving through my ankles like a furry ribbon.

"I don't believe it. Psychics don't exist."

"Believe it. Or don't. But to answer your question, I was planning on bringing Jax back to Mark's house to see if he might remember more of the murder. I was serious when I told you he saw what happened."

"Wait." Kai held up his hand. "More of the murder? You mean he's remembered some of it?"

"Yes. Bits. Mostly emotions. The images I've seen don't make much sense."

"Tell me."

I scanned Kai's face. His brow was furrowed. Eyes bright, intense, and filled with some emotion I couldn't pin down. Doubt? Anger? Impatience?

I tried to explain the images and feelings Jax had shared with me. "It was dark, obviously. Jax was outside. He seemed to know who was coming to the door. There was a sense of anticipation. Then . . . violence. Fear. Helplessness. And . . ."

"And?"

"Betrayal."

"So you're saying the dog felt deceived in some way?"

"No. It was more shocking. Jax trusted the person who came to the door. Felt they were . . . family."

"Family," Kai repeated. He seemed to consider the idea for a long time. He raked his hand through his hair and muttered, "I can't believe I'm buying this."

I felt my back go up. "No one's asking you to buy any-thing."

"Okay. Sorry. I'm just trying to get my head around what you're telling me."

"If you have a cup of coffee, and an open mind, I think I might be able to explain it to you."

After a long pause he nodded. "Yeah, okay. Have a seat. I'll grab a couple of mugs."

I sat on the sofa. Dusty leapt onto my lap a nanosecond after my rear made contact with the cushion. I chatted with the cat while I waited for Kai to return with coffee. Dusty was happy and calm. I laid my head back and relaxed into his consciousness. It embraced me like a warm cloud. His purring vibrated in my head like the lull of ocean waves.

I needed to get a cat. They were better than Prozac.

"Black is all I can offer." Kai's voice jerked me back to reality.

I opened my eyes. Kai handed me an oversized mug and sat on the sofa, turning to rest his back on the arm so he could face me.

"I'm out of milk. And sugar. And just about everything else but mustard."

"I'll live." I didn't care what kind of coffee was provided as long as it wasn't decaf.

"Okay. I need to understand this before we can talk about what Jax may or may not have seen. Do animals have a vocabulary, or is it more like a vision?"

I took a sip of coffee as I tried to think of a good way to explain it. "It's a combination. If an animal has learned a lot of words, then it's more like a mental conversation. But most of the time it's, I don't know, like sensory perception. I can see, feel, and sometimes even hear, their thoughts."

"How do you ask a question?"

"It can be tricky. Depending on the animal's intelligence, and some other stuff, I can usually just think a question, with a little added imagery, and get a solid answer. Like I did with Dusty." I ran my hand over the cat, who had settled contentedly in my lap. "He's a very smart cat. I just asked about you, while kind of showing him your face and . . ." I paused. I'd never really attempted to put what I did into words. It was proving to be both a challenge and a thrill.

Kai was waiting for me to finish.

"I don't know, questions are . . . they have a different feeling. In my head. Like opening a door or a box. I open the box with an image and a thought and wait for the animal to fill it."

I focused on Kai's face, wondering if anything I'd just said made a lick of sense. He was listening. Frowning, but listening.

"Anyway, like I said, Dusty was easy. He likes to talk. And sometimes animals just tell me things on their own. Like when you went to get the coffee, Dusty was very interested. He thought you might be opening a can of tuna. He told me that sometimes you pour the water from the can on his dry food. When you do that, he always makes sure to leave a whole lizard on the back step. Head and all. Even though that's his favorite part." I took a sip of coffee to shut myself up.

Kai's pensive look had changed. He was staring at me in flabbergasted silence.

"Um . . . anyway. I guess I'm trying to say that, normally, I can get plenty of information from a dog as smart as Jax. But right now, it's just too much for him."

Kai wrinkled his brow. "Post-traumatic stress?"

"It happens to people all the time." I searched his face for a sign of comprehension, but saw only doubt. "It may be hard to believe that a dog could be so affected, but he is."

"So you went to Mark's last night to try and jog something loose?"

"That was my hope."

"Where was the dog?"

"Jax was in Bluebell a few blocks away." At his confused look, I added, "Bluebell's my Suburban."

Kai was probably thinking, *Great, I'm sitting here with a woman who talks to animals and names her cars.*

"Anyway, I never got the chance to take him through the house. Maybe now it won't matter."

"Because you believe Jennifer Weston's suggestion that Burke killed Mark?"

"Yes. It makes sense, doesn't it?"

Kai shook his head. "No. If you're right about Jax feeling betrayed by the killer, Burke doesn't fit. He wasn't close enough."

I chose not to comment. Instead I said, "There's something else. I got one solid thing from Jax. Kind of solid. Jaguar."

"Jaguar? What, like the team? The animal?"

"The animal, I think."

"You think."

I let out a long, measured breath. "It's not an exact science."

Kai sat looking at me, those intelligent eyes probing. Uncertainty filled his face.

I returned his gaze and sighed. Of all people to reveal my ability to, I'd picked a man who dealt in tangible facts and physical evidence. How could I expect him to understand? "I'm aware that you usually don't work like this. You're just going to have to trust me."

"It's hard to trust what you don't understand."

"I'm sorry. I realize this is a lot for someone like you to grasp—"

"Someone like me?"

"What I mean is you don't get it. You're never going to get it because you can't dissect it under a microscope." I tried to ignore the warm stirring of my temper.

"I'm a scientist."

"I understand that. But you have to trust my instincts."

Kai regarded me for a long moment before consenting. "Okay, so *jaguar* points to Burke because he was Charm's handler. But why would Jax consider him trustworthy? Don't dodge the question this time, Grace."

Damn.

I hate breaking promises, I really do. But as I sat there looking at Kai's stern, handsome face, I realized my loyalties had changed. Kai believed me. Reluctantly and not completely. But enough.

"Mark Richardson was gay. He and Burke were dating."

Ignoring Kai's snort of disbelief, I plowed into the story. When I'd finished, he sat shaking his head.

"And you believe this, why? Just because Jennifer Weston swears it's true? What if she's just pointing the blame away from herself?"

"I thought the same thing. But I know she's innocent. Jax cleared her." I explained the happy reunion.

"After you found Burke's body, you said Jax told you he was murdered. You were telling the truth, weren't you?"

I nodded.

"You've obviously changed your mind. Why? Why trust him to be right about Jennifer and wrong about Burke?"

"I was caught off guard at Burke's. The smell for one, but mostly mentally. I have to be calm to face something like that with an animal so close. Otherwise it . . . it can be hard."

"That's why you gave up the vet practice. Because of the connection."

Maybe I'd underestimated Kai's ability to understand me. "Sometimes it's too much. Sensory overload."

Kai studied me for a moment. I couldn't tell what he was thinking, only that he seemed to be deciding something. I waited. Dusty had assumed the form of a loaf of bread on my lap. Front feet tucked under, tail curving along his side. His purr was a constant thrum. He had reached the meditative state achieved only by cats and *Shaolin* monks.

Suddenly, I was exhausted. I wanted to close my eyes and cocoon myself in the cat's delta brainwaves. But Kai's cell phone chirped, and Dusty and I both jumped.

Kai got up to answer, and I realized it was getting late. The morning sun streamed through the windows.

I was moving a disgruntled Dusty off my lap when Kai came back into the room.

"Grace. There's been a development."

CHAPTER 21

The tone of Kai's voice was like a seven-pointed spur in my side. I stood, drowsiness dissolving like fog under a bright, burning sun.

He took the mug from my hand. "Come on, let's get a refill."

I didn't need a refill. Released from the feline tranquilizer, my nerves had zinged back to life. More caffeine was a bad idea . . . I followed him into the small, neat kitchen anyway.

Glancing around the U-shaped room, I noticed two things: One, Kai was a neat freak. Two, he was a cook. Either that, or he had a serious knife fetish. The exterior wall, with the requisite over-the-sink window, was adorned with more cutlery than I'd ever seen. Displayed like artwork on magnetic strips were everything from colossal cleavers to delicate boning knives.

Kai's big news momentarily forgotten, I stared at the glinting blades. "Whoa. What's up, Dahmer?"

Kai smiled and handed me my mug. "More like Jack the Ripper."

My expression must have been comical because he laughed.

"Should I fling this hot coffee in your face and run?"

"Wouldn't Dusty have told you if I chopped people up? He seems to have spilled every other bean." Kai leaned against the counter and grinned over the rim of his mug.

"Probably."

"An interesting way to do background checks on prospective dates."

Not knowing what to say to that, I took a swig of coffee and changed the subject. "So what's the news?"

His smile dimmed. "I think you might have been right to believe Jennifer Weston. The license plates came back on the cars entering Mark's neighborhood. Burke's car is on the video."

"So that puts him at the crime scene, right?"

"It puts him in the area. We got some things off his body that place him in the house. Of course, he had jaguar hairs on his clothes that matched the one we found on Mark. And a piece of confetti similar to the stuff Mark used at his party was stuck in the tread of Burke's shoe."

"So that's it? He did it? Case closed?" This seemed like terrific news. But for some reason, Kai didn't seem happy.

"No. Normally, it would be that cut and dry, but a little bird told me she thought Burke was murdered. So I asked Maggie to run a more complete tox screen, and scrape his nails for trace evidence."

My lips parted in astonishment.

He shrugged. "It never hurts to be thorough. Plus, telling me Burke was murdered didn't help LaBryce, but you did it anyway. I knew you believed he hadn't committed suicide."

"Was he murdered?"

"Maybe." Kai set his mug on the counter. "There are some irregularities. It seems Burke ingested wine before he died. But no bottle or glass was found in the house. He could have consumed it elsewhere, but it was odd. The angle of the entry on the gunshot wound is also unusual. Not the typical temple shot—too far back on his skull. There also seems to be evidence of unexplained bruising around the area."

"Okay. What does all that mean?"

"Nothing. At least it didn't until about five minutes ago. We found foreign DNA on his body. I just got the results. Burke had epithelial cells from a woman under his fingernails."

"A woman?" For a moment I thought Kai was going to accuse me of being the donor. Guess I'm paranoid.

"With seven common alleles to Mark Richardson."

"English?"

"The DNA belongs to a close female relative."

"You mean . . ." I felt my mouth drop open.

"We're getting a warrant for Gardenia Richardson's DNA. Or trying to."

"Holy shit."

"Yep."

"You think she murdered Burke?"

"I think it's possible. If she knew about Burke and Mark. She would have suspected. Because of the condition of the body, time of death is less accurate. According to LaBryce, Burke sent him a text the morning after the murder to say he was going to be late. So he was alive then. Gardenia Richardson could have killed Burke anytime after that."

I tried playing the scenario in my head: Gardenia suspects Burke had killed her son. She drugs him in an attempt to make him confess and then helps him pull the trigger. Cold. Calculated. It fit her perfectly.

But then, why had she asked me to find the identity of the killer?

I told Kai about my meeting with Gardenia.

"Why would she bully me into looking for Mark's killer if she knew it was Burke?"

"Maybe he didn't confess. One thing seems off to me, though. I would think she would get someone else to do her bidding."

"Not if she wanted to keep it all a secret. Miz Gardenia

would never want anyone to know her son was gay. Silencing Burke was her only option. Even if he denied killing Mark."

We stood sipping coffee in thoughtful silence for a moment. Dusty wandered into the kitchen to inspect his bowl and, finding no tuna, took a lengthy drink of water.

Preparing for a hot day of lizard hunting.

"Do you think a judge will give you a warrant?" I asked.

"Eventually. There are some on the bench who are not fans of the governor, but they're smart enough to tread cautiously when it comes to the Clarke family."

Unlike moi, I thought. "Jesus, I wanted to poke at the woman for threatening me. Talk about stupid."

"Well, you won't have to worry about it now. Even if we get her on trial, and she gets off, the damage will be done."

The idea should have made me smile, but it didn't. "Mark has already been a victim once. It sucks that he'll have to be again."

"No way to keep him out of it. Unless Gardenia falls on her sword and claims that when she found out her son had been killed by a stalker, she confronted him and then killed him in a fit of temporary insanity."

Kai and I looked at each other, and I could tell we were thinking the same thing. That if it came down to it, that was exactly what she would do. With her team of lawyers, they could build a believable case.

"She'll get off," I said.

"Maybe. Probably," he amended. "It's way too early in the game to tell."

"At least she'll be arrested. Which means she'll have a mug shot." I smiled at that cheerful thought, and then realized something. "I'm supposed to go out there today. To the Clarke estate. Actually, to Bo Bishop's cabin in the back forty. Should I cancel?"

"Hot date?" Something in Kai's tone said he was only half joking.

"Yeah, I love men who shoot animals for fun. They're totally my type."

"Kind of a redneck, isn't he?"

"Kind of?" I rolled my eyes and went to rinse out my mug. "Did you see his artwork?"

"You mean the poster of the blonde wearing nothing but chaps?"

"I missed that one."

"It was in his bedroom."

"Eew! No. Why were you in his bedroom?"

"He was a person of interest." Kai took my mug and put it in the dishwasher.

"Seriously?" Bo had made my list, too, based on his familiarity with Jax.

"Yep. But we talked to the guard at the entrance to the estate, and he verified Bo's account of coming home somewhere between eleven thirty and twelve."

"And you had LaBryce." I gave him a pointed look.

"A suspect who threatened to kill Mark and couldn't tell us where his missing gun was." There might have been a smidgeon of defensiveness in Kai's voice. It was hard to tell; he had turned his back to me to rinse out the coffeepot.

Wiping his hands on a dishtowel, he moved to face me and asked, "Anyway, why would you cancel your appointment with him?"

"I might not be able to avoid stopping at the main house. If Gardenia knows I'm there, she'll want to talk to me. The woman's a predator—she might be able to smell my smugness."

"What time are you going?"

"This afternoon."

"By the time you get there, she'll either already know from one of her spies or we'll have served the warrant." He hung the towel on the oven door and studied me. "Are you sure that's why you want to cancel?"

"What do you mean?"

"You must get attached to the animals you take care of. It can't be easy to let Jax go."

I felt a lump clog my throat. Kai was right. It was hard. "It sucks. But thankfully, I don't foster or quarantine animals very often. Especially now that I'm . . ." I'd almost said homeless, but I realized it wasn't true. Even with her griping, Emma had gone out of her way to make me feel welcome.

"You're what?"

"House hunting. I'll find the right place sooner or later."

We made our way out of the kitchen back toward the living room. "The house across the street's for sale. If you've got a half a mil."

"Jeez. You moonlight as a heart surgeon or something?"

"Nope. I got this place for a steal. It was my parents' house." Kai pulled the slider open and Dusty slunk out. Ready for the hunt.

"You grew up here?"

"Yep. Couldn't stand to move off the beach, so I bought it from my mom." He looked around. "I've changed some stuff. You know, updated this and that."

"It looks great." I meant it. I was envious. Having a place to fix up, with my sister's help, of course, would be a dream come true. "One day."

"Well, if you get a place that needs work, you can call me. I've had to learn how to do more fixing up than I ever wanted."

He'd walked me to the door and we stood looking at each other for a heartbeat. Suddenly, I cared that I hadn't combed my hair or bothered to make sure my socks matched. I looked down at my feet, on impulse, just to be sure. Both white. Safe.

I looked back up into Kai's face, and he smiled. "After all this is over, I really do hope you call me. Even if you don't need my mad home improvement skills."

"Isn't the guy supposed to call the girl?"

"I guess." Kai leaned in and kissed my forehead. Somehow, he made the platonic gesture passionate. I felt my body go very still, my heart stumbling in my chest like it was intoxicated.

Maybe it was.

Before he opened the door, he murmured, "I'll call," in my ear.

I still had goose bumps when I climbed into Bluebell.

So completely distracted by the sensation his promise had elicited from my body, I almost didn't notice the car parked down the street.

The frigging black sedan.

Morning light gleamed off the windshield like a mirror. I put Bluebell in reverse and turned toward the sedan. A Mercedes.

As I pulled up alongside and stopped, the car's window slid down. Stein. The Richardsons' lawyer smiled at me benignly. I cranked my window down.

"Why are you following me?"

"Mrs. Richardson would like an update. Your friend is being released. No one else has been arrested. Have you made any progress?"

I wanted to laugh in his face but knew better. I counted to ten and forced myself to be polite. "Actually, I have."

He waited expectantly.

"I'm still ironing out a few wrinkles. Tell your boss I'll call her tomorrow."

"Someone might come forward by then." I had no idea what he meant. He knew it, because he continued, "To collect the reward. Buck and Gardenia have decided to offer one hundred thousand dollars to anyone who can provide information leading to the arrest of Mark's killer."

A hundred grand? I blinked at him, mouth agape.

"They are holding a press conference to announce it very soon. Gardenia asked that I be sure you were informed." With a dip of his chin, Stein raised his window and drove away.

I sat there for several seconds, trying to process this news. Why would they offer a reward if she knew the killer was Burke? To confuse things? Or possibly because the governor had wanted to, and Gardenia didn't want to refuse. That would mean he didn't know what his wife had done.

Well, good ol' Buck was in for a surprise.

Unless . . .

A horn blasted me out of my reverie. Waving an apology to the car behind me, I hit the gas and turned onto Ocean

Boulevard. Not the fastest way home, but I could go slower and think.

A hundred grand was a lot of money. Not to the Richardsons, but to a lot of people. Including me. I let myself daydream for a minute about how much of a bolster that kind of money would be for my house fund. I could get something on the beach, close to the water, and have a yard.

I was sure I wasn't the only person who would have a similar fantasy. The cops would be overrun with "tips."

Maybe that was the point. Keep the cops chasing false leads 'til the waters were so muddy there would be no hope of clearing things up.

If that was the plan, it was too late.

• • •

The press of a cold, wet nose against my cheek nudged me awake. I opened my eyes and tried to focus on my assailant. Jax let out a salutatory snort, spraying me with fine droplets of slobber.

"Eew." *Move.* I pushed at his chest. He stepped back, and I blinked at the DVD clock. Past noon. I had slept for over four hours.

Wiping moisture off my face, I sat up and swung my legs off the couch. It hadn't been my intention to pass out. I had just closed my eyes to rest for a minute.

I smiled at the Doberman. "Where's Emma?"

Emma gone. He glanced at the foyer and back.

"Did anyone call?"

That one was beyond him.

"Never mind. I'll check." *Sonja should have called by now.*

I walked into the kitchen and began fishing through my purse for my phone. A few seconds later, I spotted it on the counter. Evidently, Emma had plugged it in for me.

I scooped it up and checked my voice mail. There was one message.

Sonja's warm voice filled my ear, and I knew she had good news. "Hey, just checking in. Moss's kidneys look good. He's sleeping right now. I'll call when we know more. Don't worry, girl. He's doing much better."

I breathed a sigh of relief. If his other tests came out as clean, he would be fine. Tears stung my eyes, and I had to laugh. Jax was looking at me with apprehension.

Okay? He let out a short whine.

I patted his head and sniffed. *I'm fine.* "I don't think I've cried this much in years. Every other day, I'm boo-hooing like an idiot."

I unplugged my phone and went to drop it into my purse. It vibrated loudly in my hand. Emma must have put it in silent mode so I could sleep. I smiled and flipped it open. "Hello?"

"Miss Wilde? This is Bo Bishop."

I grimaced. "Mr. Bishop. I'm so sorry I haven't had a chance to settle on a time for today. I had an emergency to deal with."

"Everythin' all right?"

"Yes. Again, I'm sorry."

"No problem. You want to come on out now?" he drawled. "I'm finished with most of my chores."

"I can be there by one or one thirty."

"That'd be fine. You know where to find me."

I stuffed my phone back in my purse and stared blankly at the clock on the microwave. A ball of apprehension had settled in my gut as I'd spoken to Bo Bishop. Was it because I was soon going to have to give up Jax?

No. That wouldn't hit until I handed him over to Bo. Today was just a social event.

I didn't want to see Gardenia again.

Not that I was afraid of her. It was more that I was afraid if she pushed me, I'd be tempted to push back. She would soon be stripped of some of her social clout. Gardenia would lose her sway over Emma's career.

And therefore, over me.

I smiled, though it was probably more of a maniacal grin. I wouldn't have to go to the main house if I didn't want to. I wouldn't ever have to see the woman again.

"Free at last."

CHAPTER 22

I sang out loud with Janis Joplin about freedom and feeling good with a boy named Bobby as I drove toward Mandarin. So cheery was my mood that even the thunderheads looming ahead didn't dampen my spirits.

Kai had called. He had lifted a good print off the anti-freeze bottle and was running it for a match.

"Cavanaugh is goin' down, Jax."

I turned the radio to a respectable level and pulled Bluebell off the main road, rattling to a stop at the guard booth.

Empty. I stared at the gate. Closed.

"What the hell?" I retrieved my phone from my purse. One missed call. Stupid thing was still on vibrate. I wouldn't have been able to hear it ring anyway.

I tried to call Bo.

The reception was sketchy, but at least I could hear when he answered.

"I'm locked out."

"Sorry about that. You'll have to punch in the code."

After he said it, I noticed the keypad. I cranked down

my window, and hanging most of my upper body out of the Suburban, I managed to enter the numbers he gave me.

There was a buzz, and I was allowed entrance.

Following the road as it meandered under the canopy of huge live oaks, I slowed as I rounded the final turn to the grand estate. In the storm-tinted light, the mansion took on a gothic, foreboding air.

I glanced back at Jax. He sat at attention in the backseat. I could sense his interest and curiosity, but I didn't feel any familiarity. Jax apparently had never been here with Mark to visit his family.

I swept my gaze back over the majestic estate. Spanish moss swayed in the quickening wind. There was no sign of movement around the grounds or in any of the windows.

Jax shifted anxiously in his seat.

"Creepy, huh?" I eased my foot off the brake and continued past the house, out of the grove of enormous oaks, and finally bounced along toward Bo's lakeside home.

Unlike the antebellum mansion, the shotgun cabin perched at the water's edge seemed to brighten in the odd light.

Coasting slowly to a stop near the large magnolia tree that sat in front of the cabin, I turned in my seat to face Jax. "Well, whatcha think? This is going to be your new home."

Jax answered with an apprehensive whine. He wasn't sure he wanted a new home.

I smiled at him. "Don't worry. If he doesn't measure up, you're staying with me." I reached around and patted Jax on the head. "I'll be right back."

I left the window cracked and hopped out of Bluebell. Once again, I heard the hounds yapping from the kennel. Hopefully, Jax would get used to his noisy neighbors. I assessed the cabin as I shuffled through the blanket of magnolia leaves. Though the place lacked charm, and the area around it was a little cluttered, the air was clean, and there was plenty of room for Jax to stretch his legs.

It would be an ideal place for a dog with Jax's energy.

Lots of space to throw a tennis ball.

I walked up the steps to the cabin door and knocked.

No answer.

As I waited, the breeze shifted—became cooler. Thunder grumbled in the distance. Rain was not far off. I searched for a doorbell and, finding none, knocked again.

Strange. I'd just talked to him.

"Bo?"

Moving to one of the dusty windows that flanked the door, I peered inside. I could see into the small kitchen and past it into the living area. Empty, aside from the stuffed deer heads on the wall and the arsenal of firearms in the display case. I remembered Kai's comment about the redneck décor and smiled.

"Hello?" I rapped on the glass. Nothing.

I turned and looked past the magnolia toward the barn. Maybe Bo had gone up to the kennel. Trudging around the tree, through the leathery leaves, and up the hill, I called out again.

The hounds had quieted some. But the hush held a restlessness. The approaching storm was making them uneasy. Before I moved into the barn and, with it, the minds of a dozen nervous hounds, I pulled up my mental shield.

Brain buffer in place, I walked through the large open doorway. The blueticks welcomed me with happy barks and lolling tongues.

"Hi, guys." I looked around the cavernous interior. There were no separate rooms that I could see. So where was Bo? I was getting tired of looking all over hell and half of Georgia for someone who was supposed to be meeting me.

My irritation was building as fast as the thunderheads. Reminded of the storm, I tried to be more charitable toward my absent host. Who knew what kind of battening down needed to be done?

With one last glance around, I started to turn and leave when something caught my eye. A box with a bright red-and-blue label. A case of antifreeze.

I was struck with a feeling of dread so acute I was surprised I hadn't cried out.

Taking a small sip of air, then another, I tried to think.

Lots of people use this brand of antifreeze, I told myself rationally.

Instinct roared to life, drowning out weak, wavering reason.

Before my mind had given the order, my feet were moving. Propelling me out of the barn and down the hill. Something stopped me only a few feet away from the barn. I scanned the cabin and tree line, listening.

Rumbling thunder. Wind rattling through leaves and branches. Jax started barking. A slow tingle snaked up my spine. They were not happy or excited barks. They were fast, harsh, and panicked—a warning.

A cold shiver shot through to my core. I looked toward Bluebell. The view was partially obstructed by the large tree, but I could see Jax in the back. He wasn't looking at the woods or at the pasture. He was looking at me.

No. He was looking behind me.

I felt myself go still as fear seeped into me. I had walked into a viper's nest.

"Hey, there, Miss Wilde."

I tried not to jump at the sound of the drawling voice. Mind racing, I turned, struggling to conceal my horror with mild surprise.

"You startled me."

"Did I?" Eyes blazing with some dark inner fire, Bo twisted his lips into a crooked smile.

I tried to smile back, pretending not to notice the ax handle he was holding in one hand. "I knocked. I thought you would be in the cabin."

He returned my comment with a long, narrowed stare. "I reckoned you'd figure it out once you got out here."

"Figure what out?"

"At first, I didn't believe Gardenia about you being able to talk to animals."

"What?" I barely breathed the word.

"But I figure why take the risk?"

I took a small step back. *Stay calm.* I had to keep my head. *Think. Don't panic.*

"I don't know what you're talking about."

"Come on, now. Don't play dumb. You know Jax saw me kill Mark."

Jax had seen it, I was sure, but with my mind shielded from his thoughts by distance, I was spared the sight. I swallowed hard against the bile that rose in my throat. I had to think. It was hard to focus. Jax was barking like mad. Angry, panicked barks. I didn't have to be linked to his mind to know he wanted to tear Bo apart.

I wanted to give him the chance. If I could get to Bluebell . . . I glanced back. About fifty feet—it seemed a mile away.

I had to focus. *Think.* "Are you going to kill me, too?"

"I didn't want to have to. I tried to get rid of Jax without hurting anyone else."

"You were trying to kill Jax with the antifreeze." Anger momentarily seared away my fear.

"I know you won't believe this, but I ain't no murderer."

"Really? What are you?" I edged another step back.

"I didn't meant to kill Mark. But he made me so angry. I'm just tryin' to protect my family."

"How was killing Mark protecting anyone?"

"Because he was goin' to write a book. A book!" he said louder, as if I needed to understand what a book was. "About the family and all the dirty little secrets! It would have destroyed our father, his career. I couldn't let him."

"Your father? You mean Buck Richardson?"

"He's a great man. He'll be president one day." The fanatical pride in his voice chilled me more than any threat could.

"Not if you do this." I tried to ease another step backward. "The police know I'm coming out here. You won't get away with killing me, too. And then everyone will know. The controversy will kill Buck's chances."

"You think I'm stupid? I'm not gonna kill you. You're gonna get in an accident."

He saw my gaze flick to the ax handle.

"That's right." He grinned. A wicked, distorted grin.

"You catch on quick. A little bump on the head and you and your truck will end up in the lake."

"They'll figure it out," I said, trying to keep him talking. *Think, Grace! If I could just get to Jax . . .*

He chuckled. "They won't find you. That lake's an old limestone quarry. A few feet out it drops off to seventy feet, straight down." He made a whistling noise. "If they do find you, by the time they drag you out of there, the critters will've eaten you up. They won't be able to tell it was more than an accident."

Thunder cracked and roared as rain began to fall. "You're wrong. The cops are smart. They'll know I was murdered." I inched back another step, heart hammering in my chest. Fighting panic, I tried not to think about the fact that I was talking to a murderer. "They know Burke was murdered."

"What?" His eyes narrowed. I eased back another step. The hill was becoming slippery. I tried to think of a way I could use it to my advantage.

"Alexander Burke didn't commit suicide. He was killed. The cops know. And they know about Mark's relationship with Burke."

Bo's smile morphed into a sneer. "He should have let Mark be. But he talked Mark into writing that damn book. About our family! Brothers don't do that. In this family you cover for each other. You've got each other's back."

"So you killed him."

"You wouldn't understand."

"You're right. I don't. I'm sure they won't either." I pointed to the dirt road.

The bluff worked. Bo turned to see who I was talking about.

I spun and flew down the hill. Immediately, I heard footsteps closing in behind me. I wasn't going to make it.

Bo's hand clamped on my elbow but slipped off. A few more steps and he snaked his arm around the tops of my shoulders. On instinct, I planted my feet, dropped my weight, and tried to throw him the way I had practiced with Emma.

Instead of slamming into the ground, he skidded past, and went down on one knee. Which put him between me and my only escape.

Shit!

I needed a weapon. Too far to try to go back to the barn. Picturing the gun cabinet and its stockpile of firearms, I sprinted for the cabin.

Careening into the door, I clawed at the handle. Locked. Through the wind and pounding rain, I could hear Bo crashing through the leaves. No time.

Frantically, I looked around for a weapon or an escape. I caught sight of an access hole leading under the house. Like a hunted rabbit, I dove for the opening and scrambled through.

A hand snagged one of my ankles, and I was dragged backward. Spinning onto my back, I kicked out. My heel connected with a satisfying crunch. Bo bellowed like an enraged bear.

He brought his hands up to his shattered nose.

Ankle free, I crab-crawled backward farther under the house. My gaze was locked on the murderer kneeling just outside. Tears and blood streamed down his face. He spit out a string of curses and stood.

For a moment, I was relieved. Chest heaving, I tried to adjust to the dark of the dimly lit crawl space. Water ran into my eyes. I wiped it away with the back of my hand. There was only about two feet of space between the earth and the cabin. Not enough room for Bo to wield the ax handle. Under the house, we were on a more even playing field. Still, I felt trapped.

I've got to get out of here. Scanning the outer walls, I saw a shaft of light coming from another opening on the right side of the cabin.

I started toward it on my hands and knees but stopped just a few feet away. The opening was partly blocked by several pipes. I could never squeeze through the hole.

I felt another wave of panic. I was beginning to feel claustrophobic. The ground seemed to be rising up—the crawl space shrinking.

I opened my mouth to sob or scream or something else

pathetic, but choked back the impulse. Crying and screaming wouldn't do any good. The creak of a floorboard sounded
overhead. I held my breath, listening. Bo's muffled voice
traveled down through the floor.

"There's nowhere to run to. Stupid bitch. You hear?"

Footsteps echoed above me. I searched for another
escape. Then I heard something that made my heart stumble
in my chest.

The ratcheting sound of a cartridge being chambered.

Bo Bishop had a shotgun.

I crouched motionless, straining to listen over the thun-
derous beat of my heart. Would he shoot through the floor?
I could hear Bo talking, cursing, walking. It sounded like
he was moving toward the front door.

I was frozen. Petrified. Where could I go? I stared at the
opening I had come through. I couldn't go that way. Bo
would be coming out of the cabin any second.

"Move," I ordered myself in a ragged whisper. "Move if
you want to live."

My body obeyed. I began crawling furiously toward the
back of the cabin. I slammed my knee into a root and scraped
my shins on an exposed cinderblock, but my mind barely
registered these things. I had to put as much distance as
possible between me and the hole Bo was sure to crawl
through any second.

As I neared the opposite end of the cabin, I heard the
front door slam. I glanced back over my shoulder but kept
crawling. My hand sank into something wet.

I looked down. Water. I had crawled to the far side of the
cabin. The side closest to the lake. My gaze shot up. I wasn't
looking at a wall. There was no wall. A thin sliver of weak
light danced on the water's surface. What I'd assumed was
a solid exterior wall was an illusion. It was the underside of
steps leading to a small floating dock. The cabin went right
to the water's edge.

I crawled forward, fingers groping in the muck. After
only a foot, I felt a steep slope. *A few feet out it drops off.*
Sucking in a deep breath, I plunged into the cool water.

My chest and legs scraped the ground as I wriggled under the steps. I swam hard at a downward angle, kicking madly with my heavy, sodden tennis shoes.

A ghostly light materialized above me. I changed directions, knowing I was past the floating pier.

Breaking the water's surface, I gasped. The sound was muted by the driving rain. Treading quietly, I looked back toward shore. I scanned the back of the cabin. There was no sign of Bo.

I could still hear Jax barking like mad. He was desperate now. In a frenzy. I had the feeling he could still see Bo. That meant he wasn't crawling under the house looking for me.

He was waiting.

Waiting for me to come out. Like a cat waits to pounce on his prey.

Swimming around the dock toward the side of the house closest to where I'd parked, I pulled myself up the sharply sloped bank into the tall reeds. Though I knew the rain concealed my movements, every crackle of the dry stalks seemed magnified in my ears. I lay still for a moment, trying to steady my breathing. Rising slowly to my feet, I crept along the side of the cabin.

I stopped at a window and peeked over the sill. Looking past the interior of the house, I strained to see through the windows by the front door. Bo's figure came into view. He was standing with his back to the Suburban, pointing a shotgun down at the access hole I'd crawled through.

Shaking from fear and exertion, I turned and flattened my back against the wall. I was only twenty feet from Bluebell. But he had a shotgun.

No time to dwell on that. *Don't think, run!*

I surged forward and sprinted.

I had only gone a few feet when I heard the sound of boots, heavy on the ground behind me. I willed myself to run faster. To live.

I was only steps from the truck now. I reached forward and clasped the door handle. I pulled and felt the door begin to swing open.

An explosion of pain shot through my head as I was shoved forward into the door. It slammed shut. The metallic taste of blood filled my mouth. Bo pressed his weight against me, penning me to the door. He clawed his hand into my hair and yanked. I cried out. Snarling, Jax lunged at the window and dug frantically at the door.

A scene burst though my mind. Fast and violent.

A memory. Jax's memory. Mark Richardson's murder was played out in sickening clarity—

Mark holding up his hands, then backing away. Then shouting and a loud *pop*. Mark's head snapping back. His body falling, slumping back on the white couch. The murderer standing over him, a look of fury and disgust on his face. Speaking words in the same voice I heard in my own ear.

"You broke my nose, bitch."

I tried to fight off the nauseating terror that beat against the inside of my skull like the tail of a caged alligator. But the memory had been so filled with desperate emotion and crippling fear, I was paralyzed. I stood limp and defenseless as a rag doll in the hands of a cruel child.

"You are gonna pay." Bo slammed my face against the window. White light flared over my vision. Blinding pain splintered across my cheekbone.

Broken.

I could feel a trickle of blood flow from my lip. It smeared on the glass and was washed away by the driving rain.

Tired, beaten, and sopping wet. What a miserable way to die.

I felt my breath shudder out in surrender.

Jax crashed into the window. I blinked, focusing through the glass on the dog. He was frenzied. Snapping and snarling. The feral beast within him had broken free. Reaching out, I latched onto it—let his rage burn into me.

I curled my fingers around the door handle, all my energy centered on holding on . . . I only had to wait a second for the chance I hoped for.

Hand still fisted in my hair, Bo jerked me back.

I gripped the handle as if it was a lifeline. Maybe it was.

The muscles and sinew of my arm popped and tore as I was wrenched back to the ground. But the door swung open.

A snarling blur leapt out of the Suburban.

Jax's feet barely hit the ground before he lunged forward and slammed Bo sidelong to the muddy earth.

I tried to scuttle back out of the way. My arm buckled, my injured shoulder unable to take my weight.

Bo lifted the shotgun to aim at the dog. But Jax was fast. He sprang forward and sank his teeth into Bo's wrist. Screaming, he released the gun. It clattered out of his hands.

Awkwardly, I lurched forward in the dirt, my hand outstretched, reaching for the gun.

Bo brought his knees up and kicked. Jax tumbled away with a sharp yelp. Bo twisted onto his side and groped for the shotgun.

In an instant, Jax was on him again. This time he went for Bo's face. Screeching, Bo writhed and twisted, trying in vain to fend off the enraged animal. Snarling, Jax ripped at Bo's cheek, and then clamped down on his throat.

Bo let out a gurgled cry.

I scurried forward on my knees, grabbed the gun, and cradling the butt in the crook of my arm, managed to point it at Bo. Jax's feverish anger filled me. I was swept away by it. I felt my own anger surge. I wanted to kill this man. He was a murderer.

But you're not. I squeezed my eyes shut. I was shaking violently. I had to bring myself under control.

Don't kill him. "Jax. Leave him. Come." My voice was a quaking whisper. I swallowed and tried again. "Jax." My voice was stronger now. I couldn't let him kill Bo. As much as he deserved it. "Jax! *Heir!*"

The German command reached the animal's febrile mind. Jax stilled and slowly obliged, leaving Bo in a moaning heap. Blood was smeared on his face, he had one hand holding the wound at his throat.

I would not be his executioner. Neither would Jax.

I kneeled in the downpour, shivering like a nervous

Chihuahua, and knew I didn't have long. Shock could kill as surely as a homicidal maniac.

"Get up." Though I said it to myself, Bo's voice answered. "I can't. Help."

The sound of his voice rebooted my survival circuits. He sounded way too healthy for a guy who'd just had a Doberman use his throat as dental floss. I was way too close.

Dragging one foot under me, I was able to shift my weight and stand. I knew my phone got little or no reception here. Factoring in the storm, my best bet to reach help was the cabin phone. To get to the cabin, I'd have to walk past Bo. And then, I'd have to leave him outside.

This shouldn't have been difficult, but thinking about losing sight of him reminded me of every slasher movie ever made. Where the girl turns her back on the dead or dying psycho and he lurches back to life.

While I stood debating in the droning hiss of the rain, I became aware of movement behind me. If Jax hadn't been there, I don't think I would have noticed the car at all.

The sporty BMW splashed to a stop. Jennifer climbed out, her face flitting through a bevy of emotions—confusion and fear being most pronounced.

Jax whined. *Jen.*

No, Jax. Fuss!

He heeded my command to heel. But whined again, confused.

"Oh my God, Bo!" Jennifer started forward, but I aimed the barrel at her and she froze. "Grace . . . what?"

"Don't move."

She hadn't, but I wanted to be very clear.

"Okay, I'm not moving."

"What are you doing here?" She flicked a glance at Bo.

"Don't look at him, look at me."

"I came to see Bo. He called me and asked me to come by. What happened? What's going on?"

She seemed genuinely surprised, but what did I know? "He tried to kill me."

"What?"

The shock was real. But I didn't let down my guard. "Bo killed Mark. He admitted it."

Jennifer stared at Bo, shaking her head. "No. He would never . . . Bo?"

The murderer was lying on his side, curled in a fetal position. He whimpered, "Help."

"Did you . . . shoot him?" There was no accusation in her voice.

"No. But I will if he moves."

Jennifer blinked and her eyes focused. She seemed to see me for the first time. "You're hurt."

"Yep."

"We need to call 911. Can I go into the cabin and call?"

I thought about it. I desperately wanted to call the cavalry, but I didn't trust Jennifer's sudden appearance. I couldn't stand there all day, so I nodded. "Come back out of the cabin with your hands up."

She nodded and walked inside. I could just see her moving through the windows. Within a few minutes she came out slowly, her hands obediently in the air. The rain had slowed. Soon the fickle Florida storm would be over. The sun would burst through the clouds and we'd be sweltering under its bright rays.

Suddenly, I was unbelievably thirsty. My arm began to tremble under the weight of the shotgun. I could feel my lip and cheek swelling.

I willed the ambulance to fly on Mercury's wings.

"Grace." Jennifer spoke calmly from the stoop. "The police and an ambulance are on the way."

"Good."

Her arms still raised, she walked toward me the way someone would walk toward a spooked horse.

"Stop." I didn't want her to get too close.

The shocked expression had vanished. Now she just looked worried. "Please tell me what's going on."

"Bo killed Mark because he found out he was going to write a book. He thought killing Mark would keep the world from knowing Mark was gay. He was going to kill me, too."

"That doesn't make sense. If Bo wanted to kill you, why would he ask me to come meet him?"

"You tell me." I swung the gun around to her, aiming it more pointedly at her chest.

"I don't know." She looked at Bo's motionless form. He wasn't dead. I could hear him breathing. Every once in a while, he'd moan.

Jennifer sucked in a shocked breath and clamped her hand over her mouth. The sudden movement startled me, and I felt my finger jerk against the trigger. Hard, but not hard enough to make the gun go off. Thank God the gun didn't have a hair trigger. I really didn't want to shoot anyone.

"Jennifer. Don't—do that—again."

She turned her wide-eyed gaze to me and lowered her hand from her mouth. "He was going to kill me, too."

Bo stirred. "Sorry, Jen."

The shock was back. Her eyes flooded with tears. She looked at me, like a puppy that had just been kicked. I lowered the gun to train it on Bo.

Far off, mixed with the sound of the departing thunder and whistling wind, I thought I heard the wail of a siren. I let myself relax a fraction and white-hot pain speared from my shoulder into my hand.

I flinched. My finger brushed the trigger again.

The police really needed to hurry up.

"Grace." Jennifer moved closer toward me. "Here. Give me the gun. You can barely hold it."

I shook my head. Not because I really believed she'd shoot me, but because I wasn't sure I could move my injured arm.

Jennifer reached out with both hands and gently took hold of the shotgun.

"I don't think I can let go with my hurt arm."

"Can you support it with the good one?" Jennifer kept her gaze on Bo while she spoke. Smart girl.

Cradling my arm, I eased away. The motion hurt, but not as much as I expected. Jennifer kept the gun pointed at Bo, and I let out a relieved breath.

After I'd managed to call him off Bo, Jax had been standing sentinel next to me. Now, sensing the release of my fear, he let out a happy whine.

She didn't seem to notice. Her eyes were locked on Bo.

"I've got to sit down." I moved to Bluebell's open door. The step up into the cab, which I typically negotiated with ease, now looked like a mountain. I figured the bumper was as good a place as any to perch, so I walked to the back of the Suburban and lowered myself onto the wet chrome. I listened for the sound of the sirens, but they seemed to have disappeared in the wake of the retreating storm. The wind had settled into a soft breeze, the sun pierced through the clouds in shifting spotlights.

The shotgun blast ruptured the quiet.

I jumped up and spun around. Jennifer stood over Bo, her face expressionless.

"What the hell?" I rushed forward. Bo was on his back, with a hole the size of a cantaloupe where his heart should have been. "Jesus!"

"Is he dead?" Jennifer whispered.

I didn't bother to answer.

"He moved. I jumped and . . . it just went off."

For a split second, I believed her—then Jax, who had been hovering by my side, edged close to the body. He began to whimper and pace. I knew what was coming. But before I could slam my mental door shut, his emotions plowed into me. The jumbled, frenetic feelings were too familiar. My stomach clenched, bile rising in my throat to choke out air.

I stumbled away, gagging and coughing. Using the outside corner of the cabin as support, tears streaming down my face, I tried to breathe. But just as it had before, the thick, foul specter of murder threatened to overwhelm me. Clinging to the wood siding, I sputtered and spit and tried to give myself time to think.

Shooting Bo was not an accident. Jennifer had pulled the trigger—one I personally knew to be quite stable—because she wanted him dead.

Unbidden, pieces of the puzzle began to slide into place. Forming an ugly picture.

The DNA on Alexander Burke. Jennifer's bruises. Her mock romance with Mark. Bo's rant about covering for family. He had been talking about Jennifer Weston.

The specifics eluded my clouded mind, but I knew. The woman standing behind me with a gun was not a sweet girl who'd managed to escape the projects. She was a woman who used her understanding of people to manipulate and murder.

"Grace, are you okay?" Jennifer's voice remained wholesome and guileless. So far, she hadn't realized I'd seen through her charade.

"Yeah." I straightened and turned, hoping I'd schooled my features enough. "Sorry. I shouldn't have looked."

I kept my eyes averted, to prove my point and because I felt if I looked at her, she might see into my head. Jax was still pacing around the body. I didn't dare open my mind to him again. I had to stay focused if I wanted to survive. I whistled to the dog and he came to heel. I released my injured arm to give him a quick pat.

"It was an accident," Jennifer said.

Nodding, I tried to act as if I'd never had my epiphany. But I could think of no words of support or friendship. I remembered the parallel I'd drawn between Jennifer and Emma. Unsettling as it was, I forced myself to act as if Jennifer were my sister.

What would I say if this was Emma . . .

Finally, I was able to speak.

"It's going to be okay. Don't worry." I superimposed my sister's face over Jennifer's so I could meet her gaze. "Are you okay?"

"I think so." She seemed to be studying my face. Looking for something.

I redoubled my efforts to imagine Emma standing in front of me. Hoping I'd arranged my features correctly, I said, "You sure?"

"I'm okay." She motioned to the concrete porch steps. "You should sit down."

As I shuffled toward the stoop, I pretended not to notice she still held the shotgun aimed in my direction. I wanted to look harmless. Exhausted. It was way too easy. I listened again for the wail of the police siren. *Come on, guys . . .*

Understanding registered slowly, as chilling as a winter dawn. The police weren't coming. Jennifer hadn't called them. I cursed myself for a fool.

Way to go, Grace. Brilliant.

Self-recrimination wouldn't do me any good. I had to think. The "wait for the cavalry" option was gone. My mind raced—frenetic as a beehive caught in a wildfire.

I had to assume the only reason I was still breathing was because Jennifer had yet to come up with a way to get rid of me. She had killed Alexander Burke and, with Bo's help, done a fair job of making it look like a suicide.

My death would not be so easy to explain.

When I reached the cabin steps, I paused to collect my thoughts. Finally, I turned and let myself see the woman who held me at gunpoint—and let her see me.

"Whatever plan you're concocting won't work," I told her.

The innocent mask Jennifer wore so effortlessly slipped and fell away.

"Plan?"

"The police might believe you shot Bo in self-defense, but me?" I shook my head.

"I'm not going to shoot you. Bo is."

"That's . . ." I glanced at his body. "Doubtful."

"Actually, it's perfect. Now, turn around. We're going inside."

I moved slowly up the steps toward the open door and tried to gather my wits. How could I get away? Jax was at my side, but he knew Jennifer as one of his masters. If I asked him to attack, he might not obey.

I had to think of something else. As I moved through the doorway into the cabin, my gaze zeroed in on the gun cabinet on the far wall. My left arm was badly injured, but I was right-handed. If I could get to one of the weapons . . . I shook off the thought. I was getting ahead of myself. Before I could come up with a counterstrategy, I needed to know what Jennifer was planning.

"So, how is a dead man going to shoot me?"

"With this."

I turned, and saw Jennifer had shifted the shotgun to cradle under one arm; in the other hand she held a pistol pointed directly at my head.

"Where the hell did you get that?" Shock had me blurting out the asinine question.

"I set it by the door when I came in a few minutes ago. You walked right past it."

I glanced at the small table by the door, stunned.

Jennifer laughed. The sound was melodic and clear as a silver bell. It sent a shiver straight to my core.

"I thought you said you weren't going to shoot me."

"I lied." Her finger began to tighten on the trigger.

"They'll know."

Jennifer paused at my comment—I wasn't about to waste the opportunity.

"The police will know."

"Because it will leave gunshot residue on my hands?" There was a sarcastic bite to her words.

I shouldn't have been surprised she knew the term. After all, she'd staged a suicide.

"It won't matter," she said. "I'm already covered in it."

Grinning, she tilted the shotgun up in a sort of salute.

"Pistols are different. It's not the same type of residue." I had no idea if it was true, but I was more than willing to wing it.

Her eyes narrowed and she lowered the gun, tucking it into the waist of her jeans. Before I could make a move, the shotgun was leveled at me once again.

"The cops might believe you killed Bo in self-defense, but only if you have me to back your story."

She shook her head. "We both know you won't lie to the cops. Especially your cop."

Damn. I'd forgotten she'd met Kai. "I lied to him at Mark's." I knew I was wasting my breath, but I needed time to think. Then, like a bolt of lightning, I remembered—Jennifer had been looking for something at Mark's. Something he would have kept hidden in his desk . . .

The book. If Mark was writing a book, he'd have notes. Or a journal.

"Think about it," I said, trying not to sound as panicked as I felt. "You don't want to screw up like you did with Mark's journal."

"Journal?" Though her tone was questioning, I knew I had her. She wanted the book. I had to make her believe I'd found it.

"It was hidden in Jax's dog bed," I said, trying for nonchalance. "Interesting reading."

She angled her head and studied me. "You're lying."

"Nope." I could bluff my way out of this—I had to. "I have to wonder, though, why not just blackmail Buck Richardson when you found out you were his daughter? It seems a lot easier than pretending to be Mark's girlfriend."

"That was my first choice, believe me." Her gaze remained focused on my face, still searching for signs of deceit. "But Gardenia intervened before I had the chance."

"She knew about you." It came out as a statement because I wasn't as surprised as I should have been.

The reaction worked in my favor because Jennifer's scrutiny eased a little and she huffed out a chuckle.

"That woman knows about everything. I'll admit it was a good plan. Buck and Mark got to keep up appearances, and I got tickets to ride the money train."

"Forever?"

"Of course. The Richardson family would never abandon a poor girl like me. Or wasn't that in the book?"

"I skimmed a few spots. But believe me, you being the governor's daughter is just the tip of the iceberg. There's enough dirt on the family in that journal to bury Buck Richardson. The money train you've been riding . . . derailed."

"Really?" she asked dryly. "That hadn't occurred to me."

"Well, I want to live, and you want to keep the train rolling, right? We can make a deal." Now that I'd convinced her I had the book, I had to come up with a strategy. "If you let me go, I'll give you the journal."

"Where is it, Grace?"

I didn't answer right away—I was still trying to think. "Don't point the gun at me, and I'll tell you."

Quick as a viper, Jennifer racked the shotgun and aimed it at Jax. "I know about your thing with animals. Would it hurt if I shot him?"

Fear ran through me, as keen and cold as a blade. I felt the blood drain from my face. It would hurt. Shield or no shield. Not just because of my ability, but because I loved him.

I thought about giving Jax the command to attack. But even though she was threatening him, he might hesitate. The gun was chambered now, too risky.

"Fine." I heard my own voice, but it sounded dead.

"Well?"

I knew what I was going to do. "It's in the back of my Suburban."

She kept the gun aimed at Jax as she circled away from the door. "Walk. Slowly."

I did. Jax stayed at my side though his movements were jerky. I was sure he knew something was wrong. He was probably confused. I couldn't risk opening up to him. If I was going to pull off my plan, I'd have to be completely focused.

And I needed Jennifer to be distracted.

As I shuffled over the wet ground, I tried to think of something, anything I could say to accomplish that.

Though my mind seemed to be moving slower than a herd of turtles, a question occurred to me.

"Why did Bo go to Mark's house that night? I know he hadn't planned to kill him."

"Really? How's that?"

I stopped and turned slightly to look over my shoulder at her. "Jax saw what happened. Bo and Mark got into an argument, it escalated, and ended with Bo taking Mark's gun and shooting him."

"Jax told you all that?"

"He's a smart dog."

She angled her head and studied me. "Bo was supposed to drop off the suicide note."

"So you were going to kill Burke and make it look like a suicide. How were you going to get rid of Mark?"

"I wasn't. I told you the truth when I said he'd broken things off with Alexander and changed his mind about writing the book."

"Why?"

"I helped him realize Alexander was desperate and controlling. It didn't take much. A few well-timed hang-up calls followed by a couple of bumps in the night to put Jax on alert."

"You were Mark's stalker."

"Actually, Bo was."

"I don't get it. Why go to the trouble to kill Burke if he and Mark had broken up?"

She blinked at me as if I was the dumbest human on earth. "Mark needed to see how disturbed Alex was. So he would understand publishing the book was as sick as the person who'd talked him into writing it."

It was almost comical hearing her referring to others as "disturbed." I would have smiled, if it weren't for the shotgun in her hands.

"Keep walking," Jennifer ordered.

I did. As we neared Bluebell, I said, "So, Bo messed up the plan by killing Mark."

"Actually, it worked out better," she mused. "We were going to drug him and make it look like an overdose. There were a couple of snags, but in the end, a murder-suicide was more believable."

"Makes sense." I wasn't about to tell her the police were

looking more closely at Burke's death. I wanted Jennifer to feel calm and in control.

We reached the back of the Suburban, and I stopped. "I can't open it with my arm like this."

"Sure you can." She moved the gun slightly. "One shot will kill him and blow your knee off."

I let go of my left arm, letting it hang. The movement cost me. A shockwave of pain seared all the way to my fingertips. But at least I knew I could still move it, I'd have to if I was going to live. I reached out and unlatched first one door then the other, swinging them both open wide.

Jennifer had shifted around while I did this. She was slightly behind me.

"Where is it?"

Thankfully, the cargo area of Bluebell was not well organized. There was an assortment of cages and carriers. My medical kit. And my cardboard catchall box. What I wanted was next to the box.

"I think it was sitting on Jax's bag of food."

Jennifer came closer, pressing the shotgun into my ribs. "Find it."

"Okay, okay. It's just a folder." I leaned forward over the box, placing my throbbing hand next to it. I reached with my good arm into the box and rummaged around.

"Grace, if you're messing with me, you're dead."

"Just hang on." Next to the box, I felt my seminumb fingers brush against something cylindrical. With my good hand, I reached into the bottom of the box where I kept an old notebook. "Got it."

I lifted the battered journal. Jennifer's eyes locked onto it. But she couldn't take it without letting go of the shotgun. She started to lower the gun and I shifted my weight, ready to spring.

A siren howled in the distance. Jennifer's head snapped toward the sound. It was a shock to hear, but I didn't waste time pondering the hows or whys.

Leaping forward, I brought the modified stun gun around and jabbed it into Jennifer's belly.

With a jerk, she dropped, crumpling face-first to the wet earth.

The shotgun thudded to the ground next to her. I knew I couldn't hope to pick it up, so I kicked it away.

I straddled her and lowered myself to plant one knee in the middle of her back, which I knew would keep her from reaching the pistol at her waist. I held the stun gun against her cheek. Her eye fluttered open and focused on the prongs of the gun.

I didn't say anything. I didn't have to.

Jax shuffled beside me and whined. I prepared my mind, at least as well as I could at the moment, letting the white noise seep into my thoughts. With a final calming breath, I dropped the barrier between us.

Fear. Confusion. Aggression. All batted at my mind.

Jen? Jax sniffed at Jennifer's face, and sensing her anger, let out a low, short *woof.*

It's okay, boy. "Jax. Sit."

He continued to growl and pace. His eyes shifting from me to Jennifer.

I heard a chuckle, felt the vibration in my knee. "Looks like you're not so great with animals after all."

I ignored Jennifer's remark, focusing instead on reassuring Jax. The police would be there any second. Rushing around, shouting. A confused, afraid dog was a dangerous one. If he snapped, the cops would shoot him.

Not going to happen.

I focused on extending the soothing blankness of my mind. *It's okay, Jax.*

Okay?

Yes, everything is okay.

He still wasn't sure. I could feel him tense as the sirens came closer.

Finally, I gave up trying to force him to calm down by smothering him with comforting thoughts. Instead, I drew him in. Invited him to see Jennifer from my perspective. Her treachery, her greed, her cruelty.

Bad?

Pretty bad.
Like Bo?
Worse.
Help?
No, Jax. I got it. He sat and waited for further directions.
I breathed out a sigh. *You're a good boy, Jax.*
Jax, good boy.

CHAPTER 23

"You ready to face the dragon?" Wes smiled as we stepped onto the elevator at the Police Memorial Building.

"Grace isn't afraid of dragons," Emma said, moving to flank me. "Not even ones as scary as Gardenia Richardson."

"I'm not afraid of her. I just don't want to do this. I don't want my picture in the paper."

"Even for a hundred thousand dollars?" Wes asked.

I sighed, but gave him a half smile. "I guess I can pose for a couple of reporters. But after that, I have no comment."

The last week had been a blur of hospitals, interviews with police, and finally, at Wes and Emma's insistence, meetings with the Richardsons' attorney to claim the reward for identifying Mark's killer.

I had been reluctant at first. But considering the damage to my arm—I would be in a sling for another two weeks—and the fact that I was, technically, the person who had brought Bo's palm print to Kai on the antifreeze bottle, I figured I deserved it. Besides, I had a little surprise for Gardenia.

The doors slid open and Jake, who was standing there waiting, came forward. "Grace, how you feelin'?"

"Good. How's Jax?"

"He's a pain in my ass. My wife lets him sleep in the bed. She treats him like he's our kid or somethin'."

I gave him a grim nod. "Moss really misses him. If things aren't working out—"

"You kidding me? Mary'd divorce me if I got rid of him."

I felt my lips twitch. The burly detective loved Jax. Played tug-of-war with him and fed him scraps. I knew, because I'd asked—Jax adored his new family.

"Come on." Jake motioned down the hall. "Let's feed the vultures, so you can take your check to the bank."

The room was set up with a row of seats in front of a blank wall. A handful of reporters were seated, their cameramen milling around behind.

I felt my nerves begin to jangle. Public speaking freaked me out. Emma must have sensed my sudden urge to bolt, because she murmured, "Remember, you don't have to say anything. Just take the check, shake hands, and smile."

"Got it." I sounded a lot more confident than I felt.

Wes led me to the front of the room and we waited. I saw Kai come in to stand at the back with Jake. We shared a quick smile.

He looked tired. I knew he was working long hours, even though Jennifer Weston was in jail.

Jennifer had been arrested for killing Bo. They were still working on finding evidence in Burke's case.

A murmur from the reporters drew my attention back to the present. The governor had arrived with his petite, demure wife.

The woman had refused my claim to the reward, at first. Then Wes had gotten hold of Mr. Stein and it had been a TKO.

The couple approached with their attorney, who made a few comments and deflected questions pertaining to Jennifer Weston.

The governor had taken the traditional "I deeply regret having an inappropriate relationship . . ." stance in regard to Jennifer's paternity, claiming never to have known of her existence and playing the shell-shocked victim of her schemes and deceit.

The media hadn't let him off the hook. The story was too sensational. But the governor's spin doctors had managed to shine the spotlight more on Jennifer's actions than the affair that led to her birth, insinuating she had befriended Mark, then blackmailed him into feigning a relationship with her.

Wild rumors about assassination plots were given equal airtime with the truth. A smoke-and-mirrors tactic I was sure Gardenia had implemented.

Though Buck Richardson had taken a big hit, the governor had somehow managed to pull some sympathy into his corner. Many saw him and his wife as a devastated couple who'd lost their son and been betrayed not only by Jennifer, but by Bo, the orphan they'd taken in and loved as their own.

Shaking my head inwardly, I tuned out most of what the lawyer said, and before I knew it, it was time for the big photo op.

Buck Richardson and I posed with the check. Flashes strobed and cameras whirred. I moved to Gardenia, but when I took her hand, I made sure she felt the piece of paper I pressed into her palm.

Her false gratitude never wavered as she said quietly, "Grace, you surprise me."

I met her gaze. "Just wait."

After the chatter and hubbub died down, Wes made a final statement, and I walked to the back of the room. Kai angled his head toward the door, and we slipped out.

"Hey." He smiled. "Guess you can be my neighbor now."

"Maybe. Emma's doing the big sister thing. She won't let me move out 'til my arm is better, so . . ." I lifted my good shoulder.

"She almost lost you."

"Almost. But you saved me."

"Technically, you saved yourself."

"Maybe."

The antifreeze bottle had been the key. Bo's palm print

had been a match to a partial found on LaBryce's gun. Kai had tried to call and warn me. I could have saved myself a lot of terror and pain if I'd checked my missed calls.

It meant more than I could say that he'd been worried enough to come riding to the rescue.

Kai's phone beeped, and after glancing at the message, he looked at me and smiled. Oh man, did he know how to smile.

"I have more good news," he said. "You're not going to have to testify against Jennifer."

"I won't?" I asked with stunned relief. It had been one thing to tell Kai about what happened at Bo's cabin—the idea of being questioned in a courtroom full of people gave me hives.

"She's pleading guilty to manslaughter for Bo's death and accessory after the fact with Mark."

"What about Alexander Burke?"

"She's claiming it was all Bo's idea. He forced her to help him dose Burke with the drugged wine. Once Bo was able to coerce a suicide note from him, Bo drove Burke's car to Mark's to leave the note on his doorstep."

"So Bo left her there? Why didn't she call the police? Let me guess, she was afraid of Bo."

He shook his head. "She says Bo instructed her to force-feed Burke the pills while he was gone but instead she tried to revive him."

I stared at him, incredulous. "What about her DNA under Burke's fingernails? Can she explain that?"

"Of course. Jennifer claims Burke woke up as she was trying to help him, but in his confusion, he attacked her. Bo returned and struck him in the head with the wine bottle. Which explains the bruising and odd angle of the gunshot wound—they tried to cover the blow to his head with a bullet."

One of the snags she'd mentioned.

"So she's blaming everything on Bo."

"And she's doing it with the skill of an Oscar winner. As I watched the interview, I caught myself nodding my head a few times. Jennifer is easy to believe."

"She is," I agreed but still shook my head.

"I think that's why the state attorney is working a deal. Can you picture Jennifer on the witness stand?"

The jury would fall for whatever story she spun. "You don't seem upset that she's getting away with it."

"Well, she's not. She's going to prison. Not for life, but for a while. By the time she gets out, she won't be able to pull off the innocent-young-girl act."

I had a feeling it wouldn't matter. People like Jennifer knew how to dig deep and survive. She'd manage to claw her way out of the gutter.

"So, are you going to tell me?" Kai was now looking at me the way he did when he was trying to figure something out.

"What?"

"You slipped something to Gardenia." He sounded more curious than critical.

"Did I?"

"Come on. What was it?"

"Just a little note."

Actually, it had been the piece of paper I had taken from Mark's kitchen. But I'd scratched out my phony list of Jax's things and very clearly written the word *Jaguars* and the twelve-digit number from Jax's tag.

Jaguar tag.

It had floated into my head while I was in the hospital. Apparently narcotics were real eye-openers for me.

Some part of my subconscious mind had found Jax's second tag odd. Then, I'd found the notepaper in my purse and it clicked.

The piece of notepaper had been printed with the logo of an online server. Charlie Yamada's story of catching a criminal after finding evidence online was what really made me connect the dots.

Mark had stored his journal files on the Internet. The online server acted like a safe. Much more effective than a real one.

Jaguars had been Mark's user name. The number on Jax's tag had been his password.

I'd given Gardenia access to Mark's journal. I figured it was worth more than the hundred grand. After all, she could read all the terrible secrets her son had been ready to spill. And then hit the delete key.

I'd let her wonder if I'd made a copy.

Kai shook his head. "You're not going to tell me, are you?"

"I like being mysterious."

"How about over dinner? The case is almost wrapped up—"

"This must be Miss Wilde."

Looking past Kai, I saw who had cut into my dinner proposal. I'd seen the man before. He was Kai's boss. As soon as his gaze latched onto my face, I was glad he wasn't mine.

Stern lines ran parallel between sharp brows. His white buzz cut and mustache seemed trimmed with a precision laser. He held out his hand.

"I'm Assistant Chief Monroe." He shook my hand. "Thank you for coming forward with your evidence."

"Sure." We'd had to bend the truth about why I'd given the bottle of antifreeze to Kai. But the why didn't seem too important. Everyone was glad that the case was closed.

He nodded at Kai. "Sergeant Duncan tells me you have a special ability."

I felt myself go very still. In the whirlwind of the last week, Kai and I had only seen each other once outside of work. I hadn't had the chance to set any ground rules. Namely, not blabbing about my ability to anyone without my approval.

"Oh?"

"He said you're good at seeing details. Connecting them."

"I always liked puzzles."

"Well, let's hope you never have to be involved with one like this again." Monroe inclined his head and walked away.

"Think you can handle that?" Kai teased.

"Can you?" I looked up at him. "Tell me you won't be tempted."

"To what? Call you next time my only witness has four legs?"

"Or two legs and a beak."

"Wait, you can talk to birds, too?"

I laughed, and for the first time in years, I heard the rusty hinges of the door to my heart creak open. The sound was nerve-wracking. But hey, I tamed dragons. I could handle it.

Right?